# THE TIME FOR REVENGE
## WAS AT...

But as she attempted to c_____
tracted by a sudden chang_____
stead of coming at them as_____
three-dimensional wedge—the ships had formed up into a
single, vertical column.

"What is that?" Fotey Smothe cried out.

Mestoeffer said, "It's the new weapon! They're going to
fire at once!"

But even as she was speaking, the odd formation broke
apart and the Gold Fleet ships resumed their previous positions.

Dane felt as if her body were electrified. Even as she'd
seen and recognized the sign, she had difficulty
believing . . . but it had to be.

"Like a cobra ready to strike," Fotey Smothe muttered
and instantly regretted the mistake. "I've read about them, I
mean . . ."

No one but Dane was paying attention to him.

*Or a stem*, she thought excitedly. Momed! He'd boasted
that when the Fleets met, he would let her know where he
was. *"Remember the sign."* What she'd seen could not be
an accident, or a coincidence. Momed Pwanda was aboard
one of those ships. And telling her that Gold Fleet would
follow his plan for the final battle. She allowed herself a
rare, unguarded smile. Her partner had succeeded in doing
the impossible. Now it was her turn.

**Praise for**
***Legend of the Duelist***
**by Rutledge Etheridge:**

"Action-packed SF adventure . . . There are battle
scenes galore, plus some intrigue."          —*Kliatt*

*Ace Books by Rutledge Etheridge*

# AGENT OF DESTRUCTION

## RUTLEDGE ETHERIDGE

ACE BOOKS, NEW YORK

This book is an Ace original edition,
and has never been previously published.

AGENT OF DESTRUCTION

An Ace Book / published by arrangement with
the author

PRINTING HISTORY
Ace edition / August 1996

The Putnam Berkley World Wide Web site address is
http://www.berkley.com

ISBN: 0-441-00356-7

ACE®
Ace Books are published by The Berkley Publishing Group,
200 Madison Avenue, New York, NY 10016.
ACE and the "A" design are trademarks
belonging to Charter Communications, Inc.

PRINTED IN THE UNITED STATES OF AMERICA

10 9 8 7 6 5 4 3 2 1

To Nancy,
who took care of life while I was having
a wonderful time writing this novel.

To Rutledge III and Liesa,
who make it all worthwhile.

And to Rutledge E. Etheridge Sr., 1921–1992,
who knew more about war and personal combat
than anyone should have to know.

# PROLOGUE

The three hundred seventeen children of the fleet were well disciplined. Ranging in age from four to fourteen, they also ranged in performance evaluation from uncertain, to promising, to exceptional. For the eldest among them, this day was all of those things: uncertain, promising, and definitely exceptional; today would determine their final classifications, and the career paths they would follow for the remainder of their lives.

Keve Fosman sat with his fellow senior students in the last row of occupied seats, wondering if any of his peers were as nervous as he was. Mara Sanza seemed to be. She'd been shivering, sweating, and short of breath even before the air-test began. Although Keve had caught the odd hour of sleep here and there during the past week, he felt as if he'd been awake the entire time: studying, supervising the attendants who cleaned the engineering spaces, studying, listening to the advice and encouragement of his parents, studying, working . . . He couldn't remember if he'd eaten. He must have, because for the first time in his life a fantasy image of gravied meat and rich pastries left him unmoved.

An hour passed while the children sat without a word spoken, hands in laps, eyes fixed on a jeweled mosaic that dominated the stage in front of them. Keve wondered what it must be like to be one of the Generals depicted there: revered as no mere human could be, commanding more ships than he could imagine . . . hundreds of thousands, at least. If he did as well today as his parents assured him he would, he might command one of them in another twenty or so years; who could say? His evaluations had been consistent throughout his life—only "promising." But everyone said that because he worked so hard and was so enthusiastic, and had never disobeyed an order in his life, he was just a step below "exceptional." A big step, but only one.

Specially rigged circulation fans whispered quietly behind the students. At times during the hour the fans had roared, rushing bone-chilling air at high speed throughout the auditorium. At other times they'd pumped in hot, dry air that was oxygen-deficient. The children first clenched their teeth against the cold, then later took in fast and shallow breaths and itched where tiny rivulets of perspiration trickled down their backs. They shivered uncontrollably when the air changed again and the perspiration froze. During all of that time not a hand had moved, not an eye had strayed from the Generals. Not one of the students, and it was the hardest thing of all for the little ones, giggled or squirmed. This was a test, and they all knew what it took to pass.

The ordeal was especially easy for Keve because it was an everyday routine. He and his parents, both Engine-Tenders, and his younger brothers, twins, lived in a small alcove separated by one bulkhead from the ship's power plant. His earliest memories were of sitting up nights in the heavy thrum of magnetic dissonance, alternately shaking with cold and panting for breath, studying flow diagrams and dreaming of a bed of his own and a clean uniform. When the twins were born it was five people living in a space intended for three, his parents each working double shifts from then on to keep the two extra people.

The first words spoken in today's fateful class—the squadron leader herself was present, along with a panel of senior staff—came from a young officer who'd remained at attention at center stage for the entire hour. He was tall and straight; probably had never spent twenty consecutive hours crouched in a down-time flux override passage. Keve envied the young officer's self-assured bearing. Like most subLieutenants, Michael Lieter was courteous but condescending toward students who were only a few years younger than himself. Keve had encountered only one exception to that rule, one officer who treated him with real respect and friendship. Keve wished his friend were here now, instead of this one. It would help him to calm down a little.

"Who can tell me," SubLieutenant Lieter asked, "what a moth is?"

All but the very youngest in the audience leapt to attention, signifying their readiness to answer. "You," Lieter said, pointing to a seven-year-old in the third row. The remaining students, as one, sat down.

"Sir, thousands of years ago our ancestors were called moths," the girl said brightly. "The word was an insult, because it compared us to a stupid little thing that always went toward light."

"You," the officer said, pointing to an older boy sitting behind the girl. "What does she mean 'light'?"

The girl took her seat, while the boy jumped to attention. "Sir, she meant the stars. Our ancestors made their lives in space. It also means destruction, because moths fly to their deaths. And so did we."

Lieter directed his questions to progressively older children, and appropriately the answers became more encompassing. "Why," he asked, "did so many of us die in space?"

A nine-year-old recited, "Sir, in those times, the galaxies had very little order. The settled worlds fought with each other. To fight their wars they built little fleets that stayed in space all the time because travel was so primitive and slow. It was our ancestors who were aboard those ships. We were born and died on them and we never got to see our homes. All we did was fight other ships who were like us because they never saw their planets either."

Keve hoped to be called on, but knew that no questions so elementary would come his way.

A twelve-year-old added, "Sir, the worlds sent us out to die by the hundreds of thousands, offering us nothing in return except more death and sacrifice. The people on the ground mocked us and called us moths, even as we died to protect them. Eventually those tiny fleets began to think for themselves. They realized that they had more in common with one another than they did with the worlds that sent them out. And so as centuries passed they began to form associations which were independent of any planet."

"How did they maintain themselves?"

One of the youngest children, a boy whose evaluation was marked "exceptional," was given the privilege of responding. Keve was filled with pride; this was his brother Samel. "Sir, they lived as we do now, taking from the worlds what they needed, and never again trusting Grounders to lead them. And they wouldn't allow the worlds to develop weapons or ships as good as theirs. That was the right thing to do because of the way they had been treated. That is how our Sovereign Command came to exist, more than eight hundred years ago."

The boy's twin, regarded as "promising," stood in hopes of being recognized. At a nod from the officer, Tanan Fosman said, "We call ourselves . . . I mean, *Sir!* Sir, we call ourselves the Silver Fleet because our outer hulls are ti . . . tat . . . *titallium*-based, and tatil . . . that metal reflects silver light. But at the same time as us, the Gold Fleet broke from the association. That was wrong because the Gold Fleet is evil."

The officer asked the same boy, "Why do you say the Gold Fleet is evil?"

"Sir, everyone knows that! It's because they are the Enemy!"

The squadron leader came to her feet and smiled. She applauded, and was followed in the accolade by her staff. "I am pleased," she began, "with your grasp of history. The senior students will remain here. The rest of you will proceed to Mess Deck Four at this time. You will find cake and sweet drinks waiting for you at a special reception hosted by my adjutant. You will inform your parents that you have done well, and that your records will be annotated. Dismissed."

The younger children filed out quietly, in order of class

rank. When they were gone the squadron leader turned toward those remaining. Her kindly smile had vanished without a trace. "Next," she said, "we will discuss applied physics, followed by engineering, battle tactics, command theory, weaponry . . ."

Fifteen hours later the senior students received their final classifications. All were now adults. Twenty percent were selected to become Fleet officers. These could look forward to futures limited only by their individual abilities and their loyalty to Sovereign Command. The rest were assigned as general crew. Their opportunities for advancement were genuine, but severely limited. As was often the case, and was allowed for in assessing the personnel needs of the Fleet, one in three of this latter category took their own lives within hours of the announcements. Keve Fosman was the first.

# JUSTIFICATION

# 1

*Five companies. Total fifty squadrons. Total five thousand warships of the Silver Fleet. Totally boring.*

*One sees so few ships as hopelessly inadequate for any serious work against the Gold Fleet. Yet, one admits, sufficient in number for a rewarding supply run. And one acknowledges the nominal privilege to lead it. But for the love of Glory, in an out-of-the-way-and-who-cares sector on the fringes of M-419? Why here? It is to spit! How many settled planets? Not twenty thousand in the whole pathetic galaxy. And in this little chunk of it? Maybe ninety. Of those, maybe fifty worth the effort. If they're stripped clean. Maybe.*

*One thing's clear: If Sovereign Command Council ever laughed, there were chuckles aplenty when* these *orders were issued. But . . . duty, duty, duty.*

*Ah, well.*

*A long, slender arm stretched toward a communications panel. Equally thin legs dropped with a sigh onto the command desk.* "All squadrons ready?"

"Fifty targets, fifty squadrons in place and waiting," *said the panel.* "One hundred ships available as reinforcement."

*Again, to spit.* "Probability of needing reinforcement?"

"Functional zero."

*Even the nobodies were unimpressed.*

*Dull, dull, dull. Not even decent sport.*

"Go."

"There it is!"

Dane Steppart raised her arm and pointed excitedly. Her

small face, framed by just-shy-of-shoulder-length black hair, was bright with excitement. Standing next to her, Paul Hardaway grunted and turned his head to watch with his younger cousin. He was tall, described by his mother as "prematurely rangy," and fair of hair and feature.

Both children were silent as, far to the east, a thin crack of luminous yellow edged upward from behind the crest of Bowman's Plateau. Dane let go a long breath as, in an instant, the elevated plain exploded into intense streaks of light, and the gray dawn sky became a palette of dazzling color. Five sharply etched bands of radiance fanned upward from the distant plateau and seemed to shove against one another as they leapt for the sky. How fast they are! Dane marveled, seeing this phenomenon for the first time. And how beautiful! Like living beings of perfect energy.

But so fleeting!

Already, as the sun crept higher into a cloudless sky, the fabled Rainbow Ghosts were fading into nothingness. The girl sighed, her mood suddenly leaden. For such astonishing beauty to burst upon the senses, tingling her every nerve and firing her imagination—only to die away so quickly. She would *not* allow the Ghosts to depart so soon! Closing her eyes, she willed the scintillating specters into memory, where they would never be permitted to fade. With her eyes shut she could see them again, fanning brilliantly into the sky: three pure, gleaming beacons of red, violet, and blue. These were the beautiful ones, the three in the center. It was only an accident, she told herself, not an intentional cruelty of nature, that these three exquisite flares of radiance were entrapped by two outer bands; one of silver, the other of gold. Ugly colors. But fitting, nonetheless.

When Dane opened her eyes again the eastern sky was its normal morning self. The sun was fully risen now, and Bowman's Plateau had resumed its normal identity as a featureless gray monolith between two snow-capped mountains. A black desert stretched before the plateau, itself a thing of beauty. Every few years would come a rain that fell as fast and hard as a waterfall. Dane had seen this phenomenon once. Windblown paths in the desert filled like rivers with the deluge, only to be swallowed up within minutes by the deep sand. Like the Rainbow Ghosts, the rivers were gone quickly, the waters too ephemeral to do any good in the insatiable desert. But when they came, the rivers were unforgettable, meteors cutting shining paths through infinite blackness: but on land and close by, not in the heavens and unreachable.

"Time to work," Paul said, pulling at Dane's arm. Reluctantly she turned to him and nodded, unable to understand his lack of excitement. Hadn't he seen the Ghosts?

As if she'd spoken out loud, Paul said, "That happens for five days every year, unless it's cloudy. It'll be here tomorrow, the next day, the next day, the next day, and then next year, and the year after that, forever. Besides, it's just some crystallized formations up there that catch the sun. They're not real ghosts."

"They're as real as any ghosts are," Dane said.

Paul gave her a bewildered look. "What is that supposed to mean?"

"Oh, nothing. I just think you should appreciate the beauty that's out here, that's all. It doesn't take much thought."

The remark stung. Paul's older brothers and sisters often teased him that he wasn't as smart as they were. Not so, his parents assured him. It was just a matter of age and experience. So he didn't mind the taunts. But Dane was younger than he was. Which meant that even if she were smarter than any of them, and he was sure that she was, she shouldn't be teasing him. "I've been in King's Valley all my life," Paul said defensively. "I guess I 'appreciate' it as much as anyone. But it's nothing new. I've seen it enough, that's all. It doesn't mean I'm stupid."

"You know that isn't what I meant." Dane and her older brother Alfred had been raised as cousins to the Hardaways. The familial relationship was based on Paul's mother and Dane's father having been neighbors in childhood, and close friends all their lives. After her father's death when Dane was three, the friendship between the families had continued. Dane enjoyed the weeks she spent nearly every year on the enormous Hardaway farm. The trips were a pleasant break from the specialized training she practiced while at home. This, her first summer visit, was the best yet.

She had always liked Paul, despite his sometimes maddening over-sensitivity. No, he wasn't the most intelligent person on Walden. But he certainly wasn't stupid. She'd never known anyone whose obvious talents so perfectly matched a chosen career. Paul's skill at framing and woodcraft seemed uncanny at times. His private garden, tended since early childhood, invariably produced the first yields of each season, and were always the best of the best. His abilities as a tracker and stalker were legendary among the "old-timers" who came to watch him every autumn at regional competitions. He was phenomenally strong, with a capacity and enthusiasm for hard work that anyone would admire. Best of all, with the exception of her mother, he was at heart the most loyal and gentle human being she'd ever known. Although he *did* have a quick temper at times. "I've never called you stupid, Paul. Or even thought you were."

Paul nodded down to her, relieved. "All right. But look, my parents don't want me standing around 'appreciating' things when I should be working. So don't tell me I should, all right? I always end up doing what you say, and you could get me into trouble this time." His expression became serious. "Why is that, anyway?"

"What?"

"I'm sixteen years old, and you're only fifteen. Besides that, you're from the city and I've been a farmer all my life. So I'm supposed to be teaching you, remember? But ever since you got here this time it seems like *you're* the teacher. When you want me to do something, I just do it. Why is that?"

Dane felt a laugh building inside that she dared not express, for fear of offending Paul. *When you want me to do something, I just do it. Why is that?* She recalled a very strange old man, twelve years before. He was Mr. Whitlock—a "friend" her mother had presented to her one morning. Within twenty-four hours of that first meeting a confused, headstrong young girl had asked that very question. The man smiled and tousled her hair. "That's what I'm going to teach you," he said.

"Did you hear me?" Paul asked. "I asked why—"

"You always do what you know is best," Dane said, shrugging. Of course there was an explanation; she was *showing* him why. But he was untrained and would never see it. Purposely matching his puzzled expression, she eased him away from that line of thought. "I admit that I don't know anything about farming like you do, Paul. But shouldn't we be putting that, ah, *thing,* on Hokum?" She pointed at the ground beside him.

*"Thing?"* Paul asked, grinning. "It's called a yoke, Dane. And I suppose you're right." Now that he was back in charge, he tried for the self-important gruffness that his older brothers and sisters used with him. Wiping nonexistent sweat from his forehead, he said "But this business here is a waste of time. It isn't real farming."

"You're right. This is history."

"Not mine," Paul said. And he added proudly, "I was practically born in a HarvesTrain."

"That doesn't matter," Dane said. "I was born in a warm and dry cement building. But I sleep outside sometimes, even when it's cold and raining."

"Well so do I, Dane. In fact, I like it. But that's because I'm in the Dog Scouts. Did you know that I'm the best tracker in my unit? Maybe on all of Walden?"

"Yes, I knew that. Everyone says so."

"And," he said, enormously pleased, "I can live off the land better than most wild animals. But see, you're a city person. So it's different for you."

"No, it isn't. Why do you think your Dog Scouts have been around for three hundred years?"

"Same as now. For fun."

"Well, yes, but it's more than that. Experiencing discomfort and working in primitive ways are parts of every citizen's history. Three centuries ago nearly everyone on

Walden had to live like that. And remember, we're never more than a minute away from having to start with nothing and build it all up again. That's history, too."

"Yeah, yeah. 'History Mandates Preparedness,' " Paul said, shaking his head. He was in the Scouts because it was fun. Period. "You sound like Mom and Dad."

"Thank you."

Arguing with Dane was a bigger waste of time than teaching her to plow. Frustrated, Paul turned away and whistled. An old white mule looked up from nearby, where it had been nosing through clogs of dirt. Taking its time, the mule ambled toward the children and came to an abrupt stop. Here was another creature Paul knew better than to argue with; except Hokum's problem was what his father called plain cussedness. With Dane it was something he'd never quite figured out. Grumbling, he carried the heavy yoke the remaining fifteen feet between them.

Dane laughed and looked out at her surroundings. The day was already hot, with visibility perfect beneath a clear sky. Two hundred yards to the north and south of her, the soya fields began. In each field she could see men and women climbing up into one of the farm's two Harves-Trains, preparing for a new day's work. From around noon to about three o'clock the heat would be rising from the tillage to create the illusion of deep water in motion. It was fascinating to watch the barn-sized machines, which in that magic time would appear as ships sailing on a broad green sea. In their wakes the behemoths would leave bundles of cloth, gigantic sacks of coarse grain and fine meal prepared for shipment, boxes full of breads that were ready to eat and would stay warm until they reached market, and still other boxes of assorted glues, pharmaceuticals, dyes, and metal containers of liquid fuel for the standby generators. Aside from the metal containers, all of this was produced as needed within the HarvesTrains, all from the soya plants and the symbiotic *mopa* tubers that grew between the rows. In addition, the huge machines would plant and fertilize the year's second crop, corn, as the soya was reaped and processed.

Paul turned to speak to Dane and saw where she was looking. "That's *real* farming," he said wistfully. "It's what I should be doing right now, instead of this children's game. By the time I was your age I could take apart an entire engine blindfolded, and reassemble . . . hey, you're supposed to be watching *me!*"

"I saw you yoke the mule yesterday," Dane said. This time she meant to tease him as she added, "It's nothing new. I've seen it enough, that's all."

"Oh, really?" Angrily the boy dropped the yoke, which hit the ground with a dull thud. Hokum gave a confused snort. "Then *show* me, Dane." The sharp rise in his voice startled the animal so that it took a step backward and began sniffing the air and rotating its ears, searching nervously for whatever it was that was wrong. Finding nothing it could identify, its eyes widened in what Paul recognized as the beginning of a panic. "Uh-oh," he said. "Get ready to run."

Dane made a cooing sound and then mimicked the mule's snort, followed again by the cooing. Hokum stood still for a moment and then approached the girl with its head lowered. Dane continued the soothing sound and repeated the mule-talk while she scratched at the fur between the eyes of the contented beast. After several minutes she hefted the yoke, heaved it up and onto the mule's neck with one smooth movement, then belted and tightened the harness securely. Hokum seemed to be asleep.

Paul had nothing to say as he inspected Dane's work and found it perfect. He watched quietly as his young cousin attached the harness to an old wooden plow.

A shadow fell over them, and the world went suddenly dark.

Paul looked up to see dozens of stars shining dimly in a dusklike sky. "Hey! What . . . Dane, what—"

"*Get down!*" he heard as if from a distance, not recognizing the words. Instead he turned to look for the sun, and could not find it.

Where the sun should have been he saw a huge black ball, surrounded by a halo of light. *Eclipse,* he thought im-

mediately, but his rational mind told him that neither of the
moons was due to eclipse the sun for another two years.
From behind him he heard Hokum's bellow, followed by
quick clopping sounds. He watched as the mule bolted and
took off running north, toward the field. The wildly bounc-
ing plow followed along behind.

"Paul, listen to me." It was Dane's voice, insistent but
calm. "Lie down and don't move."

"What is it?" Even as he spoke, he moved to comply
with her command. In the second he needed to lie facedown in the dirt and become immobile, Paul realized what
the answer had to be. He felt his stomach turn to ice.

"Just don't move," he heard Dane repeat quietly, in the
same tone she'd used with Hokum. "You'll be all right if
you don't move."

"All right." Paul raised his head slightly and turned to
the east again. There was more light in the sky now. The
black ball was breaking up into patterns of dark shapes,
which in turn began to separate out into individual objects.
Within seconds full daylight had returned. There was no
sound except for his own erratic breathing. One of the objects in the sky grew at an impossible rate, and Paul understood that it was speeding straight for them. The ship
reflected silver light and was shaped like a dome, the bottom almost flat, but gently rounded.

"It's the *War,*" he whispered, barely catching his breath.
He spoke again, forcing the whine out of his voice, "It's the
War." His first reaction was intense excitement and a little
relief; he'd often boasted to himself and others that if this
moment were ever to come, he would face it with courage.
And now, to his amazement, he was doing that.

The object continued to grow until, at least a mile in the
air and still larger than ten storage barns, it swept soundlessly overhead and was gone. To the north of him Paul
heard the mule honking in panic as it fled, then wailing.
Then nothing. The boy fought the impulse to look, knowing
that to move was to die. And, he had no wish to see whatever might be left of Hokum. At that instant, in perfect uni-
son, the two HarvesTrains exploded, the blast splitting the

air and shaking the ground violently. Intense light followed. From every direction came waves of heat, and more light. Paul's lungs emptied in an instant, as if vacuumed. He felt his clothing soak through with perspiration, and opened his eyes to see steam rising from every covered part of him. He was unable to draw a full breath. *Where is Dane? Is she all right? Am I all right?* He wondered which would hurt more, suffocating or burning alive.

The light faded to normal as the explosions from the HarvesTrain died out like an echo. Paul took his hands from his ears. As quickly as it had begun, the fury was over—except for a subdued and ongoing roar. It was the crackle-and-hiss sound of leaves tossed into a fire, multiplied by infinity. The sound lessened as the entire soya crop was consumed in less than a minute.

In the sudden relative quiet the lingering heat was gentle, while the stench of burned vegetation and flesh filled his nostrils. With a groan he rolled over and gulped for oxygen until his dizziness passed. The initial excitement and relief he'd felt, along with the terror, were gone. Hard reality jolted the boy like sudden sight.

After an absence of more than three hundred years, history—the War—had returned to Walden.

Paul whispered to Dane, "Now, what do we do?"

Dane had made that determination the moment she'd sighted the ships above Walden. "They're gone for now," she answered simply, and stood up to brush the dirt from her coveralls. "You should go home, Paul. Your family has a shelter. Get in it and stay there."

Paul stood. The first thing he noticed was that Dane was dry. Why wasn't she steaming, like he was? It was a strange thought; but then, he wondered, what would be a normal thought right now?

"We were lucky," Dane said. "It was a very selective attack." The fallow "back yard" in which they'd been standing was an untouched ribbon of ground stretching from Paul's house westward, an eighth-mile strait between twin continents of devastation. Only moments ago the soya crop had reached nearly to the horizon, both north and south. Now it was seared to a smoldering brown carpet, shedding wispy clouds of gray smoke that rose into the suddenly breezeless air.

Paul too was surveying the damage. There was nothing left of the mammoth HarvesTrains. He had known most of the men and women working them, now dead, for as long as he could remember. Deep in thought, he realized that he had avoided looking in one direction, ever since the smoke had lifted from their corridor of safety.

"I think they made it, Paul," Dane said softly.

"You . . . you think so?"

"Yes." Relieved as she was, her amazement was greater, for the ship had passed directly over the object they were both looking at.

Paul let go a breath. The family house was still standing. There it was, half a mile away between two rising curtains of smoke, standing in bright sunshine. It looked fine. He could see two figures moving, running from the building, and knew that it would be members of his family, coming to look for him and Dane.

All of the Hardaways had been lucky, Dane thought. Today was the first of the month, which meant that all of them except for Paul would have been inside the house for the farm's monthly business meeting. They, along with any surviving crew, would already be moving into a centuries-old underground labyrinth of rooms and tunnels that would be their home for the foreseeable future.

"I always thought my parents were crazy to make us spend so much time keeping that place clean and supplied," Paul whispered.

"They're wise people," Dane said. "They'll be all right. You tell them I said that."

"I will," Paul responded automatically. Then he thought about what she'd said and turned to face her. "Where are *you* going?"

"Back to the city, of course."

"I don't think so. We've only got the one flyer, and—"

"No one flies until they're gone," Dane said. "You know that. I'll walk."

"That's almost a hundred miles!"

"Then I'd better start now, don't you think?"

"But . . . but why? You're safer here. There's enough room in the shelter for you, Dane. It was built for sixty, and . . . well, a lot of people are dead now."

"My mother needs me," she said, which was part of the truth. "Alfred is off-world, so I'm the only one left at home."

"Your mother is president of the council," Paul argued. "She'll be too busy to look after you, with all the work she'll have to do."

"You go ahead and go home. I'll be fine."

"But you're only—"

"Only fifteen? Paul, I know what to do. Travel only when there's sunlight, and stay immobile if any of the ships appear. There'll be plenty of cooked food on the way," she added with an ironic half-smile. "Don't worry."

"I'll go with you, then! You'll need someone to—"

She approached him, and stood on her toes to kiss his cheek. Even so, Paul had to bend down. Suddenly he reached beneath her arms and lifted her easily, hugging her tightly against him. Dane returned the embrace with equal fervor. Paul's lips moved to hers. Again she responded, and then quickly pulled away. Their eyes met, and it was clear that both of them were startled by what had happened. Paul set her down, and Dane backed off a pace, looking up at him.

She was not angry. How could she be, when she'd initiated the incident, and then eagerly accepted an escalation? But she was shocked at her response. It was . . . nice. She'd never thought . . . and then she was blushing as hard as he was. This was altogether confusing. At no time in her life had it occurred to Dane that she and Paul might someday think of one another as potential . . . but such a thing would not be possible. Technically, they were not related; but where it counted, they were family. Paul would understand this as well. She hoped.

"You're not leaving here. Not without me," the boy said resolutely.

Dane shook her head, clearing it. "Good-bye, Paul," she said, and abruptly turned away from him, to the west. The last thing she said to him was, "When this silliness is over, I'd like to learn more about farming."

"I'll be here," Paul said, watching her walk away with long, confident strides. He'd seen Dane every year or so since she'd been born. As the youngest of seven children, he'd accepted her gladly as a new family member—a *younger* one, which allowed him to feel older than someone else on the farm, and therefore important. He'd always felt important when Dane was around. But Paul had never seen her as she had been on this visit. She seemed grown-up, even more so than some of the adults who worked—had worked—the farm with his family. Or maybe she had simply passed him by on the road to maturity. Maybe, as his brothers and sisters said, he really was slow-witted. But he understood what he'd felt when he picked her up and she kissed him, and he kissed her back. And he understood that when they grew up he could never think of her as a potential mate. People didn't behave like farm animals, after all. But that didn't change the fact that suddenly he knew, with the life-breaking, iron certainly of a sixteen-year-old, that he loved her. And that she was beyond his reach. And that both facts would be true forever.

It came to him then, what real fear was—that Dane Steppart would be killed. Or taken away into slavery. Which was worse? He decided it was better not to consider that right now, or he'd be running after her. And maybe he would do just that. But first he would take some time and think about . . . everything. Because everything was different now. There was the War, and hiding for a while, then finding out who was dead or taken away, and then a whole world starting again with nothing, and his farm, and . . . His thoughts drifted. He assured himself that if he decided to, he could catch up to her easily enough. She could go anywhere, and he could find her; Paul Hardaway wasn't the best tracker in the Dog Scouts for nothing.

• • •

Walking briskly, looking ahead at the burned-out soya fields and the untouched pathway between them, it seemed to Dane as if a clear road had been left open for her. In the strong light of morning she lengthened her stride while keeping a careful watch on the sky.

# ⇛ 2 ⇚

Within a hemisphere of blackness that dominated all space above the massive War Table, fifty thousand ships of Sovereign Command were displayed like motes of ignited, silvery dust. Beyond these ships of the Silver Fleet were starscapes familiar to every member of both Fleets: This was Prime Sector of Galaxy S-143. The Fortress, it was called, a nebula where for more than five centuries no Sovereign ship had penetrated and survived long enough to broadcast a report. Here was the principal nest of the Enemy, the so-called Great Command, the Gold Fleet . . . where death was about to strike, on a scale never imagined by those butchers. Now!

A woman ran into the Operations Room, clutching her sides and gasping for breath. "Stop! You must not launch the attack! We have word that the Enemy is—"

*"Mother, please!"*

"But son, we're hopelessly outnumbered! You're working with faulty intelligence reports, your commanders have no coordination plans . . . And worst of all, you haven't eaten your breakfast! I tell you, all is lost!"

"Mother . . ." Despite himself, SubLieutenant Jarred Marsham began to laugh. Like his mother, Jarred had dark auburn hair and freckles that were highlighted when he laughed or was otherwise excited. The two were of identical average height. But unlike hers, his nose was prominent above a mouth that seemed to turn down, even when he was smiling. These things he had inherited from his father, the long-deceased Lieutenant Colonel Edward Jarred Berta.

Jarred punched the computer to save the simulation, and a second later the black hemisphere disappeared. But by now Squadron Leader Jenny Berta Marsham had cast a professional eye on her son's battle formulation. She wasn't pleased. Committing an error common among beginners, he'd been overcautious and splintered his primary force into far too many defensive positions. The overall attack strategy would therefore be weak, inviting instant and massive Enemy retaliation. Worse, his reinforcements were half the galaxy away, too distant to be of assistance. Why couldn't he remember the basics? Hyperspace could be maintained for only two hours of subjective time. Those two hours would bring his reinforcements only half the distance they needed to travel. Six hours in normal space would then be necessary to cool power plants and replace burnt elements. Another ten minutes would be required to run up to hyperspace again. And still the reinforcements would be two hours away from the battle. More than eight hours wasted in all, by which time her son's primary force would be lost. It was all so elementary, and so vitally important . . .

But for once she refrained from giving him a critique; Jarred was not on duty, and she knew that he was grieving over the recent death of his young friend, Keve Fosman. Still, she hoped that her silence concerning his attack simulation would not be mistaken for approval.

The Operations Room was cavernous. Silver-gray walls enclosed eighteen thousand cubic feet, most of it disorientingly, almost sickeningly, empty. All but the permanent fixtures had been removed for a ritual that would begin within the hour. Seven small communications consoles, and dozens of status panels fixed into the walls throughout, formed the decor. Centered in the room was a technological marvel called the War Table, with seats around it for one hundred ten officers. At the moment only two were present.

Mother and son were aware of this rare opportunity to speak openly and freely, the security to do so having been signaled by Squadron Leader Marsham's thoroughly unprofessional entrance into the room; obviously, she'd deactivated all of the compartment's monitors. But Jenny sensed that her son was not ready to talk about Keve Fosman, whose suicide he had discovered at the end of his last watch. And she did not want to discuss the ceremony they awaited: Today in this room, after eighty-five years of distinguished service to Sovereign Command, Major General William W. Marsham—Jenny's father, Jarred's grandfather—was retiring. With full honors, his orders proclaimed.

Jenny Marsham had serious reservations about the truth of the phrase, "with full honors," even though General Marsham had given no hint that he felt slighted. He'd debarked onto *Bagalan* three days before, brimming with good cheer, enthusiastically embracing his only two surviving relatives with an unrestrained and open joy that shocked the other officers attending his arrival. But remaining within the complementary disciplines of protocol and fear, they made no comment, and were perfect in their reception of him. All were nervously aware that had there been a breach of etiquette, Squadron Leader Marsham would without hesitation have added names to the retirement list.

Since that time the old man had spent hours with his daughter and grandson. Jenny had never seen Jarred so animated. From early childhood the boy had communicated on a yearly basis with his famous grandfather. Jarred would send a message to mark the old man's birthday, and would receive a reply on his own birthday. But this was the first time the two had met personally. And while those yearly communications had been necessarily observant of the general's rank, the conversations of the past three days had been frank, warm, and without a trace of formality. No doubt it had been a dizzying experience, probably impossible at first, for Jarred to sit, laugh, and express his ideas for the Fleet with someone whose personal command numbered three flotillas, thirty thousand ships. And of course the boy must have realized that the elder Marsham was careful in his remarks; he was, after all, a major general. But the illusion of casual conversation had had a visible and profound effect on Jarred. All his life he had admired and respected his grandfather. Now his behavior toward the old man was nothing short of worshipful. This added to her indignation over the circumstances surrounding her father's retirement.

As Jenny saw it, the insult was twofold: No officer superior in rank to General Marsham would be present at the retirement celebration; this was unheard of. Second, the ceremony was taking place aboard *Bagalan.* It was, in fact, an important ship, a top-of-the-line battle cruiser and the flagship of her squadron. Under better circumstances it would be an aceptable host and not without precedence, because of the clan connection. But presently her squadron was virtually idle. Her one hundred ships were nowhere near, were not even hunting for, the Enemy. Intolerable. The correct procedure would have seen herself and Jarred transported to a senior flagship, in action, with at least one Sovereign Command council member aboard for the observance. Major General William Wylie Marsham, one hundred years old today, had earned—and was due—no less.

She could think of only one explanation for the break from tradition: that her father had somehow run afoul of one or more council members. The offense could not have been formal in nature. Had it been, he'd have been court-martialed at once. There was more to disturb her as well. Only two decades ago the widespread Marsham clan had numbered four hundred twenty-five. At present only three were living. Why? Roughly half of the deaths had occurred in combat; perfectly natural. But the remainder had been logged under various official causes, all of them meaning "accidental." That was too much to believe. As the age-old maxim proclaimed, "Once is accident. Twice is coincidence. Three times is hostile action." And so it was logical—virtually inescapable—to assume that someone in supreme authority was carrying out a silent vendetta against her clan.

She'd been tempted an hour before to confront the general with her suspicions. She hadn't, because there was no doubt that he'd read the same incident reports she had, detailing the deaths. And yet he'd said nothing. That could only be seen as a tacit admission that he shared her suspicion—he would know what her conclusions were—but had been powerless to stop the vendetta. Her father was an officer of enormous influence; she, relatively little. What then, could *she* do about it? The only possible defense against a hostile council member was to find a powerful ally to identify that individual and intercede in one's behalf. If her father had failed to do so, could she hope to succeed? But the question was irrelevant, she reflected. If only one course of action lay open, however unlikely, it must be pursued. She would find someone with the ability to protect her son.

She realized with a start that Jarred had been speaking to her. He repeated, "Grandfather has instructed that when it's time, you and I are to escort him here to the ceremony. It's time. May I take your arm, Mother?"

"Consider it an order, Son."

"I have no doubt that all of you are expecting to hear the retirement address given forty years ago by my father," General Marsham began. "This of course is the same speech given by his mother before him, by her father before her, and by members of the Marsham clan for seventeen generations." He waited until the applause waned. "But, I have been informed that aboard *Bagalan* and all the other ships commanded by my daughter, officers in training are required to learn and to present papers on this very speech. Is that true, Squadron Leader?"

From her seat to her father's immediate right at the War Table, Jenny Marsham stood. "It is, sir."

"I see. Under these circumstances, then, I'm afraid that I must disappoint your officers and crews." Now the old man smiled for the first time. "For that is exactly the address I intend to give."

Taking a cue from their commander, the four hundred present, most of them standing—along with the crews of ninety-nine other vessels watching remotely—laughed and applauded.

Jenny snapped to attention and asked, "May your grandson deliver your record, sir?"

Like all of those in attendance or watching the ceremony remotely, General Marsham was in full-dress uniform: maroon blouse and breeches, edged and trimmed with thin silver cord. Reaching down across his chest was a wide blue sash that bore fifty-three combat awards. While inspecting his uniform earlier, Jenny had remarked that had he been taller, all ninety-five of them could have been displayed. To which her grinning father had replied that the forty-two left in his satchel had been awarded for using proper diction while issuing orders, which he pointed out was the most difficult task faced by a major general.

Answering his daughter's question, he said, "Please proceed."

At a nod from Jenny, Jarred made his way through the assembled officers to stand at the head of the table. For the next hour he read out a list of the retiree's accomplishments, beginning with the general's first assignment as a sublieutenant and continuing through his last battle action. At the end Jarred faced his grandfather and saluted, while Jenny called all witnesses to attention.

General Marsham stood and returned the salute. "Thank you, Squadron Leader, SubLieutenant. All of you, please stand at ease." After a moment, with daughter and grandson on either side of him, he cleared his throat and began the address first given more than three hundred years before his birth by Lieutenant General Rachel McNear Marsham.

" 'There are two guiding principles which have been the lodestars to my career, and which I commend to each of you in your own service to our Fleet. First, our cause is just. All of history—that which we have learned, that which we now are living, and that which our efforts shall form—bears this out: Our cause is just. The second principle is likewise borne out by this same eternal flow of history. And that is that the Enemy is goat urine . . .' "

By tradition the audience joined in here, jeering and adding their own insults.

" '. . . nearly two centuries ago. Space itself could not contain the evil of that day. For it was then that those we trusted, those with whom we freely shared our superior technology, betrayed and murdered tens of thousands of our ancestors. That atrocity by the Gold Fleet, that monstrous and shameless deed, began the war which continues to this moment.' " His voice rose to a shout. " 'The Enemy claims, and teaches its children, that the betrayal was ours. But we know the truth. We will be avenged . . . As I stand before you now, the Enemy plots to dominate the galaxies which are rightfully ours. We will stop them . . .' "

Hearing him speak, the officers of Jenny's squadron reflected that the ancient words rang as true today as when they'd first been spoken.

" '. . . that we would prefer to trade peaceably with the worlds, because we are a peace-loving people, and govern them with discipline and kindness, because we are a generous and forgiving people. But the Enemy forces us into a brutality which is foreign to our nature . . .' "

No one was aware of time passing. Every person hearing the speech realized that they had never before heard it delivered properly.

" '. . . say to you that for these reasons and more, too many to be named here, each of us is called to a noble and historic work. How fortunate we are, each and every one! For we ask, will our ancestors be avenged? Will our children be free? And we rejoice as the universe itself cries out with us, Yes! Yes! And again, Yes!' "

When it was over, when abraded throats had given their last shouts and officers stood in sweat-drenched silence, Major General William W. Marsham drew himself to his full sixty inches of height and delivered the final salute of his career. And so he stood for several minutes while his audience filed out of *Bagalan*'s Operations Room in descending order of rank. One by one, also in order of rank, the commanding officers of Jenny Marsham's other ships darkened and then switched off their screens.

"And now," the old man said when the three Marshams were alone, "one final detail." As he spoke he removed his sash and handed it to Jenny. "I've given orders that all of the clan's memorabilia are to be moved here to *Bagalan.* Please add this to the pile."

"I will. Thank you, sir." Along with the sash he pressed a folded note into her hand, which she accepted and concealed.

"Jarred, your mother tells me that you've given a name to my new command."

"It's what *I've* called it, sir. But I would never presume—"

"What is the name?"

"Ah, sir, I know how you value music. And now that you've retired, you'll have a new standard of time. And so, ah, I called the ship *Metronome,* sir."

That brought a moment's thought and a laugh. "Perfect! I am to surround myself with the music I've loved for decades, while the ship's chronometer ticks away the remainder of my life. Very well, *Metronome* it shall be."

Jarred flushed. "Sir! I never thought in those terms. Please accept my—"

"Don't apologize, young man. The symbolism is perfect. Now, will the two of you walk with me to the hangar?"

"Yes sir," Jenny said. "I've had your baggage put aboard already. But, before we take that walk, won't you consider staying with us for a while longer? If you would consent to writing your memoirs here, I can assign a team of—"

"A waste of crew-hours," he said, waving dismissively. "Out of the question."

"But, sir, future generations—"

"What about them? If my career has been worthy of study, future generations have all they need to pursue the matter. Since the moment I became a senior officer, including these last three days, every word I've spoken has been monitored. And reviewed. That," he added with a never-before-seen hint of resentment, "quite properly includes the final words I shared with your mother after the Battle of N34-V654. As she lay dying." Clearing his throat, he continued. "And of course, all of my command decisions are a matter of written record. What can I add to all of that?"

"The most important thing, sir. The thoughts that guided your contributions to our history."

He shook his head emphatically. "I gave the speech. That is enough. Besides," he added with a smile, "I'm eager to begin my retirement. And you must return to your *vital mission,* Squadron Leader. With no further distractions from me." Addressing her by rank, he let it be known that no further discussion was possible. "Now let us proceed to the hangar."

"Yes, sir."

His mention of her mother's death and the inflection of the words "vital mission" allowed some of her father's anger to escape, Jenny noted with satisfaction. It was a subtle acknowledgment that he too had felt the shame of their present location and assignment. Jenny's squadron was on detached duty to support a minor supply run in a sector of space that held no military significance whatever. The worlds involved were remote and unimportant. As a further indignity, her one hundred ships were designated as mere reinforcements, with the chances of being called to action hovering at functional zero.

*Metronome* was polished to a high silver sheen, sitting alone in the huge hangar. The sleek craft measured fifty feet in length, twenty at the beam, and seventeen in height.

"It's new, of course," Jarred said with obvious pride. "I've done all of the flight testing myself, and have inspected every inch, from bow to stern." He followed behind his grandfather as the old man walked around the craft, nodding his approval. Jarred continued, "The engineering and the power plant are the finest available. Squadron Leader Marsham afforded me the privilege of overseeing their installation personally."

"We've onloaded ten years of provisions. Although," Jenny added with a grin, "you'll have to reprovision more often, if you decide to, ah, pick up a passenger along your travels."

"Your mother was the only passenger in my life, Jenny," he responded seriously. "As I was the only passenger in her life. Along with you and your brothers and sisters." He coughed twice. "Your mother was the finest, most loyal officer and companion . . ." He stopped again, his eyes attempting to say what his voice could not.

"Of course, Father." Jenny thought angrily of the monitors within the compartment. She would have deactivated them, but the general would never approve. She smiled at him, forcing levity into her voice. "But you have many years ahead of you. You don't need to travel alone."

"Travel?" he said, returning the smile and her tone. "Why, I may just find a nice planet somewhere, take some land, and—"

Mother and son exchanged a shocked, disbelieving look. "Father! Please! Don't even *joke* about becoming a Grounder!"

"Ha! You'd both change your names if I did. Don't be concerned, Squadron Leader. I am who I've been, and that can never change. One thing more. Jarred has the potential to become an outstanding officer. But you've allowed him to become harmfully close to you. I recommend that in another year you transfer him to a new ship. I've spoken to Olton Kay-Raike about arranging a marriage for your son with one of his most junior clan members, if he deems Jarred acceptable. I believe he will. Then concentrate on your own career. You'll both benefit."

"I understand, sir."

"Now then. Give an old man a farewell hug, you two, and let me be about this retirement business."

Jenny was grateful that her father had waited until now to speak to her of this. At any time up to the moment of his retirement, the "recommendation" would have carried the weight of a direct order. Now she was free to ponder—and refuse—the general's idea. The Kay-Raike clan was rising fast in the Fleet. A marriage to one of their least officers would allow Jarred to retain his clan name. Further, an alliance with them under these circumstances could greatly strengthen the Marshams—perhaps even protect Jarred if,

as she believed, her clan was the target of a vendetta. But
the Kay-Raikes were known for their cruelty and fanati-
cism. Becoming "acceptable" to them would mean the
death of Jarred's innermost being. How could her father
even "recommend" such an arrangement? He'd done so for
the record, witnessed by the ship's monitors. That, she realized suddenly, might be the answer. Perhaps the note he'd
given her would explain.

To Jarred, General Marsham said, "May your children be
worthy of our name, as you are." The young man nearly
fainted with delight.

A few seconds later Jenny opened the door to
*Metronome* and her father climbed to the pilot's seat. He
called to them, "Give me three minutes after you leave, and
set the airlock to cycle automatically. I wish you both long
and productive careers. Good-bye." With a final wave and
smile he activated a switch to shut the door and seal the
vessel for space.

Outside the hangar, after three minutes, Jenny reached
for the control panel and hesitated.

"Go ahead, Mother," Jarred said, his voice breaking.
"It's your duty."

She nodded, not daring to express the revulsion she felt
at that moment toward Sovereign Command's policy of
mandatory retirement for all but council members. For a
major general, the age was one hundred. At the level of an
enginetender third or assistant steward, the age was forty.
Elevation in rank was the only way to avoid forced retirement.

She placed a hand on her son's shoulder and squeezed.
With the other she made the appropriate settings and threw
the toggle. A red light began blinking at once. The two
watched as indicators told of events within the hangar.
Most of the air pressure was removed before the outer airlock door opened. Sixty seconds later the door cycled shut
again, and pressure built quickly to normal once more.
With shaking fingers Jarred unlocked the hangar entrance,
and stood aside as his mother entered first into the vast
compartment.

• • •

*Metronome,* of course, had not moved. The vessel's door had been opened.

"I wanted so badly for him to take the ship and leave," Jarred said as tears coursed down both cheeks. "He was a major general. He had earned the right to continue his life."

"We both knew he wouldn't," Jenny said. "He told us so. 'I am who I've been, and that can never change.' Your grandfather was not an officer to break clan tradition, regardless of his rank. He has served, and he has gone. Both with honor." As they turned to leave the hangar she said with scarcely concealed bitterness, "Now let us return to our *vital mission.*"

After walking with Jarred to his quarters, Jenny went to her stateroom and locked the door behind her. She shut off the compartment monitors and placed her father's letter on the desk. The distinctive odor of the paper brought a smile to her lips. She recalled similar notes passed to her as a young child, leading her to birthday surprises. The paper was always coated to allow for easy and complete disposal, before her mother discovered their conspiracy. It warmed her that he had remembered the little game they'd shared.

She unfolded the paper and recognized at once the tiny, precise script.

"My Dearest Jenny,

"In death I exercise for the first time the most rare and perilous of luxuries: that is, the sharing of my thoughts with another human being. Understand me, daughter. The only things I have ever owned are my thoughts. They belonged to no one but me; this was for my own safety, but more importantly, for those whom I have loved. (As you ascend into the senior ranks, I believe that you will come to feel the same way.) Along with whatever legacy I may have at the concluding moments of my life and career, I present them to you as a final gift. It is my most cherished hope that you will find them of value.

"First. I have by now proposed to you an alliance with

the Kay-Raikes. This idea did not originate with me, but with Olton Kay-Raike, who for reasons I cannot begin to understand considers me to be a personal friend. In truth I regard him as the worst of a clan which in its entirety is a disgrace to Sovereign Command. But because of his superior rank I am forced to consider such an arrangement, and to pass the burden of decision on to you. You must negotiate with them. But as I know you have already decided, you must never complete the arrangement. Kay-Raike is old. If you are fortunate, he will be dead before he grows impatient and insists that you send Jarred to him.

"Next: There is the systematic slaughter of our clan, the cause or source of which I have failed to determine. But I have taken a step which I hope will assuage . . ."

Minutes later she carefully shredded the document and dropped the pieces in water, where they began to dissolve. Her hands trembled, and she wept. What she had just read were the first unguarded words she'd ever received from her father.

As she'd told Jarred, the general's death was true to his nature. But now she understood that there was another dimension to it. If, as they both believed, the elder Marsham had somehow run afoul of a council member, then his willing suicide might be seen as an attempt to assuage the offense; he could not honorably have done such a thing while on active duty. But would the gesture be accepted? *You can't rely on that being so,* he'd written. *Jarred needs an ally, a protector. Keep him with you until you find one.*

"I will," Jenny whispered. "Good-bye, Father. Thank you for your sacrifice. I love you."

Tumbling away from *Bagalan,* the vacuum-distorted corpse of Major General William W. Marsham began a journey that would never end. Unless, as he had thought in horror when the airlock door began to open, his body were to enter the atmosphere of a planet and be incinerated— leaving his ashes to fall as fertilizer upon land. This was a bad moment, his only brush with fear. It arose from a memory that was as clear and hard as crystal, and had never been far from his thoughts: a toddler at his mother's knee more than ninety-seven years before, standing at wide-eyed attention, repeating a solemn vow that he would never allow peace with the Enemy. Or become a Grounder. Then the joy of being swept up into a warm, scented embrace and hearing the words, for the very first time, "Willie Marsham is a good boy."

# 3

*"This is not an attack!"*

On the first day of the supply run, four silvered ships circled Vermilion City. Far beneath them, buildings exploded in a crushing wave of sound that had long ago deafened the citizens who were in destruction's path. Structures and vehicles hit by the streaking debris were torn into shrapnel as well, in turn tearing into the bodies of those fleeing, and those already dead.

*"Remain calm! This is not an attack!"*

Only those well away from the carnage heard the words, blared out at regular intervals from the lead ship. Within the targeted area the mortally wounded lay strewn over thirty city blocks, staring up with shock-vacant eyes at the silver glints of light weaving a snaking, double-eight pattern above them. Those able to move scrambled over fallen chunks of concrete and steel toward subbasement shelters whose locations they had memorized in earliest childhood. Most of these never made it to safety.

Police and rescue workers were helpless. They dared not take their vehicles into the air above the wreckage. They had seen twenty of their number destroyed, in as many attempts. Their paths into the ravaged sector were blocked by story-high clutter and street sections that had become craters. Scores of them broke ranks and ran individually toward the hordes of pleading injured. They perished at the same rate as those they attempted to help.

After one hour, the ships departed. Shuttles landed elsewhere in the city and began taking aboard slaves and other valuables.

On the third day of the supply run, Squadron Leader Buto Shimas paced a small office floor, glancing every few seconds at Council President Linda Steppart. The bald man came to a halt ten inches in front of the woman. Unconsciously, he twisted one end of his black mustache back and forth between thick fingers. His short and extraordinarily wide muscular body gave the impression of a dynamo at idle.

"You've stripped our world," Linda Steppart repeated numbly. "Why don't you just go? Take your ships and *go?* How can you do . . . there is no need for . . . this." With a thrust of her jaw she indicated the new round of destruction taking place beyond the office window. Even through soundproofing the devastation could be heard; muted thunder . . . *phoomp* . . . *phoomp* . . . *phoomp* . . . orderly, perfectly timed, like distant cannon firing an honor salute. And with each report another part of her beautiful Vermilion City returned to the dust from which it was formed. "Please, stop this. You're destroying the city!"

"Less than half of it, and most of the people have evacuated," Shimas said matter-of-factly. "We're merely finishing the work we began on our arrival. Sections of your twelve largest cities, along with all of your farms, your transportation systems, mines, universities, factories, research facilities, power plants, water processing stations, and so on. Some unfortunate citizens lost, a few hundred taken aboard for our use. And," he finished with a shrug, "that's it. Then it's over."

"But *why?* What gives you the right—"

He answered in a disinterested tone, explaining to her what her ancestors had done to his, centuries before. "I repeat," he concluded. "It was worlds such as yours that sent my ancestors to slaughter, by the hundreds of thousands. You are paying for your crimes." Shimas took a deep breath, and regarded Steppart. "Is it clear to you now? Do you now understand what every child in Sovereign Command understands before walking?"

Linda Steppart shuddered, thinking of those children and the poison forced into their minds, generation after generation. To learn hatred at such a tender age . . . "But we have done nothing to harm you. What you describe took place centuries before any of us was born. How can *we* be held responsible for—"

"You're being ridiculous, Madam President. Of course you're responsible. History teaches it. But we are not vindictive. We take what we need, and we leave you nothing to make war on one another again. We force you to live in peace. Now then, enough of that. Soon we will have aboard our ships everything we want from you. Raw materials, minerals, captives, meat stock, precious stones and metals, and any new technology we may have found interesting."

"But the destruction . . . you said you were not vindictive."

"And we are not," he said impatiently. This woman's rank entitled her to professional courtesy, but she was behaving like a dull child. "Please, Madam President, think. Suppose we were merely to leave when we're finished, as you suggest. What would happen to your little world here?"

"We would start by rebuilding the . . ."

Shimas held up a thick hand. "Really, your ignorance is appalling. Please consider. The Gold Fleet may know that we're here. If we leave you reasonably intact, they would conclude that you willingly *gave* us what we've taken, in exchange for sparing your cities and farms. Is that clear to you? They would believe that you've taken sides against them. Believe me, I know the Enemy. Within days your world would not have two molecules clinging together. You see?" He watched her eyes widen in what he took for sudden understanding. "You are very fortunate, Madam President. When one of our ships is hit, we often lose every man, woman, and child aboard. Surely you can't complain about . . . that"—he indicated the window again—"compared to the dangers that *we* face. And allow me to add yet another item to your education. As I said, we are not like the Enemy. We would prefer to come to you peaceably, and trade for what we need. You would be astonished to see the things we could sell and teach you. But then as your world began to show signs of true achievement and civilization . . ." He shook his head sadly. "You see my point, Madam President. By their cruelty, the Gold Fleet forces us to do that which is foreign to our nature. And so for your sake—"

"You have stolen or ruined everything of value we possessed. And you will now leave us . . ."

"Precisely!" he said, delighted at her sudden comprehension. "You have nothing left to steal. And, you'll be crippled for decades. The Gold Fleet will *never* come here." Drawing himself to attention, Buto Shimas said triumphantly, "Madam President, we have saved you from the War."

She was weeping. He was certain that he understood her tears. Aside from the gratitude she would now feel, of course she would be somewhat disappointed by what had happened to her pristine world. Those who made their homes on planets—Grounders—were known to grow sentimental about them. He was tolerant of such foolishness, even if he didn't understand it. Existing so remotely from any of the major routes or any area of importance, this president may have thought that her world was safe from the Enemy. How naive. Very possibly, his squadron had arrived not a moment too soon.

"Can . . . can you leave us . . . *any*thing? To help us survive while we rebuild? Something small . . . anything at all . . . no one would know . . ."

Squadron Leader Buto Shimas stared at her, aghast. "Madam President, I have the honor and traditions of my Fleet to uphold. We are not like the Enemy, which is treacherous. If they were here instead of us they might well accede to your request, merely to poison our minds against you. But we would never risk endangering you in that way. Now." He motioned for an aide, who held forth a single sheet of paper. "Once again, I must insist. You will sign this document for our archives affirming that our policies are humane and in your best interests. And you swear on penalty of death that you will not take sides against us." He offered her his warmest smile. "Then we will part, as friends."

Shimas did not mention that he would leave one ship behind for a month, to destroy or bring aboard anything of value the squadron may have overlooked. This was a new tactic, inspired by the poor performance of one ship's captain. He'd decided that the officer needed to learn personal initiative; her ship had done little but stay in the background while the hard work was being carried out. Also, she had attempted to hide a chest of precious stones from him. The punishment for theft was dishonorable retirement. He was offering her a chance to redeem herself; if Captain Lortis succeeded in making a valuable discovery here, that fact might mitigate her circumstances later on when she faced Company Leader Tam Sepal. Shimas felt himself fortunate that a Grounder had told him about the theft. Otherwise he'd have been held as guilty as Captain Lortis, once it was inevitably discovered.

Linda Steppart reached for the paper. There was nothing else she could do.

At that moment the door to the office opened and a young officer entered. "Yes?" Shimas asked pleasantly, buoyed by the thought of their impending departure. Within hours this dreary supply run would be over, and he would be free of Grounders and their ridiculous worlds. How, he wondered, could people live like this? A planet was stuck in its orbit forever, trapped beneath the same starscapes for all of a person's life, its population having virtually no control over climate—without even the most basic freedom of all, the ability to travel as a unit. And the openness! He cringed each time he experienced the nightmare of being "outside" on some planet. Nothing solid overhead . . . how could Grounders look up at their beloved "sky" without the sensation that they were falling into it? Yes, he was glad that this was nearly over.

"Sir," the young woman began, "a Grounder has come to this building, demanding to see you or President Steppart."

*"Demanding?"* Shimas repeated, laughing.

"That was her word, sir."

"I see. Lieutenant Hormat, tell the fool to go away immediately."

"Yes, sir. But, sir, she claims to be the daughter of the president."

"Dane!" Linda Steppart cried. "Let her in!" Seeing the scowl building on the squadron leader's face, she added, "Please? Look, I'm signing your document." She did so quickly and passed it to the aide beside her.

Shimas turned to face her. He said, not unkindly, "As a courtesy, I had hoped to spare you this nonsense, Madam President. Please observe." Turning again to the officer, he asked, "Lieutenant Hormat, how many have come forth and claimed relation to the president? *Today?*"

"Twenty-five, sir. The total is now fifty-three."

"Why have so many come forth with lies, Lieutenant?"

"Sir, this world was visited by us three centuries ago. These Grounders know that by our traditions, close clan members of planetary leaders are not subject to harm or capture. *If,* sir, we know who they are."

"Correct," he said, glancing meaningfully at Steppart. To the lieutenant he said, "And where are they now?"

"In custody, sir, until the president confirms or—"

"Fifty-three. We know that the president has only two children, one of whom is off-world. Why then did you see fit to disturb my meeting and bring this *particular* liar to me?"

"She . . . she seemed very convincing, sir. Very sure of herself. Not afraid, like the others."

Shimas turned to Steppart. "Perhaps, Madam President, you will save your fellow citizens from this needless charade, and give us an accurate description of your daughter?"

One of the first things Linda Steppart had done when the attack began three days before was to incinerate all pictures of Dane, as well as any correspondence that might indicate her present whereabouts. But now that she'd had a moment to think about it, she realized that it was impossible for

Dane to have traveled from the Hardaway farm to Vermilion City in three days, with the skies filled with hostile
ships. "No," she said, "I will not. Wherever she is, I don't
want you to find—"

"You trust us so little, when I have taken pains to explain
the benevolence of Sovereign Command. Again I remind
you, you and your immediate family are safe from harm or
abduction. As you have just heard verified, that is our policy. Circulating her description would have protected her,
or caused her immediate release if she had already been
taken aboard one of our ships. Nothing more. But I refuse
to go on with this nonsense."

To the officer he said, "Release those you have in custody to Colonel Barnell for immediate transport to *Pacal*.
Execute any of them who persist in these fabrications. As
for the one who demanded to see me, count her among
those who persist."

The words flashed in Linda Steppart's mind.
*Demanded . . . convincing . . . very sure of herself . . . not
afraid, like the others.* It was Dane. Somehow, it was Dane.
And he'd just said, *immediate transport. Execute.*
"Squadron Leader, I apologize. Please let me see them all.
If she isn't among them, I'll give you her description."

"With respect, sir, I believe that would be a waste of
time," the young officer said to her superior. "The one I
told you about is the president's daughter." Responding to
the questioning glance he cast her way, she averted her
eyes. "She is, sir. I don't know why I'm so certain. But she
is."

"Very well, Lieutenant. Bring her here."

Eight minutes later Dane Steppart was escorted into the
room.

Mother and daughter ran to one another and embraced
fiercely, each proclaiming in delight, "You're all right!"
and then laughing at Linda's tears.

"Of course I am," Dane said. Then she approached
Squadron Leader Shimas. To Linda's amazement, she offered the man a handshake. "I wanted to meet you, sir," she
said, giving him a bright smile. "I've just walked more than

ninety miles. The damage is much less than I expected. Thank you for your restraint."

Shimas's massive hand swallowed up the small one offered. He nodded, accepting the praise. At least *one* of these Grounders understood. "You are welcome," he said.

Linda was nonplussed, and furious. "Dane, how can you . . . This man and his crews are responsible for . . . they have . . . they're criminals! They should be tried and—"

Dane interrupted angrily, an offended expression on her face. "Mother, don't you see the obvious? No, of course you don't. I'll explain. First, what is done is done. Most of us are alive, and that is because of the squadron leader's kindness. Secondly, we are now safe. Walden will be at peace until well past our lifetimes. None of this would be possible, if not for this good man and the Fleet he represents."

Linda's mind reeled. How could her own daughter defend . . . And then she understood what her daughter was doing . . . Whitlock, the training . . . Dane was working.

Sensing what the young woman wanted from her, she continued the tirade. She dredged up every vulgarity she could recall while cursing the Silver Fleet and every person who served it, past, present, and future.

Dane held herself quiet until she recognized the moment that Shimas was about to explode. She needed him defensive and angry, but not homicidal. "Stop it, Mother!" she shouted. "Can't you, just once, behave rationally? What is *wrong* with you people? The complaints, the whining . . . You make me ashamed to be a citizen of Walden!"

Buto Shimas was torn between fury at the intractable president and admiration for her daughter. Of course the young woman was ashamed of her life as a Grounder. Any reasonable person would be. Here, he thought, is one who deserves better. This led him to reflect once again on the wretched existence these people led. And how relieved he would be to return to *Pacal* and depart. His good mood returned at once. And with it, compassion. "Perhaps," he said charitably to Dane, "you would like to come with us."

To his astonishment the girl spun around and faced him

full-on, hands on hips, laughing. "How presumptuous! Have you forgotten who I am? Are you ignorant of your own policies? You don't have the *authority* to take me. I've thanked you for your kindness. Now go away, little man."

Shimas stared at her, speechless. After a moment he turned and stamped from the room, calling behind him, "Bring the document. And the young Grounder! We're leaving this miserable rock. Now!"

Linda Steppart sank to her knees as the room emptied and Dane cast one last look in her direction. She would never forget that look, any more than she would outlive the heartbreak or the pride that filled her. There had been love in her daughter's eyes. But more than that, triumph. Dane had what she wanted, what she'd planned from the moment she'd seen the first silver ship above Walden.

Fifty-three young women with arms bound to their sides walked silently, with heads lowered, toward the shuttle. The door had just sealed when the craft lifted from Walden and streaked with others of its kind toward the waiting sky.

One block away, Paul Hardaway pulled himself and inch at a time up one last mountain of rubble. From lower back to neck his coveralls were shredded and soaked. He was bleeding from dozens of tiny shallow punctures, the result of an explosion which had vaporized a stone fountain an hour before. He could ignore that for now. But the going was slow because of a badly twisted right leg and his left arm, broken in a shower of debris in the pre-dawn hours of that morning as he entered the city. He'd set and splinted the compound fracture as well as he could while stopping for a ten-minute rest. Now the wound was beginning to fester and alternated between throbbing pain and numbness.

He arrived at the crest of the pile just in time to see the hurried procession. Dane was the last to emerge from the Capitol Building and be herded aboard the shuttle. Nearly blind with anguish, the boy hefted a fallen shard of concrete and hurled it with all his remaining strength at the disappearing vessel. Then he lifted another and pounded his head with it until he collapsed.

# **➤4➤**

Serjel Weezek of the Omnipotent Gold Fleet had decided hours before that this was the day he would go completely out of his mind. Berserk. He was thinking of his thirty years as a crew representative to the Grievance Board. Paradise. And of his five months as a ship coordinator. Hell. Madness beckoned. It was the only course for a sane person to follow.

A woman's voice droned on from behind him, mumbling and barely intelligible. ". . . confirmed for the *third* day and the *fortieth* time that only ninety-nine of them have departed. *Serj.*" The voice became clear and sarcastic. "Or should this common crew address you as 'Coordinator'?"

Weezek bit back the reply that would have given him instant satisfaction. And eons of trouble with the mindless Grievance Board. "Thank you, Crew Harter. I commend you for a highly professional duty watch. If it pleases you, you may proceed to Leisure Quarters."

"About time. As sure as there's a Nomarch, I've earned it," Harter said.

"Indeed you have. As a courtesy, would you please inform Crew Zadmark that his watch began one hour ago, and that if he is not inconvenienced would he kindly consent to—"

"That's not a part of my assignment, *Serj.*" The woman stood from her station and marched out of the room, kicking the door shut behind her.

"What *is?*" he whispered. Two and a half more years of this, Weezek reflected sourly. Supervisors despised him as a presumptuous pretender, daring to seek entry into their caste. Crew despised him on the same grounds, for daring to leave *their* caste. Not just him, though. Any ship coordinator. As if he had asked for the assignment! Never in forty years of service to the Gold Fleet had he wanted to become a supervisor. Now it was all he lived for. On the day of his ascension and transfer from the ship *D35A* to a new society of ten thousand ships, all crew everywhere would fear him like any supervisor; that is, like death itself. On that wonderful day he would return to hating all ship coordinators; his authority over them would be limited, but he'd certainly make their every moment a living misery. As to crew . . . Serjel Weezek smiled for the first time in months. Life would indeed be joyous again.

For now, there were two problems facing him. The long-range one was to placate crew and supervisors without actually going berserk. The short-range one was to discover why one of the Silver Fleet ships had remained behind after their supply run. He'd pondered the question for days, with no new information. Breakdown? Impossible. Treacherous though they were, the Enemy's personnel were nearly as skilled in engineering as that of his own Fleet. To spy? On whom? The Omnipotent Gold Fleet had no intention of establishing a presence here. Weezek and his family of one hundred vessels had been merely transiting the galaxy, not even looking for Enemy ships. Spy on whom, then? Were the People of the Dirt suddenly worth anyone's time? Why would—Coordinator Weezek sat bolt upright. Suppose the Dirts had something that the Silver Fleet could not immediately steal—and yet were not obliged to destroy. Yes! It *had* to be that! And only one thing could be so interesting: *weapons research!* Let it never be forgotten, he thought grimly, that the Razon cube itself was invented eighty years before—by People of the Dirt! For the Silver Fleet to acquire new technology . . .

Weezek's hand shot to the console in front of him. The response was immediate.

"Coordinator Weezek, you have disturbed me once too often. Your ascension is in grave doubt."

"Supervisor Yardley, please accept my apology, and allow me just one moment of your time."

"Speak."

"Supervisor, this coordinator has discovered evidence that . . ."

Seven hours later a sleep-deprived and trembling Serjel Weezek stepped out from the covered safety of a shuttle and onto the open, scorched soil of Walden. Behind him followed Supervisor Fourth Grade Yardley and seventeen crew. Glancing down at his communicator, Weezek saw its light fade from yellow to green. Which meant that thousands of miles above him, unheard and unseen, *D35A* had jumped into hyperspace, to return when the junior supervisor reported success. Weezek felt horribly exposed and alone. He was *outside*. The crew were oddly silent—a testament to their fear of Yardley, who moved without apparent concern for the open terrain. Were all supervisors equally mad, he wondered, or just the lesser ones? With every hesitant step Weezek was reminding himself not to look up; a locator he raised no higher than his waist pointed the way to the capital city.

Two hours of walking subtracted minimally from his dread of this place. Nothing he saw on the ground along the way indicated that anything had survived the Silver Fleet's assault; the butchers were efficient, as always. He hoped that their lone vessel would keep to its station on the far side of this rock.

"Faster pace, Weezek."

"Yes, Supervisor."

Later that afternoon Weezek saw something moving for the first time. It was a wild-eyed and disheveled youth who jumped from behind a boulder and threw something. Then, incredibly, he charged at them, waving one arm and limping heavily on one leg. The boy's head and clothing were filthy and matted with dried blood. He was enormous, and obviously insane.

As one, the seventeen crew of the Omnipotent Gold Fleet turned and fled in every direction. Yardley placed his hands on his hips and remained where he was, mentally rehearsing the questions he had for this Person of the Dirt. Weezek fainted.

Eighty-three miles away, President Linda Steppart stirred, faintly hearing a rhythmic pounding. The noise grew louder and more insistent as she struggled to pull free from an exhausted sleep. At the moment of consciousness she gasped and threw herself to the floor beside her bed. *They've returned!* Seething with anger, she crawled toward the chamber door to sound the alarm.

The pounding was repeated. It took several seconds for her to get beyond the image in her mind and realize that someone was knocking at the door. A quick glance at a wall chronometer told her that this was the time she'd requested for a wake-up call. She sighed, with relief and regret. Three hours already? It seemed only a moment earlier that her body had tumbled toward the bed. "Yes," she called out. "A minute."

Tired, stiff muscles protested—*You're getting old, Steppart*—as she stood and opened the tiny chamber's one closet. From it she took a vermilion overgown and pulled it around her. "Come in, Mary. Did you find any coffee?"

"It's Johann Berger, Madam President. And I do have coffee. May I enter?"

"Yes, Johann." Linda's sense of alarm returned. Berger was her chief of staff. If anyone had worked longer hours than she had during the past days, it was Berger. The fact that he was awake now, against her direct order, indicated yet another major problem.

A child-sized, balding man walked through the doorway as she opened it for him. True to his word, he carried a steaming mug of brown coffee. "It's rather thin, I'm afraid, but it is quite satisfying if you can get it down without tasting it."

"Thank you." She took a small sip and then half emptied the cup in one swallow. It scalded her throat and brought tears to her eyes. As he'd said, satisfying. "What has happened?" she asked abruptly.

"Good news this time, Madam President. Selfishly I'm sure, I had left word to wake me when it occurred. It's out in the corridor now. It appears to be in perfect condition."

"It?" And she understood. "You found it!"

"Not I, I'm afraid. Credit belongs to the workers you assigned to search through—"

"Yes, yes! Medals will be awarded, I assure you, the moment we can produce them again. Now bring it in!" This was the best moment she'd had in a long while. As with the coffee, she had no intention of taking the time to savor it.

Berger returned seconds later carrying a nondescript white metal box. "There isn't a scratch on it," he said with obvious satisfaction.

"Have you checked the contents?"

"How could I, Madam President? Fortunately you are still living, and so I have not disturbed the contents of your personal safe. Therefore you alone have the code to open this."

"Of course." Her heart was beating rapidly as she took the box. "Johann, only the two of us are present. Have you forgotten protocol?"

The small man smiled, understanding. "Your predecessor never allowed me the privilege. Please accept my apology . . . Linda."

Both knew that she was stalling, fearful of discovering that the device had been damaged. When her fingers were steady she punched in a seven-character code. The box's lid opened with a barely audible "pop."

*It looks fine,* she thought. *But . . . will it work? Dane's life—assuming she survives her present ordeal—might well depend on it.*

"All right," she said. "Let's go."

"Ah, Madam Pr . . . Linda. Your state of attire?"

"The citizens have seen much worse lately, Johann. Are you coming?"

The Capitol Building was the tallest structure remaining in Vermilion City. With the autolifts presently lacking power, the two climbed fifteen levels of stairs and out to the roof. Dawn was still three hours away, but visibility was good beneath a star-filled sky. A westerly wind caught them at once, rustling Linda's overgown and bringing with it the musty, smoky reek from dozens of small fires still smoldering. The shouts and shovels of work gangs below could be heard as citizens worked in three shifts to level mountains of debris in preparation for clearing the streets and erecting new, modest shelters against the coming winter.

Linda Steppart waited while Berger kicked aside enough rubble to give them a flat working space. When he was satisfied, she placed the open white box in the center of the small area. Now or not at all, she thought.

Working carefully in the semidark, she punched another code, this one of ten characters, into the box's front panel. Immediately a timer glowed from the interior. She entered "2" and "0," and stood up. The timer hesitated and then read out, "19 . . . 18 . . ."

At the five-second mark she reached for Johann's hand and clutched it tightly. "3 . . . 2 . . . 1 . . . 0." A bright flash stung their eyes. There was no sound at all. Had it worked? She had hoped to see it go, but the flash . . .

With her night vision ruined, Linda bent over the box and felt inside its interior. It was slightly warm, no more. She probed carefully with her fingers until she was satisfied that the message needle was gone.

She didn't know why so much—it seemed like everything—depended on her daughter's capture. Those who'd trained her said that Dane was the linchpin of their plans. That explained nothing, but Linda had long ago accepted that she could know little of what was intended to take place. Very well, she'd trusted them. Although he had never said so, she believed that fulfilling this promise to Mr. Whitlock would somehow help her daughter, his "linchpin," remain alive. It was all she could do for Dane.

Her rational mind told her that the launching of this device, whose purpose she did not know, was a poor basis for hope. But it was all she had, and she clung to it fiercely.

*     *     *

Twenty miles up from them and still accelerating, the tiny transmitter streaked outward on a preprogrammed course. The device contained no moving parts. Its form and functions were one, the product of liquid SynthTechnology long ago developed by the same small group who'd invented the Razon cube; in this case, their discovery had gone undetected by either of the Fleets. Too small to register on any watching eye or instrument, the needle flashed into hyperspace where it would traverse galaxies, in and out of hyperspace, while broadcasting on the null-band—another development that so far was safe from the Fleets.

The tone itself was a message. It would resound within microscopic implants in the tissues of hundreds of captives aboard Gold and Silver ships, some of whom had been in place and preparing for decades. They would never know specifically who the signal referred to; only that Mr. Whitlock had found someone with the abilities he had searched for, and that that person had now been taken captive. They would understand that their organization—The Stem—was ready to carry out the plan for which he'd selected and trained them. The signal also told them that their individual assignments must soon be brought to completion. For many, this meant voluntary death.

Two hours of a new workday had passed. Linda Steppart sat tiredly at her desk, reading the latest reports of the devastation that had come to Walden. With each one her anger grew, until finally she could no longer read them. Closing the folder and rubbing moist eyes, she thought beyond her own world to the uncounted others fallen victim to this war. Even those so far untouched existed in terror and isolation. The planets seldom communicated with one another, fearful of attracting Fleet attention. Civilian space travel was rare, for the same reason. But what travel there was, what communication there was, consistently revealed a picture that had not changed for six hundred years: two colossal Fleets with a hatred for one another that was beyond imagining. Millions of innocent lives caught between them, broken, extinguished, or enslaved. Civilizations by the

# PREPARATION

# ⇥ 5 ⇤

Talk among the captives was animated, to the extent that was possible with their arms and legs bound. Dane watched the others sympathetically but distantly. They were victims, taken from their homes and families by force. Who among them would believe that she was here by choice? She thought again of that strange old man, Mr. Whitlock. She had been at first frightened, then astonished, at how intimately he had come to know her mind. He understood her joys, her sorrows, her anger, happiness, fears, hopes . . . often before she herself recognized them. He usually knew what she would do in any situation, and she often found herself doing things she hadn't planned to do—realizing later he had somehow influenced her behavior. Such influence, he said, was an art. He tantalized her with the promise of secrets: What he did, she could do. Dane was an enthusiastic student. Over the years she learned how to gain entry into another mind. And how to use what she found there.

Whitlock made her an agent of The Stem, taught her about the Fleets, and gave her a job to do. *"The Fleets,"* he'd said, *"can be envisioned as the two halves of a single brain. We will become the brain stem. Once we have placed ourselves properly, neither half will be able to survive without us. Then we will vanish, and direct the fall of a dead colossus."*

Nervous laughter caught her attention. Dane knew only two of the group taken with her. One was her longtime friend Carnie Niles, daughter of Aldon and Martie Niles, both physicians from Vermilion City. Listening to Carnie assure the others that her family would come for them, Dane wondered what she ought to say. She'd seen the bodies of Carnie's parents in a pile with other medical workers, as she'd crept into the city that morning. Say nothing, she decided. Blonde and taller than Dane and much heavier, Carnie had always looked at life with hope and good cheer. It could destroy her to learn suddenly how much she had lost in one tragic day.

The other person Dane knew was seated next to her. She was Hatta Gronis, who, at twenty-five, appeared to be the oldest among them. Hatta was nothing like Carnie. Unusually tall and thin, she came from generations of bureaucrats who'd worked at the Capitol Building in mid-level positions. The woman was quick and decisive and not considered to be friendly by those who served under her. From observing all of them there, Dane estimated that Hatta was the least likely to adapt to her new status. The power and authority she'd wielded so inflexibly had been hers as a virtual birthright; everything she'd encountered so far in life had been traditional and expected.

Dane understood why all of these young women had claimed to be her. Historically, high government officials and their immediate families were safe from capture or physical harm. None of these people could have known at first that others were making the same claim. Each had hoped—naively—to be interviewed, believed, and released. But their lies were born of desperation, and were bound to · fail, as indeed they had.

Seated opposite the captives just inside the door of the shuttle's cramped hold were six crew members from the vessel she'd heard referred to as *Pacal*. These four men and two women were the real focus of Dane's attention. None of them had spoken a word, to the captives or to each other, since the trip began. All were identically dressed in maroon clothing that differed only in patches worn on both shoulders, which she assumed indicated rank. She watched how they sat, at whom they looked, how often each of them glanced up at the compartment fixtures or down at their hands, how they reacted when one of their number moved to stretch. Soon it was clear who was in charge among them.

The captives had been relatively quiet for several minutes when Hatta asked, "Where are the comfort facilities?" None of the crew members responded with anything but a blank stare. Anger flashed on the woman's face. "I asked you a question! Where—"

"Wait," Dane whispered to her. She keyed in on the fat bearded man. Subtly mimicking his posture, she said, "Perhaps one of you would tell her how long it will be until we reach your ship?" She'd been correct. The other five looked to the bearded man.

"Ten minutes," he said.

"Thank you, sir." Dane lowered her head slightly and gave him a tentative smile. "We're not yet accustomed to your level of personal discipline."

"That's to be expected," he said, and half returned the smile. One of the women cleared her throat. Dane hid a grin. From the man's quick glance at her, she was certain that this had nothing to do with any proscription against speaking with captives. The woman claimed authority over the man as either wife or lover.

Dane was gratified, but not surprised, at what she'd been able to learn so quickly. Whitlock and other of her teachers had stressed to her that there existed a "universal currency of interaction" that is shared by all peoples and all cultures, of all times. This was the first opportunity she'd had to prove for herself how true that was. Those of the Fleets were as alien to her as human beings could be. Their experiences, their expectations, their basic assumptions about life itself might bear no resemblance to her own. And yet they were clearly subject to the same core principles of relationship and communication that governed her own society. She savored this fact for long moments; it meant that what she'd learned and practiced on Walden would be, at least to some degree, effective against those whom she was pledged to destroy.

Dane was tempted to experiment further. Could she elicit

a conversation from one of the other crew members? Could she further develop the woman's irritation at the man? And then subtly intervene, making them both feel a whisper of gratitude toward her? She dismissed the thought as dangerous and premature. For now she wanted to draw no further attention. First she needed to know what these people *did* with their anger and gratitude. She'd been taught to anticipate that with some of those she would encounter, it would be safer to bring on hatred than friendship. And that with others, either was dangerous; success would then depend upon remaining invisible.

Their arrival within *Pacal* was signaled only by a subtle decrease in the shuttle's air pressure. Within seconds there was a gentle impact as the craft settled to the deck. To the captives it could as well have been a crash landing, for that light touching down carried with it the full impact of death: the death of all that they had known in life. Never again would they be anything but someone's property. Every thought for the future, every wish a young mind had made while dreaming alone or sharing that dream with a special friend, was gone.

The reality seemed to reach all of them at once. Carnie Niles buried her face in her hands and wept. Her family wasn't coming. No one ever would. Hatta Gronis moved her lips without sound and trembled. She closed her eyes and began rocking, unable to hear Dane whispering to her or feel the girl sliding her arms around her body.

When the ship was firmly docked, the bearded fat man leapt to his feet with surprising agility and addressed them all. "My name is First EngineTender Mr. Harold Chittham. You may address my by my first name: *Mister*." The other troops laughed on cue. "Your name," Chittham continued, "is Grounder. Translated, that means 'nothing.' Understand that, and you may survive. During the next few days you will be my responsibility. Be warned, I am ready for you. I expect that very soon at least one of you will test me, or otherwise cause trouble. That's good. Whoever it will be, I thank you in advance. Your punishment or killing will help the others understand us better. Now, which of you volunteers for that duty?" It was obvious to Dane that he'd rehearsed these remarks. And that the man was nervous. "No one?" he asked, letting a little of his relief slip through. "Won't you reconsider? I promise you that someone here will test me eventually. Why not now?" Seconds passed in silence. "Good. You." He motioned to one of his troops. "Untie five of them. Those five can untie the rest."

When they were all free of restraints, Chittham motioned to another of his party. The woman who'd cleared her throat before opened a satchel and dumped its contents to the floor. Chittham scowled at her. "Pass them out, Neria. Please," he said tightly. She raised her eyebrows at him as if to speak, but apparently thought better of it and bent to retrieve the scraps of cloth. Walking among the captives, she said, "Each of you take one."

"These are blindfolds," Chittham continued. "Put them on securely. I'll be inspecting each of you as you pass by me. As soon as they're tied, put your hands on someone's shoulders." Dane's blindfold was shoved into her hands. She took it and coughed. The cloth was filthy, and smelled of a sharp chemical. Just from holding it, Dane felt her eyes begin to tear. She immediately dropped the rag and made her way around some of the other captives until she could reach her hand between two of them and retrieve another. Neria did not look up to see whom the hand belonged to. This one was relatively clean. Dane fastened it around her forehead and pulled it down over her eyes.

After a minute Dane heard the fat man moving among them. There was the impact of a hand striking flesh. One of the young women cried out. "No, you fool!" she heard Chittham bellow. "Put your hands on the *back* of her shoulders!"

When they were formed up, Dane's hands were slapped away from her partner's shoulders. "You're the head of the line." She recognized Neria's voice. "Follow me." Dane reached out, but was again slapped away. "You can hear, can't you? Now let's go." She moved away and Dane followed, straining to pick out her footsteps from other sounds. By listening closely to each of Neria's footfalls,

Dane was able to recognize the moment that they came to
steps leading down from the shuttle. As she negotiated the
three steps and arrived on the hangar deck, she was surprised at the level of noise. All around her she heard people
lifting obviously heavy objects, grunting with the effort.

A sudden lessening of noise told her that they'd entered a
corridor. After a turn to the right, the corridor seemed to go
on forever. A number of people passed them, going in the
opposite direction. Neria stopped to exchange a few words
with some of these. In the brief conversations, the captives
were not once mentioned. It was as if they did not exist. Or
were beneath notice.

*"Battle Contact! Battle Contact!"*

The metallic voice was deafening, seeming to shake the
floor beneath them. It would seem impossible, but Chittham's voice was even louder. "Grounders! Hands and
knees! Move to your right against the wall. Link to the
bars. Now!"

*"Battle Contact! Battle Contact!"*

Dane was on hands and knees, crawling to her right. The
corridor became a jumble of noise with people running in
both directions. She bumped into thin vertical stanchions at
her hip and shoulder, and assuming that this was what he'd
meant them to "link to," slid one arm and one leg between
the bars and the wall, pressing her body tightly against it.
As she did so, *Pacal* veered hard to the right and accelerated. Behind her she could hear many of her group falling
out into the aisle and rolling back the way they'd come.
"Idiots!" Chittham roared, and there were sounds of bodies
being kicked. "Link to the bars! Grab them! Get against the
wall!"

"Mr. Chittham, *help* me! I don't understand this!" The
voice was Hatta's.

There was more kicking of flesh and pandemonium for
long minutes while *Pacal* abruptly changed speed and direction, once rolling completely over. Dane heard bodies
falling against every surface of the corridor. Her arm and
leg were strained and sore where they were linked to the
stanchions, but she was able to hold fast.

After a final jolt, the ship's motion was smooth again.

*"Secure from Battle Contact drill. Secure from Battle Contact drill."*

"Grounders, up!" Chittham bellowed.

"I can't! Help me!" Hatta again. And again the sound of a body being kicked, with Hatta crying out in pain.

"I said, up! I'll deal personally with any of you who don't think you can walk. *Up!*"

There was moaning and quiet cursing from the captives, but soon they were formed together and moving down the corridor with Neria once again in the lead. After only a few dozen steps, the procession stopped. Dane heard Neria open a door to their left. "Inside," she said.

This seemed to be another corridor, much narrower than the first. On either side of her Dane could reach out and touch horizontal bars running parallel about two feet up from one another. There were vertical ones as well, at roughly six-foot intervals. At every third interval the horizontal bars were gone for three feet before appearing again. With no one leading her, she continued walking until she came to the end of the corridor, which she judged from counting the spaces was approximately one hundred twenty feet in length. There was a pervasive odor of perspiration and sickness.

"Take off the blindfolds," Chittham called from far behind her. "You're home."

Dane freed her eyes and blinked them against the unaccustomed light. As her vision adapted she saw where she was: a catacomb. The bars had been bed frames. The beds were stacked from the floor to two feet below the ceiling, six high, eighteen to a block. The precise sameness stretched from where she stood all the way back to the door she'd entered through, and away on both sides. Between each block was a three-foot passageway. At a rough guess she would estimate the total number of beds to be near five hundred.

About a fifth of them were occupied, she soon saw. Men and women, in about equal numbers, were scattered throughout the compartment. Most of the ones Dane could see were young. Some were sleeping, but most were watching the newcomers. Some of them were on their sides in a fetal position. They were ill, Dane concluded, which accounted for the smell.

Chittham spoke again. "Each of you choose a bunk that doesn't have someone's belongings on it. Stamped onto its head frame you'll find an identifier. I don't care what you call each other, but when addressing any member of this crew you will refer to yourselves and each other by that identifier. Next. The *comfort facilities* . . . by the way, the Grounder who asked that question aboard the shuttle is no longer with us . . . are against each of the compartment walls. I suggest that you new Grounders get in line right away. Those who arrived ahead of you tend to be selfish about the *comfort facilities*. At least for a while." He laughed at his witticism, and was joined by the five troops. "Good-bye for now. An attendant will arrive soon to record your identifiers and give you a little information about staying alive. I'll be back in three days. You'll be used to the food by then. That's an order." Chuckling, he led his troops out of the compartment. Neria slammed the door behind her as she departed.

Almost immediately the door opened again and Chittham walked through, alone. He made his way to Dane. "Didn't think I forgot about you, did you?"

"Sir?"

"Who are you?"

She looked at a vacant bunk next to her. "CJ359, sir," she said at once.

"Very good." He grinned down at her. "May I call you CJ?"

"Yes, sir."

"You seem to have a brain about you," Chittham said. "And I like the way you tried to flatter me before. I'm going to let you try it again, more privately."

Dane felt the threat, but hid her revulsion. "Yes, sir."

"Don't eat anything until I send for you, CJ. You can adapt to the food afterward." He glanced down for a moment, then back up at Dane. His mocking expression had turned to anger. Without another word he turned and left as the captives pushed up against the frames to make room.

Shaken, Dane ignored the sympathetic comments around her and climbed into her new bed. *I'm not as clever as I thought* was the first thing that came to mind. Carnie Niles came into view and placed a hand on Dane's shoulder. "I'm sorry," she said.

A man's voice came from beneath Dane. "He's taunting you. They don't touch children. Not in that way."

"Are you sure?" Carnie asked.

"Yes. He has the authority to have your friend killed, but not to . . . touch her."

"I wonder if he killed Hatta," Carnie said to Dane.

The man's voice said, "Is she the one who's no longer with you?"

"Yes," Carnie answered.

"What did she do?"

"Nothing."

"Did she speak to one of them without permission?"

"Three times," Dane told him, remembering Hatta's voice during the drill.

"That's not good. The first offense is usually punished by intimidation. The second, by denial of what they call 'privileges.' If she did it a third time, you probably won't be seeing her again. Not soon, anyway. But I doubt if she's dead. We have a little value to these people. Not much, but some. And none, if we're dead."

"What will happen to her, then?"

"Most likely, isolation. They'll find a use for her eventually, on one of their ships."

"I see," Dane said. She was certain that the man was holding something back; there'd been a slight variation in his vocal cadence on the words "isolation" and "eventually." Whatever he was hesitant to say, she didn't want Carnie to hear it. "How long have you been here?"

"This is my third day."

"You've learned a lot."

The man laughed. "Oh, it's fascinating stuff. I find myself paying very close attention."

"No doubt. I'm Dane Steppart. This is Carnie Niles."

"You're the president's kid?"

"One of them," Dane said. "The other is off-world."

"And so are you, now." The man laughed again. "Sure, I know all about you. I'm Momed Pwanda. Look, you should both try to sleep. After your first meal you won't be able to."

"Thanks," Dane said. "I will." What did he mean, 'I know all about you'? He might know *of* her. But the way he'd said it, it didn't sound like a casual comment.

Carnie squeezed Dane's shoulder and bent down to thank the man. She straightened and bent over Dane. "He's *very* handsome!" she whispered. "But not very smart. How can he expect us to sleep? I could never sleep here. What do *you* think they did to Hatta?"

Dane took Carnie's hand and held it, saying nothing. She wanted to tell her friend not to worry, but couldn't bring herself to speak nonsense. She was furious with herself for the clumsiness she'd displayed with Chittham and Neria. Childish! It had been mere parlor-game stuff, as easy to perform as it was to see through. She'd fallen—or rather, led herself into—a trap made especially for the careless. So easy to think, "I'm specially trained; therefore anything I do is special." Like the successful artist who couldn't understand the critical failure of a painting she'd virtually slept through. Or the acclaimed lecturer discovering to his horror that while he'd allowed his mind to wander, he'd lost his audience. Or the precocious Dane Steppart, who'd forgotten for a moment that *everyone* is to some degree skilled at watching people.

Whitlock had taught her science, not parlor tricks. He and the others of The Stem trusted her. They said she was one of the very best; they were all certain that she could do the job. But for the first time in her life, Dane did not share their confidence. She'd acted too soon, and had nearly ruined everything. Suppose she made another elementary mistake? *Why* had she made it? She thought about that for long minutes. When the answer came, it shocked her. There was a factor at work here she hadn't anticipated: She was afraid. And as her mind moved in that unlit direction, she found something else. She was lonely. Why so hard to admit it? Or to admit that . . . she thought of Paul Hardaway's question, and her too-easy, offhand response. But he'd been right. Good, solid Paul was right. Despite anything else, she was still a fifteen-year-old child.

Dane reached for Carnie's other hand, and the two looked for a long time into each other's eyes.

"I know," Carnie said at last. "Me too." She climbed into the bunk above Dane, and within two minutes was snoring.

Dane lay awake thinking of her mother and Paul. As president of the council, her mother would be overwhelmed with work, but not too busy to worry about her. Somehow Dane had never given that much thought. She hoped that things were quiet out on the farm for Paul and his family. And that every now and then, he too would think of her.

*"Grounders! Up!"* was the next sound she heard, followed by the clamor of clanging bars and angry shouts that startled her awake. It took a moment to remember where she was. There was no time to wonder why her cheeks were wet.

A tall and slender woman entered the compartment, followed by six others. All wore plain gray tunics and trousers, and carried clipboards. Veteran slaves, Dane guessed.

## ⇥ 6 ⇤

*Pacal* and its Squadron formed up with the other units of Sovereign Command that had been involved in the supply runs. The four thousand nine hundred ninety-nine ships met in a designated sector of space between the plundered Galaxy M-419 and its nearest neighbor, S-1724. The mood aboard all the ships was jubilant. The operation had been a success, with all vessels but one—the ship Buto Shimas had left behind on Walden—arriving packed with commodities to be sent on to larger segments of the Fleet. However, the success of the mission surprised no one, and was not itself the cause for overall good feeling. Rather, it was the fact that the expedition was over and they were again in deep space. Far, far distant from the clutter of stars and the stench of planets.

Within hours of arriving they learned the true reason for the supply run, which most of them—privately—had considered a waste of time. First, it was not fifty planets of Galaxy M-419 that the Fleet had visited recently; it was four hundred, which meant more supplies could be secured. Second and more important—the squadron leaders purposely saved this for last—orders were read stating that these five companies would soon link to a similar number, forming a new flotilla of ten thousand ships. In turn their flotilla was to join nine others to form a new SubFleet totaling one hundred thousand—and then, incredibly, be united with another SubFleet, the one commanded by the invincible Brotman Nandes.

As these words echoed through the ships every man,

woman, and child stood up and cheered. For the news could mean only one thing: A major engagement with the Enemy was imminent. The news was savored, absorbed with a sense of awe. Even the oldest among them could not boast of having seen combat on this scale. The closest such occurrence, involving only half of one SubFleet, had taken place one hundred seventeen years before at Q17-V065. There, as history recorded, a much larger but incompetent force from the Gold Fleet had been routed and nearly destroyed. This time the orders read that there would be no Enemy survivors.

From that moment on, no other subject was discussed. Where would the battle take place? When? Who would command the two SubFleets? To whom would fall the honor of leading the first attack? How many of the Enemy would be dealt with by their own flotilla, company, squadron, ship? Would they be using, or facing, new weapons?

No one outside the Sovereign Command Council knew their full strength, which stretched across galaxies and took power over all it encountered. But guesses were ranging that from twenty to thirty percent of the entire Silver Fleet was about to go into battle—as a *unit*. The very thought of it was hypnotic, intoxicating.

Last to join the celebrating ships was the squadron commanded by Jenny Marsham. Her unit had been permanently detached from its former XF322 Company, in which she had been third in seniority. Now she was to serve XF566. The transfer could only be seen as a deliberate insult; the higher number of XF566 denoted a lower status. Worse, her new assignment placed her below someone named Buto Shimas—an officer new and untested in his post, and the most junior squadron leader in XF566. Until now.

It was Shimas who made the first and only courtesy call upon Jenny at her arrival. As he entered the Operations Room of *Bagalan,* she stood to greet him. While they exchanged pleasantries, Jenny took stock of the man before her. He was about the same height as her late father, perhaps an inch over five feet. But the word she would choose to describe him was "massive." He seemed as wide at the shoulders as he was tall, with arms and legs proportional. She guessed that there was not one ounce of fat on his body. Physical immensity, along with his bald head and fierce black mustache, gave him the look of a primitive weapon: explosive, powerful, and not easy to control. His soft manner of speaking somehow added a dangerous edge to that image. Early in their exchange of pleasantries, he expressed condolences and respect for Major General Marsham. That, coupled with the consideration he had shown by coming here instead of waiting for her to visit his own flagship *Pacal,* gave Jenny a favorable first impression.

For his part, Buto Shimas understood why Squadron Leader Marsham had elected to receive him alone. His seniority over her was unquestionably a source of discomfort. Wisely, she had seen to it that if her guest were of a mind to embarrass her, it would not be done in the presence of her officers. Of course it was a breach of protocol. Not serious, just enough to make him smile and raise her a few degrees in his estimation. In her position he'd have done exactly the same.

She invited him to sit, which began the formal part of their meeting. "I wanted to present you personally with our new orders," Shimas began, retrieving a document from his uniform blouse. "I think you'll find them gratifying, to say the least."

Skeptical, Jenny read the first few paragraphs quickly. Her eyebrows arched as the import of the orders reached her. "This is . . . wonderful!"

"An understatement," Shimas said. "I believe this explains your transfer to XF566."

"How so?"

"Obvious, I think. It means that our company of ships is to have a vital role in the upcoming engagement."

"Please explain, Squadron Leader."

"Would you address me as Buto?"

"Certainly." She made a point of not inviting the same familiarity from him. He gave no indication of resentment.

"You were at N34-V654 twenty-two years ago with your father?"

"That's a matter of record. My father was in overall command. I merely served as a ship's captain."

"Aboard *Tanal.*"

"Yes."

"Involved in both the first and the last assaults."

"You're beginning to sound like a court-martial officer, Buto. Do you have a point to make?"

"Yes. N34-V654 was an important battle in many respects. What interests me at the moment is that we nearly suffered disaster. We *would* have suffered disaster, if it weren't for the tactics that were developed during the fight."

"Major General Marsham was properly recognized for his accomplishment."

"Of course. But you were there. You were an integral part of that astounding campaign. And since that encounter you've served many times in a first-attack capacity. Both as ship's captain and squadron leader. No one in XF566 has your depth of combat experience. *Innovative* combat experience. It can be assumed that all of your captains are exceptionally well trained. And so my point is that your presence among us bodes very well for our participation in what will be the greatest victory any of us will ever know."

Marsham thought about what he'd said and grinned, relaxing. "Buto, if you weren't senior to me I would accuse you of bootlicking."

Looking at her in surprise, Shimas tensed. "And I would be gravely offended, Squadron Leader. Gravely." His eyes and tone left no doubt that he meant his words literally. Marsham instantly regretted her comment. She had spoken in jest, a response to his friendly, even familiar, overtures. But she'd gone too far. Before she could begin an apology, he went on. "I came aboard *Bagalan* to welcome you and to share the good news with you personally. As well as to pay my respects to your father. And to your mother, who I know perished from injuries received at N34-V654."

She was mortified. "Squadron Leader Shimas—"

"Please be silent. I believe that my assessment of your transfer here is accurate. Any other interpretation of my praise for your record is absurd. Further, it was my hope that I would be given the opportunity to profit from your knowledge and experience. That is still my intention. And that is all I have to say to you for now, Squadron Leader Marsham. Perhaps you will save us both embarrassment by erasing all records of this meeting." He stood and turned for the doorway.

Marsham stood also. "Sir," she said to his back, "nothing is on record. And I am trying to apologize. Will you accommodate me for a moment?" The man remained where he was, giving the impression of a powerful engine at rest, while Jenny Marsham attempted the difficult task of humbling herself.

After a few seconds he said, "Very well. You've said enough." When he turned abruptly to face her again, Shimas was grinning. "I believe we are now even in the matter of jokes, Squadron Leader Marsham. Shall we continue our meeting?"

She stared at him, running the emotional gamut from confusion to indignation to rage to hilarity. It had been many years since anyone had gotten the better of her so quickly. Now she was certain that her first assessment of Buto Shimas had been correct. She liked him.

For the next hour he briefed her on the composition of XF566 Company, and his own role in it. Naturally, he could offer her no preview of her own squadron's function. That would come directly from the company leader. She recognized a few of the names he mentioned in passing. Not from having met any of them, but from reading brief reports of their commendations and promotions. And from a much more enlightening source: gossip. The name she knew best was Tam Sepal, who commanded the entire company. This was bad news. Sepal was known to be jealous of his position and prone to destroy the career of anyone he found threatening. Worse than that, his combat record was only mediocre; it was rumored that his high po-

sition had come from the fact that a granduncle of his was a
council member.

Hoping to elicit more information from him, Marsham
said, "Buto, I say to you again that this meeting has not
been, and is not now, being recorded."

Shimas nodded, and began speaking informally. "I have
the same problem. Faulty equipment. In fact, *Pacal*'s monitors are almost always out of order."

She looked at him in surprise. "You don't use monitors?"

"Rarely. Only a few of my officers know about it, and
none of the crew. Until someone gives me a reason to acti-
vate them, I'm content to allow everyone a little privacy."
He shrugged. "Let's just say I like to live dangerously."

"Apparently." Marshal asked cautiously, "Have you discussed with anyone your idea of why I was sent here?"

"No," he replied, understanding her perfectly. "Believe
me, that isn't something I'd want Sepal to hear about, for
your sake. Do you know his reputation?"

"That's why I asked. Thank you. For the first time, I'm
pleased that I was sent here with such a junior billet."

"Someone in authority wanted you here, but acted to protect you."

"No. But it did work out that way."

"I don't know what you mean."

"I've appreciated your candor, Buto. Please don't be insulted if I'm not ready to confide in you."

"Not at all," he said, smiling. "I'm aware that I give the
impression of supreme wisdom. But actually I'm very
dense, and not at all easy to offend. But I believe I'll ask
your leave now. Again, welcome to XF566 Company."

"Thank you for coming."

They rose together and shook hands. Little was said on
the walk to the hangar where his shuttle was waiting. The
man's eyes were everywhere, looking over her crew and
*Bagalan*'s state of preparedness. The level of energy and
competence he felt all around him was amazing. He was
thoroughly impressed. But he kept that to himself, feeling
at heart that he was too junior to comment on anything so
intimate to Jenny Marsham as her personal flagship. As he

was about to step aboard the shuttle he said, "Oh, I meant to ask. How is *Bagalan* staffed for Grounders?"

"Many of them are nearing retirement. Why?"

"I'll see to it that we replenish your supply, before the most promising ones are shipped elsewhere. Oh! A thought just came to me. We have aboard *Pacal* a young woman who was brought to my attention by one of my officers. She expressed a rare understanding and appreciation for the work of Sovereign Command. I believe you'll find her interesting. That is to say, useful. Very intelligent."

"Why yes, thank you. My chief steward will send your staff a list of our needs."

"Excellent. Good-bye for now, Squadron Leader Marsham."

She shook his hand once more. "Please, address me as Jenny. Good-bye, Buto."

Shimas waved cheerfully to her as the shuttle's door closed. When he was strapped into his seat, he burst out laughing. *Oh yes, Jenny, you'll find her* interesting. *And now I'm one ahead of you in the matter of jokes.*

# ⇒ 7 ⇐

*"You are not yet under attack. Surrender your vessel."*

Ship Coordinator Serjel Weezek's stomach lurched toward his throat. It had to happen! It *had* to! The shuttle from *D35A* had lifted from the scorched soil of Walden only moments before. Why *now?* The wild boy had turned out to be sane, even reasonable and cooperative, once his wounds were dressed and he was convinced that they had no idea of who or where a Dane Steppart was. He'd agreed to lead them to his world's president, whom he identified as a man by the name of Hindman who was known to be hiding far to the north in a place called Azure Forest. Yes, he'd confirmed, Hindman had long been suspected of conducting illegal weapons research. Could that be why those "other ships" had come and nearly killed everybody? Of course it was, Yardley said. Actually *smiling* at Weezek. Then we'd better catch him, the boy said, before the damage got worse. Could Weezek's future have been brighter? That, he thought, is why it had to happen.

*"Surrender your vessel."*

Turning green, Weezek looked from the pilot's controls to Yardley. "What can we do, Supervisor?"

"Destroy that ship, Coordinator," he said simply.

"Supervisor, this is an unarmed shuttle! That's a *war*ship out there!"

"Ingenuity is the key, Coordinator. Now stop annoying me and get to it.

As he'd promised himself that very morning, Serjel Weezek went berserk.

• • •

Captain Vivian Lortis of Sovereign Command could barely contain her excitement.

For three days after her squadron had departed she'd kept *Anfer* on station above this useless planet, watching the Grounders running around like tiny animals: Tear down piles of debris. Put up new piles. Fill in the roads. Pull their dead out of the big holes and put them in little ones. Cover them with dirt. *(Barbarians!)* Watching this nonsense instead of moving on to important work. Curse Buto Shimas! Practically accused her of theft! She liked gems, wanted to examine and classify a chest full of them before turning it over to him. Could have found a new crystal, valuable to Sovereign Command. Could have. For her services? One or two for herself. No more than that. *Does that make me a thief? Hardly.*

Shimas had thought to punish her. Give her some time to worry about it. Instead . . . she couldn't stop dancing. When was the last time Sovereign Command had prisoners from the Gold Fleet? *Living* ones? And a ship! Yes, just a shuttle, not even hyperspace-capable. Yes, only a fourth-rate supervisor (if he was telling the truth) with a bruised-up face and eighteen non-officers (if *they* were telling the truth) and one Grounder. But she, Captain Vivian Lortis, she alone of the Silver Fleet's however-many ship's captains, had achieved this historic coup. Herself. The ship whole, the prisoners alive.

She'd called Tam Sepal directly. (Shimas could eat dirt and spit Grounders if he thought *he* was going to share in the credit.) The reply: *Escort en route your location. Return soonest. All precautions, all speed. Conditional Well Done.* She just couldn't stop dancing.

On her third day aboard *Pacal* Dane could bear the food without retching. It looked and smelled like liquefied raw fish mixed with cleaning fluid, presented hot in the morning and as cold gel in the evening, dished from small tanks into bowls with no eating utensils. The procedure was to drink it hot or scoop it with the fingers when cold. The erstwhile blindfolds served to clean fingers and mouth. Terrible stomach sickness and cramps had afflicted everyone but Carnie. After a mild reaction the first morning, she looked forward to the meals. For the rest of them, as Momed Pwanda had promised, the body did eventually adapt.

Dane found herself liking Pwanda very much. He was only slightly shorter than Paul Hardaway, ebony dark, with the muscular but lithe body structure of an athlete. He found something amusing about every situation, laughed easily and contagiously, and combined extreme self-confidence with gentle patience in quieting the fears of the other captives. She would put his age at mid-twenties.

His knowledge of their new environment was astonishing. From Dane's description of them, he identified both Squadron Leader Buto Shimas and the young lieutenant, Giel Hormat, whom she'd encountered in her mother's office on Walden. But he hadn't said how he knew who they were, only that he'd been taken on the first day of the raid.

Today was the day that Chittham had said he'd come back to them. On Pwanda's advice, Dane skipped the morning meal. "You'll want to be as clearheaded and attentive as possible," he said. "Worry about your stomach later."

"What do you think will happen now?" Carnie asked him, finishing her bowl of gruel and accepting Dane's with a nod of thanks.

"Orientation and assignment, no doubt," Pwanda said. "Only a few of us who arrived before you have been outside this room. It'll be good to see something else for a change."

"And smell," Dane added. "Although I'm getting used to it."

"No, you're not. Everyone's just feeling better." He grinned at her. "You'll notice that the lines in front of the *facilities* are much shorter lately."

"Dane," Carnie said worriedly, "when Chittham gets

here, maybe you'd better stay out of his sight. I still don't trust . . . Oh! Excuse me!"

"One bowl too many," Pwanda remarked sympathetically as Carnie hurried off. "I'm curious, Dane," he said in a half-whisper. "You don't seem as alarmed as the others about today. Why?"

She began to ask him what the point of worry would be, but instead asked a question that had bothered her for three days now. "Momed, who *are* you?" His knowledge had been so complete—too complete—that she'd at first suspected that he was something of a spy among them, either a long-held captive or a member of *Pacal*'s crew. But in conversation he had revealed a detailed knowledge of several of Walden's major cities and prominent persons. No one from another world, or from the Fleets, would possess that degree of contemporary information. Communication with other worlds was rare, and those from the Fleets would not have bothered to monitor and observe for any length of time. The Fleets came to destroy and steal, nothing more.

Pwanda was grinning at her. "First, answer my question. Why aren't you afraid of Chittham?"

"Fear implies some measure of respect. Not necessarily for a person, but at least for that person's ability. Chittham is a fool and a coward. He made a threat against me that he knew he couldn't carry out."

"No, he didn't."

"But you said that they don't touch children."

"I lied. But not completely. Among them, childhood ends at fourteen. You're older than that, aren't you?"

"Of course I am," Dane replied quickly. Unaccountably, she was blushing.

"And so they see you as an adult. Before we Grounders are assigned, Chittham can do whatever he likes with us."

"Then . . ." Dane felt her face go pale. "He might . . . when he comes here for us . . ."

"No, he won't. I phrased my words as I did to give the others hope. There's nothing more I can do for them. But Chittham won't harm you in any way."

"Why?"

"Because I won't let him."

"Then you *are* one of them! An officer!"

Pwanda burst out laughing. A number of the other captives turned to look. He waved at them, and said nothing further until they'd turned away again. "I'll tell you a little story, Dane. I told you I was picked up on the first day."

"That's right."

"I was passing by a hospital not far from the Capitol Building. When the attack began, I followed the crowds to a shelter below it. It was already packed with sick people who needed the space more than I did, so I left. I went to the Artifact Museum and stayed there, virtually alone. That afternoon a group of them"—he gestured to indicate the crews of the Fleet—"found me. They needed some heavy lifting done from the museum basement to one of their shuttles. They hate to be outside, you know."

"Yes."

"To make a stirring and heroic story short, I happened to overhear a conversation between two of the crew members. A particular chest that I'd carried to the shuttle was not to be logged in, but was to be taken directly to a Captain Lortis. That was all I needed to hear."

"All right; what they stole from us, they were stealing from each other. That's hardly a surprise. I still don't understand what you're talking about. What has this got to do with Chittham? Was he there on that shuttle?"

"Oh, no. And this has nothing to do with Chittham, specifically. Let me finish. On the walk back to the museum, I ran away. It wasn't difficult, with so much rubble to hide behind. I reasoned that whoever was in charge would be at the Capitol Building. So that's where I went."

"You told Buto Shimas that one of his captains was stealing?"

"I told that lieutenant, Giel Hormat. She took me to Shimas. Now he owes me a favor."

"You have to be joking," Dane told him.

"No, I'm not. Shimas is an honorable man."

"He kidnapped you, Momed. We're all to be made slaves. These people have no integrity."

Pwanda shook his head. "That's a foolish thing to say, Dane. Of course not all of them do. It's the same with us. But within their own context, Shimas is an honorable person. Hormat is also. She repaid me by telling me what to expect when I got here."

He was right, Dane realized. Her statement had been foolish. Without certain principles, without the upholding of those convictions, no organization or society could exist. Even the Fleets. Abhorrent those principles might be, but within their society—context—they defined honor. "So what is this 'favor'?"

"That's my point," Momed said. "That's why you're safe from Chittham."

*"I'm* your favor?"

"No, no," he said, laughing. "This is a beautiful thing, Dane. You see, the crew knows that Shimas is indebted to me. But I haven't asked him for anything yet."

Dane joined in the laughter. "And so until you do, Chittham and the others will worry that *they'll* be the target of whatever you request."

"Exactly. Good, eh?"

"But then, why can't you do the same thing for all of us?"

"Not a good idea. You were the one in trouble that day. When Chittham looked down at me, I shook my head. He understood and complied. To my surprise, by the way. But I don't dare risk trying that again. So you're safe for now. But only you, and only from him."

Dane was astounded. On his first day of capture, Momed Pwanda had managed to gain a measure of control over everyone under Shimas's command. And he seemed to know everything there was to know about . . . everything. Not only that, but he'd kept her guessing for three days, revealing absolutely nothing about himself that he didn't want her to know. There had been only that one break in vocal cadence, when they'd first met. Other than that, there had been not a gesture, not an eye-flicker, voice tremor, verbal slip, unconscious pose . . . nothing that her years of training could latch onto. Her training told her only one thing. One impossible thing. She looked again into his smiling face.

"Thank you, Momed. And . . . please excuse me, I don't mean to sound ungrateful. But you haven't answered my question. In fact, you've given me more reason than before to ask it. Who *are* you? And if you lie to me, I'll know it."

Big grin. "You think you will?"

"Test me."

Coming up behind her, Carnie said, "Dane, are you being silly again? I told you already. He's very handsome, that's who he is. But I was wrong about one thing. He's also *very* smart."

"Thank you," Pwanda said, bowing.

"Grounders! Up!" Chittham's booming voice filled the huge compartment. Throughout the catacomb, all the captives jumped to stand beside their beds. "Today," he said, still shouting, "you new arrivals will begin to become useful to us. All but one of you." The fat man pushed his way forward until he stood glaring down at Dane. "And that one is you, little CJ." He turned quickly and gave Pwanda a meaningful glare.

Dane looked at Pwanda, as well. He didn't seem to have moved. But suddenly he was the most innocuous and unimposing human being anyone could imagine.

"Come with me, CJ," Chittham said lowly, with satisfaction in his voice. Raising his volume, he addressed the others. "The rest of you, clean your stinking bodies. I'll be back in one hour." He turned and stomped toward the entrance, with Dane following.

She glanced back at Carnie and Pwanda. Carnie was trembling, with tears coursing down both cheeks. Pwanda put his arm around Carnie, then winked at Dane, scratching the back of his head. Dane shook her head, smiled, and returned the wink. She'd found him out. A full five seconds before he was going to confess. It was slightly insulting that to be sure she understood, Momed Pwanda had scratched his head exactly where the brain stem would be.

• • •

"That is what you want?" Buto Shimas sat back in his wide, thick chair and stroked his mustache. "CK360, are you certain of this?"

"Yes, sir," Pwanda said. The squadron leader's private office was surprisingly small and sparse. There was the desk and chair, a bank of computer screens against each of two walls, and a communications console. On the wall behind Shimas were mounted three ceremonial swords and matching daggers. That was all. Nothing on the desk except one open hand that dwarfed a keyboard, fingers thrumming rhythmically.

"I assumed that you'd want a favorable assignment," Shimas said. "Custodian, archivist, something along those lines."

"Archivist would be perfect for me," Pwanda conceded. "I was a researcher for most of my professional life. But I'd rather—"

"The personal affairs of Grounders are not of interest to me," Shimas said. "But in this case I am curious. Is this idea yours alone, or theirs as well?"

"Your generous promise was to me, sir. What do their ideas have to do with it?"

"So you haven't discussed it with them?"

"No, sir." He spoke the truth. Dane had returned under guard an hour after she'd left, to gather up her few belongings. She nodded good-bye to Carnie and Pwanda and was ushered away.

"You understand what is necessary for me to grant your request?"

"Yes, sir. Lieutenant Hormat briefed me when I told her what it was I intended to ask from you."

"Very well. Which of them is to become your wife?"

"CJ359, sir."

Shimas was not surprised. But he felt sure that this young Grounder was needlessly complicating his life. That one, a president's daughter, would be a problem for anyone. More than once he'd had forebodings about sending her to Jenny Marsham; sometimes his impulsive joking nature got the best of him. "And the other one. VH433. She is a lifetime friend of CJ359."

"Yes, sir. I feel that her inclusion in my request will help me, ah . . ."

"Keep your nose from being smashed immediately."

"Yes, sir. I'm glad you understand."

Shimas contained a smile, recalling his own brief marriage eighteen years before. There'd been no "lifetime friend" along to protect him on that first meeting with his new bride. In a sense he was sorry to see this CK360 go. But then again it was best. He'd found himself liking the Grounder, and that was always to be avoided.

"Wait." Shimas withdrew a communicator from the desk and punched in a code. "Jenny? This is Buto. Have you a moment? Quite well, thanks. And you?" He went on quickly to explain the situation, adding that of course she could refuse the two additions to her Grounder staff. He rather hoped that she would refuse all three of them. After a moment: "Yes, Jenny. I look forward to meeting with you again. Good-bye."

To Pwanda: "Very well. A husband and a lifetime friend. To assure that you won't be subsequently separated without extreme cause. Well within regulations, and Squadron Leader Marsham has no objection. The other Grounder will be told to be ready for transfer. The two of you will leave together, in one half hour."

"Thank you, sir."

"I owe you nothing more, Grounder. Dismissed."

After CK360 had gone, Shimas sat for a few moments and reflected. It had been a somewhat awkward request, involving as it did another squadron leader. But so long as Jenny Marsham had no objection, he was pleased that he'd granted it. It was as important to encourage Grounders when possible as it was to discipline them when necessary. Rewarded, they performed better. So simple. Why did so few understand that? And the information provided by CK360 had been valuable. He'd reported the theft to Company Leader Sepal as soon as he'd spoken to him privately. Sepal had listened quietly and almost smiled, which was high praise from Tam Sepal. Just an hour ago he'd called to summon Shimas for another personal discussion of the matter, aboard his flagship.

Buto Shimas stood and checked his dress uniform carefully. He selected one of the ceremonial swords and buckled it on; a summons from Sepal was always a formal event. Then, taking a towel and wiping the forming perspiration from his scalp, he left the office and locked it behind him.

≈**8**≈

From the moment he was ushered into the opulent office of Tam Sepal, Shimas knew that the meeting would not go well for him. The company leader was sprawled back in his chair, staring at him. His long, thin legs were crossed and draped across the high-sheen silvery desk. Equally thin hands were clasped together over his stomach, the thumbs tapping together in obvious irritation. Shimas took his eyes immediately from Sepal's and stood stiffly at attention, focusing his concentration on a display of battle decorations mounted on the wall far behind the company leader. From this distance he could recognize only a few of them, and identified three that he knew had been awarded for actions in which Sepal had not personally participated. His peripheral vision spied a fine tapestry on the wall to his right. It was one he'd seen taken aboard one of his shuttles during the recent supply run. He'd been so impressed by its beauty and craftsmanship that he'd sent it along to Sepal with a note, suggesting that he might forward it directly to Sovereign Command Council.

Long minutes passed with no words spoken, while Sepal's face remained still as statuary. Shimas was certain that the man hadn't so much as blinked. He almost jumped when a voice came from a panel inset into Sepal's desk. "Contact is established," it said simply.

Sepal grunted and seemed to strain with the effort of reaching forward. "Go." To Shimas he said, "Face left."

Shimas executed a sharp left turn and watched as a communications screen flicked on. The image was immediate and perfect. Captain Vivian Lortis was displayed from waist to head, in quarter scale. Shimas winced as she began speaking immediately. "Company Leader, the captured vessel and the prisoners have been taken aboard one of your escort ships. I have protested to Captain Cansalves that they are *my* prisoners, and that it is *my* privilege to bring them to you personally. I am certain that a misunderstanding has taken place. I ask you to contact Captain—" A grunt from Sepal, and the screen went blank.

"Reaction, Shimas."

He knew enough of Tam Sepal to know that in those brief and foolish words, Lortis had foreshadowed immense harm to both their careers. "First, Company Leader, it was a breach of protocol for Captain Lortis to speak without invitation."

"Good, good. Go on."

"Next. It is clear that she has accomplished an important capture. Your sending her an escort would suggest that the prisoners and vessel she referred to are from the Enemy. That the vessel has been taken aboard our ships indicates that it is a shuttle. Next. Captain Lortis reported the capture directly to you, bypassing my own authority. Next. My leaving the ship *Anfer* on that planet brought about this chain of events. Last, that Captain Lortis and I have made mistakes which offend you."

"Accurate on all points but one, Shimas," Tam Sepal replied thickly. "I am not important. It is Sovereign Command Council whom you have failed." *And you know that I speak for them,* his tone implied. Again he reached forward and activated the screen. Lortis appeared, shaken and silent. Sepal continued, "You are dealt with first, Shimas. Your decision to leave a ship behind on that planet was commendable. One sees the potential for such a tactic. It is from this moment to be made a standard policy of XF566 Company."

"Thank you, Company Leader." Shimas felt both relief and confusion. And, as he glanced quickly down at those unblinking eyes, dread. He was not long left waiting.

"And yet, one must consider your motivation during the

accidental discovery of this tactic. In doing so, one finds your actions to be unacceptable. You meant to risk an entire ship merely to punish one insignificant captain." There was a muted gasp from Lortis. "Matters become worse," Sepal went on, turning his head to face the screen but still speaking to Shimas, "when one points out that had you any understanding of the value of the tactic, you would not have assigned it to an officer whose record is at best unremarkable, and who is a known thief." Lortis had gone pale, but made no reply.

He turned again toward Shimas. "You are demoted. Beginning immediately you are assigned as adjutant to the most junior squadron leader in my company. You will ask my own adjutant who that might be, and report immediately."

Shimas found a measure of humor in the situation. If Jenny Marsham had not recently joined them, his orders would place him as his own adjutant. He said dryly, "Thank you, Company Leader."

It was Lortis's turn. Sepal faced the screen and said, "You understand of course, Captain, that only one disciplinary procedure is authorized for theft. One regrets that your most notable accomplishment has arrived so late in your career. But you are comforted in knowing that your contribution will be of benefit to Sovereign Command." With an officious clearing of his throat, Sepal continued. "Captain Lortis. At this moment you are relieved of command and ordered into dishonorable retirement. The act will be completed within thirty minutes, those minutes commencing now. I will view your retirement from here. No ceremony is permitted. Further, all of your clan will be interrogated for complicity in your crime. Further, your corpse will be recovered and at a convenient time buried within a planet. You are not fit to be dead in space." The screen went blank again.

Returning his attention to Shimas, he said, "Go."

The ship was named *Sovereign*. To any human eye, or to any detection instrument, its exterior was identical to other like-sized ships of the Silver Fleet. But within its titallium-based hull were the treasures of a hundred worlds, along with the officers whose decisions became law for all of Sovereign Command. Throughout the Silver Fleet were hundreds of millions who had at one time or another dreamed of visiting—or being assigned to—the ship.

Most would have been surprised to see how unremarkable the conference room was. A simple compartment measuring twenty feet by twenty with a standard ceiling height of eight feet, the room contained a single table large enough for eleven people, and chairs to accommodate them. Nothing more. Equally surprising to most would be the tone of the conversation taking place: informal, to the point of shouted vulgarities.

But at a signal recognized by all present, that informality ended. Supreme Generals Menta Carole and Tobok Ishmahan reached ahead of themselves to move a twin pair of levers on the table before them. The two sat closely together on one wide chair, of necessity. Their touching arms were grafted into one, ending in a double-thumbed hand that could close either way. The common uniform sleeve they shared was wrapped in two coils of ceremonial silver chain. Tobok was free to move his left arm; Menta, her right. As the levers came together, a shimmering, opaque curtain formed between themselves and the remaining nine members of Sovereign Command Council. Those nine looked across the table and from side to side at one another, masking their impatience and speaking in civil tones.

Arlana Mestoeffer was the first to speak, as was her right when the Generals were not present. Mestoeffer was ninety-three years of age and looked to be half that, with red-blonde hair and wide green-tinted eyes that missed nothing. She seldom smiled, but did so now. Although the man seated across from her had just done her a valuable service, she decided to focus the council's frustration on him. "You would have served the Generals better, Hivad, if your report had been better organized. I say this respectfully, of course."

"I second that opinion," said Fotey Smothe, standing behind Mestoeffer. Thin and dark-haired with a musculature that was unmistakable through his uniform, Smothe was described by his patron as "brutally beautiful." His eyes were a soft blue beneath graying eyebrows, drawing attention to a face that was unlined and went easily into a wide smile. He was known to be the last surviving member of an insignificant clan, an officer whose own record was virtually nonexistent. He was considered an annoyance by other council members, and tolerated only because of Mestoeffer's power.

"Of course you do," Hivad Sepal responded dryly. "That is one of the only two functions you have."

To Smothe's chagrin, even his patron laughed at Hivad's remark. "Of course," he added hastily, "I was going to comment that had you waited and prepared a formal report, precious time would have been sacrificed."

"No doubt," Hivad replied icily. That was exactly what he'd intended to say. To Mestoeffer he said, "The information came to me from more than three thousand sources representing our seven galaxies. After collating all of the data, I have presented the major points of agreement. I leave it to the Generals and my fellow members of the council to decide what further steps are appropriate. And of course a comprehensive report is now being prepared for all of you." He smiled thinly, breaking a perpetual scowl. "All of you members, I mean."

His unspoken rebuke was not lost on Mestoeffer: Why do you bring your toy to council meetings? Because I *can*, her eyes told Sepal and the others. They did not need to be reminded that Menta Carole was dying. And that she, Arlana Mestoeffer, was next to be joined with Tobok Ishmahan. Who could deny her an open dalliance when she was about to sacrifice her last vestige of privacy, forever? Today's meeting only increased her claim to that honor, which had been her sole ambition from the age of five.

Her sources had proved correct, as always. Weeks ago she'd discerned a pattern in their reports. Throughout the galaxies, ships of the Gold Fleet had begun breaking off from routine activities—and even from active engagements. This was occurring everywhere she had spies; the logical assumption was that it was happening elsewhere, as well. There could be only one reason, she'd argued: The Enemy was preparing a massive attack. She had predicted that the Gold Fleet was assembling the largest unified force in its history, and would use the Fortress in Galaxy S-143 as its staging area. As a result the Generals had recently agreed to the uniting of two SubFleets into one command.

Hivad Sepal's disjointed report had merely served to demonstrate that her analysis and recommendations had been correct. As always.

The opaque curtain dissolved as the Generals rejoined the meeting. "I have conferred," Tobok Ishmahan said, referring to himself and Menta Carole. "Sovereign Command will redouble its efforts to create and unite the two Sub-Fleets into one unit. It is clear to me that the Enemy plans to sweep us from at least one of the seven galaxies we consider important. If we were to allow them that victory, they would use the strategy again. Within fifty years we could find ourselves owning only two or three galaxies." As customary, he had spoken as the "defense" half of the Generals.

"Generals," Hivad Sepal asked, "do you see this as a sign of desperation within the Gold Fleet?" The question was critical. Given the answer he anticipated from the "attack" half of the Generals, he would deliver a blow to the person he most hated, whose position he most desired.

"No," Menta Carole answered sharply, clearly pleased with the question. "I see it as a false sense of their own strength. I see it as proof that you here have not been aggressive enough against them. I see it as an indication that some of you have forgotten that we are at *war*. I see it as your failure to remember that with the Enemy, coexistence is not our goal. *Annihilation* is our goal. Our *only* goal. Need I remind you that no ship can have more than one power plant? That two are impossible to synchronize, that even dormant, they poison one another? Need I remind you that the universe is *our* ship, and that we are its *only* legitimate power?"

While the others lowered their eyes to the table, Sepal pressed on boldly. "I agree, Generals. This of course adds to the importance of the imminent engagement. Once we have annihilated the largest formation the Enemy has ever constructed, we can proceed to press the war aggressively, as never before. Our momentum will be unstoppable. That is why we must make our new force the very finest and most deadly in the history of Sovereign Command. I therefore recommend to you with utmost respect and urging that the new force be commanded directly by the one who conceived it. I refer to our own Arlana Mestoeffer."

The curtain formed again while everyone at the table applauded. All but one.

Mestoeffer was livid. The two SubFleets accounted for only two hundred thousand ships. As head of Operations, she exercised authority over four times that number. The assignment was beneath her—but she was trapped. To refuse, even to hint at less than eager acceptance, was unthinkable; as Sepal had so skillfully pointed out, this had been her idea from the beginning. "Thank you for your confidence, Hivad," she said to the smiling head of Intelligence.

"You're welcome, Arlana," he replied, inclining his head slightly. And added to himself, *Thank you for your job.*

Reaching behind her, Mestoeffer dug her fingers into the left thigh of Fotey Smothe until his eyes teared over. Engrossed with thoughts of revenge against Hivad Sepal, she did not notice that the curtain had dissolved once more.

"I agree," said Menta Carole. "Mestoeffer, you will go at once. Your victory is to be swift, brutal, and complete." In a rare tone of kindness she added, "Bear in mind that you must return, Arlana, before half of me is dead."

*And if you die before I return,* Mestoeffer thought bitterly, *someone else will take my place.* She offered the most grateful and humble expression she could manage. As she rose from the table she mentally cursed Hivad Sepal. She vowed that she would drive his clan to extinction as speedily as she was doing the same thing to that of William Marsham.

Roughly pushing Smothe's hand away from her shoulder, Arlana Mestoeffer walked from the spartan chamber. The sound of applause and good wishes followed her down an ornately bejeweled corridor that led to her personal suites. All the way, a thought nagged at the back of her mind. Why had she acted so quickly on the information from her spies? Because it had come nearly all at once, she answered herself. And all of it pointed to the same obvious conclusion. And none of her one hundred twenty sources had ever been wrong. There could be no doubt that she had made the correct decision, had developed and pursued it perfectly. Nevertheless, something about it bothered her. Perhaps it was her lifelong aversion to depending on Grounders for anything important.

## ⇛ 9 ⇚

"I am SubLieutenant Jarred Marsham," the young man began. "I am addressed by rank and clan name, in that order. During the next one hour and twelve minutes you will learn what is expected of you aboard *Bagalan*. You are required to remember every word I say to you, and to obey without exception all of the regulations I will outline. To assist you in this you will find detailed manuals waiting for you when you return to your quarters. Further, you are encouraged to speak with the Grounders whose identifiers you will find listed in those manuals. They will help you, as well. To begin, then.

"You have been given the opportunity to atone for the crimes of people like yourselves. Your new lives here will have order, meaning, and purpose. In your own small way you will help us to pursue the Enemy to the ends of the universe, and destroy it utterly. And so be proud, Grounders. You no longer serve the petty and selfish interests of your past world. Now you serve *all* of humankind . . ." He went on for another thirteen minutes, detailing the destiny that awaited Sovereign Command and the justice that would embrace all of humanity, once the Enemy was destroyed.

"And now," he continued, "Regulations. First Heading: To whom are you responsible, and in what order of priority? Section One: Fleet Rank. All officers . . ."

Dane Steppart stood comfortably at attention in the first rank of ten, five captives per file. To her surprise, the gray tunic and trousers she'd been issued were clean, warm, and soft. Her boots were distractingly tight, but their supple composition suggested that they would adjust to her feet in time. Her hair had been cut to reach just below her ears.

To Dane's immediate left stood Momed Pwanda. She had expected him to arrive eventually, but there had been no opportunity yet to ask just how he'd managed to have himself and Carnie transferred to *Bagalan*. There was also the question of why he grinned and Carnie giggled every time they looked at her.

The huge auditorium seemed nearly empty with only fifty people there. Or fifty-one, she thought, if she counted SubLieutenant Jarred Marsham. Without appearing to do so, she was watching him in minute detail as he spoke. He used a number of intricate hand gestures that he employed most often before, and not during, the points he stressed with his voice. It was an effective technique, drawing attention as it did to everything he said, emphasized or not. He paced as he spoke, taking slightly longer steps with his right foot, always turning on the left. Those turns were executed with economic grace. Like the pirouette, Dane thought, of a trained dancer. He had the habit of looking upward to his right when he seemed to be searching for the correct word to use. Standing still, his bearing was erect and precise. Slightly more so than that of Buto Shimas. His voice carried an easy rhythm and inflections that were as defined as his posture. The freckles on his face tended to stand out at certain moments. An excellent speaker, Dane thought, hoping she'd captured enough of him to proceed.

When the lecture was concluded the fifty newly arrived captives, or "attendants" as they were formally referred to, began filing out of the auditorium. At the door Dane and Pwanda were stopped by Jarred Marsham. When the others had gone he said, "Were you paying attention?" He had not addressed either of them specifically. When neither responded, he said, "Good. But the two of you seemed to be half asleep. Normally I would question you, and punish you for poor answers. This time you'll receive a warning. While the others are having their meal and attending other lectures, you two will remain here and clean this room. All seats are to be wiped clean, and the floor polished. You'll find everything you need in that locker," he said, pointing. "I'll be back for you in six hours. Work fast."

"Yes, sir," they answered together.

When they were alone, Dane asked, "How did you get here so quickly? That favor Shimas owed you?"

"That's part of it," Pwanda said. "I'll tell you the rest later. Or maybe I'll ask Carnie to tell you. By the way, she says that today is your birthday."

"Yes, it is," she said. "I'll thank her for remembering."

From the locker they removed handfuls of cleaning rags and a rotary polisher that was explicit enough in design to require no instructions.

"All right," Dane said. "I want to know who you really are, who trained you, why you're here, and where you're from. Because I know you're not from Walden. And stop *grinning!*"

"I will," he said, becoming serious. "And I'll answer your questions. But first, did you get enough to track Marsham?"

"Yes, I think. I'll find out for sure when there's time."

"Why not now?" Pwanda asked, sweeping his arm toward the podium. "My lady, the stage is yours."

"But the cleaning?"

"Go ahead. You'd be amazed how fast I can work alone."

"No," she said. "I don't think I would."

Mounting the low platform, Dane stood behind the podium and concentrated for a minute. Beginning with Marsham's introduction, she began to work. She mimicked every movement the young officer had made during the lecture: every gesture, every facial expression, every step, while silently mouthing each word he had spoken, in the exact cadence and inflection he'd used. She went through the entire lecture more slowly than the officer had, then at double speed, and then once more, exactly as he had delivered the address. This time, her face flushed at every juncture of the speech where Marsham's freckles had stood out.

When she was finished, she looked out at the auditorium and was shocked to discover that there were not fifty attendants watching her. How dare they leave without permission! She felt a stab of anger, then worry. There would be trouble for her about this. Well, new arrivals or not, a warning would not be enough. She would punish the Grounders, all of them, and . . . it wore off slowly.

Dane concentrated again, and was disappointed; there was so little there. She'd gone through the tracking much too quickly. The process had just begun, and it was over. Unconsciously she bent her knees and put her hands to her face, rubbing vigorously. She'd have to try again later.

"Five and a half hours," Pwanda called to her from a seat far to her left. "Five and a half hours, Dane. Do you understand me?"

"Five . . . *what?*" Finally back to her surroundings, Dane looked at a wall-mounted chronometer. More than five hours had passed. The huge floor was polished, the seats gleaming. In a single instant, everything she had done and learned in that time came rushing through her mind in one seamless image. She sighed in relief. "I've got him, Momed. I've got him."

From that moment on, in the sense of the word taught to her by The Stem, she *knew* SubLieutenant Jarred Marsham. She owned him. Dane smiled to herself. So, Paul Hardaway thought *he* was a tracker!

"That was wonderful," Pwanda said. He walked to the platform and offered her a hand down.

Dane was exhausted, and grateful for his steadying hand. Her clothing and hair were damp with perspiration. "You've put all the equipment back already."

"I kept a cleaning rag out for each of us," he said, handing her one from a trousers pocket. "Our friend should be joining us soon. We'd better separate and look busy."

Precisely six hours after he'd left the auditorium, Jarred Marsham returned. He watched with approval as the two Grounders went hard at their work, too intent on finishing in time to see him come in. The woman in particular impressed him. She was bent at the knees, vigorously rubbing the cloth against the back of a seat. Even from a distance he could see that she'd been perspiring heavily. The man, by contrast, looked as though he'd been resting for most of the six hours. Jarred dismissed that thought as impossible; the job had been done better than the usual four attendants could accomplish in eight hours. These two had been busy every minute.

"I trust," he called out, pleased that he'd startled them, "that you two have learned the importance of paying attention at lectures."

Dane and Pwanda turned to face him, coming at once to attention.

"Very good. Stow your equipment and I'll take you to join the others. They're soon to be led through the ship."

As they followed Jarred Marsham out the door Dane said, "Sir, may I speak?"

"Yes."

"Sir, would it be possible for me to bathe first?"

Jarred stopped to face her and shook his head. "No. You've lost enough time already."

Dane nodded compliantly. "But if I may, sir. While the room was being cleaned, I went over everything you told us. I give you my word that I've learned a great deal from the experience. More, I believe, than if I'd gone on with the rest of the attendants. It would be distracting to me and the others if I were to join them like this." She held out her arms and pirouetted as he had done during his lecture, emphasizing her damp clothing. Her voice became a reflection of his own, as it would be if he were afraid to ask a question but even more fearful of personal humiliation. "Sir, I would be embarrassed to join the others like this. And I *will* hurry."

Jarred considered the request and decided that his initial refusal had been impulsive. After all, their work had been well above standard. Didn't his mother say that good results should be rewarded? "Very well," he said, nodding. "The two of you will want to go together. When you've bathed, open the manuals I mentioned earlier. You'll find a chart of the ship's compartments and passageways you're permitted to enter. Proceed directly to Level E, Compartment 32A. If you deviate from the shortest route you'll be stopped, and I'll hear about it. Do you know the way from here to your quarters?"

"Yes sir," Dane said. "The shortest route. No deviations."

"Good."

As Jarred walked away, Pwanda flashed Dane a thumbs-up. "Oh, yes," he whispered. "He's been tracked."

Pwanda waited by the bunks while Dane bathed in the communal shower compartment. There was no one else in the catacomb, which was identical to the one they'd been assigned to aboard *Pacal.* When she rejoined him, wearing a fresh attendant's uniform, he said, "I am in awe of you."

"For Marsham?"

"Yes."

She pulled on her boots, which already seemed to conform better to her feet. "Thanks, but the flattery isn't necessary. Somehow I think you could have done it better. Certainly faster."

"I could not have done that at all," he said seriously. "Not the way you did. Up until today, I believed that tracking was little more than theory."

"Are you serious?" Dane finished toweling off her hair and began combing it out. "Your teachers weren't very good, then. Who trained you?"

"Whitlock, same as you."

"That's ridiculous. Whitlock is a master at it. Besides, you wouldn't have been sent out if you couldn't even do tracking. It's elementary."

"No, it's impossible. Or was. Tracking was an invention of our esteemed teacher. He *believed* it was possible, but no one every actually *succeeded* at it. He didn't tell me that for years, and then only to spare my feelings when he was finally convinced that I'd never learn. Whitlock told me you'd done it several times. I didn't believe him until now."

"But . . . he said it was easy. Elementary."

"And you believed him. So to you, it was. But only to you. That's why you are the linchpin." She still looked unconvinced. "Dane, when you were leaving the tracking state before, you bent your knees and rubbed at your face. Why did you do that?"

"For circulation, I suppose."

"I thought so too, at the time. But when you heard Marsham come back, you did exactly the same thing, to one of the chairs. That wasn't something you thought about, was it?"

"No. It was just part of the work."

"Wrong. It was something you knew, subconsciously, he would respond to. And he did, also subconsciously. You had that little movement perfected by the time you finished tracking him. Where did that come from? There was nothing in his lecture that related to such a thing. Believe me, I watched him as closely as you. What you did when he came back was more than a display of compliance and hard work. It meant something personal to him. You acted that out, and it was perfect. Because you really got inside him."

"That's the idea, isn't it? Momed, are you telling me the truth? No one can do that but me?"

"Not one tenth as completely. I can go through the process, Dane. Any of us can. And yes, we experience the world through the subject's senses. But in a very limited way. We can add nothing that wasn't actually performed by the subject, except for a little intuition and practiced guesses. And the result is astounding, to those who don't have the training. But you didn't guess. You *knew*. As I said, I didn't believe Whitlock when he told me how far you'd gone in it. He hopes you can teach me."

"Me? Teach *you?*"

"Of course. That's why I'm here, Dane. If you can't carry out your assignment, it's up to me. In the meantime I'm going to watch you at work. And learn something, I hope."

"This is going to take a bit of adjustment," she said, dropping the brush into her bag of personal belongings. "Here I was, thinking that you might be of some help to me." She affected a deep sigh. "Ah well, alone again."

"I have my uses," he said. "As you'll discover."

"Maybe I wasn't as successful as you think, though,"

Dane said seriously. "There was one thing Marsham said that made no sense to me at all."

"What was that?"

" 'The two of you will want to go together.' He was referring to my coming back here and bathing. You hadn't asked at all."

"He knew there'd be no one here but us," Pwanda said. "So his reason should be obvious."

"He thinks we're lovers?"

"He's certain of it. After all, I've been your husband since yesterday."

*"What?"*

Pwanda raised both hands in front of his face. Partly in jest, but also because he was sure that Dane would hit him if she saw the grin on his face. Now that she knew what it was about. "Look, we'd better join the others, don't you think? Level E, Compartment 32A. Direct route, and no talking in the corridors. Someone could overhear."

"That won't protect you, Momed."

That evening in his quarters Jarred Marsham relaxed, deep in the spell of one of his favorite musical compositions. This was one of the pieces he'd installed into the sound system of *Metronome* as he'd prepared that vessel to be the perfect retirement home for his grandfather. Jarred felt the music as if it were a physical force, lifting him. He thought of the euphony as vast and grand, as limitless as space itself, hinting at the beckoning mystery of uncharted starscapes. Unlike more traditional music, this symphony spoke of no battles, no clashes of ships or heroic death in the pursuit of duty and honor. To Jarred the music suggested courage of a higher level than warfare. It was the courage of a mind in contemplation of itself and the universe, a search for the harmony that might exist between the two. Was such a universe conceivable? Could time and space and the human mind exist, without war? When the Gold Fleet was at last utterly gone, would his descendants look at the stars not as navigational aids guiding ships to the next encounter with the Enemy, but as objects of beauty, natural generators of the awesome power that made life in space possible? Jarred had hoped that if his grandfather had lived on and heard this composition, the old man's thoughts would have mirrored his own; that Major General William Marsham would have a glimpse of eternal peace, and eventually might forget the one force that had driven his life for one hundred years: war.

On a rational level, Jarred knew that these were frivolous ideas. Certainly not something he could discuss with anyone. At least, he thought sadly, not after tomorrow. The Gold Fleet existed; that was a fact of life. It was foolish to imagine his grandfather becoming more like Jarred Marsham. His best course in life, the only one that would benefit Sovereign Command or even himself, was to become more like Major General William Marsham. That was not easy. The old man had been the ideal warrior from the time of his youth. He'd mastered every assignment ever given him, mastered not only its strategic importance, but also its smallest detail. Jarred found himself thinking of his own duties aboard *Bagalan,* and contrasting his performance to what his grandfather would have accomplished at the same level. The contrast was distressing.

Those two Grounders earlier in the day had perfectly illustrated his own inefficiency.

In six hours they had cleaned the auditorium better than the usual team of four, in eight hours. That being the case, it was self-evident that he had failed. The job should always have been done as well and as quickly as those two had done it. It had not. Why? Because SubLieutenant Jarred Marsham had never showed true leadership. He had never analyzed the objective, broken it down into small parts, and developed the strategy and tactics necessary for optimum efficiency. Weren't battles planned along those lines? Hadn't General Marsham been spectacularly successful in war because as a young man, he had approached *every* assignment in such a manner, until it was his very nature? Yes! Why couldn't *he* be that way?

Jarred sat up in bed and switched off the annoying music. He was inspired. What those two Grounders had done, all would be expected to do. He would train them, and lead them. That was his job. He would do it better than anyone ever had.

The first step, he thought excitedly, was to learn to do everything the Grounders did, himself—a breathtaking thought in itself. No officer had ever participated directly in a cleaning detail. Except, he realized suddenly, his own grandfather. The old man would have, and he'd have done it perfectly. It was too late for Jarred to take that route. No one could match what those two Grounders had done because, obviously, they were long experienced in such work. So, how *exactly* had they gone about it? What methods did they employ that he could teach the others, so that everything Jarred Marsham led them to do, they would do with near perfection?

There was one way to find out. Tap into the monitor circuits, and retrieve the tape of their work in the auditorium. Jumping out of bed, he glanced at the chronometer. Good. Six hours until he was due on duty again. He'd watch every move the Grounders had made.

The tape was recalled and running. For a few moments he watched himself speaking to the fifty Grounders. Not bad. He looked adequately professional and sounded sure of himself. In truth he'd been frequently distracted, thinking of BN887. "Beanie" had been his personal attendant since birth and was facing retirement the next day. In his youth she'd been such fun, even making a game of bathing him. She would bend down at the knees and put the cloth close to his face and say, "Monster! Monster!" while pretending to attack with it. All through his life she'd encouraged him to pursue poetry, philosophy, and music. She had strange ideas about life that fascinated him. Despite regulations, it seemed a shame that she had to . . . *Stop that! You're doing it again!*

Moving the tape ahead quickly, Jarred slowed it at the moment he'd said, "I'll be back for you in six hours. Work fast." Not wishing to be distracted by whatever meaningless conversation newly married Grounders might carry on, he switched the sound off and watched them take the cleaning supplies from the locker. Neither of them spent more than a second examining the polisher. Yes, they'd done this type of work often. After a few moments the man made a broad gesture toward the speaking platform. The woman seemd to argue with his choice of who would work where. That can be improved, Jarred noted mentally. Have the plan laid out in advance. Perhaps have more than one locker, located strategically . . .

"*Battle Contact! Battle Contact!*"

The young officer leapt away from the console, was out the door and running with other officers before the words registered consciously in his mind. He sped past and did not see BN887, who'd come to ask if she should clean his quarters one last time.

"*Battle Contact! Battle Contact!*"

The tape of Dane and Momed played soundlessly to an empty compartment until the woman entered. Ignoring the sudden changes in attitude and velocity of *Bagalan,* she moved with unconscious surefootedness toward the bed, which was rumpled in the way it always was. But this time instead of going immediately to work as she always had for Jenny and then Jarred Marsham, she sat down. She was tempted to stretch out in a real bed for the first time in nearly forty years. What a thought! But then, she'd always been daring, hadn't she? The way she played with "Little Marshie" when he was a small boy. None of the other attendants could believe it. The way she'd taught him music and philosophy and that at rare times in human history, there had been peace. He'd promised never to tell anyone about those things, and he'd never betrayed her. Very daring. And then tonight. She'd almost gone to Squadron Leader Marsham: May I live for a while longer, please? A transfer, a new identifier, start again on a new ship? I'm in excellent health, and . . . Embarrassing to ask for the impossible, but she'd nearly gone through with it. It was important to live. Not only for herself, but . . .

As she wiped tears from her eyes and cheeks, the flashing screen caught her attention for the first time. Who was that young girl? What in the name of Glory was she doing?

The older woman watched, fascinated, and began to laugh. The child was mocking Little Marshie! Oh, she was so funny! Just the way he walked and moved his hands, and turned, and . . . she sat up straight then, light-headed and nearly in shock. *My God! My merciful God in Heaven, is she* tracking *him?* BN887 watched for a full minute before acknowledging to herself that what she was seeing was exactly what she thought it was. *Can she* really *do it? Is this the one that Brian Whitlock promised, so many years ago, that he would find and train? Has he at last succeeded? Is she the one that signal was about, the one that activated the chip I thought long since dead in my brain? Is that why God has allowed me to see this?*

Gaining control of herself, the old woman went to the console and began punching in instructions. Within seconds the image was gone from the screen. Next, she called up the monitor circuits and erased the tape completely, wiping it permanently from *Bagalan*'s memory. Acting on a hunch, she also destroyed the records of that day's activity in the attendant's quarters. To be safe she randomly selected ten compartments aboard *Bagalan* and erased their records as well, adding Jarred's quarters last. Then she created a genuine and untraceable malfunction in the system that would later be held as the cause for the tapes' erasures.

When it was done she reruffled Jarred's bed to the way it was when she'd entered, and made certain that there was no other sign of her presence there. She stood at the door and looked back once more at the blank screen. Maybe Brian Whitlock has finally done it, she prayed. She herself had been a poor student, but was so enthralled with The Stem's plans that she'd found a way to manipulate Whitlock himself into accepting her and sending her out to be captured. She'd done some good, she reflected. Jenny and Jarred Marsham both had been brought to the point that they sometimes questioned tradition—even the wisdom of Sovereign Command itself. Both were willing on rare occasions to discuss important matters with her. Jarred, especially, was showing promise. She'd been so close to reaching him! Whoever this new child was, perhaps she could build on the work already done. Then again, if she were half as skilled as she appeared to be, she was not intended to remain at squadron level. It only remained to warn her about *Bagalan*'s monitoring system.

For the first time in years BN887 laughed out loud in an officer's quarters. She no longer had any regrets about death. Now she could go into Eternity knowing that The Stem was still active, and that the plan to cripple the Fleets was going forth. And that her dear husband, whose heart she had broken, was still alive and carrying out his life's work. With a final smile toward the blank screen, Amanda Whitlock Coram closed the door softly behind her and walked down the long empty corridor, no longer alone.

*"Secure from Battle Contact drill. Secure from Battle Contact drill."*


There were no retirement ceremonies for Grounders. Breaking from protocol, Jenny and Jarred Marsham walked with BN887 to the airlock. Following them were three attendants who had been the woman's closest personal friends over the years. Dane was with them also, having had no difficulty in convincing Jarred Marsham that it would be good experience for her to witness this. If, as Jarred had proposed, Dane was to be Squadron Leader Marsham's new personal attendant, it seemed reasonable that she should witness the courtesy that the squadron leader extended to BN887.

Good-byes were exchanged in a low-key fashion, with both of the Marshams offering brief words of appreciation for the woman's forty years of service to Sovereign Command. Each of her friends was allowed a last embrace. When it was Dane's turn, she kissed the woman's cheek and whispered her thanks for providing her with a hand-drawn diagram of the ship's monitoring system, which Dane had immediately memorized and destroyed. This information would help the two Stem agents to remain alive. Dane had begged the wonderful woman to allow her to make an appeal to Jarred for her life. That was met with a

# ➤ ❿ ➤

Arlana Mestoeffer found one thing very gratifying about her new command. It was not the grand opulence of her new flagship *Dalkag,* which had been transformed into a surprisingly good imitation of her former—and future—home with the council. So good, in fact, that she'd promoted the officers who'd designed and directed the refit. It was not in discovering that the two hundred thousand ships were ahead of the old schedule for creating a new unit. More promotions, for excellent work. It was not even that since arriving aboard *Dalkag,* Fotey Smothe had been more enthusiastic and tender than he had ever managed before. Although it was Fotey who brought her the news. The poor dear had begged for a chance to do "real Fleet work" for her, as he often did. To keep him out of her way while she worked, she'd given him the "vital" task of reviewing the vast tables of personnel assignments—which would later be done competently and formally, by teams of officers trained in that specialty.

He'd stumbled upon the fact that two of her enemies, one old, one new, were assigned together in one company of ships. Jenny Marsham was a squadron leader in XF566. Tam Sepal was the company leader. This was delicious! Taking her time, savoring the distraction from her new duties, Arlana Mestoeffer planned how she would indulge in the splendid joy of striking at the two people she most despised: the deceased William Marsham, and the soon-to-be-disgraced Hivad Sepal, whose treachery had sent her away from the council.

She had a wonderful time, over five nights, telling Fotey exactly what she had in mind. The darling was so enthralled that he spent his days trying to conceive of nuances to her plan that would enhance her enjoyment. Some of them were actually good.


Paul Hardaway was amazed to be alive after the interrogation. They hadn't hurt him physically. In fact, they'd fixed his twisted leg and done something to his arm that healed the bones and took away the pain almost overnight. His back was still sore from the concrete pellets the people with Supervisor Yardley had dug out, but the skin looked good and all the little scars were gone.

What they'd done was inject him with something that made his head feel as if it were going to break right open. But then it was like a dam broke, because he felt these warm little rivers going down through his body. It felt good. He'd read somewhere that death came that way, if you died peacefully after a good life. He didn't expect to be breathing much longer. Death didn't seem important, but it was kind of a shame, because he still hadn't found out if Dane was all right. But even that stopped hurting after the dam broke.

From that moment on, everyone he spoke to seemed like the best friend he'd ever had, except one. This was a man almost as tall as he was but so thin he'd have to walk around in the shower to get wet. He wasn't friendly at all. Everybody was afraid of him, from the prisoners to the people who asked Paul the questions the stick Man told them to ask. His new friends didn't want to know a thing about farming or woodcraft; they looked like they were getting sick when he started telling them about it. He didn't remember when they left him alone. The tall man said, "He has no value to me. Send him to Shimas." Everybody laughed at that, including him. Paul asked them if they wanted to hear a good joke. He had in mind the one he'd told Supervisor Yardley about a president named Hindman and some research he was supposed to be doing. The joke was that President Hindman had died about two hundred years ago. No, they said. They didn't want to hear any "Grounder" jokes. The last thing he heard was one of them saying that they'd never find a Grounder uniform long enough to fit him. He thought that was funny, too. Was Shimas a planet somewhere? Also, what was a Grounder, and what did it wear?

It wasn't so easy for Serjel Weezek. Not until his own interrogation was over did he remember the seventeen crew, and Supervisor Yardley. All were dead now. The day after their capture, Yardley had stood at attention and activated a chip in his brain that all supervisors had. He'd died instantly and painlessly while Weezek screamed at him, wishing that his own ascension to supervisor had taken place so that he could do the same.

He'd been given the same injection as Paul Hardaway. Once the soothing heat began moving through his body, he could understand why these strangers asked so many questions. Obviously they liked him as much as he liked them, and wanted to know more about his life in the Omnipotent Gold Fleet. But why would these new friends slap him, and kick him, and tell him nothing about themselves? And why did they take him to an airlock and tell him to watch while seventeen people, vaguely familiar, were sent into space? They'd even forgotten to give suits to the group. Didn't they know what would happen? They thought their little mistake was hilarious. He didn't think it was so funny, but didn't want to offend them by telling them so. There were more questions after that, and more kicks and punches. After a while he wasn't so sure that these people were really his friends at all.

Weezek was nearly unconscious when they finally told him he could lie down. When he woke up, it was to a dark universe of pain. Either he was blind, or there was no light. He was tied at hands and feet and felt sore everywhere, bleeding from nose and mouth. Every nerve in his body was screaming at him. Many hours passed before he could piece together where, or who, he was.

Despite his suffering, or perhaps to distract himself from it, Serjel Weezek tried to recall the questions posed to him by the Silver Fleet, and his answers. With a sense of relief he realized that he'd told them little of importance. Perhaps he'd even managed to frighten them. They'd wanted to know why he and the "squadron"—really family—of one hundred ships he'd told them about, had been transiting that particular galaxy, that particular sector, at that particular time. The truth was, he didn't know. There were rumors, but weren't there always rumors? Here the physical blows had begun. *What rumors? What were they?* And so he'd listed them: rare metals discovered in an asteroid cluster at the far side of the galaxy. Or—their family supervisor was to report for promotion. Or—demotion. *Report where? To whom?* He didn't know. More kicks. *What other rumors?* He told them the most unbelievable rumor of them all— that the Omnipotent Gold Fleet was calling two hundred thousand of its ships to one sector of space. *Where?* He didn't know; he assumed that if it were true, it would be to the nebula he called Noldron, where the Gold Fleet had its greatest concentration of power. They seemed to understand which nebula he meant. *When?* It was just said, "very soon." But this, he explained, was ridiculous gossip that no one paid attention to. It was then he'd seen the seventeen crew executed. More beatings, with more questions pounding his ears like physical blows themselves. He'd wanted so much to give them answers, so they could all become good friends again. But he couldn't tell a lie. Even to make them happy. The rumor really was absurd. So much so that the supervisors had put to death a number of crew, merely to stop it. He explained to them that supervisors were not always kind. But they were always truthful. It had broken his heart that they didn't believe him.

Yes, Weezek thought with satisfaction. He'd frightened them. Two hundred thousand Gold Fleet ships, together! Of course it was ridiculous. But cowards that they were, the Silver Fleet might well disappear for a long time to come.

"Very soon." Those two words from the Gold Fleet prisoner were enough to stir Arlana Mestoeffer to a frenzy of activity. She cut in half all times allotted for arrival and assignment of incoming squadrons, companies, and flotillas. Excuses were met with instant demotion. In many cases, retirement. Postponed for now was any thought of striking at Jenny Marsham and Tam Sepal. There would be time for recreation later, when her new force was assembled and operating at top efficiency.

During the following two months the true skills of Arlana Mestoeffer were displayed at their best. She had risen to prominence from a relatively obscure clan that had never produced an officer of higher rank than lieutenant general because early in life she had been recognized as exceptionally gifted in the areas of large-scale organization and coordination. Her quick rise to command a ship was almost incidental to her career as a whole. Squadron leaders, company leaders, and then flotilla leaders became eager to have her as part of their staffs. Her own ambition was set much higher. By the time she was sixty she had reached the Fleet level. Fifteen years later she was asked by the council itself to reorganize Sovereign Command's Intelligence Division. So successful were her efforts to rebuild the organization and to cast the blame for its failures squarely on the head of the presiding head of Intelligence, that when the three-year assignment was completed she was invited to accept the job herself. As a council member. And now, the moment her new force crippled the Gold Fleet, she would return in triumph to become the "attack" half of the Generals. There was no higher rank in the universe. She would be satisfied at last.

Three months from the beginning of this new assignment, Brotman Nandes, the highest-ranking SubFleet Leader of Sovereign Command, arrived aboard *Dalkag* and formally accepted the post of first adjutant to Arlana Mestoeffer. The two hundred thousand ships were now one unit, and ready to rehearse for battle.

# B

# PROMOTION

Three weeks later found Jarred Marsham pacing the Operations Room of *Bagalan,* repeatedly circling the War Table. As he walked he kept his eyes on the display hovering over it, nodding, a serious look on his face, all the while muttering to himself. "Yes . . . Ah, how clever . . . Why, that's perfect! *Exactly* as I would have done it!"

The other person in the room was Dane Steppart. Cleaning a comm unit adjacent to the table, she was trying not to burst into laughter. Jarred Marsham was doing everything he could to attract her attention, virtually begging her to ask him about the display and his excitement over it. Even before activating the War Table he'd signaled his intentions by shutting down the compartment monitors, which he was not authorized to do, taking care that she saw him doing it. Dane worked as if unaware of his presence; the less interest she showed, the more eager he would be to say whatever it was that was on his mind. When she'd finished the routine cleaning, she stood near the table and waited for him to come around again. "SubLieutenant Marsham, I'm finished here. Will you be inspecting my work before I leave?"

Jarred glanced at her in obvious disappointment, then stood still and looked back up at the display. "No, CJ, I'm sure your work is satisfactory as always. You may return to your quarters."

"Thank you, sir. May I ask about that formation of ships?"

Jarred almost jumped. "That? Oh, it's nothing much."

"I don't know about things like that, but it looks . . .

powerful, I would say. Invincible." The ignited motes above the War Table were too numerous to count individually. Dane guessed that they represented all of the two hundred thousand ships now under the command of Arlana Mestoeffer. She knew little of Fleet tactics—although she was learning—but this formation did indeed appear to be overwhelmingly aggressive, suggesting a battle in which no quarter would be asked, or given. "Is it your design?"

"Of course it . . . Actually, no," Jarred said reluctantly. "I approve of it, though. As it happens, this is new, from First Adjutant Brotman Nandes. He's a genius."

His eyes and tone conveyed much more than admiration for Nandes. Knowing Jarred's behavior patterns as intimately as she did, she knew that he wanted to impress her not only with the formation, but with the fact that he knew of it at all. That was a significant detail. She recalled Amanda Whitlock telling her that an attendant, whose word meant nothing against a Fleet officer's, was considered a "safe" person to impress with forbidden information—as Jarred had often tried to impress "Beanie." Dane asked the question he wanted to hear in the hushed, excited voice the young officer hoped for. "Is this how we're going to defeat the Enemy?"

"Oh," he said in an attempt at nonchalance, "I didn't say that." His eyes said exactly that. They confirmed it, beyond doubt. "Besides, CJ, I'm only a sublieutenant. How could a mere sublieutenant know something like that?"

Dane smiled up at him. "A 'mere sublieutenant' couldn't, sir. I see that very clearly."

"Yes. Well, as you know, I . . . But you really shouldn't be asking me these questions. And if I am more than I appear to be, then of course that is not to be discussed with anyone."

"I understand, sir."


"I told you, Dane. I don't believe in luck." Pwanda pulled on a freshly laundered tunic and tossed the soiled one to an attendant passing by with a large cloth bag.

"Then listen. You will." When the attendant was beyond

hearing range she put her head close to his, and gave him a one-sentence whispered overview of what she'd just seen and heard.

Momed Pwanda showed her a new skill; he could grin and whistle at the same time. "Tell me about it."

They skipped the evening gruel and sat together in Pwanda's lower bunk, out of visual range from the compartment monitors, huddled together and speaking quietly. After an hour Dane was satisfied that Pwanda knew the battle arrangement in minute detail. This information was the perfect complement to a plan they'd devised after learning that a Gold Fleet shuttle had been captured. They'd realized at the time that they were making a radical departure from Whitlock's instructions, but each agreed that the opportunity could not be lost. Especially now. Their whispered conversation continued long into the night, with each adding refinements to the plan until a final strategy was agreed upon that fully incorporated their newfound knowledge. When that was done Dane and Momed wished one another good luck, and said good-bye—forever.

The following morning Dane walked purposefully down the corridor leading to the stateroom of Squadron Leader Marsham. She was met by a tall attendant heading in the opposite direction, grinning and holding a wrapped package.

"Dane!"

"Hi, Paul, how are you?"

"Best ever," he said. "The squadron leader is in a real good mood. Are you going to see her?"

"Yes. What are you smiling about? And what's that you have there?"

"It's the biggest potato anyone on this ship has ever seen," he answered proudly. "And I'm going to be the new head farmer."

"Paul, that's wonderful! How did you do it?"

The boy snickered. "Easy. These people don't know a thing about growing food. Did you know that they grow everything in water? Or something like water. Anyway, I started experimenting with nitrogen levels and pH, and ... well I don't want to get technical. It turns out that that water stuff is pretty good because you can do so much with it. More than soil. You wouldn't *believe* how fast things grow! But they never did get it balanced right, even with all their computers and that kind of nonsense. All it took was a *real* farmer. The squadron leader said if I can get the rest of the crops this good, they'll produce forty percent more food than they ever did before. And I'll be in charge of the whole operation. The vegetables and fruits, I mean. I won't even go near that other place."

She knew what he meant. The "other place" was a series of compartments devoted to raising meat. Not animals: meat. In row after row, mindless, grotesquely large carica- tures of cows, sheep, and fowl grew, attached to harnesses of tubing that provided nutrients and carried off waste. A popular Fleet joke was that Grounders should be bred that way. By contrast, Paul's new area of responsibility was a wonderland, where a fertile mind like his would find new challenges every day.

"I'm proud of you, Paul."

"Thanks. Well, I'd better get back to it. Carnie Niles is going to be working there, too. Why don't you come down there and visit me sometime? I'll show you how everything works."

"I will, thank you." As the boy walked away humming a tune, Dane smiled. Jarred Marsham had told her about Paul's interrogation. The chemical they'd used on him was highly addictive, so much so that its sudden absence was often fatal. Jarred had prevailed upon his mother to allow Paul diminishing doses of it until he was able to return to normal without trauma. A total of two months was antici- pated. The only time Dane had not seen her cousin happy was after he'd learned that she had a husband. "I'm sorry, Dane, but you're too young for that," he'd said. "I think I should kill him, is that all right?" But she'd explained to him what the marriage was, and what it was not. After that Paul decided that he was Momed's best friend.

Arriving at the door, Dane knocked.

"CJ359?"

"Yes, Squadron Leader."

"Enter."

Jenny Marsham was seated behind her desk. As usual the desk was covered with reports, evaluations, and orders for her to sign. Standing to her right and behind her was Buto Shimas. Dane had long since begun her work on the two. She now had the rare privilege, when alone with either or both, of speaking first. "Good morning, Squadron Leader Marsham. Good morning, Adjutant Shimas."

Both acknowledged her presence with a quick nod before returning to their conversation. It dealt with numbers of spare parts to be requisitioned for the squadron, prior to an upcoming Fleet exercise. Dane listened in silence while outwardly looking around the room for spots in need of cleaning.

After a few minutes, Shimas bundled his own notes and headed for the door. He said to Dane, "You had asked me about a Grounder friend of yours aboard *Pacal.*"

"Yes, sir." That would be Hatta Gronis, who'd been taken at the same time as Dane and Carnie. She'd disappeared on their first day aboard Shimas's old ship.

"She's dead. I am told that she took her own life that first night aboard."

"Thank you, sir." Dane had known that Hatta was weak. But it was far from accurate to say that *she'd* taken her life. Hatta's life had been ripped away from her on the day she was stolen from her home, and her home destroyed. Her death was yet another item to be added to the list of things these people needed to answer for.

Shimas departed and, without a word from Jenny Marsham, Dane began to put the desk in order. She worked quickly while the older woman stood to stretch. When she'd finished with the desk, Dane went to a small counter and poured Marsham a cup of steaming tea.

"Thank you, CJ," Marsham said, resuming her seat. "What was it you wanted to speak with me about?"

"Squadron Leader, we are about to return the Gold Fleet prisoner, Weezek, to the Enemy."

Marsham caught her breath. "I am constantly amazed at what Grounders come to know," she said slowly. For a full minute she didn't speak, and then, "But I suppose there's no harm in your learning about that. Yes, we are. He has been programmed to say exactly what we want said. Assuming," she added, shrugging, "that they allow him to live long enough to speak after he returns to them. How does this concern you?"

"I think you should send my husband to the Gold Fleet with him."

Marsham laughed. "So that's it. Young marriages are often difficult, CJ. But don't you think you're being a bit extreme?"

"My husband is a trained saboteur. He plans to harm Sovereign Command."

Marsham set her tea down carefully. "A saboteur? Trained? By whom?"

"What I meant is that—"

"CJ, this is foolishness. Calling your husband a 'trained saboteur' implies that he *planned* to be taken by us. How could that be possible? Grounders never know when, or where, we will visit. And captives are selected randomly."

"As you say, Squadron Leader, how could anyone make such plans? I mean that my husband was a professor of engineering before he was taken. Now that he is here, he intends to use his skills against you." All true, but for the misleading question.

"I see. CJ, I will ask once more. Are you certain that this isn't a marital disagreement carried to extreme?"

"Yes."

"Very well, then. I will report this to Tam Sepal. Your husband will be interrogated. And killed, of course."

"I've thought of that." She had. Many times, with horror. But there was no other way. "And of course he deserves whatever is done to him. But . . ." On cue, tears began rolling down her cheeks. "The moment I was sure of this, of course I had to report it to you."

"Of course. Sit down."

"Thank you, Squadron Leader. I . . . I am pleading for

my husband's life. I give you my word that he has done nothing yet to hurt this ship, or anyone on it."

"Be sensible, CJ. Do you believe that we merely send traitors away, where they cannot harm us?"

"Perhaps you could, in this case." Before Marsham could respond she continued, "I was thinking that if he's as adept as he brags that he is, and we were to send him to the Enemy, he may—" She shrugged.

"Work against the Gold Fleet?" Marsham asked, completing the thought as planned. For a number of seconds she pondered her own words. It was an astounding thought. Ludicrous, on the face of it. What could a Grounder do? But then, why not consider the possibility—at least as a symbolic gesture? Never in six centuries had Sovereign Command been able to place a saboteur with the Enemy.

"That is what I had in mind," Dane said. "And he will be alive, at least longer than if you'd discovered him yourself. As you certainly would have. There is nothing he can possibly do to hurt us, once he's gone. With luck, he may be of benefit to us."

Marsham's mind was racing. In mere months this young Grounder had more than proved herself reliable and helpful. Was it possible that she was now offering Sovereign Command an opportunity never before realized? "What reason could we give for sending him along with the prisoner?"

Dane sighed. Everything she'd learned by tracking this woman had gone into preparing for this meeting, planning every word, anticipating Marsham's every possible reaction. And it was working. "Weezek is not well, Squadron Leader. My husband can accompany him as a medical attendant. The Gold Fleet will believe that we consider him worthless and expendable, or we would not have sent him. Therefore his only value to them would be as . . . whatever it is they call attendants."

"Or they will simply murder him. The Enemy is treacherous and cruel, CJ. They are not like us at all."

"Yes, Squadron Leader. But no matter how small, this is his only chance to live. And he may be able to help us.

Please consider," Dane pleaded. "The most to be lost to Sovereign Command is an attendant who deserves death. The most to be gained . . ." She offered the words carefully, like bait into a fish pond.

Marsham considered it all, and nodded. That last part was certainly true. Nothing to lose; what was one Grounder? But perhaps something to gain . . . "You understand how serious this is, CJ. You will be required to repeat everything you're saying to me. In the presence of Tam Sepal, or even Arlana Mestoeffer. And with drugs."

"I understand." It was a major risk, involving the most stern test yet of her training. But success could mean a quantum jump ahead in her purpose here.

Responding to the young woman's distress, Marsham said, "If my superiors agree to this, I doubt if they'll question your husband in that way. Nor will they torture him, I think. The wounds or the chemical traces would show, if the Gold Fleet examines him. That would guarantee his execution. And destroy his value to us."

Dane wept with gratitude. "Thank you, Squadron Leader. My husband is a good man. But his mind was poisoned against us. It's not his fault."

Marsham shook her head adamantly. "Treason is never justified under any circumstances. But in this case it may be useful."

"I believe it can be," Dane said. She was responding to both of Marsham's statements.

"Very well. You will not return to your quarters until he is safely in custody. I will contact Company Leader Sepal at once. You may go now to my stateroom and prepare a dress uniform for me. Speak to no one until I arrive."

"Yes, Squadron Leader. Thank you." Dane stood and left the room.

The interview had gone just as she and Momed had rehearsed in whispers, in the dark of the attendants' quarters. One last hurdle remained: the interrogation.

"Like a HarvesTrain running over your head," Paul had told her. "And then it feels good. Like you're sleeping, but not quite. And then you think you're going to die. But you don't mind."

He'd been right, as ever.

While the effect of the drug deepened, Dane pushed part of herself into a small room in her mind, willing that this part would remain alert, no matter what the rest of her did. As it shut itself in, that part of her was grateful that nearly everything she'd told Marsham was true. It had to be that way. She knew already that no matter how well she'd been trained, large-scale deception would be impossible. Impossible . . . But . . . why even try?

Why would she want to deceive these wonderful people? There was her dearest friend in the world, Squadron Leader Jenny Marsham. There was Company Leader Tam Sepal, who looked ill, the poor man. He needed a few good meals, that was all. And then there was the radiantly beautiful Arlana Mestoeffer, the second most important woman in the universe, who looked like everyone's mother *should* look. But she wasn't really *there*, except on a screen. Could she be so beautiful, face-to-face? Of course she could.

My husband, Company Leader Sepal? Oh yes, I *was* surprised and a little angry when he told me we were married. But I really like him now. He's a good man, and so handsome. An engineer? Yes! A professor! And *very* smart, he knows everything. Oh, yes, that. Someone must have told him lies about Sovereign Command. He wants to hurt us. What do *I* want to do? The watching part of her squeezed something that sent a jolt through her body. Not unpleasant, but not something that she wanted to feel again. What I want to do is to become better at my job. Yes, I'm the personal attendant to Squadron Leader Marsham. Why, thank you, Squadron Leader! I will try to be even better.

Oh, yes, I am sure of it. My husband will use his training to hurt the Gold Fleet. They are so wicked! I hope he is very successful.

Oh, my, are you certain? Can't we talk some more? I would like to sleep, but I would much rather go on talking with all of you. The watching part squeezed again, harder. Please, excuse me. It is impudent for me to speak to you

like that. But you are so friendly, and I feel so . . . *Squeeze.*
I promise, I will learn to be better.

"With your permission, then?" Sepal asked the screen, as
surprised as Dane that the questioning had ended so
quickly.

"Yes," Mestoeffer said. "That is enough. Take her away.
Dispatch the shuttle as soon as its occupants are aboard."

After Dane had been half carried out of Sepal's office,
Mestoeffer continued. "I commend both of you. You, Marsham, for discovering this. And you, Sepal, for correctly
bringing it to my attention. I doubt that anything will come
of sending that Grounder to the Gold Fleet. But it can do us
no harm, and it does set a precedent. Marsham, it may be
that the most important thing demonstrated here was the
strong sense of loyalty that young one has toward you.
Imagine, betraying her own husband because she thought
he might be a threat to you. How refreshing!"

"I agree. She has adapted to Sovereign Command very
quickly."

"You might send me your personal guidelines for the
treatment of Grounders. We would all do well to cultivate
such loyalty and rapid acquiescence. It could reduce the
bother of executing so many of them, and save us time in
training replacements."

"Thank you, Fleet Leader. I will begin the moment I return to *Bagalan.*"

"No need for hurry, Marsham. A week will be satisfactory." Mestoeffer could not have been more delighted as
she viewed the screen on *Dalkag.* The affair with the two
Grounders was interesting, but in truth meaningless. "Nothing to lose" was hardly a rationale for taking action. And
what was there to gain by sending one of them to the Gold
Fleet? Functional zero. The shuttle was to be sent through
hyperspace to the Fortress, the Enemy's stronghold in
Galaxy S-143. If the vessel survived, the prisoner and the
Grounder would be useless to Sovereign Command from
the moment it was met and boarded. The shuttle itself was
the real point. Certainly, even the Gold Fleet was not stupid
enough to allow it near a real ship. They would expect an

explosive device. Finding none, they would wonder, why was it returned to us? They would study the craft minutely, discovering that the refit for hyperspace had been accomplished with obsolete technology. Again, they would ask, *why?* And go on asking, until at last they settled upon the most elusive reason of all: *no* reason. It was all to engage their poor minds with incomprehensible questions. A gesture of contempt, nothing more. The value for Sovereign Command? A confused and humiliated enemy makes mistakes.

The converse was, a flattered foe draws closer. That was the purpose for which she'd consented to attend this interrogation. Mestoeffer continued, "Sepal, it was your idea to send the shuttle back, was it not?" Naturally, this could not be done without her direct approval.

The man stared at the screen and hesitated. How much did Mestoeffer know? Her network of spies was reputed to be everywhere. He decided that the risk of lying was too great. Better merely to shade the truth. "Actually, the plan originated during a conversation I held with Squadron Leader Marsham."

"I see." Given Sepal's well-known reputation, that was a blatant admission that the thought had never entered his mind until Marsham brought it up. Interesting. Perhaps she'd inherited some of her father's talent for tactical innovation. It was regrettable that the man had been such a fool in other ways. "Your modesty is refreshing," she said to Sepal. "In fact, both of you have contributed significantly to Sovereign Command. And," she said with a smile, "to providing me with a pleasant hour. I confess to you, such times are rare."

"Thank you, Fleet Leader," Sepal replied for both of them.

"As you know," Mestoeffer continued, "I am to inspect your XF566 Company in three days. Why don't both of you plan to return with me to *Dalkag* after the inspection, and join me for dinner? The occasion will be informal, of course."

The unexpected honor was too much for either officer.

Moments passed before Marsham recovered and said,
"Thank you for the privilege, Fleet Leader. Of course, we
would be delighted." Sepal nodded vigorously.

"Good, then. Oh, and Marsham. If she is recovered by
that time, plan to bring the young Grounder with you. I am
fascinated by the depth and quickness of her attachment to
you. I would like to observe her more closely."

"Of course, Fleet Leader."

Had Dane been present and thinking clearly, she'd have
discerned that Mestoeffer's formality and courtesy toward
officers so junior to herself was out of character: awkward,
forced, and a clear danger signal. She'd have found a way
to warn Marsham.

As it was, the squadron leader left the room and returned
to *Bagalan* in a near trance. Aware of virtually nothing
around her, she was focusing on that incredible invitation
from Mestoeffer. She saw it as more than a great honor; if
she were careful, and lucky, this could be the opportunity to
save her son from whoever was behind the extermination of
her clan. *Jarred needs an ally, a protector,* her father had
written. There could be no more powerful an ally than Arlana Mestoeffer. Wasn't she rumored to be next in line for
linkage with the Generals?

And all for an idea she'd had. A simple one, really.
When had it come to her? She couldn't recall now. It . . .
yes. She'd been uncrating clan memorabilia sent to her by
her father. Models of ships commanded by members of her
clan . . . That was it. CJ and her husband had been there,
distracting her by making a silly game of arranging them on
a display table. "Surrender! You are my prisoner!" CJ
cried, and they laughed like newlymarrieds, repeating the
foolish game time after time, chattering nonsense. Marsham had ordered them away, annoyed at the chaos they'd
created. Yes, that was the moment.

Not that it mattered.

# ⇉12⇇

"Are you well, Ara?"

"Yes, Momed. Why do you ask?"

"Your hands are shaking."

"It's nothing. Fatigue."

"So early in the day? Come back after your duty and I'll examine you, if you like."

"No . . . Yes, thank you. I'll come and see you in fourteen hours. Here you are. Enjoy." The attendant passed him a bowl of morning gruel and turned her attention quickly to the next person in line.

"Thank you," Pwanda said, taking the bowl and moving on. So, he thought. My breakfast is "special" this morning: Ara giving him a bowl set apart from the others, her unsteady hands and reluctance to be examined for the cause . . . until fourteen hours later. He would be gone by then, she'd told him without meaning to. Was he to be drugged for questioning, or merely sedated to be kept silent until he was aboard the shuttle? Probably the latter, he thought with relief. There had always been the chance that he would be interrogated to learn whether he had discussed his treason with anyone but Dane. But had that been the case, a number of *Bagalan*'s crew would have come in and taken him forcibly, along with others known to be his friends. He was delighted that Dane had succeeded so well. But not surprised.

As he'd told Dane, Momed Pwanda was not a believer in luck. His education in mathematics, medicine, and especially engineering had taught him that all consequences are the result of cause—which when properly understood can be observed, measured, replicated, and predicted. Dane succeeded because she was very good at what she did. Luck did not exist. But, he thought . . . how else to explain his eight-month journey alone, across two galaxies in an obsolete ship whose defective power plant created "noise," often detecting, but never detected by, ships of both Fleets? Or his timely arrival on Walden; had it been three days later, he'd have missed Dane entirely. Or his "capture" by the same officer who would take Dane three days later.

No, he thought. That one could be explained logically enough: Both he and Dane knew they were to seek out the most senior officer of the invading force, and find a way to draw attention to themselves. That was not "luck," nor were the skills he'd learned from Whitlock and others, which had their basis in proven scientific principles. Whitlock and his long line of predecessors were dedicated scientists, shrewd innovators, and exemplary teachers. They were not, as Whitlock was said to be, wizards. But . . . what else but luck could explain the recent capture of a Gold Fleet shuttle, giving them an incredible opportunity that not even Whitlock could have imagined? Or Jarred Marsham risking court-martial to impress Dane with his unauthorized knowledge of the Fleet battle plan? In itself, that was not surprising; it could be explained in terms of ego, infatuation, the recklessness of youth . . . but the timing could only be described as . . . extraordinary?

Taken together, there were so many factors at work that seemed to be under no one's control, and yet violated the laws of blind chance, that the only explanation . . . Professor of Engineering Momed Kwasii Pwanda-Pwanda had no answer. Except that maybe there was something to luck, after all.

Finishing the gruel and returning to his bunk, Pwanda ignored the surprised looks and questions—"Are you sick? *You?*"—of other attendants who were filing out for this day's work. He could not tell them good-bye; he was not supposed to know that he was leaving. To Carnie he gave a quick hug, and wished her a good day.

His intent was to be acting in a suspicious manner, remaining in the attendants' quarters instead of reporting for his cleaning detail, when the drug took effect. In this way he would reinforce the things Dane had told Marsham about him. As the weariness began he slumped to the floor next to a panel whose interior fed power to the compartment's monitoring system. In his left hand he clutched a piece of metal he'd removed from a polisher, which would have been suitable for prying open the panel. *Good-bye, Dane,* he thought. *Next time we meet it will be across a battle line.* He added, grinning, *If I'm "lucky."*

Pwanda woke to the sound of moaning. He was loosely strapped into a pilot's seat, which was set much too low for his large frame. His hands nearly touched the floor and his long legs were bent uncomfortably beneath the seat. There was no groggy aftereffect to the chemical they'd given him, he was relieved to note. Other than the cramps in his legs, he felt as if he'd had a long and refreshing sleep. That was clearly not the case for the miserable wretch strapped in next to him.

The man appeared to be half-asleep. He was slumped forward with his chin resting on his chest, arms bound to his sides by the straps. They had made no effort to clean him after the weeks-long ordeal he'd been through. Long-dried blood caked his nose and mouth, giving his ragged breathing a strained and snoring quality. His gold-trimmed uniform was filthy with vomit and excrement. Nothing could be made of the words, if they were words, that he was half-whispering.

He was a small man. Thin and gaunt—how long had he been without food? Weezek, that was the name Dane had gotten from Jarred Marsham. So, this was a representative of the Omnipotent Gold Fleet? His appearance told Pwanda more about the man's captors than it did about those who'd sent him out. The thought produced a pang of renewed worry for Dane, which Pwanda instantly dismissed from his mind. She'd agreed that the two of them must separate.

There was nothing more he could do for her now, other than to complete his own assignment.

The straps came away easily. As he removed them, Pwanda noticed a small note pinned to the front of his tunic:

CK360

> Your treason has been exposed. Rather than exe-
> cute you, we assign you to carry out your plans.
> But against the Gold Fleet, not Sovereign Com-
> mand. We wish you success. Dissolve this paper
> in water, and accept the role of medical attendant
> to the prisoner. Controls are locked onto your
> destination. Transit time is four weeks. For your
> safety do not touch the controls. Especially do
> not trust the prisoner. The Enemy is treacherous.

Pwanda located the bath facility in the shuttle and flushed the paper away. He followed the sound of the moving water to the holding tank and noted that it was full. It was five minutes' work to find the appropriate panel and set the system to purify the water in the tank. The vessel's interior was one open compartment of twenty seats. Six doors led to smaller compartments. With the exception of the bath, all of them were stowage lockers. In them he found food, a few gold-edged uniforms, a box of medical supplies, and spare parts for the shuttle's operation. He found also a detailed manual on replacing power plant elements after each journey through hyperspace. The instructions seemed simple enough, and he assumed they had provided sufficient spares.

"Who's there?"

Pwanda returned to the pilot's station to find Weezek attempting to look around himself. Locating a cup next to his seat and returning to the bath to fill it, he nearly emptied the "clean" tank.

"Here," he said. "Drink slowly."

Weezek's face seemed to leap for the cup as it was presented to him. "Slowly," Pwanda repeated, withdrawing it as the first few drops were passed. The process took several minutes as Weezek first tried to inhale the water, then settled down to frantic sipping as his thirst was slowly eased. He was still reaching for more when the cup was depleted.

"I'm going to release you," Pwanda said. "Move slowly."

"My plan exactly," Weezek answered weakly. "Don't worry, I won't attack you. War is suspended for now, if you don't mind."

"I'm not a member of the Silver Fleet," Pwanda said.

As the bindings came off, Weezek managed to turn enough in the seat to look up at Pwanda. He faced to one side, as if able to use only his right eye. "You're not dressed like them. Who are you?"

"CK360," Pwanda said sardonically.

"You're a prisoner too?"

"I was. We're both free now, so to speak. We're heading back to your Fleet."

Weezek's mouth opened wide, causing the dried blood around it to crack. "Is that *true? How? Why?*"

"I'll explain when we've got you in better condition," Pwanda said. "We'll begin with a meal. Then a bath, as soon as there's enough water. Can you stand?"

"I'll try."

With every mouthful of food, Weezek vomited. An hour passed before the "clean" tank was filled again; when it was, nearly all of the water was needed. But finally Weezek was clean, in a new uniform, and able to hold down small amounts of food. His left eye was nearly blind, and three of his ribs had been broken and never set. There was nothing Pwanda could do for the eye, but he found bandages among the medical supplies and wrapped Weezek's chest tightly enough to promote healing and just loosely enough to permit adequate breathing.

"So you're what they call a 'Grounder'?" Weezek asked.

"That's right. What do you call the people *you* kidnap."

"People of the . . ." He hesitated until his mind caught up with his words. "Just 'people,' " he said. "You said your name is CK360?"

"It's my identifier," Pwanda said. "Grounders don't have names."

"Among us, you would," Weezek said with something that sounded like pride. "What is your real name?"

"You may call me Momed."

Weezek flushed, despite his weakness. "I'll call you whatever I . . . Whatever you prefer," he finished quickly. "I am Ship Coordinator Serjel Weezek."

Pwanda smiled. "And how shall I address *you?*"

"However you prefer," Weezek said, pale again.

Pwanda smiled once more. " 'Ship Coordinator,' I think."

"Very well, Momed."

Good. It was necessary that Weezek be afraid of him at first, to be certain that he had the man's full attention. He'd already determined that fear was the ship coordinator's primary motivating force. And that his title itself was a source of anxiety. After tracking him as well as he could, Pwanda intended to lead Weezek back to a sense of superiority. And, if possible with the mentality that apparently pervaded both Fleets, to a sense of friendship that went beyond any that might ordinarily be felt toward a captive. He knew from Weezek's demeanor that the man was not of high rank. But he might be able to bring Pwanda close to someone who was, and provide a recommendation that would allow him to begin working his way upward. He anticipated that their shuttle would be met by someone with power within the Gold Fleet; the taking and returning of a prisoner were extremely uncommon events. It seemed reasonable to assume that someone powerful would claim the right to see him first. Of great importance also was a suggestion that must be planted in Weezek's mind, planted deeply where it would remain below the conscious level until Pwanda called it forth again.

As days passed Weezek grew stronger. His left eye showed signs of improvement; he turned his head to less of an angle when looking at Pwanda. His time was equally divided between eating, sleeping, and talking. He was more than willing to speak of life in the Omnipotent Gold Fleet although, like the members of Sovereign Command

Pwanda had met, he showed no curiosity whatever about the people who lived on planets. To both Fleets, apparently, such people existed only to supply them with needed materials, and captives to train for their own uses.

Personnel of the Gold Fleet were divided into two castes: A relative few were supervisors. These made all command decisions, and exercised the power of life and death over anyone beneath their caste. The vast majority were crew, who stood watches and performed all maintenance and manual labor not left to Dirts—as Weezek finally admitted all captives were usually referred to. Dirts were not a caste. They were merely Dirts. Even after generations of service, descendants of Dirts remained Dirts. Between supervisor and crew were the ship coordinators, whose role Weezek himself seemed unsure of.

Although Weezek extoled the virtues of his own Fleet while displaying a complete and utter loathing for anything relating to his Enemy, Pwanda could see no important differences between the two. Each was dedicated to the extermination of the other in a war begun six hundred years before, following an incident in which both Fleets claimed to have been betrayed and massacred by the other. So deep was this hatred that each Fleet considered its own survival of secondary importance to destroying the Enemy. Each Fleet regarded everything in the seven "important" galaxies as its own private property. Dirts, or Grounders, owned nothing, could aspire to nothing, were worth nothing.

What most astounded Pwanda was the absolute confidence with which each side claimed supremacy: morally, socially, philosophically, historically, materially, and technologically. Each believed that it had both the right and the responsibility to prevail over all others. Dirts, or Grounders, were as dumb animals: to be exploited as need arose, but also to be "protected," both from their own dangerous ambitions and from the Enemy. The annihilation of an entire world—one of scores of thousands, after all—carried less significance to them than minor damage to one of their ships.

Despite his training with The Stem, which taught him extreme empathy, Pwanda could not understand how a mind could function in this way. He recognized, as he'd said to Dane about Buto Shimas, that such people might regard themselves as honorable, and behave accordingly. But how could the inhabitants—for such they were—of spaceborne ships believe that where and how they lived, or their history, which was less than two thousand years in all, or anything else about them, placed them above all others in the scale of the universe? He had a disturbing thought: Had there been planet-based cultures that made the same irrational assumption of supremacy? If so, these cultures had long been returned to dust, for Pwanda had never heard a whisper of such a thing.

Or was there something about living in the grandeur of open space that so corrupted the human mind that it became delusional? That it came to believe that everything it witnessed was a reflection of its *own* grandeur?

Although incidental to his real work, the questions helped Momed Pwanda pass the time while studying Serjel Weezek and waiting to become a captive again.

Dane refused the weaning process from the interrogation drug that had been offered to Paul Hardaway. With great difficulty due to her weakened state, she convinced Jenny Marsham that she could not properly do her work while under the influence of the chemical. She said truthfully that she would rather be dead than go through the next two months with an impaired mind.

Marsham was impressed again with the young woman's sense of duty. She remarked to Shimas how unfortunate it was that all attendants were not the same as that one.

After two days Dane returned to her duties aboard *Bagalan*. The weakness persisted, but she was pleased to discover that she was again able to anticipate Marsham's responses to most situations, and to exercise subtle influence over some of her actions. She sensed that the test would come soon of how thoroughly she "owned" the squadron leader.

She accompanied Marsham during a day of surprise inspections to a number of ships in her squadron, in preparation for the next day's formal tour by Fleet Leader Mestoeffer. One of the things Dane had recently allowed Marsham to learn about her was that she had a remarkable eye for detail. It was not long into the day before the older woman began allowing her to review the notes she was making while shuttling from one ship to the next. Dane added to these, observing that in one ship a particular piece of machinery seemed less use-worn than the same equipment in others—perhaps not functioning reliably?—or that one captain had presented to Marsham fewer of the ship's crew than had others—a problem with morale? Marsham contacted Shimas about the ships involved and ordered him to go over them in detail. By the end of this very full day, a number of minor problems had been identified and corrected in this manner. There was little that merited disciplinary action, but Marsham would henceforth watch these captains more closely. And was spared any embarrassment that might arise during Mestoeffer's inspection.

The following day Arlana Mestoeffer arrived aboard *Banor,* the flagship of XF566 Company. Waiting inboard of the airlock to greet her were Tam Sepal and his ten squadron leaders. Mestoeffer passed through the two parallel lines, stopping to speak a few words to each person. Behind her marched Fotey Smothe. He was prepared to whisper each name into her ear, but this service was not required. The Fleet Leader had spent an hour that morning reviewing all of their records. Especially two.

The officers wore the most perfect dress uniforms their attendants could prepare. As an optional adjunct to her own uniform, Jenny Marsham had added her clan's distinctive crest to the award patches that nearly filled a blue sash running from her left shoulder and down to her right waist. She'd been furious that morning when CJ had done her usual excellent work in readying the uniform, but had inexplicably forgotten to add the crest. And, when the omission had been pointed out, seemed hesitant to make the addition; the crest interferes with the symmetry, she'd suggested. Insolence! Had it not been for Mestoeffer's specific "request," she'd have confined the attendant to her quarters for a week.

As the Fleet Leader approached, Marsham was pleased to note that the woman's eyes lingered for a full second on the clan insignia. If she was not mistaken, Mestoeffer's smile toward her contained something personal.

The seven men and six women of Sovereign Command proceeded to *Banor*'s Operations Room, where all squadron adjutants and ship's captains from XF566 waited at attention, flanked by their personal attendants. Mestoeffer took her place at the head of the assembly and nodded to Sepal.

The space above the massive War Table became a hemisphere of blackness. Displayed within was a real-time representation of two hundred thousand ships, carrying a total of three hundred eighty million officers and crew of Sovereign Command. Although appearing to be stationary, the massed ships were in fact traveling together at thousands of miles per second as they raced through normal space to confront the Enemy. All present noted with experienced eyes the aggressive posture of the formations. There was nothing here to suggest even the possibility of accepting, or giving, quarter to the Enemy.

"I present to you," Mestoeffer said in her penetrating command-voice, "our Fleet!"

Dane was pleased to see that the formation was identical to the one Jarred Marsham had so proudly displayed for her. *We were right,* she thought to Momed Pwanda.

The applause following Mestoeffer's pronouncement was spontaneous, nearly raucous with excitement. A few brave souls among them began a hesitant cheer, which was soon taken up enthusiastically by all present. *"Sovereign Command!"* half of them shouted out, while the other half answered with *"Mestoeffer!"* The exchange grew in volume as it was repeated, time and again, until the sound was a rhythmic hammering that reverberated with a deafening cadence from the walls of the Operations Room. Fotey Smothe shook with uncontrolled delight as he shouted the name of his patron into her ear, eager to be heard above the others.

Mestoeffer raised her hands in acknowledgment. Beside her, Sepal leaned down to the War Table controls. A moment later the two hundred thousand motes moved minutely back and forth in their formations. The effect suffused the silvered display with an aura of living power and deadly purpose. Though ears were ready to burst and throats were hoarse from shouting, the rhythmic roar screamed to new heights.

At last Mestoeffer brought her hands down slowly to her

sides. Following her signaled command, the cheering dimmed until it was gone. At the last whispered chorus, the displayed ships ceased their movement. The room itself seemed to tremble with reluctantly dissipating energy.

Mestoeffer was hard put to restrain the feelings the cheering had evoked in her. Decades had passed since she had witnessed the pouring out of such raw emotion on this scale. And never, never, had it been directed toward herself. The blood coursing through her veins was charged as it had not been since the day of her first Enemy kill.

"Thank you," she said finally. "I know that each of you will show the same enthusiasm when we first close with the Enemy." As the cheering threatened to erupt once more, she raised her hands with palms outward. "I tell you all," she said with rare unguarded sincerity, "that your welcome and your response have exceeded my previous estimation of your readiness and resolve. In that light, I promise you that conditional upon today's inspection, XF566 Company is to be granted a place of prominence in the first skirmishes of our coming victory."

The applause threatened to explode anew until Tam Sepal, unable to bear it again, motioned the assembled officers to silence. "On behalf of all of us," he said, "I thank you for the honor." Inwardly, he was appalled. A "place of prominence" guaranteed fast-track promotions for the survivors. More to the point, it guaranteed casualty rates of seventy to one hundred percent. And always, the company flagship—his ship—led the first attack. "We are humbled, and grateful," he added.

Sepal's quavering voice betrayed him. Marsham and Shimas lowered their eyes in shame. For Mestoeffer, the man's disgusting show of fear utterly deflated the exultation she'd known a moment before. It was as if an extraordinary and uplifting experience had come to overwhelm her senses, and then vanished like air into space. She felt cheated.

"We will proceed now," she said coldly, "with the inspection." Turning abruptly, she left the Operations Room. Following closely behind her was Fotey Smothe, who cast a bewildered glance back at the gathered officers before disappearing from sight. Those officers looked around themselves, most of them understanding what had happened, and hurried to fall in by rank to accompany their superior. Tam Sepal left the room on thin and visibly trembling legs. Dane watched him go, thinking that if dead men could walk, she was seeing one do so now.

"It was a disaster, Buto, a disaster!"

"Your ships did very well, Jenny," Shimas reminded her. "Not one of your captains was ordered into retirement. The company average was three per squadron." And for the most trivial reasons, he thought to himself. Aloud, he said, "Of course, the Fleet Leader's decisions were correct."

"Of course," Marsham replied automatically. "Buto, what helped us was your thorough reinspection of those ships yesterday. I thank you, formally. Your record will be updated."

"I'm grateful, Jenny. But please remember that I was acting on your order." The two were seated in Marsham's stateroom, dressed in casual uniforms. Shimas had long ago given up wiping perspiration from his scalp. Now he wore a towel draped across his head, gathered together in the back over his wide shoulders. He smiled for the first time that day. "If I were still your superior officer, I would document *your* record. After all, it was your idea."

"Yes, it was," Marsham answered. She raised her own cup and gestured toward Shimas's. Instantly, Dane refilled both.

"And your invitation to dinner with Mestoeffer?"

"There's been no cancellation. I'm due to leave here in an hour." She turned to Dane. "CJ, is everything ready?"

"Yes, Squadron Leader. Your uniform is freshly prepared. May I be excused to bathe and clean my own clothes?"

"Go ahead." Marsham rose from the table and extended her hand to Shimas. "You'll pardon me now," she said. "Duty calls."

"Will you let me know when you return to *Bagalan?*"

"Yes, if you like." She noted that Shimas held her hand

for a second beyond a formal handshake. She added pressure to her own grip.

"Adjutant Shimas?"

Dane's voice seemed to startle both officers. "Yes?"

"Shall I notify your attendant to wake you when we get back?"

"Ah . . ."

"That won't be necessary," Marsham answered. "I'm sure you'll be tired by then, and I want you fresh for tomorrow's work."

"Yes, Squadron Leader." As she walked back to the attendants' quarters, Dane found herself thinking about Shimas and Marsham. She'd seen the mutual affection growing between the two, but was certain that this was the first time it had been physically acknowledged. There was something else about Marsham, though, that was bothering her. Each time recently she'd seen the squadron leader looking at her son, there was a hint of worry in her expression. Somehow this seemed to be about Jarred's own prospects for marriage, although Dane had never heard the subject alluded to by either of them. It occurred to her that she knew little about that part of life among these people. No doubt it was important to them, but they never discussed it within her hearing. She needed to learn about this, and quickly.

One hour twelve minutes later, the shuttle from *Bagalan* drew into an open airlock-hangar of *Dalkag*. From the moment she and Dane stepped out of the small vessel, Jenny Marsham was astounded by what surrounded her. Even a hangar on Mestoeffer's flagship was fabulous, something from a storyteller with too vivid an imagination. The floor and walls seemed fashioned of genuine silver, whose muted sheen was interrupted by inlaid murals of various metals and slabbed stone that exactly duplicated the maroon of the uniforms now authorized by Sovereign Command. The designs were simple, most of them suggesting ships in conflict, others the profiles of officers who had distinguished themselves in battle over the centuries. One mural set above the exit door was larger than all the others. This was a mosaic, done in precious stones of varied color and size. Depicted were two faces, one female and one male, pressed together and facing the viewer. Marsham knew what it represented. This was the finest likeness she had ever seen of the reigning Generals. The venerable faces projected confidence, strength, and wisdom, with eyes looking ahead and reflecting back a future that was more glorious than the observer could imagine. It was an inspiration to witness, a stunning achievement in art. All this, she thought, in a hangar!

Dane was equally in awe. Not from any sense of beauty, but from the knowledge that every precious gem and every scrap of metal so gaudily displayed had been stolen from worlds left shattered; worlds whose people still mourned their dead and missing, people whose every waking moment was a struggle to recover from the brutality thrust upon them. She was reminded again that the Fleets produced nothing except death, destruction, and misery. For the rest of the way to Mestoeffer's dining room she kept her eyes downcast, noting only the bejeweled path they followed there.

*Dalkag*'s chief steward bowed to Marsham as she approached. To Dane's initial shock, the officer looked remarkably like Momed Pwanda. He was taller and heavier, but with proportional body structure and a face of the same shape and strength, lacking only the fierce intelligence of Momed's eyes. She thought briefly of her partner, a man who found humor in every circumstance, recalling how subtly and easily he could disguise the fire inside him whenever a member of the Fleet approached. She pushed those thoughts away and concentrated on the matter at hand.

"Welcome, Squadron Leader Marsham," the man said in a surprisingly high-pitched voice. "I will announce you at once. May I take your sword?"

Marsham hesitated at this departure from protocol, but handed the ceremonial instrument to the man without comment. Her uneasiness was allayed when she looked past the steward and saw that all of the guests she could see had met with the same request. Or had they? She recalled suddenly that Mestoeffer had designated the evening as informal. Glancing down at CJ, she also recalled that she had not mentioned this fact to her attendant. It was not CJ's failure.

There must be no further mistakes this evening, Marsham told herself. In a uniform pocket she carried a message that had been received on *Bagalan* only moments before her departure. It was a dispatch from Major General Olton Kay-Raike, the man with whom her father had discussed a marriage for her son. In his renowned brusque manner, Kay-Raike had demanded that Jarred Marsham be sent immediately to one of his ships for "evaluation." To protect her son, she'd ordered *Bagalan*'s memory purged of the message. She could later say that due to a malfunction, it had never been received. But in the meantime she was hoping to speak privately to Arlana Mestoeffer, in hopes that the Fleet Leader would put an end to the entire matter.

Befitting her junior status, Marsham was the last to arrive. As she was announced, all heads turned toward her, and then quickly away. Mestoeffer was the only person she could see in the opulent room whom she had met before.

Arlana Mestoeffer watched Marsham enter the room and nodded to her. She smiled graciously at the returned silent greeting. Noting that all of the assembled officers now looked toward the latest arrival with new interest, she was pleased. Now, she thought, the interesting part of the evening would begin.

Dinner was served almost immediately, with Marsham seated at the far end of the long table from Mestoeffer. Dane stood behind Marsham and served her from platters circulated by other attendants. The foods nearly caused her to swoon. There was new lamb, roast beef brimming with juice, steaming loaves of crusty breads, a selection of cheeses, and a host of vegetables and fruits, many of which she could not identify. Also present were whole potatoes so large and aromatic that she knew they were from Paul Hardaway's "farm" aboard *Bagalan*. None of the meats tempted her. But the vegetables and fruits, steamed whole or sliced and raw, and the breads made her grateful that she had steeled herself for this moment by saving her evening gruel for the minutes before she'd left her quarters. Otherwise her hunger for real food would have been audible throughout the dining room.

As the last to be served, Marsham looked up toward her host while all conversation at the table ceased. Mestoeffer stood and raised a glass to her guests. "Welcome, all of you," she began, "and thank you for accepting my invitation." Without drinking from it, she set the glass down again. "We do not often discuss matters of duty at gatherings such as this," she continued. "But an unpleasant matter has arisen, and I bring it to your attention for reasons which will become clear to each of you. Afterward, I assure you, we will have a pleasant evening. I direct your attention to the one seat at this table which is conspicuously empty." All heads turned toward the vacancy. Marsham realized at once that it represented Tam Sepal. No one spoke as Mestoeffer resumed her chair and nodded to the man seated to her right.

"I am former Fleet Leader Brotman Nandes," the man began, "now honored to serve as first adjutant to Fleet Leader Mestoeffer." Like Buto Shimas, he was bald and heavily mustached, a style he himself had made popular. This evening his voice was uncharacteristically flat. "Fifteen hours ago Fleet Leader Mestoeffer had the extreme displeasure to witness an act of blatant cowardice." He waited until the murmuring swept the table and ebbed away. "By coincidence we have among us tonight another witness to the event. Squadron Leader Marsham, would you please stand?"

Jenny stood self-consciously.

"Of course your testimony is not needed to reinforce that of Fleet Leader Mestoeffer." Muted laughter greeted this self-evident statement. "However, she asks that you make yourself available to answer any questions that these honored guests may put to you, informally."

"I will, sir," she answered, beginning to feel sick. There could be nothing "informal" about cowardice. Unless it was specifically ordered so. She took this to mean that whatever was to follow would not be according to tradition.

"Good. Please sit down." Nandes continued, "The act I refer to took place before an assemblage of officers from XF566 Company. Therefore every man, woman, and child in that company will be required to view what you are about to see. Chief Steward?" At the cue, the lights dimmed throughout the room. An image formed above the dinner table. It was of Tam Sepal. The image rotated slowly to face each of the guests. Like meat on a spit, Dane thought.

Sepal's voice declared, "You know who I am. Now you will know *what* I am. I am a coward. For years I have concealed this fact from those around me. My promotions and commands were all the result of fraud on my part. But inevitably, the cowardice that is in me, the cowardice that may well permeate my entire clan, has been revealed. I have no place in Sovereign Command. I am not fit to address you further." The image faded.

*Scripted,* Marsham thought in disgust. And drugged. Tam Sepal had a distinctive way of expressing himself. None of it was evident in the speech she'd just heard.

Again an image, this time the interior of an airlock. Tam Sepal stood in dress uniform at attention—more rigidly than his weak legs would normally allow, Marsham noted—while a sublieutenant removed the man's ceremonial sword from its scabbard and threw it across the floor. She tore away his insignia of rank. This was followed by ripping off the sash that crossed his thin chest, and then the uniform was cut away from him. In a few moments Sepal was naked except for his boots. His tattered clothing and decorations were dropped at his feet as the sublieutenant, obviously embarrassed by this duty, withdrew from view. With a precision of movement he had never shown before, Sepal turned to face the outer door of the airlock. A hissing sound arose as pumps began slowly withdrawing air from the small compartment.

The officers assembled at the table drew in a collective breath. This phase of retirement was normally completed swiftly and humanely. But as they watched, the scene played itself out over long minutes. Sepal collapsed as breathing became at first difficult, and then impossible. He writhed on his back, his face contorting, skin turning to red webwork as blood vessels burst. His eyes . . .

Marsham turned away, as did many of them. The drama went on for minutes longer before the image faded into darkness. The room lights were on again instantly. All turned toward Mestoeffer, who was standing again. Before speaking, she played again in her mind the short speech Sepal had given. She lingered over the words, "cowardice . . . that may well permeate my entire clan . . . revealed . . ." Those words had been her own contribution. Their coming from Tam Sepal's mouth signaled the beginning of the downfall of his entire clan, most notably its head, Hivad Sepal—the man who had tricked the Generals into sending her here. She said, "I know that this was difficult for you to watch, as it was for me. But considering what lies ahead of us, considering the parts we all must play in the greatest victory in history . . ."

Marsham turned at the sound of Dane, sobbing quietly behind her. "CJ!" she whispered. Dane nodded and regained control of herself.

"I claim this coming victory," Mestoeffer was saying, "for every human being alive. From Grounder to despised Gold Fleet member, to each of us in Sovereign Command. After the Enemy is defeated and has joined its cousins among the rocks and slime, leaving the freedom of space to its betters, justice will rule the seven galaxies. And beyond! I promise this to each one of you, and to a thousand generations of Sovereign Command yet to come!" Her practiced voice dropped from its crescendo to a personal tone. "In light of this, we are all obliged to examine ourselves, and those who serve under us. Nothing less than total commitment will be acceptable. Are we agreed?"

The applause was loud, but without energy. Exactly as she'd wanted. They were shamed, as they should be. But the next time she gave that speech, it would be as part of the Generals. Then the reaction would be very different, for nearly everything she said would have been accomplished.

By her. "Very well, then. The chief steward has provided us with a sumptuous dinner. Enjoy!" Now she raised her glass again, and drained it. Every officer at the table returned the gesture.

The meal passed quickly, most appetites lost before it began. Only Arlana Mestoeffer and Fotey Smothe allowed their plates to be refilled, each attacking the food with enthusiasm. When she was finished, Mestoeffer looked up at the silent faces watching her. "And now," she said with a perfect host-smile, "I am pleased to tell you that we have fine entertainment ahead of us."

She gestured to the chief steward. As he relayed the order, an attendant appeared from outside the room and brought in a narrow platform, half the height of the dinner table. This was placed at the far end, behind Marsham.

"Squadron Leader Marsham," Mestoeffer announced, "has brought to my attention a Grounder of exceptional ability. Would we all like to see a demonstration of her talents?"

The mood in the room shifted dramatically. When the cheering began, it was genuine and enthusiastic. Eager and expectant smiles turned toward Dane.

Marsham was mortified, suddenly realizing how badly she had misjudged her relationship with this woman. She began a carefully worded protest, but was interrupted by Mestoeffer. "Squadron Leader, your humility is endearing, but hardly appropriate for an informal gathering such as this. You've boasted to me about your Grounder. Very well, back up your boasting. Please, have her mount the table. Show us a few tricks she can do." Spirited applause greeted her remarks.

Marsham turned to Dane, unable to meet her eyes. "CJ," she whispered, "I never—"

"Don't be concerned, Squadron Leader," Dane whispered back in a voice Marsham had not heard from her before. It was eerie: penetrating, but lifeless. Dane stepped up on the platform and onto the table. Walking to the center, she turned to face them individually. Precisely as had the image of Tam Sepal.

Fotey Smothe grinned hugely and winked at her.

"Very well!" Mestoeffer said, laughing along with her toy. "And so, what will it be, honored guests?" she asked cheerfully. "A song? A dance? . . ." Peals of laughter rolled down the table, arriving as thunder in Dane's ears. "Grounder poetry?" Mestoeffer continued, as her audience groaned. "Come now, shout out your requests!"

Earlier, Dane had been weeping as she'd watched the ordeal of Tam Sepal. He was the officer who'd led five companies of ships to devastate Walden and forty-nine other worlds. She'd watched the man as he died a slow and agonizing death. She'd seen every second of his torture, watched him writhe and contort, and she'd felt—nothing. Nothing at all. Her tears had been for herself; that she could witness such a thing and feel nothing. She'd wept for her childhood, forever lost.

Through the songs her mother had taught her, through the poems she had memorized as a toddler to win a smile and embrace from her father, Dane endured the officers' jeers and mocking laughter. A child might weep in humiliation. Dane's eyes were stone dry.

When the evening at last drew to a conclusion, the guests began filing out in descending order of rank, thanking their host and looking forward to their own commands and a long night of sleep. Marsham was the last to exit. As she reached the door, Mestoeffer placed a hand on her shoulder. Marsham could barely contain two opposing impulses: to attack, or to recoil.

"A word, Squadron Leader," Mestoeffer said with a smile. When they were seated again at the table Mestoeffer said, "Have your Grounder serve us tea."

They and Fotey Smothe drank in silence until Mestoeffer spoke again. "I knew your father," she began. Marsham nodded. She had already reached that conclusion. "Members of my own clan were at the Battle of N34-V654," Mestoeffer continued. "Many of them are alive today because of the brilliance of Major General Marsham, and the excellent training of his ship's captains."

"Thank you, Fleet Leader." Marsham's heart felt like a dead thing in her chest.

"I meant to thank him personally, but never had the opportunity to do so. Not properly." She placed an affectionate hand on Fotey's shoulder.

The meaning was not lost on Marsham. Her father had spurned Mestoeffer's advances. And so had begun her vendetta against the Marsham clan. That, and that alone, was the reason that hundreds of her clan were dead.

"There is a way I can repay the debt," Mestoeffer went on. "At first I considered giving you Sepal's XF566 Company. Certainly, you're qualified to fill the position. But a better thought occurred to me." Mestoeffer stood, and by protocol the two others did as well. "Squadron Leader Marsham, I hereby relieve you of your present command. When you leave here, return to your flagship and assemble your personal belongings. You will then report immediately back aboard *Dalkag* with your personal staff. And of course, with your son." As she subtly emphasized the last three words, Marsham nearly fainted. "You are hereby elevated in rank to acting lieutenant general. The promotion will become permanent as you prove satisfactory to me on my own personal staff. I have no doubt that you will prove satisfactory. Have *you* any doubts, Marsham?"

"No, Fleet Leader. I am honored."

"You might lift your head when you say that," Mestoeffer laughed. "Very well. Go now. I will expect you to be in my staff room at the beginning of tomorrow's first watch. You are dismissed."

The shuttle was waiting in the ornamented hangar. As soon as the vessel was sealed and Marsham had taken the controls, the door opened and they departed. Less than a minute later Dane sat next to her.

"CJ! What do you think you're doing? I know that you're disturbed by this evening's events. But do not presume—"

Dane silenced her with an abrupt gesture that caught Marsham by complete surprise. "Be quiet, please, and listen to me," Dane said gently, in the strange voice Marsham had heard her use earlier. It was disturbing, as if spoken from beyond space, beyond death. Marsham was too shocked to interrupt her young attendant as Dane continued on. "We have only twelve minutes before reaching *Bagalan.* We must speak quickly, and privately. It's about your son. He needs protection. I can help you." Without a further word, Squadron Leader Marsham reached forward and disabled the shuttle's monitor.

. . . . . . . . . . . . . . . . . . . . . . . . . . . . . . . . . . . . .
. . . . . . . . . . . . . . . . . . . . . . . . . . . . . . . . . . . . .
. . . . . . . . . . . . . . . . . . . . . . . . . . . . . . . . . . . . .
. . . . . . . . . . . . . . . . . . . . . . . . . . . . . . . . . . . . .
. . . . . . . . . . . . . . . . . . . . . . . . . . . . . . . . . . . . .
. . . . . . . . . . . . . . . . . . . . . . . . . . . . . . . . . . . . .

# ⇥14⇤

Paul Hardaway was curled on his side and sound asleep, snoring lightly. He woke at the sound of someone approaching from behind him. Whoever it was moved with the stealth of a forest animal. He tensed his body, ready to spring. After a few moments his practiced senses identified the intruder, and he relaxed.

"Hello, Dane."

"Hello. Sorry if I startled you."

"Don't worry," he said, grinning in the darkness. "You can't sneak up on a Dog Scout." He sat up in bed and faced her. "What are you doing down here?" "Down here" was a series of twenty large compartments used to produce food for *Bagalan*'s crew. Much of it was Paul's domain; among the other attendants involved in growing fruits and vegetables, he was chief. Days ago he had obtained permission to sleep on his "farm," to keep a constant watch on some of his newer experiments.

"I'm leaving, Paul. I wanted to say good-bye to you properly this time." Her eyes were more adjusted to the darkness now, so that she could see him as a dim outline.

"What? Why are you—"

"There isn't much time. I wanted to tell you that everything you said to me on Walden was right. I *was* a child. I realized that very quickly. But I'm different now. Really. So don't worry about me anymore, all right?"

"You're going?" Sitting up in the bed, he was on a level with Dane's face. It was too dark to see her distinctly.

"Yes, right now. I'll be fine, and so will you."

"This time I'm going with you." He moved as if to stand, but relented to the pressure of her hands on his shoulders.

"You can't, Paul. Listen, I also wanted to tell you that in a few weeks you'll be feeling differently than you do now. Don't worry about it. It's only—"

"You mean the medicine? I stopped taking that two days ago. And stop arguing with me." He lowered his voice to a barely audible whisper. "I know you, Dane. You've got both Marshams doing what you want, just like you used to do to me. That means you can take me with you, if you want to. You said I was right before. Well, I'm right this time, too. You're going to need me. So go and do whatever it is you do, and arrange it. I'll get my stuff and be wherever you say, in ten minutes. Where do you want me to meet you?"

She'd never heard him speak so rapidly, or argue a decision so insistently. It was good that he'd lowered his voice; the monitors were sensitive. She answered in the same whisper. "Paul, they won't like you, where I'm going. They're—"

"Whatever they are, you'll take care of it. And I can help you. For instance, an attendant told me that before you left *Bagalan* you asked her about the Fleet marriage customs. She said it sounded important to you."

"I didn't get much of an answer."

"She didn't know much about it, Dane. I found someone who did. Want me to tell you?"

Surprised by Paul's initiative, Dane asked, "Can you do it quickly?"

"Sure, I can. Here's how it works. Clan and rank are tied up together. When two officers marry, the junior one takes the senior's clan name. That can be changed later if the junior becomes the senior, but it's complicated and not done very often. Also, officers can't marry without their commander's permission, or while they're under investigation for a court-martial offense, or while they're on temporary duty. But once they're married, only death can end the arrangement without written approval from the council. Is that helpful?"

"Yes," Dane said, thinking of her patron's new assignment. She anticipated greater opportunities for her work in the transfer, but diminishing ones for Jenny and Buto.

"Good," Paul said. "Now, look. You told me you were in a hurry. So let me get packing. Where do we meet?" He removed her hands gently from his shoulders and stood. A moment later he'd pulled a tunic over his trousers and was bending to pull his boots on.

Other than considerations for Paul's safety, Dane could think of no reason to refuse. That was a matter for him to decide, ultimately. In truth she was relieved. She could not bear the thought of leaving Paul alone again, knowing that he'd once nearly killed himself trying to find her, and might try again. And it would be good to have another real friend nearby, particularly one who seemed to sense what she needed. Carnie, as a "lifetime friend," was already packed and ready to debark from *Bagalan*. "All right, Paul. Be in the attendants' quarters, level three, forward, in fifteen minutes. If you're stopped on the way, don't argue. Come back here. I'll speak with the squadron leader and see what I can do."

"I want to be head farmer on the next ship, too," he said aloud. Lowering his head to hers, he whispered urgently, "It's important."

She laughed at him in the darkness, and kissed his cheek. "You do love to work, don't you?"

"More than you know, Dane. Except for taking care of you, it's the only thing I look forward to. Someday you'll see just how good I am. At both."

"I believe you, Paul. And thanks. I'm going to get ready now."

"I'll be there in ten minutes."

The quick shuttle trip to *Dalkag* was accomplished in near silence. Dane, Paul, and Carnie sat by themselves at the rear of the vessel, clutching their small bags of personal belongings. Jarred Marsham piloted the craft while Jenny Marsham and Buto Shimas sat together behind him. The officers had only one case of clothing each, the cases tied down between themselves and the attendants. The remainder of their effects were to be sent from *Bagalan* later.

The airlock-hangar they were assigned to enter upon arrival at *Dalkag* was not the one Jenny and Dane had seen before. This was on the opposite side of the huge ship, far away from the finery and splendor that led to Arlana Mestoeffer's living and working areas. The scene greeting them was very different from the formality used to welcome invited guests. Here, no pomp or decoration of any sort greeted their arrival. The hangar was stacked with crates of items and materials not yet stowed away into the massive supply system of the ship. Suited workers were busy throughout the compartment, moving the supplies onto waiting motorized sledges.

No one was standing by to receive the new arrivals. The moment the hangar was sealed and pressurized again, Buto Shimas stamped angrily down the shuttle steps and took rough hold of the first worker he saw. Lifting the man from the floor with one huge hand, Shimas ripped away his suit's faceplate. "Squadron Leader Marsham and her personal staff have arrived," he seethed, barely able to control his voice. *"Where is her honor escort?"*

"I . . . I don't know, sir! We were told to expect nine supply shuttles this watch. We thought you were the last of them."

"They're all Grounders," Jenny Marsham said from behind him. "Let him go, Adjutant Shimas."

As the man was lowered to the floor, Shimas growled, "We're due in the Fleet Leader's staff room in one hour. You will lead us there."

"Sir, I can't." As the wide face below his own reddened dangerously, the man said hastily, "Sir, I've never been near that part of the ship. None of us has. And . . . with respect, sir, we're not permitted to leave this area."

Shimas released him. "Very well," he said. "Go about your duty." As the man hurried away, Shimas turned to Dane, who was just outside the shuttle door with her companions. "You three, bring our cases." To Marsham he said, "I'll go ahead of you, Squadron Leader, and find the way."

The trek through *Dalkag*'s labyrinthine passageways began, with Shimas returning often to indicate the way. They passed a number of junior officers, none of them authorized to leave their duty stations, who fairly jumped out of the way as they saw Shimas striding toward them again. Before long Dane and Carnie struggled with the cases on their backs. Paul carried the heaviest of them easily, offering one hand of support in turn to the others.

Fifty minutes had passed before they found the first of the jewel-laden corridors that led to Arlana Mestoeffer's offices and suites. Shimas stayed with them then, as their destination was nearby. They turned left at a final intersection and nearly collided with First Adjutant Brotman Nandes.

"Well, what have we here?" Nandes laughed. "Running is better suited to childrem, isn't it, Squadron Leader? Oh, my mistake! You have no real rank, have you? I believe you are an *acting* lieutenant general?"

"Yes, sir," Marsham said, containing her anger. "Please excuse us. We're due in the staff room in five minutes."

Nandes ignored her, turning on the three attendants. "Grounders are not authorized here without permission. Whom do you belong to?"

"They're with me," Marsham said. The omission of the "sir" was deliberate. "We haven't yet been assigned quarters."

Nandes turned to her. "Get them out of here. You can find them and your other belongings later, when you have time."

To Dane, Marsham said, "Go back to the hangar, you three. I'll send for you."

"Wait," Nandes said. "I recognize that one from last night. Your personal attendant, correct? She will remain with you, on the Fleet Leader's orders. She believes that the other officers would enjoy seeing this attendant again."

Paul glared at the man until Dane caught his attention and shook her head from side to side. Turning, he hefted two of the cases and left, followed by an exhausted Carnie Niles with the third.

"And what about you?" Nandes said to Shimas. He

grinned at Shimas's bald scalp and heavy mustache, which mirrored his own. "Are you here with Marsham?"

"I am Buto Shimas. Adjutant to *Squadron Leader* Marsham." Without conscious thought Shimas relaxed his right arm and tightened his back, preparing a blow that would decapitate Brotman Nandes.

Sensing disaster, Jarred introduced himself quickly. "Sir, I am SubLieutenant Jarred Marsham. It's an honor to meet you. Sir."

"SubLieutenant," Nandes repeated. "Well, SubLieutenant Marsham, perhaps you'd better run along and accompany your little Grounders, don't you think? I'm sure they could use help with those cases."

"Yes, sir." He turned and hurried off.

"Now if you two will straighten your uniforms and follow me," Nandes said abruptly, "we have a meeting to attend."

Dane noted that the first adjutant seemed relieved, as if he'd been given an unpleasant order and was pleased to have it done with.

The meeting was a lengthy one, with Arlana Mestoeffer giving a long and animated address on subjects ranging from Fleet readiness to the dangers of lax discipline, to the state of fear and desperation she promised them was presently rampant throughout the Gold Fleet. "No doubt by now they've had ample time to think more clearly about the impossible task they've set for themselves," she commented. "And no doubt they have considered abandoning the idea of assembling their forces in unprecedented numbers. For now, a false sense of pride will keep them together. Therefore it is our utmost imperative to engage them before they scatter throughout the galaxies like the cowards they are. To this end I have this morning dispatched twelve thousand additional ships to go out in units of fifteen, as scouts. Half are proceeding toward the Fortress, to penetrate deeper than the ships we presently have monitoring there. Some of these or the other six thousand will find concentrations

of the Enemy. Before being destroyed, they are to broadcast . . ."

Easily ignoring the smirking glances cast her way by the
officers in attendance, Dane captured every word, gesture,
and nuance of Mestoeffer's speech—and the reaction.
When the Fleet Leader announced her unilateral decision to
commit an additional twelve thousand ships to going out
virtually alone to find the Enemy, a wave of unexpressed
resentment swept the room. Dane understood. These were
high-ranking and seasoned veterans of war. All of them had
more direct combat experience than did their leader. They
expected to be consulted before such a wasteful tactic was
employed. And wasteful it was. All of them believed, as
Dane knew from observing Jenny Marsham, that the Gold
Fleet had built its concentration within the nebula they
called the Fortress, in Galaxy S-143. The nebula was already being watched; they would know when the Enemy
moved. But those newly sent ships would be helpless,
wherever they were found. There was no need to risk an additional twelve thousand ships.

Dane took this in with a smile: Following so hard on the
undignified death Mestoeffer had meted out to Tam Sepal
the night before, this was a profound mistake. To Dane it
was more welcome evidence that Mestoeffer's officers
were coming to distrust her judgment. Morale within the
greatest force ever assembled by Sovereign Command was
disintegrating.

In her peripheral vision she saw Marsham, who smiled
encouragingly at Dane's intense focus on the Fleet Leader.
The previous evening Dane had told her a little about tracking, never mentioning that Marsham herself had been
tracked. She described it to the older woman as something
done on Walden by professional entertainers; that by
watching very closely one could detect small signs from the
observed that, when presented dramatically to an audience,
seemed to reflect a magical ability. A parlor trick, she said,
but sometimes valuable. She explained that because of her
anger toward Mestoeffer, she had concentrated very hard
during the dinner and thought that she detected something

in the Fleet Leader's expression and voice that was so hostile toward Marsham, Dane feared that both the squadron leader and her son could be in danger.

Marsham had been deeply impressed, and was eager to hear more. Dane explained to her that if she again focused deeply while watching Mestoeffer, she might be able to find something to suggest a way that the Marshams could be safeguarded. Taking the next step, she'd won Marsham over completely when she tearfully proclaimed to the older woman that her own allegiance was to Jenny and Jarred personally—above even the loyalty she felt toward Sovereign Command itself. Dane knew very well that secretly, Marsham felt exactly that way toward her son. She played on that fact without revealing it, until Marsham openly conceded her worry. In the end she was willing to help Dane in any way possible.

As she continued tracking Mestoeffer, Dane became annoyed at herself. She was not concentrating properly. In the back of her mind was a persistent twinge of guilt she'd first felt the night before: If it became necessary for her progress, she would attach herself to Mestoeffer by betraying Jenny and Jarred Marsham. But as the meeting progressed, another possibility presented itself.

What happened next took Dane by complete surprise. First Adjutant Brotman Nandes led the spirited applause after Mestoeffer's concluding remarks. Then, with her permission, he gave his own address. The officer paced the floor like a caged beast. No, Dane decided after a few moments. Not caged. Indeed, while tracking him she felt herself become a hunter carefully stalking a skilled and deadly predator on the prowl. He was fascinating to watch. He spoke with subdued power, like a whispering volcano, of the long history of the Silver Fleet and its great heroes. He seemed to take a perverse pleasure in mentioning William Marsham along with the finest of them. His audience appeared to stiffen its collective spine as he led them to explore anew the concepts of honor, courage, and dedication to cause. Far from evoking the resentment that Mestoeffer had, he drew from his fellow officers a sense that he and they were in perfect harmony. They feared Mestoeffer, but they revered Nandes. Which, Dane wondered, would prove to be the more powerful motivating force among these senior officers—all of whom had been personally selected by Mestoeffer?

Nandes next spoke of the value of tradition, linking it to every great victory achieved by Sovereign Command. At the end he emphasized passionately one particular tradition that was as old as Sovereign Command itself: that the strength and experience of superior—*as well as subordinate*—officers must be respected.

Of all those hearing his speech, only one did not seem to grasp the significance of this last assertion. This was the one officer his closing remarks had been directed toward. Dane saw early on that Arlana Mestoeffer had not been listening—that her first adjutant had known this would be the case, and used it to demonstrate his last point. The Fleet Leader did nothing more than nod her head politely when Nandes was finished, and lead the necessarily restrained applause.

After Mestoeffer passed to her senior staff a list of the twelve thousand ships to be subtracted from their rosters, the meeting was brought to a close. Marsham and Dane were last to leave the room. When the two of them were alone, Marsham looked hopefully toward her attendant. Dane averted her eyes; her mind was racing. She would need to confirm everything she suspected by acting out the tracking she'd done. As quickly as possible. But she had little doubt that whether he had thought consciously of it or not, Nandes would soon be contemplating the unthinkable—something that probably had never occurred to any field officer in the history of Sovereign Command: nothing less than the assassination of a council member.

"You'll need privacy to sort all of this out," Marsham suggested in a quiet voice.

"What? Oh, yes. Yes, I will."

"I'm going now to find Jarred. Then I'll locate the chief steward and have him assign quarters to you and your friends."

"Thank you." One thing was already clear to Dane. As distasteful as the prospect was, she needed greater access to Brotman Nandes. If successful, she could do much more than solve the Marshams' problem. She might solve her own, as well.

During the next week she availed herself of every opportunity to be near the first adjutant. She found that within the jumble of impressions she'd first formed of the man, some were accurate, and some entirely wrong. It was true that he was contemplating the assassination of Arlana Mestoeffer. But—surprising to Dane—Brotman Nandes was an eminently likable, though distant, person. Of particular importance to her short-term plans, he harbored a profound respect for Major General William Marsham; and despite the impression left by his initial meeting with her, he felt the same toward the general's daughter.

Dane reported these latter observations to Jenny, and advised her to look for small opportunities to exchange a polite word in private with Nandes. She suggested that Jarred seek the older man's advice on occasion; rigidly observing protocol, but speaking honestly about the doubts and frustrations so common in a young officer's mind. Both Jenny and Jarred were reluctant to accept her advice, their own impressions of Nandes being quite the opposite of Dane's. But because they trusted her judgment, they made tentative overtures to the first adjutant. Over the following days Dane was gratified to see the beginnings of a solid friendship.

But if she were to choose one word to describe Nandes's impact on her overall plans, that word would be "dangerous."

# ⇶15⇷

Pwanda and Weezek had come free of hyperspace seven hours before. By now the two were working together smoothly, and had no difficulty replacing power plant elements in preparation for the final jump. After they'd completed the task, they sat and waited for the cooling to finish and the preset controls to send them on their way again.

Through the craft's viewscreens stars once again beckoned like gems, but in patterns Momed Pwanda had never seen. Ahead, impossible to determine the light-years of distance, a billowy nebula seemed to arise from an invisible platform. Viewed from this perspective, it appeared to flow upward into a mass and become thin as it fanned to the right. Like a lion's head, he thought, caught in left profile as it stared out to contemplate diamond-flecked emptiness.

"See that formation?" Weezek asked from beside him. "That's where our greatest concentration of strength is."

"The nebula?"

"It's called Noldron, in honor of the first of our Nomarchs."

This was the first mention Weezek had made of the title. "That would be your ultimate commander? Supreme leader?"

"The Nomarch is the Nomarch," Weezek said simply. As if reciting, he added, "It was Noldron who united us eight hundred years ago, and created the Great Command. All Nomarchs are directly descended from Noldron, and take the name."

"The nebula's impressive."

"Yes. We've owned it for centuries. The next time we leave hyperspace, we'll be deep inside it. Assuming the Silver Fleet has done everything right."

"They have so far," Pwanda observed. "Does it disturb you that the Silver Fleet knows so precisely where your strength is?"

Weezek laughed. "Sure, they know. But what does it matter? They're all cowards."

Minutes later, the starscapes vanished again.

Two hours later they reappeared, in new patterns. "We're home," Weezek said, grinning. "No Enemy ship has ever penetrated here and survived."

"If that's the case, we'll be detected soon."

"Oh, I'm certain that we have been already. And identified. Otherwise we'd have been dead the moment we left hyperspace. We'll be joined very soon, I'm sure. But before that I'd like my meal. Now, Momed."

"Yes, sir." As Pwanda had planned, Weezek was no longer afraid of him. He believed that the Grounder saw himself as dependent on him for life itself. But Pwanda knew that once they were boarded, Weezek would have little if any control over what then transpired. Pwanda could only hope that as Weezek was questioned, his own role in recent events would appear to be both innocent and beneficial: a castaway from the Silver Fleet, skilled in medicine and perhaps useful in tending to other captives. Or better yet, able to meet high authority and answer questions concerning his former captors. He knew now that the capture of a ship and personnel was more than rare. Weezek and the people with him had been the first living prisoners taken by the Silver Fleet in centuries. He was more confident than ever that this would bring powerful members of the Gold Fleet to witness the coordinator's return.

Weezek had been led to believe that Pwanda was from a family of attendants, all trained to serve a company leader; that in gratitude for his family's prior service he had not been executed for an indiscretion, but instead sent away. And as he'd planned, Weezek now bore a genuine sense of gratitude toward him. During the past two weeks Pwanda had convinced the coordinator that he had suffered a major relapse and was certain to die soon; that only by remaining at his bedside constantly, administering muscle manipulation and putrid-tasting concoctions of liquefied foods of no real medicinal value, was he able to try bringing the man back to a state of health. Weezek accepted Pwanda's efforts as an extraordinary feat of skill, dedication, and luck, which had preserved his life. Most gratifying to Pwanda was his success in planting within Weezek's mind a suggestion that he and Dane had formulated.

A gong-sound echoed through the shuttle. Contact. Through a viewscreen Pwanda saw a moving, distant point of reflection. As the point drew closer he saw that it was not one, but dozens of ships from the Omnipotent Gold Fleet.

"Don't do anything aggressive," Weezek said to him in a half-whisper.

"I won't, sir. But what exactly did you think I might do to frighten them away?"

"What? Oh. Nothing, I suppose." Weezek laughed along with Pwanda. It helped to lessen the sense of impending doom that had overtaken him the moment the ships came into view. He'd remembered in that instant that despite what he'd said to Momed, he was as despised by his own Fleet as anyone could be. Neither crew nor supervisor, accepted by neither caste, he could hope for sympathy only from other coordinators—who were as despised as himself. And a faint hope that would be, in itself.

The ships really did reflect gold light, Pwanda saw. Unlike the rounded inverted-bowl shape common to all vessels of Sovereign Command, these were elongated in one direction and flat on top and bottom. They reminded him of the smooth oval stones he'd found in fishing streams as a child.

The comm speaker blared. "Confirm your identification."

Weezek hurriedly sat in the pilot's seat and replied. "Shuttle Fourteen from ship *D35A*," he began, and proceeded to name his family of one hundred ships, his community of one thousand, and society of ten thousand.

"Confirmed. Who is on board?"

"Ship Coordinator Serjel Weezek, Supervisor. And one Dirt, Momed."

"Your shuttle was sent out from *D35A* with yourself, a Supervisor Yardley, and seventeen crew. Where are they?"

"All dead, Supervisor. They died heroically."

"Let us hope so. You were to discover new weapons technology. Success?"

Weezek sneezed and accepted a cloth from Pwanda. "That was a ruse, Supervisor. A trap. I tried to warn Supervisor Yardley, but—"

*"Success?"*

"None." He covered his mouth and nose with the cloth, sneezing and coughing until his eyes watered. Pwanda handed him a fresh cloth, and he nodded thanks.

"Others aboard with you and this Momed?"

"Nud . . . nud . . ." Maddeningly, the sneeze wouldn't come. *"None."*

"Cargo?"

"None."

"And *no* weapons?"

"None."

The voice snickered. *"Value?"*

"That is yours to determine, Supervisor. I am a recent prisoner of the Silver Fleet. Momed has served their high-ranking officers for twenty years. He knows a great deal about them."

"Purpose for being here?"

Pwanda bent over and put his face close to Weezek's ear. "Sabotage," he whispered, grinning.

Weezek flushed crimson and broke into a coughing fit. When he found his voice, he made the sound of a hose rupturing. "Shhshh!"

"What was that reply?" demanded the comm unit.

"Your pardon, Supervisor. I have been ill. My purpose is to rejoin the Fleet and to provide any information I can. The Dirt is a highly skilled physician. Among his own kind, of course."

"Stand by for boarding. We will find you lying facedown on the floor, hands extended and empty."

"Yes, Supervisor." Weezek breathed a sigh of relief and shot an angry glance at Pwanda.

Pwanda handed him a cup of water. "Sorry, Ship Coordinator. You seemed nervous."

"Of course I did! That is the proper attitude while addressing a supervisor."

"Then it was a pretense?"

"What? Well . . . yes. Of course it was!" Weezek puffed himself up. "You would do well to remember that."

"I will. Thank you, sir."

Weezek relaxed somewhat and smiled. "Momed, you've given me valuable service. It's unfortunate that I haven't taught you much about us in return."

Pwanda nodded. The ship coordinator would be astounded to learn how much he'd "taught" Pwanda about the Gold Fleet. And about the coordinator himself. "Security considerations, sir. I understand."

"Exactly. And so when we're taken aboard that ship, follow everything I do. If I seem to be frightened, remember that it's expected."

"I understand, Ship Coordinator."

"Now let's get down on the floor. When they arrive, answer their questions quickly. Don't move until you're told. And then move very slowly. And whatever you do, don't make jokes!"

"I understand, Ship Coordinator."

An hour later Momed Pwanda was still lying facedown on the shuttle's floor, surrounded by four full-suited crew of the Gold Fleet. Their voices were muffled through the faceplates they wore, but their words were distinct enough. "Where is it?"

Another boot drove into Pwanda's ribs. "Where *is* it?"

Weezek had stopped protesting this treatment of Momed long ago and now sat silently, bound to a passenger seat.

For his part, Pwanda was carefully considering which of the four he should attack first. Suited as they were, they would be slow to react; their suits would be torn bags of broken bones before any of them could reach the comm unit. But this thought was only for distraction, and amusement. Soon they would grow tired of their sport. He only hoped that this would be before he was seriously injured.

*"Where . . . is . . . it ?"* The voice was female, and her boot was heavier than the rest.

"I don't know what you mean," Pwanda said again. And added, "But if you'll stop this kicking competition, I'll name the winner and help you find whatever it is you're looking for." From behind him he heard Weezek groan as the woman's boot found him again. "You're the winner," Pwanda told her through clenched teeth. "Now tell me what you're looking for."

"An explosive device! *Where is it?*"

"There isn't one," Pwanda answered. "If there were I'd have found and deactivated it long ago. I'm afraid of those things."

"Stand up," the woman said. As Pwanda came slowly to his feet, she swung an arm at his head. Clutching his sides and pretending to collapse in pain, he ducked under the blow and went to his knees. The arm swept over him and the woman stumbled, losing her balance in the bulky suit.

Her three companions laughed as her feet tangled and she sprawled to the floor. She stood up awkwardly and faced Pwanda. "You all saw that! He *attacked* me!"

"Then you should have kicked him harder," another female voice said. "That's enough, all of you." She removed her faceplate to reveal a laughing, middle-aged face. "Mertaugh, you're pathetic. The Dirt's been playing a game with you, and you lost." She turned to Weezek. "The two of you will be searched and taken aboard *C65C*. If we find anything here after you're gone, Coordinator, you'll wish the Silver Fleet had killed you. Now, then. Do you have anything to tell me before you go?"

"Nothing," Weezek said. "Except that I'm grateful to be—"

"Save it," the woman snapped. "For the Nomarch."

*"What?"*

"His Glorious Presence is among our ships, Coordinator.

Noldron himself, aboard his own flagship, with his full court of fancy high muck-mucks."

"But . . . *why?*"

"Isn't it obvious? The Nomarch is thrilled at your arrival, and can't *wait* to be as impressed by your heroism as we are. No'ln Beviney is with him, of course." The one called Mertaugh took her eyes from Pwanda at last, and joined in the laughter.

A happy group, Pwanda thought dryly. But he was learning more than he'd known before. Despite Weezek's manifest lack of humor, it seemed that they appreciated it. At least some of them did. He heard another groan from the ship coordinator, and turned to find that the man had fainted.

"It's delicious!" Dane said, savoring the taste of a steamed carrot. Until recently, even grass would have been tempting, compared to the gruel she'd subsisted on since leaving Walden. But after she'd moved the Marshams into the protective orbit of First Adjutant Brotman Nandes, her diet had benefited from the gratitude of the former squadron leader. Still, there had been nothing to compare with this steamy delicacy that warmed her mouth and tantalized her senses with aromatic sweetness. At that moment she was certain that if she closed her eyes and opened them again, she would be looking from the Hardaway kitchen out over the small personal garden that Paul had cultivated since early childhood.

"Here, try one of these," Paul said. With a thin knife he sliced away a piece of roasting mushroom and passed it to Dane. He watched eagerly as she tried it, enjoying her pleasure.

"Paul, you're a magician."

"No," he said. "I'm a sorcerer. Sorcerers are more powerful than magicians." With a grin he added, "And more evil sometimes, too."

"What do you mean?"

"Oh, nothing. It's just that I feel . . . I don't know. Strong. That's it. When I'm down here with my crops I don't think about being on *Dalkag,* or about being in space at all. I don't think about the Gold Fleet or the battle that's coming up."

"What do you think about?"

"Home, sometimes," he said, and turned from her back to the cooker. "People. The ones that lived, and the ones that didn't."

"So do I, Paul. More often than I should. That makes you feel strong?"

"No, that's not what I mean, exactly. When I'm down here I feel strong because I can *do* something. It's about the people at home." When he turned back to her, he bore an expression Dane had never seen on his face before. He raised his voice, and she understood that he was speaking for the benefit of the monitors. "I made a lot of those people happy with the things I grew. Now I can do the same for these people. Do you understand?"

She didn't, but nodded. This was a strange conversation. She'd never heard Paul speaking like this. "It's good to stay busy."

The odd expression left his face, and he smiled again. "That's right. A good sorcerer should always be cooking up something special. That's what I do here, and it makes me feel strong."

"He feels strong and I feel fat," Carnie said cheerfully, approaching the two. "Paul, which of the plants are we supposed to pick for the Fleet Leader's dinner tonight? You told me two of the vats, but there's going to be a hundred ten people there. Should I tell the other attendants to go ahead and harvest . . ."

"I told you, go to number Seven if you have to. But don't touch my herbs!" Dane smiled to herself. Shy around most people, Paul had rarely shown his annoyance to anyone but her. It seemed that he'd taken a liking to Carnie Niles. "Here, I'll go with you. Excuse me, Dane, I've got to go now. Come down here any time." Grinning again, he said, "Especially if you need something from the good sorcerer. Like I told you once, I'm good at growing things and taking care of you." He bent to kiss her cheek and whispered, "Maybe they're the same thing."

Suddenly Dane understood exactly what he'd been trying to tell her.

Reading her eyes, Paul straightened and nodded.

Dane said aloud, "Thanks, Paul. I'll see you soon. Maybe in a couple of hours. Good-bye, Carnie. And you're not getting fat. You look wonderful."

Waving good-bye, Carnie called back, "What does it matter? As long as Paul loves me."

"You stop that!"

Dane watched her friends leave the compartment and shook her head in wonder. Paul was right again. His courage made him special, and his work made him strong.

On the long walk back to her quarters, she fitted Paul's unspoken offer into the equation that had been troubling her for days. Over the past two months Jenny Marsham had been humiliated publicly and often, to the point that she now seemed likely to do something rash. That would be a disaster for Dane. Marsham knew little of her skills, and nothing of her work. But under interrogation the older woman would certainly mention "my little Grounder friend CJ, who's like an advisor to me." This time, Dane knew, her own interrogation would be ruthlessly thorough.

During the past weeks, concern for Jarred and the quiet support of Buto Shimas and Brotman Nandes had been all that kept Marsham from losing her composure completely, and denouncing Arlana Mestoeffer before other officers or the ever-present monitors. Day by day the indignities grew. This evening threatened to be the final blow that would send her beyond reason: Olton Kay-Raike had arrived aboard *Dalkag*. Tonight's dinner was to be held in honor of the newly promoted Senior General.

Marsham had gone pale and speechless when she'd heard of his arrival. Later she'd expressed to Dane her certainty that as the dinner progressed, Mestoeffer would announce that Jarred was to be transferred to Kay-Raike. And that far from retaining his clan name as promised, he would be ordered to marry a woman superior to himself in rank; Jarred would no longer be a Marsham. And because Jenny could not marry without permanent rank, once the transfer was announced this evening by Mestoeffer, the Marsham clan would be officially dead. Even her secret ally could not intercede.

Nandes's support had been expressed to Marsham privately. Dane now understood that the first adjutant had at the beginning enjoyed what he'd mistaken for a good, if somewhat harsh, joke on a new comrade. But he was sickened at the continued humiliation heaped upon an officer of Marsham's reputation. This was made worse as time went on, and Mestoeffer continued to treat him and all of her staff with disdain. Never openly, as with Marsham, but in subtle and insulting ways that left him furious. Nandes was not the type to display his anger toward a superior officer in any form, to anyone. Outwardly he was the perfect first adjutant. Only because she had tracked him a number of times, because she *knew* him so intimately, was she aware of this closely held sense of outrage. Dane saw building in him daily the fury that had first been signaled in the address he'd given not long ago. Dane was extremely careful with him on this point. She'd long been certain that he was planning to assassinate Mestoeffer, and she'd seen nothing to indicate a change of mind. And so she had to exercise extreme care. If Nandes thought for even a moment that she or anyone else suspected his intentions, lives would be forfeit immediately. The first adjutant was determined to succeed, determined to survive the crime, and determined that no other officer would be stained with his guilt. It was his plan to lead the Fleet to victory in the upcoming engagement. Following that, he intended to take his own life, and carry the secret—and the shame—with him into death.

Dane felt herself standing between two massive tectonic plates, irrevocably destined for collision. Her own position between them offered no place of safety. The danger she was in formed a circular path—each threat leading to the next, and the last leading back again to the first. She needed Brotman Nandes to protect the two Marshams, and thereby protect the work she was doing. She also needed Arlana Mestoeffer alive, to continue the erosive effect her leadership was having on the assembled two hundred thousand ships. Nandes planned to kill her and take her place. This must not be allowed to happen. The first adjutant was thoroughly a professional; under his guidance, Sovereign Command could well emerge from the coming battle as the clear winner, no matter how successful Momed Pwanda might be in influencing the final battle formation of the Gold Fleet. And yet if Nandes failed in his attempt to assassinate Mestoeffer, he would be exposed. His new ally, Jenny Marsham, would certainly fall under suspicion. And with her interrogation would come the exposure of Dane Steppart— and possibly The Stem itself.

Dane arrived at her quarters still lost in thought. Thanks to Paul, she knew how to save Jenny Marsham. At least for the moment. And in doing so, to preserve herself and her work. Again, only for the moment. The question was, could she go through with it? *All the way* through with it?

# ➤16◄

For many months President Linda Steppart had rested from each day's labor by climbing to the top of the Capitol Building and watching the stars above Walden. Her son Alfred was home now, having spent three years off-world as a pilot. His had been a dangerous task, smuggling agents and instructors of The Stem from world to world as Brian Whitlock needed them. It had saddened her to learn from Alfred that Whitlock was ill, but more important was that her son was home again, and safe.

But Dane . . . She was out there somewhere, living and breathing among people who cared nothing for her. Who cared nothing for any . . . what was it that Buto Shimas called them? Grounders. Would she ever again be safe, or home, as Alfred was now? Had other agents of The Stem reached her? Was she eating well, resting enough? Did she remember her birthday?

Steppart recalled the night that seemed so long ago, when she and Johann Berger stood on this same roof and launched that transmitter. It was to tell the captive agents, those who were fitted with microreceivers, that Dane was among them now. Had any of them heard it? Did they know that Whitlock's "linchpin" was in place? She'd been so relieved to see—or rather, hear—the device streak from Walden that night, broadcasting to hundreds of implanted chips throughout both Fleets. That relief had been short-lived. And irrational. As if she'd expected everything to come to a climax then, and be over by now. Silly. But mothers were entitled to be silly sometimes, weren't they? Even those who were presidents.

She could no longer imagine what good the transmitter would do. There were too many ships, too many galaxies, too few agents. And only one Dane Steppart.

But where?

She watched a meteor flash from east to west, like a stream of glittering water appearing magically in a black desert. But the river was swallowed up by the dust as quickly as it came, and left no trace of the good it might have done. "Liar," she said angrily. "Dane is stronger than that. Show me my daughter."

A voice came from behind her. "Did you say something?"

"Just thinking out loud, Johann. What is it?"

"I thought you might like some coffee. Bad as usual, but hot."

"No, but thank you. I believe I'll go to bed now. The sky doesn't know anything worthwhile."

"Madam President, have you been sleeping enough lately?"

"Never mind. I'm just being silly."

Uncounted light-years distant, the transmitter continued broadcasting the single pulse it was programmed to send out. Then, abruptly, it stopped. For ten days the device sent out a new pulse in response to a null-band signal from the small group who had invented it. After ten days the old pulse resumed. Linda Steppart might have been comforted to know how many agents of The Stem heard the new signal. And how close many of them were to bringing their assignments to a conclusion.

Jenny Marsham saw her worst fears becoming reality as the dinner party aboard *Dalkag* began. She had been trying to focus her attention away from the wizened old man who sat to the right of Arlana Mestoeffer at the long table. Senior General Olton Kay-Raike, at one hundred nineteen years of age, looked as though the flesh had long ago been removed from his face and replaced with a sickly mask. But it was not his appearance that repulsed her. It was what he represented: cruelty unmatched, and a mind still laser-sharp. It was rumored that the death rate among attendants assigned to his personal flagship was higher than eighty percent per year. But worse than that: Fewer than half of his new officers survived one year on that ship. It was said that Kay-Raike loved the sight of human death. Enemy, Grounder, or his own personnel, man, woman, or child, it didn't matter. It was the only thing that made him smile.

Arlana Mestoeffer had made a point of repeating the rumors to Marsham just prior to the beginning of the dinner. "They're all true," she'd said, "but not important. What matters is that no clan achieves better results in battle than the Kay-Raikes. You should be proud that the Senior General has an interest in your son. Of course, I haven't yet decided whether . . . What is his name? Gerard? No, Jarred. Yes, whether Jarred should have that honor. How would you advise me?"

Marsham's throat had closed up. Only the earlier assurance of CJ had seen her honorably through that encounter.

Now, as the dinner was being served, she looked away from Mestoeffer and Kay-Raike. At that moment her son passed by the open door to the corridor. Marsham knew that he could be there for only one reason. She glanced anxiously up toward CJ, who was filling the plate of the guest of honor, while Mestoeffer briefed him on the many "tricks" she could do. As she continued on to Brotman Nandes, the young woman returned her glance. Marsham froze. Instead of the encouragement she'd desperately hoped to see, the attendant's face was distressed and apologetic. "No," she whispered to herself and shook her head. Jenny Marsham took in a deep breath and released it slowly. What had she expected? What could an attendant do? What could she possibly say, to change what now seemed inevitable? And yet somehow, Marsham had relied on her. It defied explanation. But the girl had been correct in everything she'd told her up to now, including the prediction that Brotman Nandes would become her ally.

So. It was over. When her own food arrived, Jenny Marsham scarcely noticed it. She ate mechanically, waiting for the moment she was dreading, when Mestoeffer would rise and make the announcement of Jarred's transfer. Although it was treason, she was resolved: The moment she learned that Jarred no longer bore the clan name, she would denounce Arlana Mestoeffer to her face. Coolly. Professionally. And publicly. Torture and death would follow; they would come quickly, and be welcomed. What would be the point of living? She no longer had a command; her value to the Fleet was gone. She was forbidden to marry and continue her clan. She would no longer be able to help Jarred. And she could not live with the knowledge that the boy she loved so dearly was to be transformed into the likeness of the Kay-Raikes. Death was the only course. She hoped that Shimas would understand.

While she was lost in her misery, seeing or hearing nothing around her, an officer standing to her left took her arm and shook it roughly.

"Are you deaf, Marsham?" the woman demanded. "Go!"

"What? What do you mean? Go where?" She was startled to see that nearly everyone was standing, and that most of them were shouting or glaring at her. "Go where?"

"To the corridor, fool! Didn't you hear the Fleet Leader? Go and meet the Senior General's doctor when he arrives in the corridor, and tell him what's happened! Go!"

Still confused, Marsham stood. Immediately she felt CJ take her arm and lead her hastily out of the dining room. Jarred was standing in the corridor.

"What is going on, Mother?"

"I don't know. There's a doctor coming . . . I don't know." She felt CJ take her arm again and pull both of them close to a wall as another officer ran out of the dining room and ran past them. "Out of the way, Marsham, I'll get him!" the man shouted angrily, and disappeared around an intersection. "It's General Kay-Raike," she heard CJ saying. "He's collapsed. First Adjutant Nandes says that he's dead."

"Dead? But . . ." Jenny Marsham stared in shock back toward the dining room. Slowly the color returned to her face. "Dead. No transfer. Dead." She turned to look down at her attendant for long moments while the blood again drained from her face. She saw that the girl was as near to fainting as she was. "CJ . . . ? You?"

Jarred spoke from beside her. "Mother, what are you suggesting?" His face was flushed, the freckles on his nose and cheeks standing out prominently. "That *she* caused that old man to collapse?" Turning to Dane, he said, "What did you do, CJ, kiss him? His heart couldn't take it?"

"Jarred, this is not a moment for levity."

"Mother, I helped General Kay-Raike out of his shuttle. That is to say, he had me *carry* him out. I mean no offense or disrespect, but he looked as though he'd died years ago. You should see his medicines! One so he can get out of bed, two so he can breathe, one so he can eat, one *after* eating, three more for sleeping, and the doctor said he's got to have them all, or . . . anyway, I had to change his uniform twice before the dinner, because—"

"That's enough, Jarred. Who ordered you here?"

"General Kay-Raike told me to stand by outside the dining room. He seems to enjoy treating me like an attendant. Or did."

"The order no longer applies, then. Return to your quarters, unless you have other duties at the moment." The doctor came bustling around the corner at that moment, led by the officer who'd passed them earlier. Jenny turned and followed the two men into the dining room.

When she'd gone, Dane said, "Thank you, SubLieutenant Marsham. I thought I was about to be accused—"

"No, she was merely upset. The death of such a fine officer is a blow to all of Sovereign Command." With his eyes he drew Dane's attention to his left. She turned her head to see the chief steward standing at the doorway, watching them.

"You," the large man said to Dane. He approached, carrying a plate in one hand and a glass in the other. "The Senior General is confirmed dead. You served him his meal. I am instructed to see that you eat the remainder of it."

"But sir, why?"

"Acting Lieutenant General Marsham has ordered it."

"Good," Jarred said. "This will take care of any ridiculous thoughts that might come up."

"Where?" Dane asked.

"Here, with me as your witness." He sneered down at Dane. "You don't expect to eat in *there,* do you, Grounder?"

Dane shrugged. "No, sir." She took the glass and drained it of water, then took the plate. Most of the food was untouched. It took her several minutes to finish it.

"Good," the chief steward said. "Now you will remain here for observation." He took the plate from her and left the corridor.

"That was a lot of food," Jarred remarked. "The old man could never have finished it all. You look a little pale, CJ. Are you all right?"

"Overfull, sir." The meats had nauseated her. Her stomach was churning warm and sour as Paul had said it would. This was from the antidote; the herbal poison, which she had not put into the food as planned, had no effects other than to kill. She had trusted Paul, had gambled everything on someone other than herself. It was only her own conscience, at the last moment, that had prevented her from going through with it. No matter what, she understood now, she could not commit murder. But Paul had been there for her, again. Her admiration for her older cousin rose still higher. By contrast she felt only contempt for the man whose life she'd nearly helped to end. Kay-Raike's existence had cost humankind tens, perhaps hundreds, of thousands of innocent lives. His death had saved not only the two Marshams, thus protecting her own work, but possibly thousands of attendants who served on his ships.

In Dane's mind, Senior General Kay-Raike had been both Fleets personified. Taking his life would have been no more than the next logical step on the path she was creating toward the destruction of those Fleets. But in the end, she could not do it. Was that a failure on her part? She couldn't answer that. All she could be sure of was that she now knew more about herself than she had before. "Too much to eat," she said to Jarred. "That's all."

"I thought so. Well, I've been ordered back to my quarters." He turned to go and stopped a few paces away, then came back to Dane. "By the way, don't let it worry you if my mother seems distressed. We're both deeply disappointed that I won't have the opportunity to learn from a great officer like the Senior General. Bad luck, I suppose. Ah, well." With a secretive smile, he turned and walked away down the corridor.

Dane stared at Jarred's retreating back. If the chief steward had still been there to see her expression, he would certainly have summoned a doctor. She knew Jarred's face as intimately as she knew her own thoughts. His smile had been so transparently clever; he believed he was hiding something. To Dane, it made everything clear. There had been a slight variance in his voice and expression when he'd spoken about carrying the old man out of the shuttle, and then about acting as one of his attendants. She'd thought little of it at the time. Now she understood. Risking everything that for a few moments he would remain unobserved, he'd managed to substitute something of no medicinal value for one of Kay-Raike's medications. Jarred's courage came as no surprise to her; he was his mother's son. But he was younger, and bolder; and more foolish. She knew that he'd taken the risk not out of fear for himself, but because he understood that his transfer would have destroyed Jenny Marsham. The question, over which Dane could have no influence, was how thoroughly the Senior General's death would be investigated. As before, an interrogation of the Marshams could destroy her own plans.

She stood silently in the corridor as Kay-Raike's personal physician blustered past her again, this time in near panic. Dane guessed that he did not look forward to leaving *Dalkag* and returning, as a failure, to the Kay-Raike clan. He was followed by two attendants carrying the general's body on a stretcher. Staring vacantly upward, the man looked as if he'd been recently exhumed after years in an earthen grave—and not heading, as he was, for the deeper grave of space.

*Dalkag*'s officers came next, led by Arlana Mestoeffer and Fotey Smothe. Mestoeffer's expression was unmistakable. She was frustrated that her amusement with the Marshams had been interrupted. But Dane had no doubt that the "game" she enjoyed so much was far from over. Smothe, as always, tried to mimic his patron. The procession wound around the jeweled corridor's first intersection and snaked away. Marsham was the last to follow. She passed Dane without a glance, but there was no mistaking the relief that straightened her posture and livened her gait.

# ⇥17⇤

"Go on," the Nomarch giggled. "Do it again."

He was a young and odd-looking man dressed in loose robes of purple and gold that hung about his frail body. The robes partially hid the chair he sat on, a stout platform with wooden legs that retained a fine grain while appearing to be lightly plated with gold. A thick curtain hung just beyond him, reaching forty feet from side to side, with a high-reaching slit directly behind the chair. He was flanked by two women in uniform.

This was the room where court was held aboard *Noldron*, the flagship of the Nomarch of Great Command, the only vessel of the Gold Fleet to bear the name of a person.

Twenty feet from the Nomarch, Momed Pwanda stood stripped to the waist, feet apart and arms raised before him in a classic fighting stance. Around him circled three burly crew. They moved much more warily than they had before.

"Go on! Go on!"

The largest of the three, who was also the quickest, ran at his target with arms outstretched. Pwanda waited until the man was fully committed to the charge. Bending his left knee, he dropped his body down on that side. The man rushed ahead and tripped over Pwanda's extended right leg. As he tumbled forward, another of the three made an equally inept rush. Pwanda reversed himself, and the woman fell over his left leg. The third crew threw himself at what he hoped was Pwanda's center, only to find himself grasping at empty air as he joined his companions.

The story of Pwanda's "attack" on Crew Mertaugh had

amused the Nomarch so much, he'd asked for a demonstration. He seemed fascinated by what Pwanda called wrestling.

"Again! Again!"

"I wonder," said a tall woman standing to the right behind the gilded chair, "if the Nomarch might be growing bored with this?" Pwanda noted again the air of authority about her. She appeared to be in her mid-thirties, with short golden hair and large clear eyes that seemed to be everywhere at once. "How long," she asked, "do these people expect the Nomarch to be tolerant and remain patient?"

The Nomarch nodded his head. "Yes, No'ln Beviney. This Nomarch agrees. How long is patience to be tolerated?" He glared at those across the floor from him, suddenly irritable.

"I apologize," the woman to the left of the chair said. "Naturally, the Nomarch wants to proceed with Fleet business."

Ignoring her, the young man in the seat looked at Pwanda. "Can you teach everybody in the Fleet to do fighting stuff like that?"

"Yes, Nomarch," Pwanda answered. He felt as if he should bow or salute, but no one else had. Even the other captives behaved with an odd mixture of fear and informality while around him. The Nomarch looked to be about twenty years old. His eyes were a dim blue, and seemed nearly to touch one another above a thin nose that ended very close to where it began. Weezek, he reflected, had meant it literally when he said that all Nomarchs were descended *directly* from the first one. Apparently this was a family tree with no branches, no forks. "If I can teach them anything, that would be my privilege."

"Good," the boy said. "This Nomarch needs his fighters to be the best, doesn't he, Beviney?"

"Always the best, Nomarch. I believe I was instructed to ask questions of the coordinator at this time."

"Then why aren't you?"

"I apologize, Nomarch. I allowed myself to become fascinated with the Nomarch's comments."

"Not your fault. Well, go on."

Serjel Weezek felt hands against the back of his shoulders and stepped two paces forward rapidly, to avoid being shoved again.

"We have before us a coordinator who has accomplished something that no one in the Great Command has ever achieved," Beviney began.

"A hero? Oh, good! What did he do?"

"Nomarch, he is the first of us ever to surrender an intact vessel to the Enemy. He did so without resisting, and without having been fired upon."

"That doesn't sound very hard. Why is he a hero?" As other members of the court began to laugh, the boy joined them. "This Nomarch was being witty, wasn't he? The coordinator is not a hero. He is . . . funny?"

"He is pathetic," Beviney said.

"Pathetic!" the boy repeated angrily.

Beviney proceeded to launch questions at Weezek, all of which he'd answered before the Nomarch arrived. His replies, punctuated by vulgar insults programmed into his mind by the Silver Fleet's interrogation drug, were cut short by each succeeding question, until he'd—almost—told his entire garbled story in five minutes. Pwanda was relieved that he'd revealed no hint of the suggestion that he himself had put into the coordinator's overburdened mind.

"So the Nomarch sees," Beviney concluded, raising her voice to rouse the boy to alertness again, "that while a prisoner of the Silver Fleet this coordinator remained intoxicated, and so he was unable to bring any useful information back with him. Worse, he insults us. Worse, he claims to have a poor memory of the things he revealed to the Enemy. Worst of all, he has disgraced a tradition that dates back to the time of the first Nomarch. And for what? All he's brought to us is a shuttle refitted with ancient technology. Nothing of the weapons research he was ordered to find. Nothing of value whatever. And so naturally, the Nomarch will want to hang—"

"Him," the boy interrupted, pointing toward Pwanda.

"This Nomarch sees *him* as valuable. The coordinator brought him, and should be thanked."

Beviney flushed and for a moment lost her confident expression. "The Nomarch's amusement is valuable," she conceded quickly. "But of course the Nomarch believes that surrendering a vessel is a treasonous act which should be—"

"Excuse me!"

Every eye in the room turned toward Pwanda. Even Weezek, who was listening with a growing sickness to his sentence, was outraged. Before anyone could respond, Pwanda went on. "Supervisor Beviney," he began, guessing at her title, "the Nomarch's fighters have nearly exhausted me. Before I collapse from fatigue, would you please tell me if the Nomarch wishes to see more of what I was doing?"

"Yes!" the boy shouted. "That is what this Nomarch wants to see more of!"

"Yes, but first the Nomarch believes that—"

"Yes, yes, Beviney, you can hang the coordinator."

"The Nomarch has ordered it!" Beviney proclaimed to the court.

As Weezek fainted again, the boy continued. "But only for a little while. If the coordinator gets dizzy, bring him down at once. This Nomarch has heard that being hung can be unpleasant." Turning back to Pwanda he said, "Go ahead! Do it again."

As the three crew surrounded him and glared with anger at the prospect of more bruises, Pwanda considered his situation. He'd learned a great deal from listening to Weezek, and from noting what the man would not discuss in any detail. The Nomarch was one subject he had never mentioned at all, until that brief mention of the title and its association with the nebula. And no wonder. Was Noldron's condition widely known, or merely speculated about? Clearly it was the supervisors who made the decisions, and Beviney seemed to be the most senior among them. It was a risk to offend her as he had. Pwanda admitted to himself that the act had been more impulsive than reasoned. On the way to the Nomarch's presence he'd been led through a small room in which four people were hanging. All were alive, suspended by their heels. He'd assumed that the punishment was to the death, and had wanted to prevent Weezek from suffering the torment; he had to keep the man alive for a while longer, if possible. It was odd. He'd made the attempt but actually had done little to help Weezek; he realized too late that their method of hanging was not always fatal. The only thing he'd accomplished was to offend Beviney, make everyone else angry, and probably all for nothing.

And so he'd made a mistake. How to correct it? By finding a way close to Beviney. Only one way suggested itself immediately, and Pwanda hoped that one risk following another would not be too much. If luck exists, he thought, it had better be in this room. Right now.

"I mean no offense," he said to the room in general. "But these three are nearly as tired as I am. I wonder if the Nomarch would prefer to see Supervisor Beviney fight against me?"

"Yes! This Nomarch was going to say that!"

Beviney took a step backward.

"You can fight better than crew or People of the Dirt, can't you?" the boy asked, as if suddenly worried about her. "All supervisors can, can't they?"

"Of course, Nomarch."

"Oh, good! Then go ahead."

Without another word and with eyes that bore into Pwanda like weapons themselves, Beviney stepped forward. She charged immediately, so fast that he was beginning to drop on his right knee before his mind caught up with his reflexes. He twisted just in time to catch her charge against his left shoulder. The two went down together and rolled several feet. Pwanda was able to reach around Beviney's lower back and pull her close, controlling the way they would finish the roll. When they stopped, Beviney was sitting on Pwanda's chest, looking bewildered and at the same time triumphant.

The room erupted in applause.

"Ha! Again?" Beviney challenged, jumping lightly to her feet.

Pwanda stood up slowly, as if sorely bruised. He'd guessed correctly. This woman loved to compete, and loved to win. And wrestling was something new to them all. "Face you again? Only if the Nomarch requires it, Supervisor."

"It is required!" the boy shouted, pounding his chest in delight. "Again! Four more times!"

The results were evened out over the next three clashes. On the fifth and final match Beviney won again. She leapt to her feet and offered him a hand, pulling him to his feet. "It looks as though I'd better teach *you*," she said, grinning and flushed.

"Yes, Supervisor. I admit, you surprised me."

"This Nomarch was not surprised! Supervisors are the best of the Gold Fleet, and the Omnipe . . . Ombitu . . . the 'Nippunt Gold Fleet is the best in the universe. And everywhere else, too! No'ln Beviney, you will have a reward."

"Thank you, Nomarch."

"And so will . . . What is your name?"

"Momed, Nomarch."

"Mo . . . Nomarch? Did you say your name right?"

"Yes, Nomarch."

"Then you must be this Nomarch's brother!"

Beviney burst out laughing. But instead of joining her, the boy scowled. "This Nomarch is *not* being witty!"

"But . . . but Nomarch, your skin is light, and his size . . . and he's a Dirt."

"Are you stupid? He was stolen from us by People of the Dirt. This Nomarch saw it happen before he was born, when he was asleep. You will teach him, No'ln Beviney. If he is as smart as this Nomarch, then this Nomarch has a brother."

Beviney nodded, and smiled with a genuine amusement that left Momed puzzled. "Yes, Nomarch."

"Good."

Beviney squeezed Pwanda's hand before releasing it. She left him there in the middle of the floor and again took her place behind the boy's chair. "The Nomarch has waited very patiently for his meal," she said loudly. Her face was still bright with triumph.

"Yes," the boy agreed. "This Nomarch is hungry. And tolerant!" He stood from the gilded chair and walked back behind the flowing curtain, followed by Beviney and the other members of his court.

Soon the room was empty but for Pwanda, a revived Weezek, and seven crew. One of them grinned at Pwanda. "It seems you'll be here for a while. The Nomarch has found another sibling."

*"Another?"*

"Three sisters and two brothers, in the four years I've been here."

"What happened to them?"

"No'ln Beviney taught them." The woman smiled. "But it turned out that they weren't as smart as the Nomarch. They were, ah, reassigned."

"I see."

"Let's go. I'll show you where the other Dirts sleep."

"Thank you. As you can see, I'm very tired." Pwanda's fatigue was not physical. He needed time to sort through the incredible meeting with Beviney and the Nomarch, and to put all of it into some kind of logical order. It promised to be a long night.

"No bed yet," the woman said. "First you'll teach us how to . . . what did you call it?"

"Wrestle."

"Yes, that's it. Also, teach us when it's good to lose." She led the way out, laughing with the others.

"You can count on it," Pwanda said, following them. "I'll make it my top priority."

Twelve nights later, Momed Pwanda lay in the bed assigned him, which to his surprise had been moved that morning into a very small but private room; another sign of his success with No'ln Beviney. As he waited for sleep he mentally composed a letter to Dane:

My dear Fellow Conspirator,

Greetings from the bowels of *Noldron,* a fearsome vessel which is the very heart of the Omnipotent Gold Fleet. I trust that your own nefarious doings are proceeding as planned. There is much to tell you. Some of it is amusing, some of it interesting, and the last of it concerns the decisive moment that you and I have trained for.

First, about my captors. The Gold Fleet is *funny.* This is one reason that ship coordinators such as our friend Weezek are treated with such scorn. You see, they are not permitted to join in the merriment. Coordinators are required to be serious: the glue, if you will, which binds together the castes of supervisor and crew, each of which seems determined to obliterate the other with the sly remark, the telling look, the formal address delivered with dripping sarcasm. (Although crew must be circumspect; to be caught in this humorous mode while speaking to a supervisor is to be hanged by the heels. Usually the punishment lasts for a number of hours, and brings on temporary debility. In extreme cases, it is to the death; and is a most cruel way to leave this life. The victim, of course, never knows the length of the sentence until the punishment is, or is not, terminated. Supervisors consider this to be the epitome of jocularity.)

To summarize: The Nomarch—ultimate leader—is, let's say, *unique,* the supervisors are egomaniacs, coordinators are hapless intermediaries, and the crew are a bunch of whining jokers whose admiration belongs to the moment's most witty supervisor.

And yet, somehow, it all works. Beneath the humor and their odd social arrangements, these people are deadly efficient. They speak of the worlds they've torn apart with the same pride and the same moral blindness that afflicts the Silver Fleet. Their battle drills are carried out with impressive speed and precision. Except for *Noldron* their ships are essentially engines and weapons (very little space for personal accommodation), and seem to be somewhat more maneuverable than those of the Silver Fleet. My own humble estimation is that evenly matched, number for number, the Omnipotent Gold Fleet will justify its name.

The one weakness I see in them is their absolute conformity. All Gold Fleet ships but this one are identical, and their basic strategies have not changed for centuries. (Why should they? They're successful.) This factor affords me the opportunity to introduce a new element into their Fleet: confusion. That process has begun.

Aside from being the brother-apparent to the Nomarch—you wouldn't believe me if I explained that—I am currently in the favor of their most senior supervisor, No'ln Beviney. (All hereditary Senior Supervisors aboard this ship are called "No'ln" something. They're from one of four families that have "served" the Nomarchs personally for hundreds of years. As to their title, it's new. You see, the Nomarch's name is Noldron. Until he was eighteen he couldn't pronounce . . . never mind, long story.) Oddly, it is not my mind that first impressed No'ln Beviney, but my wrestling ability. She defeats me a number of times daily. Since I allow no one else to win a single fall against me, she has proclaimed herself to be the Champion of the Universe. (Did I mention that they're funny?) The important point, and I know this came as a shock to her, is that she *likes* me. As if she had a choice in the matter!

But the woman is not to be underestimated. I have tracked her to the limit of my poor ability (no monitors here!), and believe that her elevated rank is due to two extraordinary talents she possesses: the skill to deal effectively with the Nomarch, and total confidence in her grasp of every element of battle. There is no doubt that when the Fleets collide, Beviney will be in firm command. Make no mistake, she is formidable.

However, be comforted: Her corruption is well underway. She loves games, and has come to rely on my advice for their winning. Most notable is a game I adapted for them from one I mastered long ago, called Disks. In its present form it is a relatively simple board game involving thirty "ships" per side, on a grid of fifty by fifty squares. I am unbeatable. Why? Because the real game is my application of pure mathematics, pitted against their traditional battle strategies. Which must win? Mathematics. That is to say, me: forty percent of the time against Beviney, for obvious reasons, and one hundred percent of the time against anyone else. (Except for the Nomarch. He kicks the pieces around the board with his feet—honestly!—and is always declared the winner.)

As the game increases in complexity, so will Beviney's reliance on me. And so will the new element of confusion. The point being that when the battle is met, I will be at her side—as you are to be at the side of whomever will command your own Fleet. Now: Can I influence the final formations going into battle, as we discussed? I'm much more optimistic now than when we last spoke. Remember the sign; when you see it, you'll know.

An interesting note, though it won't surprise you: No'ln Beviney is certain that *your* Fleet was the first to assemble in unprecedented numbers. I wonder where the misinformation came from, on both sides? (I am chuckling.) So you were right, after all. Our dear teacher didn't predict this battle. He *caused* it. Whitlock *is* a wizard!

Finally, and in all gravity: This is the most important thing I have to say to you. Scouts of the Gold Fleet have found you. Even now we are leaving the nebula you call the Fortress, and coming against you. "Our" leading formations have already met and destroyed a number of "your" surveillance vessels. The real carnage will begin within three weeks. No'ln Beviney is spoiling for the fight.

I pledge to you that the Gold Fleet will emerge from this battle crippled, disorganized, demoralized, and ready to begin its ultimate demise. I expect the same from you, if not so poetically. (Want a hint of how I'm going to do it? *"Those who sleep when destiny calls are trampled beneath the march of history."* Good, eh? It's an old proverb I made up recently.)

Be well, Dane, and success. I promise again that when it matters, you will know where I am. *Remember the sign,* and the plans we made. Hello to Paul and to Carnie.

Momed

Sleep proved elusive as he contemplated the final paragraphs of the letter that would never be sent. For centuries their war had raged on, destroying everything and everyone in its path. It could not be allowed to continue. A turning had to be forced, and it was, thanks to The Stem. The price of war had to be made too high for both combatants. Whitlock had told him there would be a battle, but not that Whitlock would *cause* the battle. Was The Stem morally justified, to bring events to this point? He supposed that it no longer mattered. What was done could not be undone.

Despite his years of preparation for this moment, Pwanda could not avoid a queasy feeling in his stomach at the words "within three weeks." He knew of this timetable from Beviney, but her input really hadn't been necessary. No one needed to be told. Like a great cloud hung over all the universe, what was coming had to be visible to every person in the two Fleets—and beyond. Four hundred thousand ships with murderous intent now hurtled toward one another on an unstoppable path. The cloud was dropping swiftly. No living human being, or any yet to be born, would be left untouched by it.

And so Pwanda was certain that every eye must see that cloud as clearly as he did. It was close now, and its arrival was inevitable. Within three weeks.

# 4

## CONFRONTATION

# ⇥18⇤

The staff meeting took place in the largest and most opulent of *Dalkag*'s many auditoriums. Beneath a thirty-foot jeweled mosaic of the Generals, Arlana Mestoeffer stood in her finest dress uniform. Across her chest was the traditional blue sash, which in this case bore two additional lines of silver trim denoting the rank of council member. Displayed on it were awards from her own campaigns, along with dozens more designed for her by Fotey Smothe.

As jubilant as she was, she could not match the fierce exhilaration of the one thousand officers standing at attention before her. Every back was laser-straight, every eye clear and lit by the gleam of invincible will and the joy of coming glory. There was actually little in her spirited address that inspired them to this pinnacle of warrior's rapture. In truth only half of them, the officers invited aboard from other ships, paid close attention to the words and stale clichés the officers of *Dalkag* had heard so many times recently. Rather, it was the imminence of combat on an unimaginably grand scale. Even Mestoeffer's opening proclamation, "Good news! Hundreds of our scouts have been destroyed!" did little to dampen their enthusiasm.

One officer watched the proceedings remotely, in every sense of the word. Brotman Nandes sat at his stateroom desk, palming his clean-shaven scalp in turmoil. The screen opposite his desk glowed with the brightness of the jeweled mosaic bearing the majestic faces of the Generals. He had long ago extinguished the sound of Mestoeffer's voice, unable to bear it any longer. The sight of her standing beneath those two illustrious faces, knowing that she was slated to replace one of them, burned like acid in his stomach. But then his eyes moved down the screen and drank in the sight of his true comrades-in-arms. How proud they were, he thought, how dedicated and ready to begin the greatest adventure of the past six hundred years. As he watched them, his chest swelled with pride, he felt his pulse quicken and eyes narrow with the fierce determination they shared together. That they *owned* together. And then Mestoeffer caught his attention with a dramatic gesture, and ripped away his pride again.

He stood and paced the spacious compartment, making way for his desk to be cleaned. Seventy-three years. Seventy-three years he had served Sovereign Command. Never had he disobeyed an order. Never. Hundreds of them he had accepted, knowing that they lacked wisdom. Did he disobey? No. He improved upon them, turning a superior's blunder into victory; never once claiming credit for himself. Surely that was the honorable course. It was the course he desperately wanted to take with Mestoeffer. To accept her orders, obey them to the letter, and yet embellish them to limit their harm, and to make them work for the benefit of his comrades. His Fleet. His Sovereign Command. And yet for those same great purposes, the only three left in his life—comrades, Fleet, Sovereign Command—he could not allow Arlana Mestoeffer to continue in her position.

She had assembled the new Fleet in good order, with brilliant organization. That was her particular genius, and he readily acknowledged it. He'd had not the slightest hesitation in relinquishing his own one hundred thousand ships to her direct command. That was before he knew her.

Now too many of his fellow officers feared her. It was not the good fear that sharpens the senses and challenges the mind and body to dare toward perfection. That fear he loved, for it always had made him a finer officer. *That* fear he cultivated in his own commands, because it made the mediocre good, the good best, and the best legendary.

The fear that Mestoeffer inspired was abusive, degrading. It was irrational and unpredictable. She had no respect for her staff, and all knew it by now. Rather than inspiring her most senior officers so that they in turn could inspire others, she kept them looking over their shoulders, wondering who was coming along to replace them in her favor. They were jealous and suspicious of one another—and of those who served under them. The undignified and demeaning death given to Tam Sepal was duplicated daily aboard other ships, despite his direct order that it was not to be done. The squadron leaders and ship's captains wanted to impress Mestoeffer, and succeeded. But not for long. They themselves were retired the moment Nandes learned of the executions. And yet they persisted. This was only one symptom of a sickness that was spreading throughout his beloved Fleet.

Everything he'd ever known about duty, honor, and courage screamed in his mind that he must make the sacrifice—forgo his own claim to those virtues and do what needed to be done: Kill Mestoeffer. Take total command and lead the Fleet to its rightful victory. And then die, knowing that he was disgraced and that the legacy of unassailable integrity he left behind would be a pitiable fraud. It was the right and only thing to do.

And yet—below those screaming thoughts was another voice, speaking to him quietly and surely. He could not do it. He could not take that one step that had never been taken before. He could not assassinate a council member. Sovereign Command itself would cease to have meaning if such an act were ever discovered. The investigations would never cease. The slightest mistake, and anarchy would replace the one solid, inviolable institution in the universe. He could not risk that. Not even for two hundred thousand ships, the more than three hundred eighty million people aboard them, and the victory that was theirs by right.

In misery, Brotman Nandes watched the screen before him. He had to let them down. Every one of them. This thing was beyond him to do. He could not violate the council. He knew that now, and would have to live with it. If he could.

"Was there anything else, sir?"

His mind groped for many moments, until he remembered who she was and why she was there. "No. The stateroom is perfect as usual. Were you saying something just now?"

"An old song, sir. It's a habit of mine while I work. I'm sorry if it disturbed your thoughts."

"Don't be ridiculous. I haven't the time or patience to listen to Grounder songs."

"Good night, sir."

"Yes, yes, good night."

Dane left the stateroom hastily, glad to be gone. Brotman Nandes was the most dangerous person she'd had to work with. He had the potential for explosive bursts of emotion, but she believed that many years had passed since he'd allowed emotion to guide his behavior. From Buto Shimas, who had once idolized the man, she'd learned that twenty-seven years before, Nandes had been in an engine room when the ship he served aboard took a direct hit from a Gold Fleet adversary. Gravely wounded, he'd left his injured wife and two sons to die in the resulting fire while he dragged himself nine hundred feet through burning compartments, over piles of dead shipmates, up ladders that burned his hands to bone, and finally back to the ship's Operations Room, where he found his company leader and four senior officers dead. Nandes assumed command and led his company in a fifteen-hour, savage fight. During that time Nandes issued orders from a prone position where he lay strapped down in gathering pools of his own blood, refusing medical attention until the last Enemy ship was annihilated. When it was over he lapsed into unconsciousness and was expected to die within minutes. But a year's time found him recuperated and in command of a full flotilla, ten thousand ships.

Not all of the man, however, emerged from that fight alive; his wife and sons were gone, sacrifices to his own sense of duty. From that day forward Brotman Nandes had time, thought, patience, or care for only three things: comrades, Fleet, and—most especially—Sovereign Command.

Dane knew that just beyond that extraordinary sense of

duty was a dam holding back twenty-seven years of scald-ing emotion, ready to burst through and drown him at any time. She'd seen the fury in him just now as he'd watched Mestoeffer. This time, the dam had held. But the subliminal reinforcement she'd given him in the song would not be strong enough to hold back the flood for much longer. That meant disaster. If Nandes proceeded with his on-again, off-again plan to assassinate the woman and replace her in command, the Fleet would be too strong. With Nandes in control—with the respect and absolute trust he drew from his officers, with his fierce intelligence and unflagging rage for victory—he could well be unbeatable. The Silver Fleet would win. He was, indeed, dangerous.

And yet his presence was needed. Nandes alone demon-strated the courage to stand up against Mestoeffer. Without him her disdain for heeding the advice of her staff, her own insecurity, and her lack of battle experience would virtually guarantee a Gold Fleet victory.

Neither alternative was acceptable. And so Dane contin-ued to watch him, using all of her skill and most of her en-ergy to keep him within the delicate state of chaos that formed the center of his existence; neither giving up and ending his own life, nor going forward and taking Mestoef-fer's. The risk to herself was that each time she worked with Nandes it was necessary to become less subtle. Like a sick person becoming enured to a medication, he required more and more each time. Eventually he must detect what she was doing. She could only hope that before he did, both Fleets would have lost more than either could bear.

Beginning the long walk back to her own quarters, Dane was met by Buto Shimas coming in the opposite direction. "Hello, sir."

"Hello, CJ." Shimas looked at her searchingly. "You've just come from the first adjutant's stateroom?"

"Yes, sir."

"What kind of . . . ah, does he seem to be well?"

"I didn't ask, sir, but I would guess that he's well. Tired perhaps, if I may comment."

"You may. Very well, that's all." He left her then and

hurried on toward Nandes's stateroom. He'd been told to
report just after Mestoeffer's address was over, but had no
idea of why he'd been summoned. Could it possibly be that
Nandes was offended that Shimas no longer shaved his
head and wore a mustache, as the first adjutant did? Two
months ago the thought would never have occurred to him.
But lately officers had been summoned to see Mestoeffer
for the most bizarre reasons, ranging from the poetry of
Fotey Smothe to lectures on the relative merits of obsolete
weapons that hadn't been used since she herself was a
ship's captain. Nothing the Fleet Leader did or said surprised anyone now. It was whispered that even Brotman
Nandes was behaving erratically. Shimas didn't believe it.
The offense he'd taken at the first adjutant's initial treatment of Jenny Marsham was long past. He refused to hear
anything negative about the man he'd admired for so long,
but could think of no good reason that would cause Nandes
to call him to his stateroom.

As he approached the first adjutant's stateroom, Nandes
ran out the door and brushed past him. "Stand by, Shimas.
I'll be back."

"Yes, sir." He spent the time outside the door picking out
subtle patterns in the ceiling's jewel-work and wondering
about the strained, manic look on his superior's face.

Two hours later Nandes brushed by him again and entered his stateroom, shutting the door behind himself. Another half-hour passed before he was called.

"Come in, Shimas."

"You wanted to see me, First Adjutant?"

"You're here, so obviously I did." Nandes was once
again at his desk, which was covered with neat stacks of reports. Freshly scrubbed and in a crisp uniform, the first adjutant retained no hint of the strain Shimas had seen in his
features before. "Do you practice the saber, Shimas?"

"Ah, I prefer the broadblade or daggers, sir. They're lifelong interests of mine."

"Oh? Well, they're good too, I'm sure. Against a skilled
and determined partner, a match can be wonderfully refreshing."

"I've found that to be true, sir." Apparently, the whispers were accurate. What would come next, he wondered, Smothe's poetry? But the first adjutant ignored him then, seeming to forget he was present.

Nandes selected one of the reports from the shortest stack and perused it for several minutes, while Shimas remained at attention in front of the desk. "Yes . . ." Nandes said quietly. "Perfect." Looking up at last, he said, "You were demoted by Tam Sepal for risking one of your ships unnecessarily." He referred to Shimas's leaving one ship behind when his squadron completed its supply run, in hopes that the remaining ship would discover things of value previously hidden by the world's inhabitants.

"Yes sir."

"Do you refute the charge?"

"No, sir." The maxim was that nothing is true until it enters the record; and that nothing is recorded unless it's true.

Nandes picked up another report. "And yet Sepal immediately made it his company's policy to do precisely the same thing, under the same circumstances. That's interesting."

"Yes, sir."

"Stand at ease, Shimas. Now tell me exactly what you did. And why."

Shimas told the story, leaving nothing out. He related his desire to force Captain Vivian Lortis to use more personal initiative, and his knowledge that she'd stolen from the stockpile of goods the squadron had accumulated from that planet.

"And so your selection of that particular captain was to improve her performance? Or, given the danger and potential gain involved, was it to allow her the opportunity to enhance her record before facing Tam Sepal on the matter of theft?"

"Both, sir."

"As I suspected. Good. I approve of both motives."

"Thank you, sir." Shimas was relieved. He recalled that when facing the question of what to do with Captain Lortis, he had asked himself what course of action would have been taken by the man now seated in front of him. He was gratified to learn that he'd been correct.

"Shimas, I'm facing a similar situation. From a total of eighteen thousand ships sent to watch the Fortress, three hundred eleven left their posts without direct authority."

"They deserted?" As any officer would be, he was horrified at the thought.

"No, they did not. I've reviewed each of their circumstances. In every case, the captain involved acted correctly. All of these ships were from different special reconnaissance units of fifteen. Each of them saw the fourteen ships around them destroyed. Each of them had been hit by Enemy fire and was unable to broadcast back to the Fleet. And therefore each was correct to break off from the fight and return to us as quickly as possible, both to warn us and to protect themselves. As I say, they were correct. I do not approve of losing ships for no purpose. I believe you would concur in that?"

"I would, sir."

"Good. Here is the situation. First, those captains have lingering doubts concerning the propriety of their actions. I have no such doubts. Second, the Fleet Leader has ordered me to give each of them my personal attention, and I quote, 'for the benefit of the Fleet.' Do you understand?"

"Yes, sir." There was no question that Mestoeffer meant dishonorable retirement.

"Really? I did not understand the Fleet Leader's order, and yet you do?"

"I believe I misspoke, sir."

"Yes, you did. I did not ask directly what the Fleet Leader was referring to, nor did she elaborate. Therefore, and third, I must carry out her order. *As I understand it.*" He paused, looking to Shimas. "And so, lastly. 'For the benefit of the Fleet,' I am combining these three hundred eleven ships into a new and irregular unit. Each of the captains has demonstrated not only personal initiative in the face of Enemy fire, but also a somewhat ambiguous tradition. All of them now have the rare experience of having fought alone. But neither their confidence nor their standing in the Fleet is what it needs to be. They need the opportunity to redeem themselves. Both in their own minds, and to the Fleet. Wouldn't you agree, Shimas?"

"Yes, sir. With all points. First Adjutant, may I ask a question?"

"Go ahead."

"I believe that my own circumstances are similar to those of these three hundred eleven ship's captains. The tactic I employed on the supply run was counter to tradition, but later judged to be sound and adopted as policy. Also, I find myself in need of, as you say, 'redemption.' Would that be the purpose for this discussion?"

"It would."

It was all clear to Shimas now. In the same way that he had given Captain Lortis a second chance, Nandes was offering one to him. A smile split his wide face. "Sir, may I formally request a transfer aboard one of those vessels?"

"What a ridiculous notion! No, Shimas, you may not."

The words arrived like a physical blow. "Yes, sir."

"Those ships are already well crewed and staffed. Given your former rank and status, your presence on any of them would be a rebuke to its captain. And redundant."

"I understand, sir."

"You do? Good. Then report by tomorrow's first watch to your former flagship, *Pacal*. You'll find all the necessary records there waiting for you. When you've reviewed—"

"Sir?" The conversation had taken a sharp turn, and left him behind.

"Shimas, you're trying my patience. You said you understood. Did you misspeak again?" Nandes raised a hand, ending Shimas's reply before it began. "Never mind, just pay attention. When you've reviewed the records of your three hundred eleven captains, contact me here. Your new command will report directly to me, for now. Is *that* understood?"

"Yes, *sir!*"

"Good. As I said, this is an irregular unit. I rather like the name 'Buto's Bandits.' But we'll have to come up with an appropriate title for you, later. Get your Bandits in line quickly, Shimas. We have very little time. You're dismissed."

As he turned to leave, Nandes said, "Oh, one last point. Never again tell me that you understand me when you don't." The first adjutant smiled for the first time. "That's my game, not yours."

Grinning so hard it hurt, Shimas said, "I understand, sir."

# ⇥ 19 ⇤

The board game of thirty ships per side was so instantly popular throughout *Noldron* that it took no formal name. It was simply referred to as "the game," or "it." As the battle drew nearer by the hour, the Fleetwide responsibilities of the No'ln supervisors had become frantic; and so had the pace of the game. It was the approved way to relax while still sharpening the mind for combat.

So when No'ln Beviney marched into his room and said to Momed Pwanda, "I can't sleep. My mind is going too fast. It's the work and the stimulation. It never stops. There's so much to do. I'm too exhausted. I'm too excited. Momed, why are you just sitting there? Let's play it!" there was no mistaking her meaning. Pwanda reached under his bed and drew out the board and playing pieces she'd ordered made for him. As he recalled, it was his turn to lose. But this day he had other plans; it was time to solidify his value to her, and to introduce a new complication into her strategic thinking. Within a minute the game was ready, perched on a table recently added to his room. Pwanda sat on the bed while Beviney stood, as she preferred to do while directing combat.

"No'ln Beviney," he began, "I think you have too much ability to continue to play at this level."

"What do you mean?"

"If I may demonstrate. Would you let me use your battle computer?"

"That's cheating! Momed, your crushed ego is no concern of mine. We'll play as always."

"What I have in mind is to set the game's solution into the computer. You'll see very quickly that the game is too simple. Barring mistakes, the first player to move must always win."

"Then why don't *you* always win?"

"I'm not a computer," he said.

"That's true. But I reject your premise. Battles are won by ingenuity, daring, and courage. Not the order of first moves." Nevertheless, she passed him the small unit that by tradition she kept on her person at all times, but had never used.

As he went about programming it, Pwanda said, "All of the playing pieces are identical for each side."

"Of course. They simulate real ships. Why else would your game be so well received?"

"But suppose that one ship had an ability not shared by the others?"

"Then the game would not be valid, obviously. As I said, the pieces mirror real ships. What would be the point in giving one of them an ability not shared by the others? If that 'ability' is an advantage, it's only logical that *all* ships have it. Otherwise I'd have one good ship on the board, and twenty-nine needlessly inferior ones."

"This ship, *Noldron*, protects the Nomarch."

"So?"

"So *Noldron* must be in some way superior to your other ships."

"The shields are better."

"But since energy production is finite, the extra power to the shields comes at the sacrifice of speed and maneuverability?"

"Obviously. And is therefore not useful to the other ships."

He made no reply for twelve minutes while Beviney impatiently paced the room in nervous exhaustion. "There, I'm finished. I set the computer to play against itself. Please observe."

For an hour they played out the rapid strategies generated by the battle computer. In each game, the first player to move won.

"That proves nothing," Beviney said in irritation. "Of course the machine can't play better than itself."

"No one can play better," Pwanda said. "And that's my point. Would you care to compete against it?"

"Yes! I came here to play, didn't I?" She suffered crushing defeat in four consecutive games.

"You're the best player aboard *Noldron*," Pwanda said with a straight face. "You can't beat the computer. Do you see what I'm getting to?"

"Certainly I do. Computers are hereafter forbidden to play the game."

"Or," Pwanda said, avoiding a laugh that was too close to the surface, "We can improve the game so that it *will* be ingenuity, daring, and courage, and not the order of first moves, which determines the winner."

"So the game will be more difficult. It still remains just a game. I'm not impressed."

"But as you've pointed out, No'ln Beviney, the game mirrors the Fleet, in small scale. Therefore if we can improve the game, you can use the same principles to improve your Fleet."

Her wide, clear eyes focused on Pwanda's face. "You have my attention."

"Why don't we introduce one ship on each side with *Noldron*'s enhanced shield capability?"

"And corresponding lack of speed and maneuverability?"

"Exactly. This ship must be hit three times, instead of the customary two. And let's say, three ships per side with no shields at all, but better speed. These move two spaces, instead of one. And another four with little speed or shields, but more power available to the weapons systems. One strike from these ships is a kill, except against the shield-enhanced ship. That requires two."

"This is becoming interesting."

When the program was reset, they repeated the earlier procedure. This time the computer played itself to a draw and flashed "*No Solution*."

"Now," Pwanda said, "you have a situation in which the computer really can't play better than itself. So we need three additional elements."

"And those would be?"

"As you've already pointed out, No'ln Beviney. Ingenuity, daring, and courage. Those are qualities that no machine can duplicate. Watch." He set the computer to play against himself. And after a long and close game that held No'ln Beviney spellbound and brought numerous shouted suggestions from her, Pwanda won.

"You did it!" She was flushed with excitement, and perspiring.

"Not without your help, No'ln Beviney. Thank you."

"Let's try again."

They began again, with No'ln Beviney pacing the small floor and shouting out orders like the experienced combat commander she was. Pwanda took advantage of her pacing to reset the computer to adjust for her infrequent mistakes. When it was over they had won, barely, with Beviney ending the game drained in mind and body.

"I'm afraid," she said in exhaustion, "I'll have to sleep now. That's unfortunate. There's so much to think about."

"Please accept my apology, No'ln Beviney."

"For what? You've given me a wealth of ideas for the Fleet. If you weren't a Dirt, you'd be promoted for what you've done. By the way, you can forget that nonsense about being the Nomarch's brother, because he's forgotten about you. But I've learned by now that you do have value. As a Dirt."

"Thank you. I apologized because it took me far too long to develop these ideas. I mean no offense, but not even *you* could extend these new principles into the Fleet before the battle."

Beviney laughed. "Why do you continue to underestimate me, Momed? You know so little. Our engineering is exactly the same, aboard all of our ships. Once I decide how many ships per unit to modify, the transformations and testing can be accomplished within a matter of a few days. By then I'll have drawn out new strategies to take advantage of them. Long before we meet the Enemy in large numbers, everything will be in place."

Pwanda noted with satisfaction that she made no mention of consulting the Nomarch, or anyone else, before going forward. "I am astounded, No'ln Beviney. And I am deeply grateful that I'm no longer with the Enemy. Their defeat is assured, thanks to you." Grinning, he added, "I'm glad you are who you are, and I'm just a Dirt. The game has tired me out so much that I can't think anymore. Fortunately, the future of the entire Fleet doesn't depend on what I do in the next few hours."

Beviney nodded absently in acknowledgment of the praise that was no more than her due. She was looking toward the far end of the room, her large eyes seeming to focus on something beyond the walls of *Noldron*. " 'Those who sleep when destiny calls are trampled beneath the march of history,' " she intoned. "I seem to remember reading that, long ago." Facing Pwanda again, she said curtly, "No one in the Fleet is going to have much sleep for a while. Give me back the battle computer, Momed. Be ready to come instantly if I call for you."

"I will, No'ln Beviney."

Pwanda could hear her walking away down the narrow corridor, yawning and rapidly punching keys on the computer. As the sound of her died away, he lay back in his bed and relaxed. She may not think sleep is important, he thought, but I do. The formula was simple: $E+F+C=M$. That is, excitement plus fatigue, plus confusion equals mistakes. "C" and "M" were his gifts to the Gold fleet, ones he could not afford to keep for himself.

Seated across a wardroom table from Buto Shimas, Jenny Marsham spoke with a mixture of pride and sadness. " 'Buto's Bandits'? He really said that?"

"He did," Shimas said, nodding soberly and unable to smile as she wanted him to. His own emotions were identical to hers: pride that he had gained such a promising command, and sadness that the two were parting company. The evening meal was completed, with only the two of them lingering at the table. Shimas had already packed his belongings, and for a number of reasons intended to leave right away for *Pacal*.

He knew what the answer to his next question must be, but would never forgive himself for not asking. "Jenny, may I have your permission to ask Nandes to transfer you to *Pacal*?"

"No. Mestoeffer may be willing to let you go, but not me. That's the practical side of it. The other side is personal. My position as *acting* lieutenant general means nothing. Therefore, with your new command, you outrank me again. That would be especially true if I were sent to *Pacal*. If I ever marry again it will have to be to a man junior to me, or I can't continue the Marsham clan. You understand that, don't you?"

"Yes, I do. You're telling me that you want to marry me, by telling me that you *can't* marry me. I am lifted up and destroyed, all in one movement. A brilliant tactic, Jenny, but frankly I'd hoped for a more romantic response."

"'Romantic'? Buto, I'm sitting here telling you how wonderful it is that you've got your career back. And if that's not enough, now you know how I feel about you. How much more romantic can I be?"

"I'd like to know the answer to that question."

She winked at him. "There. How's that?"

"All right, all right," he said, laughing. "You win. But—"

"Let's leave it at that."

"Very well, Jenny. For now." He stood. "Will you walk with me to the shuttle?"

"You know I'd like to, Buto. Unfortunately I'm due at another very important meeting in ten minutes."

"You don't mean—"

"Yes, again. Fotey Smothe has dreamed up some new verses. I'm ordered to sit by his side while he recites them, and duly record his brilliance for posterity."

The blood rushed to his face at the thought of an officer like Jenny Marsham reduced to writing down the vacuous excretions of a moron like Fotey Smothe. Before he could stop himself he blurted out, "You should be commanding a full company, and here you are tied to the mindless babbling of an imbecilic Grounder!"

"Buto!" Desperately trying not to laugh, Marsham shook her head sternly. She could almost hear the compartment monitors recording their every word. "I know you're upset, and I know you didn't mean that." Despite herself, she chuckled. "You shouldn't call him a Grounder," she said. And by omission, agreed with everything else he'd said.

"It's true," Shimas said angrily. "The Fleet Leader might dress him up in a uniform, but that doesn't change what he is."

"You can't be serious!"

"Yes, I am."

"How do you know this?"

"I know, and that's enough." In fact, he didn't know. But everything about the man annoyed him, and that was enough to call Fotey Smothe a Grounder. But it was a stupid and impulsive—and dangerous—thing to say. Shimas raised his voice to a near-shout. "So whoever's watching can either erase the monitor tape right now, or Mestoeffer will know that *you* know about her toy, and she won't trust you to keep *everyone* from knowing it. That would make the Fleet Leader *very angry*, wouldn't it?"

"Buto!" Marsham could hold it in no longer. She laughed out loud until she had to stop and catch her breath. The sudden release left her shaking while she stood up and fought for control. Reaching across the table, she pulled him forward until their faces were together. "Go on, you rogue," she whispered. "You know where I'll be." She kissed him hard and gently pushed him away. "Be a good Bandit."

Overwhelmed by their first kiss and still rocked by powerfully conflicting emotions, Shimas didn't see her turn and leave the wardroom. When he realized with a start that he was alone, he glared angrily at one of the monitor cameras and stomped out of the room.

Two hours and fifteen minutes later he stood in his old office, aboard *Pacal*. It was a good beginning. The honor guard meeting him at the hangar was well drilled and crisp in uniform and demeanor. The parts of *Pacal* he'd passed through looked good, nearly as good as when he'd left the vessel to become Squadron Leader Marsham's adjutant. And someone had rushed his belongings to his quarters and office ahead of him, so that he now stood before three ceremonial swords and matching daggers newly polished and mounted on the office wall. And in the correct order.

Reverently he pulled *Kosai*, the uppermost broadblade, from its mount. It was the most ancient of his blades, dating back through his clan to before the very formation of Sovereign Command. He had no idea how old it was, beyond that. Or on what world it had been crafted. What world . . . Many years had passed since he'd contemplated the fine instrument in that way. Yes, he thought. *Kosai* was forged by a Grounder. Probably an ancestor of his. As he held it the blade seemed to slide of its own volition from the lustrous black scabbard, until three inches of laser-honed steel caught the light and shone brilliantly at him. Silver, he thought approvingly. In those days Grounders made good weapons. Because in those days Grounders were *us*. An odd and unsettling thought came to his mind at that moment: that somewhere, out there living the miserable life of Grounders, were distant cousins of the Shimas clan. It was a sad thought. If there were a way to help them . . . but no, there wasn't. There never would be.

At a knock on his door, he turned. "Yes, enter."

A man walked in, carrying a sheaf of reports. "Welcome home, sir," he said cheerfully. "These are the last of the personnel reports signaled here by First Adjutant Nandes."

"Thank you, Colonel Barnell. It's good to see you again."

"And you, sir. Well, well. The mustache is gone. And you've got hair again!"

"Astute observation, Colonel. Your point?"

"Oh, nothing, sir," Barnell replied with a smile.

"Good. Please set the reports on the desk with the others."

Clive Barnell was a strongly built man of average height, with unusually long arms. The two officers had served together for nearly ten years. When they'd met, Shimas was a ship's captain and Barnell, a major then, his new navigator. A scar running from the bridge of his nose and across his left eye attested to Barnell's status as Shimas's favorite sparring partner with the broadblade. The wound was an accident, the result of a momentary lapse on his part during a spirited match with real blades. Barnell refused to have the scar removed. He'd worn it from that day onward as a badge of honor; he was the only officer Buto Shimas had ever deemed skilled enough to face him with true blades drawn. But no one, not even Barnell, could safely spar with Shimas when he wielded the daggers.

"The ship seems in good order," Shimas commented as he took his seat behind the desk.

"You didn't have the opportunity to meet Squadron Leader Dage, did you, sir?"

"No. Apparently she was to report immediately to her new billet upon receiving a copy of my own orders. Things are changing, Clive. I left here a few months ago, and now I've returned. In neither case was there a proper change-of-command ceremony."

"I can only guess that time is precious, sir. We haven't long until that great day arrives."

"Indeed. Well, I'd better get to these reports. Have an attendant bring me something to eat in about ten hours, would you?"

"Yes, sir. The usual?"

"Sounds good, Clive."

"And sir?"

"Yes?"

"Thank you for keeping me aboard as part of Buto's Bandits."

Shimas grinned along with his old friend. "Word travels fast, doesn't it? Listen, Clive. I'm anticipating that the first adjutant will have us assemble our force somewhat away from the main body of the Fleet. Give us an area of space about three hours out."

"Toward the Enemy's approach, sir?"

"That's a stupid question, Colonel Barnell. I haven't been gone *that* long. Dismissed."

"Sorry, sir."

Barnell's tone was apologetic, but Shimas saw the grin on his face until it was hidden from view by the closing door. "You'll lose that smile when we spar next time," he said, glad to be home again.

The hours went by without Shimas noticing the passage of time. When an attendant arrived with a tray of food, he was amazed to note the hour. The personnel and incident reports had all been read by this time, and he had spent the last hour writing out drills and maneuvers to help him visualize what "irregular unit" might mean. Certainly the first adjutant had been alluding to something more than the numerical composition of his ships. If he could begin to anticipate what that something was before contacting Nandes, much the better.

The three hundred eleven ship's captains were all that Nandes had indicated and more. All of them had excellent combat records and higher-than-average evaluations, leading up to the moment they'd each made the fateful decision to break off from a lost fight and warn the Fleet of the Enemy's approach. There was not a slacker among them. Shimas found himself smiling and rubbing his hands together. Whatever Nandes had in mind, it was going to be great fun. If only Jenny Marsham could be there to share in it.

# ⇥20⇤

Brian Alvarez Whitlock was a man of extraordinary academic and intellectual accomplishment. Psychologist, author, researcher, lecturer, and teacher, he had traveled to hundreds of worlds in his eighty-one years of life, risking interception and capture by the ever-present Fleets. Those few who knew him for what he truly was considered him an adventurer of extraordinary daring and courage. More than that, they knew him as the brainpower behind a centuries-old secretive organization whose interests and intrigues now spanned galaxies. Brian Alvarez Whitlock was the leader of The Stem.

But his varied accomplishments were instantly forgotten when one met him personally for the first time, for few could recall ever having known a human being with a head as large as his. Whitlock's deep-set brown eyes were a full handbreadth apart, so that anyone speaking to him had the disconcerting experience of looking first into one and then the other; it was impossible to look into both at the same time. His graying brown hair was shaggy and ended above ears that emerged from the sides of his head at right angles, as if designed to limit his walking speed by offering stout wind resistance.

That initial impression was so distracting that early in his teaching career, Whitlock developed the habit of using his first address to a new group of students to get past it. He told them his hat size, how he managed to lie down without breaking his neck, and encouraged them to draw caricatures of him, if they were so inclined. Because after that first lecture, he promised, any reference to the subject would be met with permanent dismissal from his class; what he had to teach them was too important to be interrupted with frivolity. Such was his academic reputation even so early in his career that no serious student ever risked banishment from a course whose successful completion opened the way to acceptance into the most exclusive graduate programs.

As years passed, the ploy became unnecessary. Whitlock became adept at finding just the right words, tones, and body postures, different with each class or individual, to move past the matter of his physical appearance within minutes.

It was this skill in controlling the reactions of strangers, along with his pioneering work in human motivation and emotion, that first brought him to the attention of the organization he would eventually lead, and call The Stem.

Whitlock found himself in wholehearted agreement with two of the organization's four purposes: (1) To identify, recruit, and train individuals of exceptional aptitude. (2) To infiltrate those specially trained agents into both Fleets. (3) Using these agents, to effect a change in behavior and attitude within the command structures of the Fleets, in order to (4) Bring the War to an eventual end.

His agreement with the first two purposes was absolute; they could be accomplished. But the last two he found wholly inadequate. The organization had existed for more than two centuries. In that time, its success in placing agents had been good. But any progress in bringing the War to a conclusion was too small to be measured.

Nevertheless, he agreed to design new training techniques and to become personally involved in the selection and preparation of agents. As his status increased over the years, he argued with increasing fervor for a more aggressive use of those agents. After more than a decade with the organization he was able to force the change, for four reasons: By this time he had a small but passionate following among its leadership. Second, the plan he'd developed had become more acceptable to conservative elements as the level of skill among the agents grew beyond anything accomplished before. Third and most tellingly, the War was becoming more destructive and deadly with each year because the Fleets were not stagnant. They grew continually, exponentially, tearing apart more and more worlds to sustain themselves.

And fourth, Brian Alvarez Whitlock was an unabashed scoundrel.

Whitlock's coup d'état was delivered at a rare convocation of ninety-three of the one hundred thirty organizational leaders. His plan exploited the fact that a quorum was present, and that his work and ideas were well known to all present. Everything depended on his belief that his value to them was too great to be easily dismissed. The coup was a gamble, but one he felt compelled to take: Because the Fleets were expanding so rapidly, he could calculate with great confidence that no more than eight decades would pass before every settled world in the galaxies would have been victimized at least once.

All of the worlds had basic communication and space-travel capabilities. These were maintained at relatively primitive levels, to avoid attracting the attention of the Fleets. More than a century had passed since any planet had succeeded in extending itself into the unsettled reaches of space. Invariably such attempts had led to Fleet attacks against the transiting colonies, and against the worlds that sent them out. Thus, human expansion had come to a stop; not for fear of the great unknown, but for fear of the all too familiar.

Now, with the Fleets growing as they were, no world, however primitive or remote, and thus far safe, would be left untouched. Which meant that humankind was facing a permanent division into two categories: the Fleets, and those condemned to serve them in perpetual slavery. Whitlock believed that this point would be reached within eighty years.

Measured against that scenario, his own career meant nothing.

And so when Brian Whitlock was recognized to speak, he presented to the assembly an ultimatum: Accept his resignation then and there, or decide, then and there, between the old ways and the new ideas he represented. He was able to mitigate the anger that flashed among the participants by pledging to abide by the majority decision. To both sympathetic and derisive laughter, and whispers that Whitlock was inviting humiliation, the balloting began.

When the results were announced, the majority decision had gone, by two votes, in Whitlock's favor. Everyone present was shocked at the way the numbers fell, with the exception of the man who'd demanded the vote and taken steps to ensure its outcome. More than half of the participants smiled grimly and recalled a private plea that morning from Whitlock: Although he would fail, he must bring the matter to a contest; could he, to avoid embarrassment, count on that *one* vote in his favor?

A woman stood and said, "We've been had, but the decision is binding until we convene a quorum again. As you all know, security considerations dictate that these meetings never occur more than once in any ten years. And so we can only hope that a sly wizard named Whitlock will have the same success against the Fleets that he's had against us. Personally, I think he will." The name stuck. Thereafter he would be referred to as the Wizard, as often as by name.

It was at that meeting, in his first address as unchallenged leader, that Whitlock added another name to their lexicon. He described the Fleets as a living entity, a mind—not two, but one—continually at war with itself, taking nourishment from its body with no thought to replenishment. Eventually the body must die; as indeed, the worlds were dying. The mind, he pointed out, connects to the body through the brain stem. Without it, the mind perishes. And so by analogy this organization must become that stem—must become so vital to the Fleets that without it, the Fleets could no longer exist. Or as he would later come to phrase it more succinctly and dramatically to new agents, *"The Fleets can be envisioned as the halves of a single brain. We will become the brain stem. Once we have placed ourselves properly, neither half will be able to survive without us.*

*Then we will vanish, and direct the fall of a dead colossus."*

He announced the details of his plan to force a turning point in the War. When objections arose he drew out his calculations, challenging anyone there to refute them. No one could.

"Eighty years," Brian Whitlock told them in summation. "Within eighty years, not even a tick on the chronometer that measures the span of humankind, the Fleets will have consumed all that has ever been built, or accomplished, or dreamed. Unless we act."

Forty-three of those years passed. During that time The Stem trained and placed thousands of agents. Whitlock oversaw the training while concentrating on a search for one person; someone with a unique combination of abilities that he believed must exist among the thousands of billions of people spread among the galaxies. He needed an individual with the capacity to gain *absolute* empathy: to breathe, to move, to think, to act, within another human mind; and then *in place* of that mind, without detection. All of those who passed Stem training were gifted in that regard. But none could go far enough to do what must be done. In none of them had he found the nascent ability to *instinctively* identify and become attached to the individual within one of the Fleets who would, at the one critical moment, be in a position to determine the outcome of the confrontation he was planning. This would have to be accomplished without knowing the full details of Whitlock's plans, who the people involved would be, how to reach them, or specifically what it was that must be done to bring about success. Each step would have to be performed without error as events unfolded and circumstances changed from one moment to the next—like a juggler, blindfolded and spinning in free fall, but still able to catch the ball, the wineglass, and the knife. Additionally: He needed someone who could train the next most able agent to work in harmony, as an assistant. His colleagues told him that the combination of abili-

ties he demanded could not exist in one individual. He refused to believe them.

He refused to believe them because his strategy contained a flaw so critical that he could not go forward without that person. In forcing the Fleets into a major
confrontation, the risk was that one side might win a clear
victory and emerge as the single unchallenged and invincible force in the universe. In which case he himself would
have brought on the permanent division of humankind into
Fleet and slave. And yet without that confrontation, the
eight decades must end as he'd predicted. Every passing
month provided more proof.

And so for those forty-three years he'd waited to execute
his plan while searching for the irreplaceable human factor
that could tilt the odds in favor of The Stem. Two years
into that time he found something he'd never expected
from life: One of his students professed love for him. Her
statement so shocked him that for weeks he could think of
nothing but her. He fell in love and married, finding a personal joy and contentment he'd seen in others but never anticipated for himself—only to have his beautiful Amanda
leave him within a year to enter directly into the work that
framed both their lives. Broken but not destroyed, he continued training and sending out his agents, while traveling
at great peril to hundreds of worlds in search of that one
special person.

Of the thousands of promising reports he read from
agents assigned to help in his search, one caught his attention more than any other. Whitlock rearranged his travel
plans and made the journey to a world called Walden.
There he was introduced to Linda Steppart, who in turn introduced him to Dane. Within weeks of meeting the three-
year-old girl he was convinced that she was the one: a child
who might never fully grasp her own abilities, but who
nonetheless could do all that must be done. He had found
his linchpin. Now he needed to provide Dane with a coun-
terpart, chosen specifically to supplement her unique per-
sonality and abilities.

Seven years into Dane's preparation he found the other

person he needed: a young mathematical genius with less empathic capacity than Dane, but with more confidence and a fuller understanding of his own talents. And unlike Dane, he could take a direct role in killing, if necessary. Whitlock remained with him for five years, until Momed Pwanda reached the point where only Dane herself could complete his training. The rest was up to her.

During the years he'd spent looking for his linchpin, Whitlock had refined his calculations to the point of prediction; given sufficient data, he could determine within better than sixty percent accuracy which area of which galaxy was due to be hit. After a number of attempts, he reluctantly abandoned the practice of warning the potential victims: There was no adequate defense they could prepare; and on a number of occasions the warnings were detected by the Fleets, nearly leading to the discovery of The Stem. But still he continued those calculations, looking for any added edge.

On the day he processed new data and saw that Walden in Galaxy M-419 would likely be attacked within a year, Whitlock came close to panic. Dane was barely fifteen years old. Her skills were not fully developed. She had not completed the education of Momed Pwanda—she did not even know yet that she was expected to train someone else. Whitlock had intended that Pwanda and Dane would train together for whatever time was necessary to bring their talents into perfect synchrony. But it was too late for that now; she would have to teach him under less than ideal conditions.

This was a major setback, but Whitlock could see no alternative. Events had moved ahead of him; it was now or not at all.

He sent out a prearranged signal on the null-band instructing certain of his agents to begin the task of convincing each Fleet that the other was massing its forces in unprecedented numbers—knowing that when either Fleet moved to respond, the other would follow. Thus, carefully thrown rocks of misinformation would trigger an avalanche of activity.

# ⇒ 21 ⇐

During three days of nonstop drilling, Buto's Bandits worked to perfect the new combat formations and procedures designed jointly by Brotman Nandes and Buto Shimas. The experience was new to all involved. Because the unit ranked numerically between a squadron of one hundred ships and a company of one thousand, the potential uses for the three hundred eleven ships appeared by turns to be unusually promising and dauntingly limited. But as the hours and drills became history, a new unit identity began to emerge. As a whole, the unit could drive like a wedge into Enemy formations with three times the firepower of a squadron but without the complications of a company maneuver. Or if called upon by the Fleet, it could break up into three traditional-size squadrons and replace any whose losses had been particularly heavy.

But the beauty of the arrangement, in Shimas's view, was that very small units of ten or twenty ships could be dispatched for surgical penetration of Enemy formations, or to chase after and destroy Enemy stragglers, or to do long-range reconnaissance work without significantly depleting the main force.

The ideas and refinements flew fast between Nandes and Shimas during the first adjutant's personal visit, and thereafter in their frequent comm links. As both officers became more enthused by the seemingly endless potential, neither could understand why no unit of three hundred had been formed before. Nandes promised that the error would be quickly and permanently rectified after Buto's Bandits distinguished themselves in the coming battle.

*Pacal* at last stood down from the drills while officers and crew indulged in the rest they all needed. After touring the ship and speaking with his senior officers, Shimas was about to touch his head down on a mattress for the first time in forty-six hours when there came a knock at his stateroom door. "Yes," he said tiredly. "Enter."

Lieutenant Giel Hormat stepped through the doorway and stood at attention next to Shimas's bed.

"What is it, Hormat? And why do you have the energy to grin like that?"

"Sir," she began, "a Grounder has arrived on this ship and is demanding to see you."

Groggy as he was, Shimas's mind instantly flashed back to the final day of the supply run he'd led months before. "I suppose you're going to tell me that she's claiming to be the daughter of a president?"

"Not this time, sir. But she did ask me to use the word 'demand.' Shall I have her executed at once?"

"Lieutenant, do I look to be in a mind for levity?"

"No, sir. Please excuse me."

"Very well, you may leave unscathed this time. I'll need a minute to get dressed again and throw water on my face. Then send her in."

"Yes, sir."

A minute later Dane walked in as Shimas was toweling his face dry. "Sir, I don't know your new rank. How am I to address you?"

"'Sir' will do. Why are you here?" She was unusually pale and seemed to be as fatigued as he was. He assumed that she bore a personal communication from Jenny Marsham. She looked as though the news might be bad.

Before answering, Dane looked upward at the monitor cameras and raised her eyebrows.

"Never mind them," Shimas said impatiently. "They're malfunctioning, as usual." As he spoke he looked around the stateroom. Almost nervously, Dane thought. "Whatever you have to say, say it." His right hand clenched and opened repeatedly, as if grasping an object and releasing it. She'd never seen him so fatigued.

"Yes, sir," Dane said. "I've come with a message from First Adjutant Nandes."

"Oh? I see." Shimas pushed thoughts of Jenny Marsham from his mind as his concern switched from her to his ships and the first adjutant. Obviously whatever the message was, it was too sensitive to risk sending over the standard comm link. Or even entrusting to one of his officers—who, Shimas understood immediately, might well repeat it to Mestoeffer. CJ was the logical courier. She was known to have a phenomenal memory, and to be completely trustworthy. He believed he knew what the message would be about. During the recent drills Nandes had come aboard *Pacal* and approached him with a suggestion that made Shimas extremely uncomfortable. He had changed the subject as diplomatically as possible. But Brotman Nandes had never been one to accept evasion as an answer.

"The first adjutant has asked me to voice-record this for you while you listen, and to instruct—these are his words, sir, not mine—instruct you keep the tape on your person at all times until you replay it. And then to destroy the tape after listening to it a single time in complete privacy."

Shimas nodded, certain now that he was correct. "That wouldn't be necessary if I had your memory."

Dane couldn't resist the opportunity. "Those were the first adjutant's words also, sir."

"You are authorized to smile when you say that, CJ. Otherwise I could take offense."

"Yes, sir," she said, smiling.

"Very well, there's a recorder on my desk. Go ahead."

Dane spoke for twenty minutes. Hearing her, Shimas felt a growing sense of desperation. Nandes was extending an invitation to commit treason—no, not quite treason; but on the very edge of it. As Dane went on he found himself shaking his head in wonder that she could recall every word, no doubt having heard them only once. At times she almost sounded like Nandes. When it was over he stared at the ceiling, unconsciously flexing his right hand as he had before. He knew that Nandes trusted CJ, but would never have believed that Brotman Nandes would trust *any* Grounder, or any person at all, so much. Hearing the words forced him to make a decision: Report the first adjutant to a courts-martial officer, or become his accomplice. How could an officer like Nandes even consider—or risk—such a thing? Using CJ as a courier was a smart move after all, Shimas reflected. Nandes could easily deny the whole thing; who would take the word of a Grounder over his?

He was too tired to give the matter the full attention it deserved. For now he would sleep, and play the tape once when he was fully alert and able to ponder the full weight and consequences of what the first adjutant was proposing. Maybe he could think of a way out of it.

"Thank you. Was there anything else?"

"Yes, sir. Acting Lieutenant General Marsham sends her respects, along with those of SubLieutenant Marsham."

"That's a very short message, CJ. Has your memory been exhausted?"

"No, sir. That was the entire message. Other than to ask if you have a reply."

"I see. Well, yes, I do. Tell Squadron Leader Marsham that I return her courteous gesture. But the next time she needn't be so wordy."

"Yes, sir, I—"

*"Battle Contact! Battle Contact!"*

Shimas was past Dane and gone from the stateroom before the second word had blared from the speakers. *Pacal* accelerated and turned so quickly that the floor seemed to be dragged from under her. Narrowly missing the desk, she fell heavily and rolled herself into a sitting position with her hands braced against the desk. There were bars along each wall of the stateroom, as there had been in the corridor of *Pacal* the first hour she'd come aboard and been thrown about during a contact drill. *This is an unlucky ship for me*, she thought, releasing the desk and allowing herself to slide down the steeply tilted floor. As her feet reached the wall, she linked securely to the bars. At that moment *Pacal* reversed its angle. Within a second Dane's free arm and leg were dangling down toward the opposite wall, which was now where the floor should be. She knew a number of older attendants who could actually sleep in this position, no matter how the ship was maneuvering. She envied them.

*Pacal* rolled completely over, and then seemed to slam side-on into a celestial barrier that refused to give an inch. There was an explosion at the moment of impact. Dane's head crashed against the bar, she heard a shout, and all was blackness.

"How many now?" Arlana Mestoeffer demanded. In the pseudospace above the War Table, formations of gold and silver motes met one another in breaking patterns, like meteor storms colliding.

"Five hundred Enemy," Nandes said. "I recommend again that you dispatch reinforcements immediately."

"No. The remainder of the Gold Fleet could be directly behind those attacking ships. I will not split our formations."

"Fleet Leader, our long-range reconnaissance ships all agree on the position of the Enemy's main force. They are still days away. This is a small advance group, nothing more. I strongly recommend that you either reinforce our ships, or call them back here."

"My order stands," Mestoeffer said. "You're so proud of that new unit of yours, let's see if those deserters can hold together and fight this time."

"The last casualty report—" Nandes began. She was looking away from him, as if bored. He waited until she faced him again.

"Yes, yes, go on."

"The last casualty report," he continued, "confirms that we've lost nineteen ships over the past one hour. *Pacal* has been hit but is still operational. Buto Shimas has taken direct command of the ship, in the Control Compartment. He's suffered a broken leg and facial lacerations. There are hundreds of other injuries throughout the ship, with fifty-six dead. Also confirmed are thirty-one Enemy targets killed. Our unit has proved that it can fight, Fleet Leader.

But if that kill ratio continues, we will lose every one of those ships. We've got to reinforce them immediately. There is no reason to continue with—"

"No!"

Nandes's face turned red. Not only was she wrong, but speaking to him in that manner with other officers present was inexcusable. "Fleet Leader, I insist that you send—"

"You *insist?*" Mestoeffer glared hotly at him. "First Adjutant Nandes, you will leave the Operations Room immediately. Report to your stateroom and remain there until I call for you. Dismissed!"

Rising in anger, Nandes pushed his way past Mestoeffer's senior staff and left the room. Those officers looked away from each other, none wanting their expressions to be seen.

Nandes slammed open the door to his stateroom and went immediately to his own smaller version of the War Table. Activating it, he opened a comm link. "Buto, can you hear me?"

Long seconds passed before there was an answer. "Yes, First Adjutant. I'm here."

"What is your present situation?"

There was a short laugh. "Personally, sir, I'm having a wonderful time. I regret that you can't be here with us."

"So do I," Nandes replied sincerely. "If you need to break the link, do so immediately. But if you can, give me your present status."

"Forty-two . . . One moment, sir." Evidently Shimas had placed his hand over the transmitter; his voice was muffled and barely intelligible. "CJ, what are you doing here? No, I don't need . . . Hold on to something! Your head is bleeding enough as it is. Strap yourself into that seat and don't . . . Hold on! *Brace for evasion and roll!*" The link was severed for a full minute before Shimas's voice came back. "Sorry, sir. As I was saying, forty-two of us are gone from three hundred eleven, and sixty-one of the Enemy from five hundred. That ratio does not favor us. When can we expect reinforcements?"

Looking at his own display, which confirmed everything

Shimas had said, Nandes sighed. "There will be no reinforcements, Buto."

"Understood," came the calm reply. "In that case I'm
going to try the Sphere, while we have the numbers. This
should be interesting."

"I concur. I'll be watching. Contact me when you can,
Buto. In my stateroom. Use my private band."

"Yes, sir." There was a note of surprise in Shimas's
voice, Nandes noted, but the man had not asked why a first
adjutant was not in the Operations Room at this critical moment. Good, for the moment. But bad, because it meant that
Shimas had understood the tape he'd sent—and seemed too
willing to agree to his proposal. What he'd proposed had
been a test of the officer's loyalty to Sovereign Command.
In this, Nandes was deeply disappointed.

Severing the comm link, Nandes focused his attention on
his display. As he watched, Buto's Bandits began a maneuver they'd recently devised, one that had never been tried in
actual combat. For that reason it was a gamble, no matter
how well it had worked in drills. Nandes understood and
agreed with Shimas's reasoning: The tactic required a minimum of two hundred ships—more than they would have
before long, given the present kill ratio. If Shimas was successful, that ratio would change drastically in a very short
time. That would also be true if the tactic failed.

As one, two hundred ships of Buto's Bandits disengaged
from the Enemy and within a minute had formed two con-
centric spheres of one hundred ships each. Nandes counted
sixty-seven Enemy vessels trapped within that two-layered
sphere. The one hundred ships forming the inner ring
would now reduce their weapons' range to reach no farther
than the center of the kill zone. Within that area the Enemy
vessels were taking intensive fire from all one hundred of
the circling Silver Fleet ships. The outer layer of the sphere
protected the inner ships by pouring out their own lethal energy into any Gold Fleet vessel to approach within range.

Nandes watched the action, unaware for more than a
minute that he was holding his breath. The Sphere was not
designed or intended to remain together for long. When the

killing within the inner formation was complete, the ships were to return to a standard formation and continue the fight—until the Enemy again made the mistake of concentrating too many of its ships into one relatively small area. At that time the Sphere was to be ready for use again.

Seventeen minutes after it had formed, the Sphere disbanded. Nandes was startled by the sudden voice from the comm link. "Sixty-seven Enemy dead, First Adjutant. Four ships lost to us. Buto's Bandits out." Before he could reply, the link was severed. Nandes pounded his fists on the console. *Yes!*

The Enemy ships tried once again to form up. As quickly as before, the Sphere surrounded the formation and cut it to pieces. "Eighty-three Enemy dead, First Adjutant. Fourteen ships lost to us. Buto's Bandits out." *Yes!*

Within an hour the rout was complete. Turning together, two hundred eighty-nine surviving Gold Fleet ships broke off from the fight and fled at full speed. "Permission to pursue, sir? They've only been out of hyperspace for a short time. They can't enter again for hours," came Buto's excited voice. Nandes opened his mouth to shout, "*Yes!*" and instantly thought better. There was only so far he was willing to go. "Make your request directly to the Fleet Leader, Buto."

"Yes, sir."

Immediately, Mestoeffer's voice came on over the same band. "Permission denied, Shimas. Keep your ships where they are. First Adjutant, your every word has been recorded. Report to my stateroom at once."

"Understood, Fleet Leader," both officers replied together.

Nandes stood slowly, switching off the display. The blood that raced through his veins burned hot with battle lust. His hands trembled with the desire to be in command of his own Fleet once more, chasing down those fleeing cowards until every one of them was reduced to twisted scrap and Enemy blood. What he had just witnessed was—a poem! A thing of beauty! The Sphere had worked far beyond their expectations. And it could not have been employed at a more critical moment. The victory won this day—more psychological than real, but profound nonetheless—could mean that the opening phase of the coming battle was intractably set. Unless he was mistaken, the Enemy would not risk mounting an initial attack with its usual ferocity. They'd be forced to come warily, leery of any other new troubles awaiting them. What Buto's Bandits had accomplished placed the entire Gold Fleet on the defensive, and gave the opening advantage squarely to Sovereign Command. Now it was Nandes's duty to ensure that Mestoeffer did not squander that advantage.

He left his stateroom smiling, eager to explain to Mestoeffer the importance of what had taken place. And to concede in all humility that her decision not to withdraw or reinforce had been correct. He planned to avoid the phrase "blind luck."

Dane opened her eyes and was certain that she was having a dream. She knew instantly from the familiar smell of the place where she was—or dreamed that she was. This was the cavernous attendants' quarters aboard *Pacal*. Adding an unpleasant reality to the scene was a fat, bearded face hovering above her own, a face she'd seen too often in the past.

"Well, little CJ, you've come back. Did you miss me so much?" This man was the first of *Pacal*'s crew she'd spoken to, on the shuttle ride up from Walden the day she and fifty-two other women had been taken. First EngineTender Harold Chittham was also the person who'd kicked and harassed a terrified Hatta Gronis so unmercifully that she'd taken her own life that first night aboard.

Ignoring him, Dane closed her eyes as if she were asleep again. Her head throbbed with a dull pounding that emanated in waves from her forehead. Other than that and a muscular stiffness she felt from everywhere at once, she seemed to be unhurt. In fact she was oddly refreshed, as if she'd slept for a long time. Good. She'd needed it. The past three days, and then the fight and those strange things that happened when she arrived in *Pacal*'s Control Compart-

ment . . . Dane jumped as she felt a hand on her knee, only
to discover that she was strapped down. She shouted as
loudly as she could, "Get away from me!" and opened her
eyes to see a female attendant back away a pace, blushing
furiously.

"Oh! I'm sorry," Dane said. "I thought you were Chittham."

The woman laughed. "You poor thing! No wonder you
screamed. But don't worry, you must have been dreaming.
Chittham suffered a broken back during the fight. He won't
be around here again."

"He's dead?"

"Not yet, but soon. You're pale again. How are you feeling?"

"Confused. A headache. But all right, I think." Then it
was a dream. Or partly a dream. "Do you know how long
I've been down here? I'm sorry, I don't know your name.
I'm Dane Steppart."

"Oh, I know who you are. Everyone does. What I don't
know is why he sent you here, after what you did."

"Who do you mean, and what did I do?"

"My name is Vonnie Penn, by the way. I am . . . or was,
a doctor. I've been looking after you. Before you ask,
you've had a concussion. I don't believe it's serious, but
you'll be sore and groggy for another day or two. And
you've been down here for about thirty-six hours. Who I
mean is Buto Shimas. What you did is save his life."

"I don't remember anything like that."

"Why don't you try? It could help you."

Dane closed her eyes again, and tried to recall what had
happened. She was in Shimas's stateroom when the alarm
sounded. The ship was pitching around, and she fell, then
linked to the bars. There was a crash. The next thing she remembered was hearing Shimas calling her, and she'd gone
to the Operations Room. He wasn't there. Suddenly she
was with him in the Control Compartment. *Pacal* rolled
again, and there was another crash. A quick movement to
her left caught her eye. Something was moving fast and she
jumped to push it away, but she was upside down and

falling. Whatever that moving thing was, it was suddenly in her hands. The next memory was of being here, knowing where she was but mistakenly believing that she saw Chittham. She snapped her eyes open, half expecting the doctor to be gone.

"Is your vision clear, or blurred?"

"Clear, Doctor."

"Please, it's Vonnie. You don't remember what happened with Shimas?"

"Only part of it."

"Well, I'll give you the story as I heard it. *Everybody's* talking about it, you know. Chittham testified under interrogation that he'd taken one of Shimas's daggers from his office. He did it to impress Neria, that's his wife, with his courage."

"What does that have to do—"

"Let me finish, Dane. He was in the process of returning it when we were attacked. Chittham was thrown against a stanchion and broke his back. Later on when the ship took a fast roll, the knife apparently fell out of his uniform blouse and flew across the compartment. When you caught it, the blade was less than six inches from the back of Shimas's neck. From what I've been told, it was traveling fast enough to sever his spinal column. He'd have died instantly."

Dane shuddered. Without knowing specifically why, she knew it was vital that Buto Shimas remain alive. To have come so close . . . And then she thought more about what she'd just heard. "I caught a flying *blade?*"

Vonnie chuckled. "No, you caught it correctly, by the haft. *While* the ship was spinning. That part I'm sure of. Every officer who was there has been talking about it ever since. I've never heard so much respect given to something done by a Grounder. Are you trained in that sort of thing? Acrobatics, maybe?"

"No, I'm not."

"Then do you believe in miracles?"

"No."

"You should. You just performed one." Vonnie put a

gentle hand on Dane's shoulder. "Look, I have to go for now. Try to sleep. I'll be back in a few hours."

"Thank you."

Dane felt her energy draining again, but fought against the seductive call of sleep. She needed to understand what had happened. For three days before the fight she'd been without sleep, staying nearly every moment at the bedside of Jenny Marsham. There was no doubt in Dane's mind that the woman had been poisoned. Nor was there any doubt about who had ordered it; Mestoeffer had forbidden any of the staff physicians to examine the ailing woman. Dane was able to smuggle in herbs from Paul's garden and medications stolen by Jarred, who was also forbidden to see her. On the third day Marsham passed the danger point and was able to sit up and speak coherently. When Dane told her that she'd been called upon to carry messages to Buto Shimas, Marsham ordered her to carry her respects to him, but to say nothing of her illness.

So. She'd been exhausted, then injured. Delusional? Possibly. Or simply dreaming that Shimas had called to her, as she'd dreamed of seeing Chittham. But why *that* dream, and why then? There had to be a reason . . . something about Shimas that she'd observed . . . something that had not reached her conscious mind. Dane forced herself to concentrate. When she'd told Shimas of the messages from Nandes, what was he doing, what were his signs, how was he moving? For the time being she could retrace the encounter only mentally, which imposed limits on successful tracking. But she remembered. Shimas had been worried about something before she'd delivered the messages. The way he'd looked nervously around the stateroom. One of his prized daggers had been stolen; of course he'd have known about that. Wasn't there something odd in his bearing . . . Yes! While they spoke he'd clenched his right hand repeatedly, as if closing it around the knife. She'd been too tired then to focus in on the movement. And his nervousness . . . not fear. It was more like anger, and a determination not to be caught off guard. Putting the two together, it seemed probable that he'd been concerned about an assassination attempt; and that subconsciously, she'd understood this. But who was he worried about? The answer had to be Mestoeffer. If she'd had Marsham poisoned, it was not beyond belief that she'd also ordered the death of Shimas, whom Marsham loved. But . . . he could not have known about Jenny's sickness. Why then, would he expect an attempt on *his* life? And why, since she could order their retirement at any time, would Mestoeffer resort to . . . There were things she was missing. Something that could fill the gaps . . . The answer flashed through her mind like an explosion. *Of course!* Yes, she'd missed things. *Many* things. How could she have been so careless, for so long?

"Is anyone here?" Dane called out for minutes, with no answer. Desperately, she struggled against the straps holding her down. The pain in her head became unbearable, until she lost consciousness again.

When Dane woke again she knew exactly where she was, and with whom. The answer she'd found before now sat next to her cot, smiling down on her as if enjoying her helplessness. She could feel the shuttle's vibration beneath her as it lifted off from *Pacal* on the return flight to *Dalkag*. Although she could not see well from her position, she knew also that Buto Shimas was at the controls of the craft. And that the three of them were alone.

"So," she whispered, so quietly that the eyes watching her were forced to read her lips. "Tell me how you've overcome Arlana Mestoeffer. And what is your real name?"

A soft chuckle preceded the answer, given as quietly as her question. "You know, do you? I can't say I'm surprised. Don't worry, Dane, Arlana is well cared for. And my 'real' name is no one's business but mine. The one I bear is taken from one of my favorite childhood novels. *The Strange Life of Fotey Smothe*. It fits very nicely."

"Whoever you are, leave Marsham and Shimas alone."

The handsome face split wide in a broad smile. "We'll talk."

# 22

Brotman Nandes sat in a small chair several feet to the right of Arlana Mestoeffer's desk. Facing both of them, Buto Shimas stood at attention while the Fleet Leader considered the testimony of both officers. She reviewed her notes for several minutes before pronouncing sentence.

"Each of you has committed acts which constitute insubordination. Let me review. First Adjutant Nandes." As she spoke his name, Nandes rose to attention. "You disputed my orders in the presence of my staff. You then attempted to contact Shimas without my knowledge or approval. As I listened, you encouraged him to attempt a battle maneuver which had never been properly tested or evaluated by me. Do you dispute any of this?"

"I do not, Fleet Leader."

"Very well." Looking away from him, she focused her attention on Buto Shimas. "And you. You were aware that when the first adjutant contacted you, he was not in the Operations Room with me. You thereupon conspired with him to withhold your ongoing situation from me, and to accept his leadership in place of mine. You yourself ordered that maneuver. As with the first adjutant, you were aware that I had neither evaluated nor approved it. Do you dispute any of this?

"I do not, Fleet Leader."

"Very well. You are both guilty, and have earned dishonorable retirement." She paused, waiting for a reaction. Neither officer spoke or changed expression. "However," she continued, "my response is mitigated by four factors. First, neither of you has attempted to deny or excuse your actions. Next, you have apologized to me, and to my staff. Next, the maneuver in question was successful. Had you brought it to me for evaluation, I would certainly have recognized its potential and would have authorized its use. Next, both of you are integral to the operation of this new unit, which may prove useful in the days ahead.

"Therefore. The two of you will remain at your present stations until our victory has been accomplished. Following that, I will decide the final outcome of this matter. Your performance in the battle ahead will be taken into consideration at that time. Am I clear?"

"Yes, Fleet Leader," Nandes answered for both.

"Very well. You are both placed on probation from this moment. Be advised that any further insubordination will be dealt with immediately, to the full extent of my authority. You are dismissed."

"Yes, Fleet Leader." Brotman Nandes and Buto Shimas looked neither at one another nor at Arlana Mestoeffer. Shimas was thinking how close they'd come to committing treason; not in this foolishness dreamt up by the Fleet Leader, but in the secret proposal sent by Nandes through the attendant CJ—the essence of which was that when the great battle began, Buto's Bandits were to obey Nandes, and not the Fleet Leader. This incident showed how dangerous such actions would be.

As the two exited the office, Fotey Smothe stood up from his own chair at the back of the room and approached Mestoeffer.

"I'm deeply disturbed by this meeting, Arlana. Deeply."

"Oh? Tell me about it, dear one."

He showed her the notes he'd been taking. "I can't think of a word that rhymes with 'wonderful.'"

"You wanted to see me, sir?"

"Yes, CJ. Come in."

To Dane's surprise, Buto Shimas stood to greet her as he would a Fleet officer. She knew that his left leg had been broken, but neither his expression nor movement gave any hint of it. His facial wounds had been tended to, and were nearly healed. "Please, sit down." After they were both seated, he began. "There was no opportunity to speak with you before I left *Dalkag*. I had you brought here to *Pacal* to thank you personally for saving my life."

"That was my duty, sir. And I have to admit, a great deal of luck was involved. You don't need to thank me, but I'm glad to be able to speak with you privately again." At this she raised her eyebrows, as she had at their last meeting.

Shimas understood. "Yes, privately. Go ahead, CJ."

"After we returned to *Dalkag* I was able to rest for a day, and clear my mind."

"Good. How are you feeling?"

"Fully recovered, sir, and thank you. I wanted to speak with you about that day in the Control Compartment. Something came back to me that I hadn't remembered before."

"Yes?"

She went on to reconstruct the scene minutely, and again Shimas was impressed with her incredible memory for detail. As she continued speaking, his broad face reddened with anger. Both of his hands clenched and opened again in a rhythmic pattern of which he was completely unaware. When she finished and was silent again, he was tempted to ask, "Are you sure?" But the question would be meaningless and insulting. This was CJ; she was sure.

Buto Shimas required several minutes to compose himself, and to think this through. She'd given him enough both to ask a vital question, and to answer it. When at last his color was returned to normal and he could trust his voice, he said, "I see. This is something that must be dealt with immediately. Thank you, CJ. Again. I owe you a great deal."

"I should have remembered before, sir. You don't—"

He silenced her with an abrupt gesture. Bending his face to an intership communications console, he spoke a few words.

"Should I leave now, sir?"

"No. I need you here."

Ten minutes later a smiling Clive Barnell entered the office. "Yes, sir? I was about to go off duty, but I suppose for an old friend—"

"Stand at attention, Colonel," Shimas said quietly.

"Yes sir," Barnell answered, showing his surprise. "May I ask—"

"You may not. CJ, tell this officer what you just told me."

"Sir?"

"Tell him! To his face!"

Dane turned to Clive Barnell and repeated what she'd told Shimas, in exactly the same words she'd used before.

Barnell's expression went from surprise to confusion to anger, and ended with amusement. When the recitation was complete he said to Shimas, "Sir, I appreciate your sense of humor as much as anyone. But isn't using a Grounder to play a joke on an old friend a little extreme? Even for you?"

"I'm not laughing, Colonel. The story is true."

"It seems highly unlikely, sir. But if you're serious, then I assume you want me to find out who—"

"I know who, Colonel. You're going to tell me why. Now, if you please."

Barnell flushed. "Even if this Grounder is telling the truth, and we both know they're all liars, you think it was *me?* You can't be serious!"

"That is not an explanation," Shimas said.

"Sir, this is the most ridiculous thing I've ever heard. I deny it absolutely. How could you possibly believe that I would . . . Even if I . . . which I did *not*, the word of a Grounder is no proof at all!"

"I agree, Colonel. No proof at all. Nevertheless, it happened. And it *was* you."

"Sir, I protest this inexcusable—"

"Quiet!" Shimas glared the officer into silence, and went on calmly. "I've worked with bladed instruments since I was old enough to walk. I should have realized at the time that a dagger cannot possibly 'fall' with the force that every witness says it did, no matter how hard *Pacal* was hit. This woman saw an arm completing a fast arc at the same moment the knife 'fell' at me. She has told me, and you, that she did not see whose arm that was. But other than myself, Colonel, only you could throw a dagger with that speed and accuracy. You saw Chittham fall and injure himself. You saw the knife jolted from his uniform blouse. And when *Pacal* began to roll, you seized the opportunity."

Shimas stood and went to the rack of swords and daggers on the wall behind the desk. "By the way, Colonel, I believe I know who ordered the attempt. I was expecting it. But not from you. And I do appreciate how frightened you must have been when you were approached. But you should have come to me, Clive. I would never have betrayed you like this, no matter what the threat. You owed me the same loyalty."

"Sir, I—"

"This," Shimas said, taking a dagger from its sheath, "is the one. It has a name, Colonel. *Honto*. Clan tradition says that the name means 'truth.' That's ironic, don't you think?"

"Sir, I—"

"Would you care to hold it again?"

"Sir, I have never touched that—" Shimas whirled and threw. Before Barnell could flinch, the dagger slammed flatly against the center of his chest, with enough impact to knock him back against the wall.

Dane gasped. For a horrifying second she thought the blade had pierced the man.

Barnell regained his balance, one hand held over the spot where the knife had broadsided him. His face was a mask of shock and anger.

"You have a choice, Colonel," Shimas continued in the same calm tone. "You will confess what you've done, and confirm who ordered you to do it, and face immediate retirement. Or, you will face me." After a moment of silence he crossed the floor to stand four feet from Barnell, who backed against the wall. Shimas lifted *Honto* from where it had fallen and took a step forward. Reaching, he took Barnell's arm and raised it. He placed the dagger in the colonel's right hand and closed his fingers around the haft. "There. You tried to kill me with this once before," he said softly. "Try again." He placed his own hands down by his sides.

"Sir," Barnell said. "I protest. Formally. I am a respected officer of Sovereign Command." His voice took on a pleading tone as he looked into the unyielding eyes of Buto Shimas. "Sir, we've been friends for ten years!"

"Yes," Shimas replied, "we have. Make your choice, friend. Now."

Barnell slumped. He lowered his eyes, and looked as though he would faint. "Sir, I *planned* to come to you. But my wife, my daughter, were threatened. When Chittham fell, and I knew the monitors were off . . . I just acted on impulse. I'm glad I failed. You know how much I respect . . . but my wife, my . . . I know you won't forgive me. But at least understand how sorry . . ." His arm shot forward, an expression of pure terror on his face.

Shimas deflected the blow with an easy sweep of his left arm, then moved so quickly that Dane had no time to turn away. The weapon had scarcely flown from Barnell's grasp when Shimas's right hand flashed forward and took Barnell by the throat, lifting the taller man until he dangled several inches above the floor.

Dane left her chair and was screaming before she caught herself. "Sir! Please, don't!" Cringing, she saw that massive hand close around Barnell's throat, and heard a clean, sharp *snap!*: a dry log cracked open by fire.

Barnell fell to the floor, limp.

Shimas turned from the crumpled, still figure. To Dane he said, "If I'm anything at all, CJ, I'm disciplined." With that he grinned and raised his closed left hand. Putting a thumb over his index finger, he squeezed. The knuckle popped with the same sound Dane had heard a moment earlier.

"He thought he was a dead man," Shimas explained, "and fainted. When he wakes up he'll be confused and in shock, but he'll remember who ordered him to kill me. And he'll tell me. For the record, I don't believe in traditional interrogation. Not for personal matters."

Dane took her seat again, shaken by the violence. She'd shouted on impulse. But now she realized that it might be better for her if Barnell had died. On awakening he would confirm to Shimas that Fotey Smothe had been behind the assassination attempt. Dane had not told Shimas about this for two reasons. To do so would have revealed too much of herself to him. And until she knew more of Fotey Smothe—she was certain that he was not from The Stem— she didn't want Shimas to go after him. One, or both, would be killed.

But there was nothing she could do now to prevent him from learning the truth.

Responding to a summons from Shimas, Lieutenant Giel Hormat arrived in the office. "Take him to one of the medical staff," Shimas ordered, pointing to the fallen Colonel Barnell. "He's to speak to no one without my direct authorization. And I want to know of anyone who asks to see him."

"Yes, sir." Hefting Barnell onto her shoulder, Hormat left the office.

"Now, CJ," Shimas said jovially, taking his seat behind the desk. "As I said, I owe you a great deal. First for saving my life, and now for identifying the assassin. What is it I can do for you?"

"Sir, any attendant would have done—"

"I disagree. You're ordered to ask for something." A broad smile crossed his face. "But think before you do. The last time I granted a request to a Grounder, you ended up married to him. Apparently that didn't work to anyone's satisfaction."

Actually it did, Dane thought with mixed feelings. It was still a sore point with her that she had not been consulted by Shimas before Momed's "request" was agreed to. As if her life and intimacy belonged to someone other than herself— to be given away as a "favor." But then, in the minds of Shimas and Marsham she would always be a Grounder. No matter how valuable she became to them. It would be good to remember that. "I really don't . . . Actually there is one thing, sir," she said, as if just thinking of it.

"Name it, CJ."

"I know it sounds foolish, and it may not even be something you can do."

"Am I to guess?" he asked, somewhat impatiently.

"No, sir. But it was . . . I don't know, *exciting* to be there in the Control Compartment during that fight with the Enemy."

Shimas nodded, his eyes expressing both agreement and appreciation for her understanding of Fleet life. "Yes, CJ. That is what every good officer lives for."

"Would it be possible when the real battle begins . . . I know I shouldn't ask, but you ordered me to . . . may I be *there*, in the Control Compartment or Operations Room with you, when you face the Enemy again?" This was the question she'd prepared to ask from the time she'd been ordered to report to Shimas aboard *Pacal*. She'd understood right away what the visit would be about; Momed had explained to her about Shimas's sense of honor, even toward Grounders. It was after Shimas had called for her that she'd recalled seeing the dagger thrown—not falling from Chittham's blouse—that day. It gave her another way to earn his gratitude. Dane was aware that it defied logic to ask to be with him, specifically, at the critical time that was fast approaching. His rank and position were relatively low within the Fleet; his command included only two hundred fifty-one surviving ships from his original unit. And yet she sensed—she knew—that a moment would arrive when the final outcome of the battle would depend upon Buto Shimas. At that moment, she had to be there to influence his decisions. Somehow. "As I said, sir, perhaps I shouldn't ask."

"Frankly, CJ, I wouldn't object at all. You have a talent for watching my back when it counts. But you're assigned to Squadron Leader Marsham, and through her, to *Dalkag*. Only the Fleet Leader could approve your transfer here." Shimas held up his hands and smiled. "But who knows?

Maybe we'll get lucky again. Maybe the Enemy will attack us before you leave here today."

Dane was disappointed. Given what she knew was coming—and wishing she understood how she knew—something had to be arranged. One possibility presented itself. And as she thought about it, it seemed a more promising solution than the one she'd come here to pursue. But this was neither the time nor the place to explore the idea. "I understand, sir. May I have some time to think about your order?"

"Yes." Shimas seemed genuinely disappointed. "But I doubt that you'll see me again until after we've destroyed the Gold Fleet. The shuttle will be ready when you arrive at the hangar."

Recognizing the dismissal, Dane stood up.

"I'd like you to deliver something for me on *Dalkag*," Shimas said. "Privately." Before he reached into a desk drawer, Dane knew what it would be. "Please give this directly to Squadron Leader Marsham," he said, handing her a sealed note.

"Yes, sir, I will." Dane slipped the note into a tunic pocket. "I'm sorry I won't be here to watch you in action again."

"There may come a time, CJ, when Squadron Leader Marsham and I are stationed together again. Then we'll see about your request. Except of course, in that case *she* will be commanding the battle. That's something I'd like to see, also." Shimas blushed to have spoken so personally. "Good-bye, CJ," he said abruptly.

"Good-bye, sir."

"Come in, come in!" said Fotey Smothe. "And welcome to my poetry room." The man bowed and made a sweeping gesture with his right arm, inviting her in. The small room was even more odd than what Jenny Marsham had described to Dane. But it was not at all, as Marsham had proclaimed, "nauseating." The walls and ceiling were a soft lavender in color, varying subtly in shade to form barely discernible patterns that suggested clouds, and movement of light. A thick carpet covered the floor. Soft gray and flecked with white, it was sculpted to form long, thin peaks that, even as she watched, seemed impossibly to be flowing. It was an ocean, beneath a strange and beautiful sky. At one corner of the room was a platform raised six inches from the floor. It was just large enough to hold two ornately carved wooden chairs that were cushioned in the same color and patterns that formed the walls and ceiling.

"Do you like it?" Smothe asked, smiling with obvious pride. "I designed it myself, of course. Arlana says that it makes her sick. But I find it very restful."

"It's beautiful," Dane said sincerely. "The Fleet Leader was generous to give it to you."

"No need to be formal," Smothe assured her. "This room is mine alone. Absolutely no monitors. Even Arlana doesn't infringe on my privacy here. To do so would inhibit my ability to create the marvelous poetry she so enjoys."

Dane decided to test his claim to absolute privacy. "You're from a world that's predominantly seagoing?"

"You're a clever child, as I'd surmised. The answer is yes. Of course, I'm speaking from old memories. Elloree no longer exists as it did when I was young. But my world of origin was generally poor in minerals and soil quality. The mountains were better than the flatlands, but were too harsh for most people. Our oceans, though! They were magnificent. Until I was seven years old, I never touched a foot to dry land."

"Then you're accustomed to Fleet life."

Smothe frowned. "First you doubt my word, and now you insult me by comparing the splendid fleets of my youth with these garbage barrels. Why is that? Do you expect me to shout in anger, to reveal my secrets in an unguarded moment?"

"Sir, I—"

"You're transparent, dear, and you're beginning to bore me. But I'll play along. Would you care to sit?" He ushered her to one of the chairs, and took the other for himself. "Now. Yes, I love ships. But not *this* kind," he said, scowling and gesturing to indicate all of *Dalkag*. "This life, these people, are disgusting. They have no poetic soul, no appreciation of how truly beautiful life can be. They live in metal coffins that fly through nothing, and they believe this to be the ultimate existence. What blind arrogance! Tell me something, Dane. Have you watched a sunrise since you've been aboard? Seen a great cloud drift alone over a calm gray sea? Heard a bird sing? Smelled an ocean breeze?"

"No."

"But you miss all those things, don't you? You long to witness them again?"

"Yes. Very much." Suddenly Dane saw in her mind the Rainbow Ghosts, and the magical rivers that formed and disappeared on the black desert sands leading to Bowman's Plateau. Their memories still filled her with awe. And like the more common wonders that Smothe had described, the ones she'd always taken for granted, they were gone forever.

"You long for them because you *can*, Dane. As I do. These people," he sneered, raising his eyes to look back at the door, "these people are terrified of such magnificence. All they appreciate is destruction. Killing, and more killing. They never get enough of it." Abruptly, he smiled. "There now. Do you see that we can speak freely here?"

"I am speaking freely, sir. Why wouldn't I?"

Smothe regarded her. "All right. I don't need you to tell me what you don't want to say. I don't need you at all, Dane, and it's in your best interest to remember that. I'm sure you understand that with one word from me, one whine or pout that you'd looked at me in a way that hurt my feelings, Mestoeffer would have you killed. Or 'retired,' as they say here aboard this stinking tub of blood."

"Yes, I believe that."

"Good. Now I'll tell you something else. I ordered Marsham and Shimas assassinated because they suspect that I'm a Grounder. They can't prove it, of course, but why allow the annoyance of rumors? I watched him tell her about me, and then destroyed the tape." Smothe grinned. "In fact, Shimas virtually *ordered* me to do so. Am I not an obedient servant? And no, Arlana doesn't know about the attempts. This is personal. I poisoned Marsham myself, and had no difficulty finding an assassin for Shimas. Believe me when I tell you that these murderers are happy to jump through their own backsides to do what I ask them to do. Especially if it's to kill someone."

"I see."

"Now, then. You asked me to leave Marsham and Shimas alone. I won't ask you why. But I will consider it. I want something in return."

"I have a high regard for both of them," Dane said. "Naturally, I would ask anyone not to harm them. But I can't imagine what I could possibly do for you, that you can't do for yourself."

"For your sake, you'd better be wrong. But we'll come back to that. First, let me tell you what I'm about. As you know, I'm a Grounder. I am sixty-one years old. At the age of fourteen I stowed away aboard a spacecraft. At that age, I'm afraid, my beauty was matched only by my recklessness. I wanted to be a smuggler, you see. A pirate of legendary courage, daring against the Fleets. But my career as a pirate was cut short. The ship was captured in space. And so for forty-seven years I have lived among these criminals, remaining alive by making myself as valuable to them as I possibly could. Much as you have, I'm sure." He held up a hand. "I don't want an answer, Dane. You don't trust me, and I don't care to hear any more of your sly evasions. As I was saying, I developed my talents to the fullest. Other than my poetry . . . and I do *not* mean that trash I give to Arlana. Other than that, my talents are of a physical nature, guided by a truly poetic and romantic soul. But don't misunderstand me. I'm not proud of being a whore, even if I'm the best. Thousands of times I've been too disgusted with myself to draw another breath. But not now. Now I have a mission in life. Would you care to know what that is, Dane?"

"Yes, I would."

"I thought you might. Seven years ago I was sent to Arlana Mestoeffer. As a gift. Since coming to know her, I have decided that she is my mission in life."

"I understand, Mr. Smothe."

"No, Dane, you do not. I have nothing but loathing for the woman. My purpose, the one and only thing that moves me from one moment to the next, is to see Arlana Mestoeffer in supreme command of the Fleet. She must be united with the Generals."

Dane was taken by surprise. "But why?"

"Revenge," Smothe said. "Cold, pure, and deadly revenge. A quick story, Dane. Forty years to the day after I was taken, the ship I was on participated in a supply run. I happened to see which world it was that we were 'visiting.' It was Elloree. My *home*. It was learned that the Gold Fleet had been there only nine years before. There was nothing left to steal. Did the benign Sovereign Command simply leave, and move on to another victim? No. As a 'warning' to other worlds about dealing with the Gold Fleet, Elloree was taken apart. The squadron was there for six weeks. Not a man, woman, or child was spared."

Dane wanted to sympathize, to find a way to ease the pain that was so clear in him. But her training cautioned her not to respond until she knew more about this man; despite his apparent candor, he was attempting to deceive her about something. "May I ask a question, Mr. Smothe?"

"If you must."

"Who gave that order?"

"Yes, you can imagine how much I wanted the answer to that question. And once I had access to Arlana, it was easy to find out. The order to make an example of my home world came directly from the flotilla leader. At the time, he was a major general. By the name of Olton Kay-Raike. When he came aboard recently I did my best to influence Mestoeffer toward ordering his retirement, and giving me the privilege of carrying it out personally. Under other circumstances she might have given him to me, as a gift. Unfortunately she wanted him alive. As an instrument of revenge against the Marshams, you understand."

"I see."

"And so when that wretched man died, I was greatly relieved. By the way, it was I who convinced Mestoeffer not to pursue the investigation too thoroughly. Are *you* relieved, Dane?"

"Why would I be?"

"Oh, no reason that comes to mind. Getting back to my story. The genocide on Elloree was displayed on the ship's screens. All of us Grounders were forced to watch, for several hours a day. It became too much. When I was ordered to go back to the screens once too often, I decided to kill myself. I went to the attendants' quarters and slashed my face until it looked as I felt inside. But I did not have the courage to complete the job. I'm a coward, you see, and when the knife was poised at my throat there was nothing in my mind about the death of my world, or the future that lay ahead for me. All I could feel or think about was the pain from the lacerations, and the blood that filled my eyes and mouth. Not long afterward, my captors gave me a new face. Because, you see, I was valuable. It happened that the new face was so beautiful that my patron, one of Mestoeffer's clan, sent me to Arlana. The first thing Arlana did was to record the death of my 'old' self and order me to take a new name. I chose the one I now bear. Next she directed that my face be surgically rebuilt again. To 'protect' me, you see. And to suit her idea of male beauty. My new patron gave me a Fleet uniform and assured me that I would be with her until it came time for my retirement. Which, of course, she would order the moment she became bored with me. It was then that I contemplated suicide for the last time. But you see, Dane, I knew that I could never go through with it. So I thought of something better. I became determined to live. Because I had a mission. I tell you with no false modesty that I've helped her. I've had dozens of people killed who could have come forth with testimony that might have threatened her advancement to supreme command of the Fleet." The words had poured from him so rapidly he was nearly out of breath. Before going on, he paused while his breathing returned to normal.

"Now. Why must Arlana become one of the Generals? Very simple. You must know by now that my beloved patron is a fool. No, don't answer me. She is a brilliant administrator, but her grasp of military operations *as* military operations is about what you'd expect from a barnacle. Do you know what that is?"

"Yes, Mr. Smothe."

"Then you understand. My revenge is that by elevating Arlana Mestoeffer, I will cripple Sovereign Command. I live for no other purpose."

Dane was stunned. Outwardly, it would seem that she and Fotey Smothe were natural allies. But his was a goal he pursued alone, with single-minded determination. She saw now that her instinct had been correct; no matter what he revealed to her, she could not trust him to know who she really was, or why she was there. If he saw her as a threat—or competition—he would have her exposed and killed without hesitation. "You said you believe that I can do something for you."

"Yes, that. As I told you, I am a coward. Immediately after we defeat the Gold Fleet, Arlana will return to the council to be united with the Generals. At that time she will have no further use for me. But I do not want to die. I want to go on and find another mission in life. Before that moment arrives, I expect you to have found a way to preserve my life."

He was lying about something, Dane thought again. But about what? It was impossible to be sure, for now. Smothe was an accomplished actor with more than forty years of experience living the roles he created for himself. He was good. She would need time to track him fully before she could detect specific lies from him. "I'm just an attendant, Mr. Smothe. But of course if I can help you, I will. As long as I'm required to do nothing disloyal to Sovereign Command."

Smothe laughed. "Would I suggest such a thing?" His smile disappeared as suddenly as it had come. "I've watched you, Dane. You manipulate these butchers as easily as I do. Actually more skillfully, because you have none of the power I have. But neither do you have a mission. Your talents are wasted on trying to maintain your own life. I won't reprimand you, however. I intend to use you. I will accept your promise to help me to the full extent of your ability, when the time comes. In return I will take no further action against Marsham or Shimas. That is, provided that they never again breathe a word of rumor concerning my humble origins. Do we have a bargain?"

The moment had arrived for Dane to further her own plans. "You can watch Squadron Leader Marsham as long as she's aboard *Dalkag*. But how can you know what Buto Shimas says, or does not say?"

"You want him transferred back to *Dalkag*?"

"Me? That is not for an attendant to suggest, Mr. Smothe. I only thought that for your own peace of mind, it might simplify things for you."

Smothe's handsome face darkened. "I am not as easily manipulated as they are, Dane. You want Shimas here because of Marsham's affection toward him. You believe that if she's happy, her treatment of you will improve. That is a selfish motive. However, I do see the merits of what you suggest." He hesitated only for a moment. "All right, I'll see to it. But I remind you, keep them quiet. For their lives, and for your own."

"I understand, Mr. Smothe."

He leaned forward and placed a hand on her shoulder. "You're an intelligent woman, Dane. For your sake, I advise you to find a purpose greater than yourself, and to make that your reason for living. Or in the years ahead you'll find yourself as I was, anxious to die but afraid to do it."

"I'll think about that, sir. I've enjoyed meeting you."

When she'd gone Fotey Smothe paced his room, deep in thought. He had not intended to tell the young woman so much about himself. But as the conversation proceeded the words seemed to pour from him like the spring waters of beautiful Lake Murmur: every year rising above its dam, and emptying itself into the placid Gray Sea. He himself had held back the waters for too long, denying nature its due. When they began to break free he could not stop them. Nor, he thought, should he have. It felt good to have told his story, finally, to someone. Yes, very good. His mind and spirit were soothed, and calmed as they had not been in many years.

Perhaps they would speak again. And why not? There was no danger of her betraying him; who would believe her? Similarly, who would believe Shimas or Marsham, that Fotey Smothe was a Grounder? He'd acted impulsively to have them killed. But when he'd gone to *Pacal* to fetch Shimas and force a confrontation that would end in the officer's forced retirement, he had changed his mind. And so he'd tricked Dane; in exchange for her promise to help him, he'd conceded nothing. She was a talented young person, no doubt of it. But she was naive.

However, she had potential. He was convinced that she'd poisoned Kay-Raike. Why? Obvious. To help Marsham and that silly brat of hers. But as time passed, Dane Steppart might go beyond petty murder and strike at the Fleet itself. If so, she could be very effective.

Yes, he would talk with her again. She must be encouraged to learn patience, attach herself to someone important, and go on to great things. As he had.

Smothe returned to his chair and lifted from beneath it a sheaf of papers. He looked at the words he'd written. Then with a mischievous grin he sat down and began composing. What could rhyme with "wonderful," to describe Arlana Mestoeffer? "Thunderful," he wrote, and laughed. "Plunderful." What else? Oh yes! "Blunderful." He went on, for once having a wonderful time writing for dear Arlana.

# ➡23⬅

Twenty-one hundred Gold Fleet ships broke free of hyperspace and flew like a horde of celestial arrows, straight and true, into the heart of Buto's Bandits. Caught too late to flee toward the protection of the mother Fleet, the two hundred fifty-one ships of Sovereign Command formed up together and charged as one lethal unit into the thickest Enemy concentration. They passed once at full engagement speed through the startled lines of attackers, all weapons firing, and took a heavy toll on the frantically maneuvering Gold Fleet ships. But the end of the fight was determined from the beginning; the advantage of nearly nine ships to one could not long be denied. Ninety-three of Buto's Bandits survived that first pass through the Enemy formation. Instead of turning to repeat the procedure, they scattered and continued on, hoping to reach the safety of hyperspace before they were overtaken. Forty-one made it. The superior numbers of the Gold Fleet pursuers made short work of the rest.

The Gold Fleet lost four hundred twelve, an insignificant number to warriors who had won their revenge, and who now turned and began their run for hyperspace. Having just left it, they would need hours to cool the power plants and replace burnt elements. But they had the advantage of distance from the main body of the Silver Fleet; they were out of instrument range before reinforcements could arrive to engage them.

Only a small shuttle, ignored in the chaos of twisted metal and free-floating corpses was left to find its way back to Sovereign Command. Inside the vessel were two people, but only one sound. For the first time since the age of one, Buto Shimas bellowed with uncontrollable rage.

"We've arrived, sir," Lieutenant Giel Hormat said quietly, her hands automatically going through the steps necessary to shut down the shuttle's power plant and secure the vessel's controls. Beside her Buto Shimas nodded.

"I can see that, Lieutenant. Find quarters for yourself and get some rest."

"Yes, sir."

He waited until she'd left the shuttle before standing up and straightening his uniform. When he was satisfied, he unlashed the case of his belongings and hefted it, preparing for the fifty-minute walk to *Dalkag*'s nerve center.

"May I take that for you, sir?"

Shimas turned to see a tall Grounder standing in the shuttle doorway. He recognized the young man as a friend of CJ's. "Are you permitted to leave this area?"

"I was only here to onload vegetables for some of the other ships, sir. I'm finished now."

"I see. Yes, then, thank you." He handed the case to Paul Hardaway, who slung it onto his back and left the shuttle.

As Shimas stepped onto the hangar floor he saw Jenny Marsham waiting for him. "Go on ahead," he called out to Paul. "Take it to my old quarters."

"Yes, sir."

"Buto . . ." she began.

"Thank you, Jenny. There's no need to say anything about that. Except . . . please tell me. Were there any survivors?"

"Yes. Forty-one escaped into hyperspace. I'm sorry, but *Pacal* was not among them."

"Only forty-one," he sighed. "I lost *Pacal* and two hundred nine others. If I'd been there . . . where I *should* have been . . ." Feeling the rage come at him again, he lapsed into silence.

As they began walking, Marsham said, "We're at full alert now. No one expected a major assault so soon."

"I should have," Shimas said bitterly. "That was my responsibility. After what we did to them the first time, I should have moved the unit closer."

"You could not have done that without orders. And I know you made the request."

"Yes. Twice. But it was my—"

"Buto, we're about to begin the largest campaign in Fleet history. Are you going to be ready for it, or are you going to lose yourself in doubt and self-pity?"

"I appreciate what you're trying to do, Jenny," he said, looking straight ahead. "But it's not necessary. I've still got forty-one ships. When they get back I'll be ready. I'm ready *now*. What I want to know," he rumbled from deep in his throat, "is *why* I was ordered back here."

"I have no idea, Buto. I won't pretend to be sorry that you're still alive, but you know I would never have done anything to take you from your command. As if I could."

"Yes, I know that. The order was personally sent by Mestoeffer, and specified that I 'report immediately.' There was barely time to pack a few uniforms and my swords. I just want to know *why*."

*"Battle Contact. This is a drill. Battle Contact. This is a drill."*

Ignoring the officers and crew running by them in both directions and the sudden changes in course and angle, Marsham and Shimas continued walking, occasionally using the bars for support. "This is ridiculous," Marsham said. She spoke freely, knowing that her voice would be overwhelmed by the ambient noise, and not recorded. "Whoever heard of announcing that it's a drill before it begins? And whoever heard of two officers like us with nothing to do *during* a drill?"

"You're right."

"Buto," she said suddenly. "There must be twenty vacant staterooms within five minutes of where we are at this moment."

Shimas looked at her in surprise, and smiled. "We *should* be doing something important, shouldn't we?"

"I agree." Marsham thought for several moments. "But

then again . . . not when we're both angry. And now that I think of it, I do have something to do."

"What?"

"Bring you to the first adjutant. He's expecting you."

"He'll be busy for a while, Jenny."

"Not for six hours, he won't. No drill lasts for that long."

"Six hours?"

"Yes," she said, winking at him. "And not a second less. When it's the right time."

He laughed, sliding an arm around her waist. "Marsham, what am I going to do with you?"

"If I have to explain, Shimas, we'll need at least eight hours."

They finished the walk to the first adjutant's office as the drill ended, each uplifted simply to be with the other. It did nothing to reduce the sense of loss and anger that Shimas felt, but it gave him something else to think about for a while. Which he knew was exactly what Marsham had intended. They arrived just as Nandes was returning from the Operations Room.

"Your pardon, Marsham," he said. "I need to speak with Shimas privately for a moment. Please wait here."

"Of course, sir."

Inside the office, Nandes said, "What can you tell me, Buto?"

"Nothing that you didn't hear on the comm links, sir. My shuttle was half an hour from *Pacal* before the attack began. I'm afraid I saw less of the fight than you did on the War Table."

"I understand. And I know how you feel right now. I lost all but two ships from my first squadron command, at N66-V04."

"Thank you, sir. Before you call in Squadron Leader Marsham, there are two things I'd like to say to you, alone."

"And they are?"

Shimas mouthed the word, "Secure?"

"As I said, I wanted to speak with you privately. I've rewired the office personally. No more surprises."

"There was an incident in *Pacal*'s Control Compartment—"

"Yes, I heard about that. Marsham's attendant caught a falling knife before it reached you. Remarkable."

"That wasn't an accident, sir. That was a deliberate attempt on my life."

Nandes sat back in his chair. "I see. Please tell me about it, Shimas."

Shimas gave him the entire story, including CJ's participation and Barnell's initial denial.

"You were willing to take the word of a Grounder over a Fleet officer's?"

"Personally, yes. Officially, no. If Barnell had not confessed and tried to kill me that second time, I'd have had no choice but to let him go."

"With no real evidence against him, he was a fool to confess."

"Yes, sir. But I know Barnell. Killing me wasn't his idea. He was ordered to do it."

"Interesting. Do you know who was behind the attempt?"

"I had a strong suspicion, sir. I expected Barnell to confirm it. But he didn't wake up before I was ordered to leave *Pacal*, and now of course he's dead. But upon reflection I'm convinced that I was wrong about who gave him the order. So no, I don't know who was behind it."

"Whom did you suspect?"

"Fotey Smothe."

"Smothe? But why?"

"I insulted him."

Nandes chuckled. "It must have been a very imaginative insult."

"Yes, sir. It was something I'd shouted out in a moment of anger. But as I said, I'm sure I was wrong. I don't believe he has the courage to try something like that."

"I agree. Smothe's a harmless idiot. But Shimas, as serious as this is, something is bothering you more."

"Yes, sir. That's the second thing I wanted to discuss with you. I owe you an apology."

"For what?"

"Sir, I gave Barnell a short lecture on loyalty. I've since thought a great deal about that. Your suggestion to me regarding Buto's Bandits was completely out of line. I should have confronted you about it immediately."

"Go on, Shimas."

"We both know that I disagree with much of what the Fleet Leader does. But I owe her my loyalty, above what I may owe you. I did both of us a disservice by not making that clear to you when you visited *Pacal*."

"And so you suspect me of disloyalty?"

"I did, sir. But after dealing with Barnell, I looked into your record. In more detail than I had before. I discovered what I should have realized from the beginning: that you are not capable of a dishonorable act. You might bend Mestoeffer's orders for the benefit of the Fleet, as we've discussed. But you would never act for personal motives."

"I see. Your conclusion, then?"

"You were testing me."

Nandes said nothing for several moments. Finally he opened a locked drawer and retrieved a file. Placing it on the desk between them, he said, "Let me tell you a story that you, uniquely, will understand and appreciate. When I was a young ship's captain, a superior officer sent me secret 'suggestions' that I was to obey her, and not her own superior. I didn't know what action to take, if any. So I never challenged her. She was furious. That blunder nearly cost me my career and life. I was willing to give you another chance, as she gave me, and as you gave your Captain Lortis. But I'm relieved that you've finally brought the matter to me. For the record, everything I communicated to you is in this file. Take it with you, read it, and destroy it."

"Thank you, sir. I hope you'll accept my apology." Shimas noted the first adjutant's kindness in not stating the obvious: He had failed the test, as Nandes himself had. But the warning was clear: Never again accept an illegal order, whether a "suggestion" or not.

"Your apology is accepted, Buto. The matter does not exist. As for the other, I don't need to tell you to be careful.

I'll look into it, discreetly. Now, was there anything else to be said privately?"

"No, sir."

"Then please ask Marsham to join us." He stood and switched on the room's monitoring system.

When they were seated, Nandes said, "I have spoken to the Fleet Leader about your futures."

Marsham sat forward, hopeful that her new ally had come to an agreement with Mestoeffer.

"I proposed to her," Nandes continued, "that each of you be returned to the position of squadron leader. She has agreed, partially. Shimas, your unit will be brought to a strength of three hundred, when your forty-one ships return. Marsham, I, ah, do not yet have your final orders." Which all present knew meant that Mestoeffer was delaying, for her own personal reasons.

Nandes looked uncomfortably at Shimas. "Your two requests to the Fleet Leader to move your unit are on record, and known throughout the ship. I ask you formally, do you wish to remove them?"

Shimas stiffened his shoulders and flushed. Now he understood. Mestoeffer was offering a trade. His ships would be reinforced, and Marsham would be given a squadron command. *If* he agreed to remove evidence of Mestoeffer's incompetence—and accept the responsibility himself, for the loss of two hundred ten ships. This was one thing that Mestoeffer could not order; his requests were on record, and widely known. His forced retirement now would leave no doubt in anyone's mind about Mestoeffer's motives. And invariably, the controversy would become known to the council. "How would you advise me, sir?" he asked, with little effort to hide his anger.

"This is a formal matter between yourself and the Fleet Leader, Shimas. I can't offer you advice. But I know that you'll want to give it your full consideration."

"I will, sir," Shimas said with gratitude. Nandes's careful choice of words gave him time before having to announce his answer to Mestoeffer. His first impulse had been to refuse outright and take the consequences. Two things prevented him. First, Jenny Marsham's career was involved; he had no doubt that Mestoeffer wanted her here now for exactly that reason. Second, he did feel that the responsibility was his. As the commander in the field, he should have made the move under his own authority, as days passed and more outrider formations of the Enemy drew within attack range. And again, accept the consequences. He'd have been retired at once, of course. But then the two hundred ten lost ships of Buto's Bandits would be alive. With a new name and new commander, but alive. He was confident that he would accept the responsibility himself and withdraw his requests to move the unit. But first he wanted to hear what Jenny Marsham thought.

Nandes said, "Very well." Addressing both, he continued. "That's all I have for now. In the meantime, Shimas, your duties will consist of—"

He was interrupted by the sound of a buzzer and a particular light flashing above the comm unit. "Yes, Fleet Leader?"

"This is Fotey Smothe, First Adjutant. The Fleet Leader sends her respects and informs you that she has suffered a strained voice. She asks that I relay a message to you."

"Please extend to her my best wishes, Smothe." Nandes understood completely. During the just-completed drill, Mestoeffer had shouted herself hoarse for nearly an hour.

"She can hear you, First Adjutant, and nods her thanks. The Fleet Leader informs you, sir, that upon further consideration she would prefer to speak personally with Acting Lieutenant General Marsham and former Squadron Leader Shimas. Those officers will report to her stateroom at once."

So, Shimas thought. I didn't jump to accept her offer, and now we're to hear her threats. It was all he could do to remain seated and quiet. As if standing too close to an overheated power plant, he could feel the eyes of Mestoeffer and that moronic Smothe on his face. Marsham reached for his hand and squeezed with surprising strength for a person her size.

"I understand, Smothe," Nandes said angrily. He'd been

asked to present the question to Shimas. Although uncomfortable about it, he had done so. And quite properly, he'd given Shimas time to consider his answer. But in typical fashion Mestoeffer was interfering, showing no regard for the personal dignity of her officers.

Rising, the two officers nodded to the first adjutant and left his office. Nandes watched them go, angrily tapping his fingers on the desk. His mind traveled back to the drill, and he heard again the frantic, undecipherable shouts that dominated what should have been a simple and orderly Fleet exercise. And then Shimas's apology brought back to him his own previous thoughts toward Mestoeffer. Shimas was right. If he were ever to commit a dishonorable act, it would not be from personal motives. It would be for the benefit of Sovereign Command.

Dane jerked out of a dream, her face covered with perspiration. Sitting up and looking around in the darkness, she saw just enough to assure herself that she was still in her quarters. In her mind's eye she could still see the Fleets. They seemed to fill the entire universe with flecks of gold and silver that went on infinitely in every direction, drawing close to each other and closer still with every heartbeat. Until at last they met in an explosion that was ten trillion suns going nova at once, overpowering the universe with heat and blinding light until everything that was had ceased to be.

She heard Whitlock's voice as he had spoken throughout the dream: *"There will come a time, Dane, in the emptiness, when there is no darkness anywhere. Then you will see clearly, and you will know what to do."* Terrifying, because the dream was taking shape, becoming nearer with every breath. She'd seen the ships as clearly as if they'd been displayed above the War Table. Comforting, because her mentor was there, promising that she would know what to do when the time arrived. She hoped earnestly that however many agents of The Stem were aboard ships of both Fleets, they also would know what to do when four hundred thousand ships collided in war.

Momed Pwanda had taught her so much that she hadn't known before, about The Stem. Until he assured her that it was so, Dane would never have believed that hundreds, perhaps thousands, of agents were implanted with microscopic receivers. Or that a new transmitter was to have been launched from Walden soon after her abduction, broadcasting on what he called the "null-band"—whose functioning Professor of Engineering Momed Kwasii Pwanda-Pwanda himself did not understand. But he knew that when the proper signals were received they would soon afterward be acted upon; that for this reason, the battle would begin before either of the Fleets expected it to. And would end with them having reason to fear the settled worlds for the first time in nearly two thousand years.

Dane stood and dressed in the subdued illumination cast by a wall chronometer. How much time was left? Already twenty-one hundred advance ships of the Gold Fleet had mounted an attack, with most of them escaping. When would they meet the main body? They knew when the Gold Fleet had left the Fortress. Assuming staggered hyperspace jumps for each of the Enemy's units and maximum normal-space speed for the entire body, and factoring in their own advance, it would be at least four days, according to Marsham: The Enemy would never dare to commit its entire force to hyperspace at one time; the number of ships involved would guarantee disaster. The next minute, according to Mestoeffer: The Enemy was not bound by the same laws of physics that governed Sovereign Command.

As if Whitlock had mentioned him by name in her dream, Dane was more convinced than ever that Buto Shimas was the key to her success. She had persuaded Fotey Smothe to bring him back to *Dalkag*, and his departure from Buto's Bandits had occurred not a moment too soon. Everything depended on his being in a position of Fleetwide influence at the critical moment. And on Dane Steppart being with him. How could Marsham be persuaded to release her to Shimas?

The question became meaningless when Dane left her

quarters and learned shortly afterward what had begun while she was asleep and dreaming.

" . . . reporting as ordered, Fleet Leader," Marsham said. Beside her, Buto Shimas stood at attention, his eyes never leaving Fotey Smothe.

"In her stead, I welcome you," Smothe said. "As you know, the Fleet Leader has suffered an injury caused by severe fatigue, and her unending dedication to our victory." He glanced quickly at Arlana Mestoeffer, his eyes lovingly reproving her for working so long without proper rest. She nodded in return. Around her throat was a lavender towel that gave off a warm and vaporous herbal aroma.

Smothe continued, pleased that Nandes had failed. Now Arlana would understand that Fotey Smothe was her best advisor. "The Fleet Leader recognizes that her time has been too limited to give the two of you the recognition your services have merited. Therefore she has directed me to inform you that conditional upon your . . ." He paused significantly. "*Conditional* upon your desire to proceed in the best interests of Sovereign Command . . . " Again he paused to be certain that he was understood. "Proceeding in the best interests of Sovereign Command, Acting Lieutenant General Marsham's rank is hereby made permanent. The two of you are to be married within the hour."

Both officers took in a sharp breath. Jenny had refused to marry Buto when he was superior to her in rank, because she was determined that her future children would bear the Marsham name. Her rank, being made official, removed that obstacle. Shimas came from a clan with thousands of members, and therefore had no objection to his children bearing the Marsham name.

"Unfortunately," Smothe continued, "your time together will be limited by the new duties that each of you is hereby ordered to assume. Lieutenant General Marsham, you will report in two days' time to the flagship *Brishe*. There, you will assume command of XG212 Company. I believe you're familiar with that unit's informal name."

Marsham was astonished. XG212 was a senior company,

one her father had commanded more than forty years before. Many older officers still referred to it as Marsham's Maniacs. Jenny had been born on the flagship *Brishe*.

"The Fleet Leader suggests," Smothe added, "that your son, *Lieutenant* Marsham, accompany you to your new command, for further training."

"And you, sir," Smothe said to Shimas, "are also to report to XG212, and remain there for a brief time, until your surviving ships have returned to us."

"*If* they do," Mestoeffer rasped. "They're known to run at the first signs of . . ." Losing her voice again, she waved Smothe to continue.

"Of course, Fleet Leader. While there," he said to a stunned Shimas, "you will once again serve as adjutant to Company Leader Marsham."

Measuring his words carefully, Smothe said, "I believe we are all in agreement that this will be in the *best interests* of Sovereign Command?"

"No," Shimas said. "We are not." Taking pleasure from the suddenly pale face of Fotey Smothe and the flash of worry from Mestoeffer, he went on, "There is a matter which must be dealt with first. Not long ago I forwarded two urgent requests to the Fleet Leader."

"Yes?" Smothe said icily.

Going ahead with what he'd already decided to do, he said, "They were sent in error. I formally ask that they be removed from the record."

"Might we discuss this first?" Marsham asked at once.

"You are out of line!" Mestoeffer rasped, her voice cracking.

"I apologize, Fleet Leader."

"There is no need for discussion," Shimas said. "The error was mine. I would appreciate the opportunity to correct it, before I leave this ship."

Smothe glared at him, furious to have been treated so lightly. "I'm sure the Fleet Leader does not know what you're referring to," he said, as he'd planned. "But no doubt she will accept a written explanation from you, and proceed accordingly. In the best interests of Sovereign

Command." He looked toward his patron, who nodded. "The Fleet Leader wishes you to go now. Write out your explanation, Shimas, and bring it here. Then each of you record your marriage with the appropriate personnel. Best wishes, of course," he added dryly.

As they turned to go, Smothe called to them at the door. "There is one other matter," he said as they stopped, "so trivial that I nearly forgot. Company Leader Marsham, you have a personal attendant . . . what is her identifier? Oh yes, CJ359. She is to remain aboard *Dalkag*."

Marsham was taken aback. CJ had proved invaluable to her, and to Shimas. But her mind was focused on the futures, suddenly bright, that awaited both of them. And *Lieutenant* Jarred Marsham. "Of course," she said. "If the Fleet Leader orders it."

"She does," Smothe said.

Watching the two officers approach, Dane knew a part of what had occurred. Although neither would believe that their joy was so apparent, there could be no mistake. "May I offer my best wishes?" she said, smiling at the two.

Marsham blushed. "CJ, how could you possibly know already . . . never mind. Go to my quarters at once and prepare the finest dress uniform you've ever done for me. *With* the clan crest."

"Yes, Squadron Leader."

"It's 'Company Leader' now," Shimas said proudly.

"Oh?" In that instant, Dane knew that her plans had gone dreadfully wrong. A promotion for Marsham meant a transfer. Worse, their marriage could mean that Shimas was leaving, as well.

"CJ," Marsham said, "are you all right? You're terribly pale."

"I'm fine, Squad—Company Leader. I had a disturbing dream, it's nothing. May I congratulate you on your new assignment?"

"You may. Go on, now. Get the uniform ready."

As she walked away, stunned, Dane heard Marsham say to her husband-to-be, "I'll miss her, Buto."

# ⇒24⇐

The collision took place exactly on schedule as Momed Pwanda watched on the screen that was the latest addition to his crowded room. One moment the Gold Fleet ships flew in tight formation, seemingly motionless, more orderly than the stars and the spinning galaxies that lay beyond them. The next instant one of their number seemed to reverse course and go tumbling in one direction after another, brushing against other ships as they maneuvered to escape the erratic missile. And in the next second those stricken vessels careened out of formation, all damaged, none having moved fast enough.

As he watched, this grouping of ships broke from their formation on the far right flank of *Noldron*. They scattered, as if suddenly penetrated by the Enemy, to gather again in ranks closer to the bulk of the Fleet.

*"Full Alert! Full Alert!"*

Pwanda switched off the screen and lay back, strapping himself to the bed. He wondered if it would be remembered that the stricken ship, *B333C*, was one of the dozens of vessels he and No'ln Beviney had toured in the past days. She had been proud to show him the astounding transformations the ships had undergone in the short time following her order to modify them for the coming battle. And he had been equally proud to examine the work, and to praise her for it in the presence of the ships' personnel and other No'ln supervisors. But eventually she'd grown impatient with his detailed inspections of the altered power plants and maneuvering controls. Aboard *B333C* she'd finally left him behind, as a lesson, with instructions to follow her back to *Noldron* in a separate shuttle. Five more times the pattern repeated itself until she no longer seemed to mind his tardiness, and remained with him. Six of them should be sufficient, though. Until the explosions began.

He drifted into a light sleep and was unaware of the passage of time until he heard *"Secure from Full Alert! Secure from Full Alert!"* and was awake. A quick glance at the chronometer told him that for seven hours, the Gold Fleet had conducted a pro forma search for an Enemy presence. And of course, had found none; the procedure was mandatory when a vessel was inexplicably damaged. He was confident that no piece of *B333C*'s maneuvering controls would be found large enough to betray his work.

An hour later, yawning and standing to stretch, Momed Pwanda switched on the screen again and set it to view a formation of Gold Fleet ships that was far in advance of *Noldron*. As he waited he broke out the game board and set it on the table, absently moving the pieces in random patterns. From the corner of his eye he saw the second series of collisions occur, precisely as had the first.

*"Full Alert! Full Alert!"*

He glanced up at the chronometer. Exactly on schedule.

Seven hours later *"Secure from Full Alert! Secure from Full Alert!"* sounded. Pwanda switched off the screen on which he'd viewed the chaos: formations of ships breaking and coming together again; whole units disappearing into hyperspace, reinforcing the units already dispatched ahead of *Noldron* to probe for Enemy positions; the ships seeming to become more numerous as *Noldron* moved itself to the very center of the Gold Fleet. All of this activity was mandated by regulation; suspicious damage was always treated first as an Enemy attack, even when it was clear that no enemy was involved.

Present company excluded, Pwanda thought.

Again looking at the chronometer, he judged that it was time. Within a few seconds he'd rearranged the game board to the start position.

The door to his room flew open and No'ln Beviney marched in. "I can't sleep, Momed. My mind is going too fast."

"Is it time to wrestle?"

"Are you insane? I'm exhausted! Let's play . . . Good, you have it set up. Well, go on, go on, make the first move!" For the first time in days she took the chair, a sure sign of the fatigue that was manifest in the dark circles beneath her eyes, and the tremor in her hand movements.

Pwanda nearly felt sympathy for her, until he recalled the trips they'd made together. He'd been forced to witness the executions of thirty-one captives, eighteen crew, two ship coordinators, and one junior supervisor. They all served aboard ships that had not completed the transformations in time. Beviney had personally selected the victims to serve as warnings to the rest. As Pwanda made his opening move in the game, he reflected that sometimes he needed to remember who these people were. It did not ease his feelings about the injuries his sabotage may have caused. But it helped to keep them in perspective.

He asked, "What were those drills about, No'ln Beviney? It's unusual to have two of them so close together." The first ten moves went by quickly, as each staked out a familiar playing situation.

"Routine, nothing unusual," she said finally, concentrating on her next move. It was a foolish gambit, a mistake she would never have made under other circumstances. Pwanda overwhelmed the piece easily in the next three moves, and was in line to attack her main formation. "These game pieces"—he pointed—"that you modified for speed make a real difference, don't they?"

"Yes, yes," she said distractedly. Her response to Pwanda's game attack was so weak that he was forced to begin his own mistakes, to prolong the game. Twenty-two minutes later he looked up at the chronometer.

*"Full Alert! Full Alert!"*

*"No!"* Beviney was out of the chair and into the corridor within a second. Pwanda stood up and moved the table aside, removing his tunic and beginning a series of calis-

thenics that he hoped would allow him to sleep again. It was going to be a long day.

Four hours later he was satisfied. Crossing the empty corridor to the bath compartment, he washed down as *Noldron* continued its defensive maneuvering. Shortly afterward he was in bed again, waiting for sleep. He was hungry, but he knew that it would be a long while before the mess decks were serving food again. It would be even longer before the next "accident."

*"Secure from Full Alert! Secure from Full Alert!"* brought him awake again. Another seven hours had passed. *I'm sleeping far too much*, he thought, as he rose to slip on his trousers and tunic.

"Why can't I *sleep*?" Beviney shouted as she kicked the door open.

"Perhaps something from a doctor?" Pwanda suggested, stretching and yawning.

Beviney eyed him murderously. *"You* can sleep! If I were just a Dirt like you, then yes, I'd take something from those idiots. But *I* have to be alert for the next time this happens!"

"The next drill?"

"They were not drills." She was wavering on her feet, and sat down heavily. "They were exercises in chasing down out-of-control ships, and time wasted by stupid regulations."

"I don't understand."

"Of course you don't." Beviney rubbed her face with both hands and put them wearily down on the table. "I noticed something, Momed. Those three ships we lost—"

"We lost *three ships?*"

"Yes. They're ruined, and will take weeks to repair. We've taken their personnel aboard other ships and abandoned them for now."

"That's unfortunate."

"Three damaged ships out of a force this large is not a serious matter. Normally. But all three of these were ships I recently inspected. All three had been modified for speed."

"You mean . . . ?"

"Yes! The bunglers! I should have executed them all!"

The outburst seemed to drain her. Pwanda listened to her explain quietly in engineering terms how she believed the three ships had crippled themselves. He frowned thoughtfully. "Yes, of course you're right. But this is terrible! The controls will have to be dismantled in every one of those . . . How long will it take you to inspect the ones you caused to be altered?"

"Months," she said, raising her hands to her face. She rubbed her eyes and leaned forward to put her elbows on the table. "There are thousands of them, in all. But of course we don't have the time. All we can do is isolate them in their own formations while they inspect themselves. But they're not drilled to work together, which means that in just a few days they have to rejoin their regular units and I don't know the trouble that will cause because I'm so tired I can hardly . . ."

"Whaa . . . ?" Beviney jerked her head up from the table.

"You slept." Pwanda said, sitting on the bed and hoping she wouldn't remember his nudging her arm repeatedly.

"How long?"

"A little more than an hour. Are you feeling any better?"

Her eyes were streaked with red, and seemed to have trouble focusing. "No. My neck is stiff and my head is throbbing."

"I brought you some food from the mess decks," he said, taking a tray from his bed and putting it on the table in front of her.

She stared down, grimacing. "That is *food?*"

"It's what they serve us Dirts," Pwanda said. "I'm sorry, it was all I could get."

"Never mind," she said, rising wearily. "I'll have something that's fit for people sent to my quarters. I think I can finally fall asl—"

*"Full Alert! Full Alert!"*

*"No!"*

Exactly on schedule. Three, this time.

• • •

"Come in, come in!" said Fotey Smothe. "And welcome again to my poetry room. I apologize for not seeing you sooner, but my duties to the Fleet Leader must come before pleasure."

The moment the door was shut, Dane whirled on him. "Mr. Smothe, I thought we had a bargain."

"So distressed, little Dane! Please, tell your Uncle Fotey all about it." He led her again to the two chairs on the platform. "Now, what is disturbing you?"

"Company Leader Marsham and Squadron Leader Shimas have been transferred. They're scheduled to leave *Dalkag* in sixteen hours. Why?"

"For their happiness, of course. Don't you approve? And please mind your tone."

"Sir," she said carefully, "it isn't for me to approve or disapprove of things like this. But I understood that you wanted them kept aboard *Dalkag*."

"So that I could watch them" Smothe said, nodding. "That is no longer necessary. Their word would mean nothing against Arlana's, who of course would deny any lies they might spread about me. And they both understand a little of my power now. But, Dane, their transfer is not what disturbs you. You're afraid of being left here, alone, so to speak."

"Was that your idea?"

"Yes, it was. As you say, we have a bargain. I will do nothing to harm your former patrons. In fact they are safer now than they have ever been, at least for now. I confess in all modesty that your Uncle Fotey played a large role in bringing that about. And when the time that we discussed arrives, you will be nearby, where I need you to be. You see? A bargain indeed, and perfectly kept. But you needn't be alarmed. I intend to watch over you as your own mother would."

Given his smug arrogance and the limited time involved, Dane had no choice but to deal directly with him. She said, affecting anger, "I don't need an uncle, thank you, and I have a mother."

"I advise you for the last time, little Dane, to change your tone."

"Certainly, sir. Is this better?" While Smothe watched in growing disbelief, Dane began to repeat the words he had spoken at their last meeting. She did so in a perfect female equivalent of his own voice, matching his inflections, his every gesture and facial expression. After ten minutes he felt himself drowning, circled by sharks.

"Stop!" Without success, Smothe tried to conceal his alarm. "That is interesting, Dane. You'd have been a fine professional entertainer."

"I agree, Mr. Smothe. And I'm very vain about my talent. For that reason I tape all of my performances before presenting them to an audience. Would you like a copy? Or perhaps the Fleet Leader would? I'm sure she'd find it amusing. And convincing."

"She wouldn't be interested in a child's game."

"I disagree. I think the Fleet Leader will find it fascinating. Do you doubt that she will recognize you in the performance? Or that she'll have to conclude that what I'm saying, I first heard you say? How else would I know so much about your background, your surgeries, and the people you've killed in her behalf? How else would I know that"—using his voice again, she said—"*I have nothing but loathing for the woman.*"

He stared at her coldly. "It would mean your death."

"And yours. But more than that, Mr. Smothe. When the tapes are circulated, it will mean the Fleet Leader's disgrace. And the end of her ambition to assume a place with the Generals."

"Is there any reason you should leave this room alive?"

Dane smiled at him. "If I don't, you'll never find the tapes. Not before one of them is delivered to your patron." While he stared mutely, she went on, "I share your desire to see Fleet Leader Mestoeffer united with the Generals, Mr. Smothe. I give you my word, that goal does not conflict with mine."

"Which is?"

"Which is, like your real name, no one else's business.

It's important that Marsham and Shimas remain aboard *Dalkag* with me. Further, that Shimas be appointed as battle advisor to the Fleet Leader. That's all you need to know."

"I see. Either I cooperate with you—"

"Which is little more than keeping our arrangement, *as agreed.*"

"—or Arlana learns more about me than she needs to know. In a way that no amount of charm can overcome."

"Yes, sir." In a more conciliatory tone, she said, "Mr. Smothe, an alliance between us is natural, and mutually beneficial. I need your help. You need mine, and I assure you that I can do more for you than you suspected."

"An alliance?" He was startled by the suggestion. For several seconds he looked down at his hands. "I've always worked alone . . ." Looking up at her again, he said, "But . . . circumstances do change, don't they?"

"They've changed for both of us, Mr. Smothe. Everything we've worked for depends on your decision. Either we succeed, or we die. Together."

Smothe thought about it. What choice did he have? Yes, they would form an "alliance." But he knew, and it disturbed him deeply, that this young woman was indisputably the senior partner. Nodding, he said, "Yes, I agree." With a tight smile he added, "I've underestimated you, little Dane. But I never make the same mistake twice."

"I'm glad, sir. I wish you a pleasant evening."


"And so you retain the ranks I gave you," Mestoeffer said eight hours later. "But for the time being, Shimas, you're needed here on *Dalkag*."

Frustrated by yet another assignment abruptly taken away, Shimas said, "May I ask why, Fleet Leader?"

"It occurred to me that when you were aboard your own ships, they performed brilliantly. When you left, they were cut to pieces and ran away. That is a testimonial to your skill, and I intend to make use of it. For now you will serve Sovereign Command as my advisor."

Hiding his disappointment, Shimas said, "Thank you, Fleet Leader."

"Naturally," Mestoeffer continued, "I do not wish to separate the two of you. Marsham will remain here, as well. But when the battle is over you will have your positions as promised. I have had the necessary documents drawn up." She handed each of the officers a set of orders; signed, but with no date. "I trust that your marriage is going well?"

"Yes, Fleet Leader, thank you," Marsham said. "May I say how relieved I am to know that your voice has recovered?"

Buto Shimas bent forward and coughed into his hands. "Pardon me, please!" he said, working to control the laughter that still threatened to gush out of him.

"That is all for now," Mestoeffer said, arching an eyebrow at him.

When they'd gone she said to Smothe, "Fotey, I trust you have a good reason for this."

"I do, Arlana. You won't be disappointed."

"For your sake, I had better not be."

"And really, what does it matter? You have what you wanted from him."

"Or I would never have listened to you." She smiled and took his hand. "But it *was* your idea that convinced him to withdraw those requests, wasn't it?"

"I live to serve, dear one."

"Now, what are you planning, you scoundrel? Why do you want that big fool to advise me in the battle? Or *think* that he will advise me?"

"For your amusement, of course. Let me give you a hint: birthday surprise."

"How thoughtful. But my birthday is not for another four months, as you well know."

"Dear one, I can't wait that long," he said, meaning it.

As they returned to their new quarters, Shimas said quietly, "She's playing with us again, Jenny."

"No, I think it's simpler than that."

"What do you mean?"

"She's finally come to recognize your value." She took his arm and moved close. "At least, part of your value."

"Grounder, what are you doing down there? Come out and let me see you."

"Yes, Lieutenant Jaff." Miwan Ogaja pulled her head back from beneath a power-feed cooling unit. Trails of perspiration rolled down her face.

"Oh, it's you. Why aren't you with the captain?"

"He ordered me here, sir. To clean."

"To clean? You? I see. Very well. But finish quickly. We have an inspection in one hour."

"Yes, sir. That's why I was ordered here. I'm working as fast as I can."

"Get on with it, then. But don't stay too long in that heat."

"Yes, sir."

Ogaja bent back to her work, which was nearly complete. Her hands shook as she made the last of the fastenings secure and tested it by leaning her weight on it. Good. She wished that she knew more about the ship's systems, but this would have to do. One thing she was grateful for was the heat that was drawing moisture from her every pore. Otherwise Jaff would have recognized her tears, and asked more questions; like most of the officers aboard *Cantal*, he often treated her as more than a Grounder. She would miss them, in a strange way. But there was no time for that anymore. Now that the work was done, all she could think about were her two babies—though they would not be so small now—back on Plaisse. It had been eight years since her capture, but she always thought of them as infants—and never allowed herself to think of them as other than alive and growing happily with her sisters. Although of course she could not know for certain; like her husband, they could have been . . . She refused to think about that. Each time she pictured her twins, their sweet eyes crinkled with delight and their chubby fingers reached out to her, asking to be held and loved. And she would reach back, taking them up together and whirling around while they laughed and laughed. Even Whitlock, that strange and reserved old man, admitted that they were the most beautiful children he had ever seen.

Ogaja sat up and pushed her back against the unit, feeling its warmth as she would feel the warmth of her babies. She'd begun to say good-bye to them the day the signal had been received by the implant buried deep in her brain. Somehow, in saying good-bye, she felt closer to them than she had in years. *Remember me*, she thought, raising her head and looking upward at the cold gray pipes that lay between them.

Minutes later the drug she'd swallowed eased her gently into a dreamless sleep, and a painless death.

Superheated fluid dissolved the body of Miwan Ogaja instantly as the cooling unit ruptured and sprayed the compartment, igniting the other three charges. *Cantal*'s overheating power plant shifted automatically into shutoff mode. It made no difference. The circulation pumps she'd jammed open continued cycling at fifty thousand revolutions per minute. Within seconds the coolant-starved pumps began to disintegrate from the unrelieved friction and flung their shattered remains deep into the power plant. The explosion ripped the unit into shrapnel and tore the compartment into useless debris.

More than a week, Ogaja had known, would be required to repair the damage. *Cantal* would be of no value to Sovereign Command for at least that long; it was as much as she could do. She died knowing that she'd acted before it was time. *Cantal* was neither in the great battle, nor engaged in a supply run. But she could no longer bear the loneliness. Whitlock, wherever the old wizard was, would have to understand. Miwan Ogaja had waited long enough to be free.

Throughout the seven galaxies serving as battle arenas for the Fleets, silver and gold ships numbered nearly two million. The average complement per ship was nineteen hundred, for a total of three billion eight hundred million people. Approximately twelve percent of these had been taken from ravaged worlds; they were Grounders, or Dirts, numbering nearly one-half billion. Of that total, one in more than thirteen thousand had chosen to be captured. Thirty-eight thousand in all, they were agents of The Stem, ten percent of whom had volunteered to receive the microscopic implant. Many of these attached themselves to Fleet personnel engaged in intelligence work, and when a predetermined signal was received were able to influence the perceptions of each Fleet: Each became convinced that the other was massing for a major confrontation. Other agents, waiting for an entirely different signal, had convinced their captors early on to assign them work in the engineering spaces of their ships. They had years to learn more about destruction than had Miwan Ogaja, and weeks to complete their preparations.

Aboard the ships that were about to begin the largest single confrontation in human history, this second group of agents began to fulfill their commissions. Most would wait until the battle began; some did not.

Similarly trained operatives in both Fleets whose ships were approaching, plundering, or departing from worlds made the final sacrifice. More than four hundred vessels assigned to supply runs died in cataclysmic explosions that left no part of the ships large enough for investigation.

"I don't have time for this! Are you sure you know what you're doing?"

"I'm trying, No'ln Beviney," Momed Pwanda said. "I've done this before many times, on—"

"On Dirts! How can you be sure it will work on real people?"

"I'm not. But he didn't respond to your own methods of interrogation. I thought this might help. Do you want me to stop?"

"No. No, go ahead. But hurry! I have other things to do. Why are those Fleet units bothering *me* for answers, anyway? I have enough responsibilities with the battle ahead. *They're* not involved in it. Why can't they deal with their *own* problems?"

"Because you have the coordinator here, and he is the one who first discovered evidence of—"

"I know that. Get on with it."

Pwanda bent over the unmoving figure of Serjel Weezek. "You can hear again," he said softly, rubbing his fingertips gently over the man's temples.

Reacting to the physical stimulation, Weezek said, "Yes, Momed. I hear you."

"Serjel, you're still on that planet. The tall boy told you something about weapons." Pwanda was sickened by Weezek's appearance. The ship coordinator had been hung by his heels for nine hours while he was questioned and beaten. His nose and mouth were once again caked with dried blood. Both of the small man's arms were broken, his fingers were crushed, and the ribs Pwanda had bound up so carefully were shattered again. His left eye was a gelled mass in its socket. For nearly an hour it was all Pwanda could do to take away the man's pain without medication. When he was at last able to talk, Beviney had been called back to the doctor's table.

"Yes," Weezek said. "The boy told Supervisor Yardley about a President Hindman who was doing weapons research. But we never found him."

Beviney shouted, "You're lying!"

Weezek jumped at the sound of her voice, and began weeping. "Please . . . please, don't . . ."

"It's all right," Pwanda said soothingly. "The only voice you can hear is mine. There is no one else. There is no pain." He shot an angry look at Beviney.

"Thank you, Momed. I'm so glad you're here. You're my only friend."

Pwanda cringed. *Friend?* Would a "friend" use the ship coordinator as he was? Pushing aside the tremendous guilt that lay like a rock in his chest, he continued. "He was a strange boy. A strange boy who yelled and threw things at you." These were the words that should release the suggestion he'd put into Weezek's mind as they'd traveled together.

There was no immediate reaction. "Yes," Weezek said after a few seconds. "He was very . . . Yes! I remember now, Momed!"

Beviney opened her mouth, and closed it again as Pwanda warned her with a look. He was angry enough to attack her, and never mind the consequences.

"The boy," Weezek continued, "did lead us to Hindman. He was much younger than I'd expected a president to be. And a physicist. Under torture he admitted to Supervisor Yardley that on thousands of worlds, they were developing something that was started eight years ago. Hindman was engaged in the final phase of the research. Before he died, he told Supervisor Yardley that soon . . ."

Ten minutes later, it was over. Weezek had performed flawlessly.

"We were lucky," Pwanda said after he'd led Weezek into sleep, and the doctors came in to begin repairing the damage he'd suffered. Guilt made Pwanda refuse to leave Weezek, forcing Beviney to remain there as the coordinator received the care he needed. "The beatings he received from the Silver Fleet, *and his own people,*" he said, glaring at Beviney, "apparently damaged his memory. Does any of that help you?"

"Help? A weapon like that on 'thousands' of worlds? Momed, it's a catastrophe."

"But it does explain why the Great Command has lost so many ships recently on supply runs."

"Yes, his testimony confirms it. Whatever they were working on, it's operational now. On at least one hundred nineteen worlds that we can verify. And we know the same thing is happening to the Enemy. Can you believe the treachery of those Dirts? Attacking *us?*" Beviney shook her head wearily, as the evil of the universe seemed too much to bear. "Well," she said. "I have no time to deal with this now. I'll send the information along to all units, particularly those engaged in what you call 'supply runs.' For now, this is their problem."

She rubbed her face and looked at Pwanda with red-run eyes. "In the meantime I have ships of my own failing because of incompetent engineers, thousands more that I can't depend on, and, and . . . and a battle to win that's less than thirty hours away. And I can't *sleep!*"

Concerned about one potential consequence of The Stem's success thus far, Pwanda chose this moment to test her. "With all of your problems, No'ln Beviney, would it be prudent to postpone the battle?"

Her facial expression answered his question eloquently. She said, "You're not one of us, Momed. What could you possibly know about pride?"

"Nothing, I suppose," he answered, satisfied. "But I do know how to win."

"That you do, second only to me. Momed, your friend is sedated. These doctors will take good care of him, or I'll hang them all. So let's go. I want you to learn the Battle Control Center."

"The next time we gather together like this," Arlana Mestoeffer told the assembled one hundred officers in her dining room, "I will be bidding you all farewell." From the guests came polite, if strained, sounds of disappointment. "At that time," she continued, "our victory will have been won. Tonight I feel as though we are accompanied at this table by generations of our ancestors, who lived, fought, and died without knowing a triumph of the magnitude . . ." For more than an hour she continued, while most of the attending officers sipped mild stimulants to keep them awake for another of her endless speeches. She ended the address by pledging to all present that when she returned to the council and assumed unity with the Generals, each of them would be remembered.

As she sat down, Brotman Nandes rose and lifted his glass. "To the Fleet Leader," he offered, "and to Sovereign Command."

The officers stood and saluted Mestoeffer with their own glasses while Fotey Smothe whispered in her ear, "Nandes is out of order, dear one. You and Sovereign Command are one and the same." She squeezed his hand while acknowledging the applause that followed.

Seated at the far end of the table were Jenny Marsham and Buto Shimas, who waited while Dane filled their plates.

"CJ," Marsham whispered, "what is wrong with you? Your hands are shaking."

"I . . . I don't know," she whispered in return. "Something . . ." At that moment she pitched forward, falling against the broad back of Buto Shimas and crumpling to the floor.

Shimas left his seat at once and bent over her.

Mestoeffer's voice filled the room. "Is there a problem?"

"The attendant has fainted," Shimas called back. "It's nothing, Fleet Leader."

"Remove her, Shimas. She's disturbing my guests."

"CJ—" Shimas began.

Dane opened her eyes and beckoned him closer. "The knife," she said softly, not moving her lips.

"Yes, I remember," Shimas answered. "You must have been hurt more than we thought."

"No!" Dane insisted, barely audible. "*This* knife! The one beside your plate!"

"Shimas," came Mestoeffer's voice, "take her out of here."

He lifted Dane and carried her out to the corridor. "Can you stand?"

"I'm fine now, sir," she said as quietly as before.

When he'd set her down, Shimas asked in a whisper, "What were you talking about in there?"

"Your dinner knife. There's something wrong with it."

"How do you know that?"

"I don't understand it, sir. But it's the same feeling I had before, aboard *Pacal*."

Reddening, Shimas said, "I see. Can you make it back to your quarters?"

"Yes, sir. But please, don't use—"

"I understand, CJ."

When he returned to the officers' table and took his seat, Marsham asked, "Is she all right?"

"The concussion she had before," Shimas said. "I sent her to lie down." As he spoke he surreptitiously covered his dinner knife with a napkin and slipped it into a pocket, taking care not to touch the blade.

Three hours later, having threatened a doctor into secrecy, Buto Shimas confirmed what he already knew. The cutting edge of the knife was coated with a clear and instantly lethal poison. Marsham gasped and squeezed her husband's hand. Any food he cut with it would have killed him.

Seven levels below them Paul Hardaway finished folding a large sheet of paper and placed it on his head. "There," he said to a giggling Carnie Niles. "My sorcerer's hat."

"You are so handsome," she teased. "Ask me again and maybe I'll marry you."

"I told you to stop that!"

Dane Steppart opened her eyes to see Buto Shimas standing near her bed. "Company Leader Marsham has ordered you assigned to me," he said. "And you're going to have your request. When we go into battle, you'll be in the Operations Room with me." Reaching down to cover her small hand with his own massive fingers, he grinned. "Watch my back, CJ. You're good at that."

"I will, sir." She did not tell him that while the knife was poisoned, his food had contained the antidote. He was too valuable to her to take a chance.

Light-years from the empty space between galaxies where the future of humankind was about to be decided, Brian Alvarez Whitlock opened his eyes for the first time in months. His nurse slept in a corner of the room, snoring loudly. Whitlock didn't hear the man. Nor did he recognize the room around him, where for more than forty years he had slept between journeys. He heard nothing, but saw clearly, as if looking through the ceiling ten feet above him. A cloud. As large as the universe itself, a dark cloud lowered slowly. Already it touched every living human being, and still it came closer. The cloud was divided into halves. Between them, like the stem of a flower, was the only light he could see. The halves came together and touched. Closing his eyes, he felt himself rise from the bed and fly toward that welcoming light.

# 5

# DESTRUCTION

# ⇥26⇤

## DAY ONE—Justification

Within a hemisphere of blackness that reigned above the massive War Table, two hundred thousand ships of Sovereign Command were displayed like motes of silvery dust. Beyond these ships of the Silver Fleet, like stars born from nothing, tiny flecks of gold were appearing. By the hundreds.

Around the table stood the twenty-nine officers of Mestoeffer's senior staff, along with Buto Shimas.

"They're coming into display range," she said for the third time since the first of the flecks had appeared minutes before. She alone was sitting. As Fotey Smothe's skilled hands massaged her shoulders from behind, she thrummed her fingers rhythmically on the newest set of battle orders she'd authorized. "They're four hours away, is that correct?"

"Approximately four hours out of weapons' range from our most forward observers," Brotman Nandes said. "The War Table is receiving this data from them. At this time, as agreed, I recommend that we come to a stop and advance five companies to—"

"Not yet," Mestoeffer interrupted. "We should wait for a while longer."

Standing to either side of the seated Mestoeffer, Nandes and Buto Shimas exchanged a glance. This was the plan she'd authorized thirty minutes before—the seventh revision she'd ordered in as many hours, and the only one that he thought sensible, given the way she'd scattered the

Fleet. His idea was that five thousand ships advancing on the first Gold Fleet arrivals would tell them very soon whether the ships were a part of the main Enemy body, or an advance party detached from it. If an advance party, it would have no choice but to retreat. But if not, and they waited too long to find out, the Enemy could have its greatest strength poised against Sovereign Command's center formations. It was vital to find out immediately, because Mestoeffer had ordered their flanks to wait at distances far beyond what Nandes considered prudent; against his advice, she'd splintered the main force into far too many defensive positions. And so if the Enemy rushed their center in full force, Sovereign Command would suffer irreconcilable damage before those flanks could arrive to help.

Similarly, Shimas's instinct told him that what they saw emerging from the emptiness was the first unit of the main Enemy body. Twice in the recent past his own ships had fought against numerically superior numbers of Gold Fleet ships and given better than they'd taken. The Enemy would not repeat again the mistake of risking its ships in small confrontations. He believed, as Nandes did, that they could expect at least one hundred thousand Enemy ships to come directly at their thin center and pass through once, as a unit, in what they hoped would be a deadly surprise. And then form up and return for a second attempt, while the remaining half of their forces appeared and did the same. If successful, the Enemy would have forty percent of the Silver Fleet trapped between its two halves, in a kill zone that could not be escaped. And would then flee the carnage they'd created, before Mestoeffer's dangerously scattered reserves could arrive.

Shimas said, "Fleet Leader, I concur with the first adjutant that—"

"Your opinion was not asked for, *Squadron* Leader," Mestoeffer said. "I will decide what to do, and when."

Standing far behind the group of officers, Dane heard enough in Mestoeffer's tone to know that she was too nervous to hear, or understand, any argument. The Fleet Leader would rely on her own impulses, mercurial as they had been all day, until the first action was underway. And then she would either regain her composure and listen to Nandes and Shimas—or fall apart completely and allow the Enemy to decide the battle on the first day. This Dane could not allow.

If Shimas was right about the deployment of Gold Fleet ships, it meant that Momed Pwanda had not been successful in organizing them as they'd discussed. Until she saw the sign that Momed had promised, she would have to assume that he'd failed. For the time being it seemed to Dane very likely that Shimas was right. She caught Fotey Smothe's attention and looked first toward Mestoeffer and then Shimas. Her mouth formed the words *"Help him."*

Smothe looked back at her and shrugged.

Dane put on a facial expression he recognized as his own and mouthed the words *"' . . . contempt for this woman . . . '"*

Glaring back at her, Smothe thought furiously. After a moment he bent down to whisper urgently in Mestoeffer's ear. "Why not allow the fool to make his mistake now, dear one? Let them all see that he deserves instant retirement. You have nothing to lose, and wouldn't his death and disgrace be a wonderful surprise for your friend Marsham? Happy birthday!"

Brought back to more familiar modes of thought, Mestoeffer responded immediately. "Very well, Shimas," she said, "on your advice. First Adjutant, advance the companies."

Nandes issued the order.

Above the War Table five thousand silver motes detached themselves from the center formation and accelerated toward the nine hundred approaching Enemy ships, which were now a clearly defined unit. Beyond that unit, nothing showed. As the minutes passed, Mestoeffer's forward observers could be seen to join the five advancing companies.

"If they run soon," Nandes reminded the assembled officers, "we'll know that they're alone and unprotected. If they allow us to get anywhere near weapons' range before turning away, we'll know it's a trap and that the main force is not far behind them. At that time we will bring the companies back and call in our flanks. And then we, not the Enemy, will initiate the attack."

"*If* I order it," Mestoeffer said.

For Mestoeffer's benefit, Shimas said, "At our present rate of closure, those nine hundred Enemy ships will be close enough within the hour to see our entire formations. And of course what they see, all of their ships will see."

"Your point?" Mestoeffer asked impatiently.

"At the present time we're seeing through the 'eyes,' if you will, of our five companies. Those units are all that the Enemy can detect at this time."

"I know that! Now what is your *point?*"

Nandes spoke slowly, as if explaining a battle simulation to junior officers. "If we stop our main body right now we'll prevent those Enemy ships from learning where we are so quickly. This will force their leadership to choose between sacrificing them as scouts, calling them back prematurely, or coming ahead in force and telling us where *their* strongest formations are." As we had agreed, he added silently.

"Then you advise retreat?"

"No, Fleet Leader. I suggest that we allow more distance between ourselves and the five companies." He chose his next words carefully. "Otherwise the Enemy will see that we are not, ah, planning to meet them at our center."

Mestoeffer flared. "The positions I ordered are valid, as my own combat experience proves."

"Of course. I merely point out that by—"

"Secondly, it will never be on my record that I allowed the greatest force ever assembled by Sovereign Command to *retreat*."

"Perhaps my explanation was unclear—"

"Your suggestion was very clear, Nandes, as the record will note. I order a ten-percent increase in speed for *all* ships. Including those five companies. Immediately."

Controlling his anger, Nandes said, "Then you will call in the flanks now?"

"And invite encirclement by the Enemy? First Adjutant, I'm beginning to believe that your record of victories was attained by accident. Now understand me very clearly. *I* command here. And I will have your *immediate* acknowledgment of that fact, or you will resign your commission. Now give the order! Ten-percent increase in speed!"

Buto Shimas read the indignation and resolve in Nandes's face, and acted quickly to diffuse a confrontation that could have only one ending. "With your permission, Fleet Leader, First Adjutant," he said, crossing to the Fleetwide comm link. Both officers nodded tersely as he repeated Mestoeffer's order. The command was followed by a moment of acceleration as *Dalkag* responded smoothly, along with nearly two hundred thousand other ships of Sovereign Command.

While all officers' eyes were on Mestoeffer and Nandes as the two continued to glare at one another, Dane saw it happen above the War Table. "What is that?" she called loudly, pointing.

Within the five thousand silvered motes advancing against the Gold Fleet, one segment of ships was breaking formation, opening a large gap between them and the others. Several of these moved erratically, in no discernible pattern. None of the officers answered her question, or made a guess to explain the unprecedented maneuvering. Of all present in the room, only Dane knew precisely what had occurred; Momed had advised her to expect this.

"Isolate those ships on the display," Nandes ordered. The images of the thirty ships involved were instantly duplicated away from the companies' formations, in an isolated spot above the War Table. "Reverse the sequence," Nandes said. The thirty motes stopped and began retracing their movements of recent seconds. As they drew closer to one another, a flash occurred at the center of the gap they'd created. The flash shrank in on itself until it too was seen as a ship.

"Reverse," Nandes ordered. The sequence presented itself as it had the first time, when all eyes but Dane's were averted. Now it was clear, and was confirmed by the incoming comm link, a woman's voice heard by all.

"Fleet Leader, this is XG390 Company, Lieutenant General Hopkis. One ship, *Brosie*, has detonated. Cause unknown. Repeat, cause unknown. We are *not* taking Enemy fire. Five ships damaged in the explosion. Two are disabled with significant personnel casualties."

"An accident," Mestoeffer replied. "Proceed as before, Hopkis."

"Understood, Fleet Leader. I'm dispatching four ships to retrieve the survivors. Estimated time to match velocities and roll rates, evacuate crews, one hour fifty minutes."

"No. That's too long. Proceed as before. We'll effect rescue when the situation permits."

"Fleet Leader, those ships report a loss of airtight integrity. They have a few hours, at most."

"Proceed as before, Hopkis, and do not argue—" Smothe squeezed her shoulders, and Mestoeffer looked around herself. The assembled officers were staring at her with stunned expressions. "Oh, very well," she said angrily. "But I authorize you one hour, no longer."

"Understood."

The link had no sooner been severed than Smothe said, "Now what?" He was pointing at the Gold Fleet unit, where the same events were repeating themselves. But instead of one mote disappearing in a sudden flash, there were three, all within two minutes. Again the ships surrounding the detonations moved away, many of them clearly out of control. Before anyone could speak, yet another Sovereign Command ship flashed and was gone.

"Hopkis, what are you *doing* out there?"

Shimas said, "I'm reestablishing the link now, Fleet Leader. There, go ahead."

"Hopkis—"

"I'm here, Fleet Leader. Another ship, *Sempas*, has—"

"We saw it! What is your explanation?"

"We're investigating now. But as you know, we're operating past maximum allowable. Under these circumstances, even a slight problem with those power plants could be enough to—"

Nandes said, "Cut your companies' speed to one-quarter, General. Take readings on all your ships' power plants. Report back in ten minutes." Allowing no time for Mestoeffer to override his order, he severed the connection and keyed the Fleetwide comm link. "All ships, functional stop." Then, turning to face her as *Dalkag* decelerated, he said, "Fleet Leader, these are standard precautions. And we don't want to overrun our own ships. We'll know more in ten minutes."

Mestoeffer had heard nothing of what he'd said. She was watching the display, tapping her fingers against the table. "I know what's going on," she said at last. "Why am I the only one to see it?" Looking up at Nandes as if surprised to find him there, she said, "First Adjutant, bring our ships to a stop. Have those companies decrease their speed and proceed with caution. I want reports from Hopkis. We'll need to know more as soon as possible."

Nandes remained where he was, embarrassed.

"Why are you standing there? Issue my orders!"

Nodding, he returned to the comm unit and repeated the orders he'd given less than a minute before.

"The Enemy unit has slowed also," Shimas reported.

"Good," Mestoeffer replied. Standing, she said, "First Adjutant, monitor the situation from here. Call me immediately with any change. I need privacy to consider this new development. Apparently *you* are going to be no help to me." Gesturing for Fotey Smothe to follow her, she left the Operations Room.

Shimas's voice was a startling break in the silence that followed Mestoeffer's abrupt departure. "At present speeds, First Adjutant, our advancing companies and the enemy unit will close to weapons' range in seven hours nineteen minutes."

"Very well." Addressing all present, Nandes said, "Stand down and take a rest. If there's no change in the situation, you'll have six hours. I advise you to sleep while you can.

Shimas, go with them. I'll need you fresh when the fun begins." He smiled. "Again."

Surprised at being singled out, Shimas said, "Yes, sir." It
was good to know that whatever Mestoeffer might feel, at
least her first adjutant considered his new role as battle advisor to be justified. Still, he longed to command Buto's
Bandits again. Where were the surviving forty-one ships?
That was where he belonged, not aboard *Dalkag* as a buffer
between Nandes and Mestoeffer. He wanted a new flagship, his unit brought back to full strength, and himself taking the fight into the heart of the Enemy—when the "fun"
started again.

Dane followed him out. She was grateful that she'd been
there to witness the last moments of five agents of The
Stem. For the rest of her life she would remember that
when their time came, five anonymous men and women
whose courage would never be known did not hesitate to
make the ultimate sacrifice. Their acts had caused both
Fleets to hesitate, and in so doing may have prevented a
victory by the Gold Fleet—a victory that must be won by
neither side. It was fitting that a witness be there to mark
their passing.

She turned her thoughts to what she'd just seen in the
face of Brotman Nandes. There was every reason to believe
that if he lived one more day, Arlana Mestoeffer would not.

# ⇒**27**⇐

## DAY TWO—Preparation

"Sabotage?"

"Yes, Fleet Leader," Nandes said. "A large portion of *Brosie*'s power plant has been recovered and examined. There is evidence of a sudden overload. Normally, as you know, the plant would simply reduce its operation to within safe margins. But in this case we suspect that the shutoffs and overrides were deliberately prevented from functioning, by manual jamming in advance of the overload."

Sitting at her stateroom desk, Mestoeffer's posture showed fatigue. Her face was worn and drawn. "You *suspect?*"

"Yes. The unit was shattered, of course, and nearly melted down in the explosion. Not enough of it was intact to conduct a complete reconstruction of what happened. But evidence points to sabotage, as I believe occurred on *Cantal*. Additionally, we know from our last report from the council that the same thing may be happening on ships currently assigned to supply runs. The points of similarity are—"

"You're boring me, Nandes. *Cantal* was a minor incident, and not sabotage. The council has concluded that a negligent head of engineering was at fault, and I concur. She is no longer a problem. As for the ships on supply runs, they can deal with their own incompetence. Now, regarding *Brosie*. 'Evidence' and what you may 'suspect' do not account for what happened. We lost two ships in a matter of minutes. The Enemy lost three. It is not remotely possible

that all five were simultaneous acts of sabotage. What officer would destroy a ship as it was preparing for battle? In-
sanity might explain one such occurrence. Not *five*, in *both*
Fleets. A more reasonable explanation, as I suspected immediately and have now concluded, is that a new weapon
exists. The Enemy's losses suggest that it is not yet perfected. Apparently as the weapon was employed, it detonated. What is your response to that, Nandes?"

"Fleet Leader, General Hopkis was very specific in her
initial report. Her ships were not being fired upon."

"Not by anything she was familiar with, you mean. I've
explained to you what happened. I expect you to tell me
how we can adapt."

Nandes was caught by surprise. What Mestoeffer was
suggesting seemed impossible, even laughable. But as he
thought about it, he realized that it was her, more than the
idea she presented, that he was so ready to reject. Every
major advance in weaponry had seemed impossible at one
time, and had been met with initial disbelief by those it was
used against. He recalled that within the past century alone,
weapons' range had nearly quadrupled. Was it so unreason-
able to believe that the Enemy was on the brink of a new
step forward? No. And if that were true, then Mestoeffer's
explanation of events made strange, but plausible sense.
There could be, then, only one response. "We have no
choice, obviously. If this weapon exists and is not yet perfected, we cannot allow the Enemy additional time. I recommend that we pull in our flanks and order an immediate
full-Fleet attack."

Mestoeffer shook her head. "You're offering an opinion
before you've considered all factors. As usual. When will
you learn to think like the Enemy? Consider this: Having
this new capability, what is the best way to lure us into a
reckless attack? The best way is to do exactly what they've
done. Fire the weapon to demonstrate its existence. At the
same time provide evidence that it's still in development. I
would wager that those three ships they 'lost' were old
shells, with no one aboard. By this deception we are invited

to conclude, as you did, that an 'immediate attack' is the only solution. That could be a disaster."

"I respectfully disagree, Fleet Leader. If greater range is the only advantage—"

"On the other hand, the new weapon may *be* unstable. If so, then *waiting* would be disastrous."

"Either we attack or we don't," Nandes said, tired of her insults and irritated at her dismissive tone toward him. Obviously, she'd made her decision. "Which do you recommend?"

"I don't 'recommend,' First Adjutant. I command. How long before our companies are in range of that Enemy unit? I refer to the *old* limit, of course."

"One hour eleven minutes, Fleet Leader."

"And how far beyond that unit do you estimate the main force of the Enemy is?"

"Six hours minimum from us, or our advance ships would have them in view by now. My best guess is eight to twelve hours."

"Good. It is time for us to do something bold, something they cannot possibly be expecting."

"Time for . . . ?" With a sudden insight, Nandes understood what she had in mind. "Fleet Leader, you're talking about *five thousand ships*. We can't do that!"

"Not all of them, Nandes. Three thousand ships, three companies. General Hopkis can decide which two to retain, and which three to send. If you're right about the Enemy's location, they can enter hyperspace and—"

"And come out of it scattered, surrounded by sixty-five Enemy ships to their one. Fleet Leader, it would be another six hours before they could enter hyperspace again. They wouldn't last six minutes in that environment."

"They'll last long enough to inflict damage, and to deliver our message. That we also have a new long-range weapon. It's called 'daring.'"

"It's called 'suicide.' We might want to send in three or four, to send us back a picture of their formations. But three thousand? That's insane!"

"Nandes, you forget who I am! My tactic will confuse them. A confused enemy makes mistakes."

*If so, you're* criminally *confused*, Nandes thought. His mind raged. For all of his career he'd been able to accept bad orders and to somehow make them right. This time . . . this time there was *no* time. How many ships had he ordered into certain death? Over the decades, hundreds. How many had been unnecessary? None. Not one. Once again, Mestoeffer had plunged him into a moral dilemma. This was something he could not do. And yet if he refused to relay her order, he would lose his commission—and his life. He would no longer stand between Mestoeffer and the calamity she was certain to bring down on all of them. Drawing in a deep breath to steady his anger, he said, "Fleet Leader, I urge you in the most urgent and respectful terms to reconsider. The deliberate sacrifice of three thousand ships, for nothing, would devastate the morale of this Fleet. And if I may speak bluntly, it would also weigh heavily against you with the council."

Mestoeffer's eyes widened. "How dare you threaten me!"

"I mean no threat, Fleet Leader. As your second in command, it's my duty to give you my best appraisal of the situation. I'm telling you that all of us, including you, would be harmed by this." He could not stop his hands from tensing.

"Then you refuse my order?" Mestoeffer felt trapped. The thought of having to explain herself to the council was deeply disturbing. Suppose they didn't understand? They weren't here, facing the problem *she* was facing. And she knew that Hivad Sepal would attempt to characterize an ingenious tactic as a mistake—as Nandes was doing now. She was well aware of the treasonous grumbling that had occurred after she'd sent out an additional twelve thousand scouts to locate the Gold Fleet. But that had had a measurable effect, and most had returned safely. This was not so easy to quantify. With no precedent to cite, she could well have a difficult time convincing the council that spreading confusion within the Enemy had been worth three thousand ships. Yes, her ascension to the Generals could well be jeopardized. And yet . . . if she yielded to this present threat by Nandes, she could expect other threats to follow; her ability to command would be diminished. And that, also, would reach the council. So be it, then! This command was hers . . . "I ask you again, Nandes," she said icily. "Do you refuse my order?"

His mother had once told him that an officer who sacrifices honor for victory is worthy of neither. He'd never questioned the truth of those words. But he was no longer dealing with the honor or victory of Brotman Nandes; this was the survival of Sovereign Command itself. If she refused to accept the compromise he was about to offer . . . "Fleet Leader," he said carefully, "I don't believe you've issued an order."

"No," she said, "I have not. And you have not advised me what we can do about this new weapon. Other than to launch a suicidal attack."

He felt a moment's relief. Whether she'd recognized it as such or not, she'd accepted his compromise. And, in typical fashion, had turned it into a personal insult. "I still recommend the attack. The weapon, if it exists, has no advantage other than enhanced range. That advantage will cease to exist when we close to our own weapons' range."

A light above the stateroom comm unit came on, accompanied by the sound of the buzzer. "Yes?" Mestoeffer responded.

"Fleet Leader, the Enemy unit has stopped."

Nandes asked, "Merely stopped? They are not retreating?"

"No, First Adjutant. General Hopkis requests instructions."

"Tell her to hold her position," Mestoeffer said. "Report any further changes to me—to *me*—immediately."

"Yes, Fleet Leader."

"Nandes," she said, "we may have a respite. I have exhausted myself, and intend to sleep. You will give further thought to your recommendation, and be ready to advise me when I return to the Operations Room. I want something worthwhile from you next time. For once. Is that too much to expect?" She would not allow him to answer. "If it is, report to the nearest airlock and let us all be rid of you. Now go, you're dismissed."

Nandes entered the Operations Room, deathly fatigued. He had never been so close to mutiny—to murder—in his life. His hands still trembled. He could not say what he'd have done if Mestoeffer had ordered those ships sacrificed. He realized, now, just how low he'd come. Aside from eliminating his worth as an officer, she'd pushed him beyond the ability to predict his own behavior. He had become, like the new weapon that might or might not exist, unstable . . . unreliable . . . a danger to his own Fleet. Standing quietly in the doorway and observing the assembled officers speaking among themselves, so calmly and confidently, he acknowledged that he was no longer fit to serve them as first adjutant. He knew that they should have helped him more, when Mestoeffer was so clearly in error. Only Shimas had. But that also was his own failure; they did not help him because he had not given them the leadership they needed, and deserved. He watched them for several minutes as from a great distance, missing his wife and sons more than he had ever before in the twenty-seven years they'd been dead.

Close by in the huge compartment and unnoticed, Dane studied the first adjutant's posture and facial expression. She saw a man at the very edge, and had tracked him successfully enough to understand. The opposing concepts of duty fighting one another in his mind were so powerful that he could no longer control them. And both were so much a part of him that he could not allow either to lose.

Whatever he did now was beyond her ability to influence. But she realized that it made no difference. If he allowed Mestoeffer to continue in command, he would go mad with guilt. If he assassinated her, his brilliance would mean nothing to the Fleet; for again, he would go mad. Whatever he did, he was lost. Momed Pwanda had taught her that some of these people did have a sense of honor.

The first adjutant's was fatally strong. It was that sense of honor that, as she watched the dimming of proud eyes and the disintegration of a warrior's soul, killed Brotman Nandes.

With a sadness she did not want to feel she watched him turn and leave the room. He was the first senior casualty of the battle.

"When does the game start?" the Nomarch asked impatiently. In each of his thin hands was a figurine: a flat-oval gold replica in his right, and a larger, silver-domed model in his left. Both were mangled where he'd banged them together. At the foot of his chair was a box filled with reinforcements.

"That is a good question, Nomarch," No'ln Beviney said. "May I be excused to go and find out?"

To her vast relief he said, "Yes. But first give this Nomarch some more ships. They break too much."

"They certainly do," Beviney answered reflectively. "And too unpredictably."

"Is that a funny word?"

"No, Nomarch. It is not."

"This Nomarch understands. When are you going to find out about the game?"

Beviney gave him two fresh figurines and left the room. She trotted through three connecting corridors leading to the Battle Control Center, hoping the pace would help to revive her. Supervisors and crew alike emulated her running when she came into view; all wanted her to know that they too were on urgent business.

The nerve center of *Noldron*'s command and control capabilities was darkened when she arrived, as it always was. At intervals in the ceiling were soft red lights that cast an eerie glow onto the personnel and instrument consoles spread throughout the compartment. The distinctive lighting served no practical function; it was traditional, dating from a time and reflecting a purpose that history no longer recorded. Beviney found it comforting. This was the one place on *Noldron* that she did not need to worry about

being interrupted by the Nomarch; he was terrified of the
darkness and "those strange-looking people who live in
there."

Rubbing her eyes to clear them, she glanced up toward
the overhead status-board to see that nothing had changed
in the four hours since she'd last been here. All that could
be seen were the nine hundred ships she'd sent out as
scouts, and the five thousand opposing Silver Fleet ships.
All were motionless, about one hour out of normal
weapons' range from each other. She assumed that the Silver Fleet was stopped for the same reason she was. In the
space of a few minutes she'd seen three of her own ships
disappear, and two of the Enemy. She assumed also that the
Enemy had ordered as many interrogations and hangings of
ships' personnel as she had. *I hope they're having the same
luck we are*, she thought tiredly. *None.*

"No'ln Beviney!"

She turned at the enthusiastic greeting to see Momed
Pwanda sitting at a position-display table far to her left.
Across from him were five supervisors, all studying the
table surface, too intent to notice her presence.

"Come join us!" As she approached the table Pwanda explained, "I've reinvented the game again. Now it's possible
for up to six sides to play. But," he said, grinning, "I don't
think it's fair for all of them to band together against me."

"You're winning, I assume?" Beviney asked.

"So far," Pwanda replied. "You're not going to help
them, are you?"

Beviney could see that the game was far advanced.
Pwanda had seventeen ships remaining from a beginning
roster of thirty. He was facing a total of fifty-one, which
were split into five groups and attempting to penetrate his
solid defenses. It was obvious that the five forces needed a
single leadership if they hoped to win. She was tempted to
assume that role, and remove the self-confident smile from
Momed's lips. But instead she motioned him to go ahead as
before. As minutes passed and he claimed more game
pieces, an odd coincidence came to her mind: Pwanda's
forces had been outnumbered five to one at the beginning

of the game. Just as her own scouts were outnumbered by the Enemy.

She continued watching, nearly gasping at times as she saw him take moves she could not have predicted, only to see them proved correct, time after time. How, she wondered, do I ever beat this man? Of course, she was tired now; her perception was not what it normally was. But for the first time it occurred to her that Momed Pwanda was even more cunning than she'd imagined. Not only at the game itself, but at choosing when to lose. The thought angered her, but the anger died quickly. How could she fault him? It was natural for him to be afraid of her, as any Dirt would be. Or anyone else. As proof, the Enemy had sent five thousand ships to meet her nine hundred. An overwhelming force.

Or so they believed.

Impulsively, she reached down and ran her fingers along the table's control console. The game pieces vanished, along with the grid that Momed had put there. The five supervisors shouted angrily until one of them looked up and realized with a start who it was who'd shut down the game. "No'ln Beviney!" the man said, as all five snapped to attention.

Beviney said, "Move away. And watch carefully."

Hoping that he hadn't been too obvious, Pwanda continued the game he'd been playing with Beviney all along, a game not of ships, but of minds. "A match, No'ln Beviney? Between us?"

"No," she said, adjusting the controls again. "We've waited long enough for something more interesting." As she spoke, the table came to life again. "This is a real-time display in three dimensions. Nine hundred of us facing five thousand Enemy. Your little game is over, Momed Pwanda. It's time to show me what you can *really* do."

# ⇛28⇐

## DAY THREE—Promotion

Arlana Mestoeffer arrived in *Dalkag*'s Operations Room
out of breath, pulling Fotey Smothe by the hand behind her.
Her eyes went immediately to the display above the War
Table. "How long ago did this begin?"

"Seven minutes, Fleet Leader," Buto Shimas said. "Four
seconds before I called you."

"Who asked you to . . . where is that useless Nandes?"

"The first adjutant is ill," Shimas answered, appalled by
her language. "The doctors say that he is not responding to
any—"

"Never mind. How long until those ships close to effective range?"

"Nineteen minutes seventeen seconds, if they don't slow
again. There is still no sign of the Enemy main body."

"I can see that," Mestoeffer said, taking her seat at the
table's head. She touched her shoulders, and immediately
Fotey Smothe began massaging them. "Very well. Order
the five companies to full engagement speed. No, wait!
This could be a trap. We'll wait to see how close they
come."

"Our ships are stopped," Shimas reminded her. "They'll
need a good speed to coordinate their maneuvering."

"Yes. Yes, they will. But I don't trust the Enemy . . .
very well, order them to one-quarter speed."

"Twelve minutes eleven seconds to range," Shimas said
at once. His pulse quickened in anticipation as he watched
the silver motes accelerate. Almost immediately, the oppos-

ing gold forces responded with an increase in their own speed. The killing was about to begin. At last! "Fleet Leader, I recommend at this time that we call in our flanks, and order a general advance."

"Now? No, not yet. We'll see what happens first."

"Our center is vulnerable to a full attack, as you and the first adjutant have discussed. I believe the Enemy will be shortly behind those ships."

"Don't be stupid, Shimas. I've already told you that this could be a trap. If it is, we will not be caught in it. If it is not, those five companies won't need our help."

"Fleet Leader, it's vital—"

"Quiet!"

At their last meeting, Dane had deferred to Momed Pwanda's grasp of war strategies and tactics in the battle formulations they'd discussed. But her own understanding had been growing over the weeks, aided by the access Jarred Marsham had given her to his mother's notes and essays from past battles. She could see that Mestoeffer was making an elementary mistake, one Jarred himself was prone to make in his simulations: forces spread too thin and wide, unable to support one another quickly. Like Jarred, Mestoeffer showed a deep fear of being encircled by Enemy formations. Also like him, she was too willing to ignore the obvious in order to defend against the unlikely. Dane decided it was time to call on Fotey Smothe again.

But as she attempted to catch his attention, she was distracted by a sudden change in the Gold Fleet advance. Instead of coming at them as a forward-pointing pyramid—a three-dimensional wedge—the ships had formed up into a single, vertical column.

"What is that?" Fotey Smothe cried out.

Mestoeffer said, "It's the new weapon! They're all going to fire at once!"

But even as she was speaking the odd formation broke apart and the Gold Fleet ships resumed their previous positions.

Dane felt as if her body were electrified. Even as she'd

seen and recognized the sign, she had difficulty believing . . . but it had to be.

"Like a cobra ready to strike," Fotey Smothe muttered, and instantly regretted the mistake. "I've read about them, I mean . . ."

No one but Dane was paying attention to him.

*Or a stem*, she thought excitedly. Momed! He'd boasted that when the Fleets met, he would let her know where he was. *"Remember the sign."* What she'd seen could not be an accident, or a coincidence. Momed Pwanda was aboard one of those ships. And telling her that the Gold Fleet would follow his plan for the final battle. She allowed herself a rare, unguarded smile. Her partner had succeeded in doing the impossible. Now it was her turn.

Looking at Shimas, she saw the officer's frustration. And was pleased. This was a time to let Mestoeffer be Mestoeffer.

"Would you explain to me, Momed, what that was about?"

"I'm testing the controls, No'ln Beviney. They do respond quickly, don't they?"

"Of course they do. The ships are set for remote guidance override, and they believe that I'm controlling them. But I warn you not to overuse it. Remember, you're not *there*. Set the formations, and change them as you need to. But let the individual ships maneuver and fire within the formations as *they* need to. And if they break to run for hyperspace, do not interfere. I'm curious about you, but not enough to waste nine hundred ships."

"I understand. Three minutes forty seconds to range."

"I can read, Momed. Concentrate on what you're doing. Forget that I'm here until I push you off that chair."

In the vanguard of the Gold Fleet were forty ships whose other capabilities had been diminished to attain greater weapons' range. These fired together, a full two minutes before entering Silver Fleet range. They concentrated their lethal energy on ten second-echelon ships of Sovereign

Command. Within thirty seconds all ten targets were reduced to speeding shrapnel, damaging nearby vessels as they maneuvered to avoid the sudden maelstrom.

Responding to Pwanda's control, these same forty broke away from the others and retreated to a relative position that would keep them within that two-minute safety zone. Again they fired together, and ten more second-echelon ships of Sovereign Command erupted into deadly debris.

The Silver Fleet dispatched two squadrons of one hundred ships each to go after the forty long-distance snipers. Exactly as Pwanda had hoped.

The instant the two squadrons formed up together and were clear of the rest, eighty speed-enhanced Gold Fleet ships went to their new maximum normal-space drive and speared into them. Armed hummingbirds among eagles, he'd thought of them when he planned this attack. And so they were. Too fast and maneuverable to be handled with traditional methods of intercept and destroy, the eighty ships passed cleanly through the combined squadrons in a fraction of a second, lashing out on all sides before reversing course and stabbing through again. A third pass met with more resistance as the Silver Fleet ships closed up to present the hummingbirds with an impenetrable wall of eagle flesh. But again, maneuverability triumphed. The Gold Fleet ships seemed to turn at right angles as they found gaps in the closing ships and plunged through them. They departed the trap at full speed, having lost eleven. Sovereign Command's casualties were thirty-three killed, seventy-four damaged and dropping away from the formation; in effect, more than a full squadron was lost.

But Momed Pwanda was not finished with them yet.

As the speeding hummingbirds streaked away to safety, the long-range shooters went to work again, even as they were pursued and saw their two-minute margin of safety reduced to one. Ten more Sovereign Command vessels erupted in as many seconds, followed almost immediately by ten more.

At that moment the three-dimensional wedge, consisting now of seven hundred eighty ships facing six times its number in a headlong rush, turned away—eighty-three seconds before the Sovereign Command vessels could begin effective fire. Forty more snipers formed at the rear of the retreating Gold Fleet phalanx and poured maximum energy into ten, then ten more, and ten more pursuing ships.

Slower than their comrades and unable to keep pace, these forty dropped away and raced toward an area not yet contested. At Pwanda's signaled command they ceased firing, hoping to be ignored in the melee long enough to complete their mission or, if necessary, escape into hyperspace. Already prepared, they needed only a few minutes. But another two squadrons, fresh and unbloodied, turned and raced for them.

"Forget them!" Mestoeffer shouted into the comm unit. "General . . . General . . ."

"Hopkis," Buto Shimas said.

"Hopkis! Hopkis, you're losing! Forget all those stragglers and concentrate on *them*." With both hands she pointed at the larger concentration of fleeing Gold Fleet motes.

"Which ones, Fleet Leader?" came the calm reply.

From behind Mestoeffer, Shimas said, "General Hopkis, the Fleet Leader is indicating the main body of Enemy ships."

"Understood." Four seconds later the two squadrons, and the ships chasing after the first snipers, changed course again.

Watching the display, Shimas winced at the elementary mistake Mestoeffer was committing. The five companies could easily afford to detach those ships long enough to engage and destroy over one hundred Enemy stragglers. But they could not afford to allow those stragglers to remain alive as they passed them. Once between the five companies and the main body of the Fleet, those ships would be free to come farther in, to discover and report back their complete formations. "Fleet Leader, I recommend—"

"Casualties, Shimas?"

"One hundred three lost, one hundred eighty-eight badly damaged and unable to continue. Enemy casualties, eleven lost."

"Disgraceful! Even you could do a better job."

Ignoring the remark, Shimas said, "If I may, we can't allow those stragglers to be bypassed. I recommend—"

"The Sphere, Shimas. That was your tactic, wasn't it? General Hopkis is familiar with it, isn't she?"

"Yes. I agree, Fleet Leader. When we've overtaken them—"

"We can't wait that long. Order it now."

Taken by surprise, Shimas said, "Fleet Leader, we can't use the Sphere at this time. We haven't overtaken any Enemy ships."

"I said now!"

Shimas looked around at the other officers there, all greatly senior to himself, and all as aware as he was that this was a wasteful maneuver that could accomplish nothing. None of them met his eye, or spoke out.

Mestoeffer pounded the War Table. "I said now! *Now!*" Suddenly her face turned red, and she gripped her throat with both hands. "Aaah . . . aach . . ." She could manage no more than a whispered croak.

"Her voice!" Fotey Smothe said, alarmed. "You have destroyed her voice again!"

Mestoeffer pushed herself back from the War Table and stood. She pointed at the displayed ships and moved her hands emphatically, describing a sphere.

"I understand," Shimas said, seizing the initiative. "Get them all." Ignoring her further attempts to give the order, he turned and walked to a mounted comm console. "General Hopkis," he said, opening the link, "the Fleet Leader orders you to pursue those ships that have broken away. Do not allow any of them to pass you."

"Understood," came the relieved reply.

Mestoeffer was shaking her head, circulating among her personal staff and pulling at the uniforms of one officer after another. The few who spoke repeated Shimas's initial reply, assuring her that General Hopkis would get them all. Bright red with frustration, she glared at them, and then looked beseechingly at Fotey Smothe. "Yes, dear one," he said quietly. "I'll take you to a doctor at once." And caught her, as she fainted into his arms.

Momed Pwanda saw the Silver Fleet ships turning again toward his slower units and let go a long breath. He had no choice now, and ordered them into hyperspace. With silent thanks.

Standing next to him, No'ln Beviney nodded. "It's a shame, Momed. You almost did it. Another half-hour and we'd have slipped them past the Enemy."

"Thank you, No'ln Beviney. It was worth the try." He'd wanted to impress her, and had. But he'd nearly been too successful. Before they found all of the Silver Fleet, he needed to be more firmly in command of the Gold. As he'd said in his "letter" to Dane, Beviney was formidable. She might lack skill in the game he'd invented, but she'd never lost a battle with real ships.

Surprising him not at all, she took over the controls and ordered the remaining ships to run for hyperspace as well. "That was brilliant work," she said. "You destroyed or badly damaged nearly three hundred Enemy ships, from the five thousand sent against us."

During the next few minutes the Gold Fleet lost four more vessels as they broke away from the battle and disappeared from all displays. "Phenomenal," Beviney said, turning off the table. "Our total cost was fifteen. And some of them could have been from their own engineering mistakes. Phenomenal."

Pwanda was satisfied. His only reservation was the possibility that Dane Steppart had been aboard one of the three hundred. But her location was not something he could know, or take into consideration.

"Momed, how are you feeling?"

"Tired, but exhilarated."

"Can you remain here for a few more hours?"

"Certainly."

"Good. I want you to set up the final battle orders for my review. Exactly as we . . . " Beviney smiled. "All right, exactly as *you* planned."

"I will. Thank you for the honor."

"You've earned it. For now, I feel a long, deep sleep coming on. The best in a very long time. Thank you, Momed. Call me if you need me. Oh, and send out another thousand ships. Same composition as before."

"Yes, No'ln Beviney."

As the other supervisors gawked in amazement, she kissed his forehead and left the Battle Control Center.


The voice was barely a whisper. "Shimas?"

"I'm here, Fleet Leader. One thousand Enemy ships have appeared on the display. They're holding their positions, as we're holding ours. Still no sighting of the—"

Mestoeffer waved him to silence. She was lying in her bed, covered by a thick blanket. Aromatic lavender towels covered her eyes and throat. She looked little better than Brotman Nandes had three hours before, when Shimas had gone to pay his respects. He'd found the first adjutant sitting in his stateroom chair, looking upward, his eyes vacant and lifeless. Only his lips moved; there was no sound.

"I . . . I . . ." Mestoeffer's voice was gone again.

"Shall I?" Fotey Smothe asked, standing beside his patron. Mestoeffer nodded. "The Fleet Leader has sent the following dispatch to the council," he said. "Begin text. 'I have been informed that without my knowledge, two of my senior staff have forwarded to the council a report of a recent incident, message reference number as indicated below. That report is erroneous. I hereby correct the record.' She goes on, sir, to record the times and date involved, the message reference number, and the names of her fellow council members to whom this was sent."

Shimas nodded.

Smothe cleared his throat and resumed. "Continuing text. 'The incident in question began when I offered a jest regarding the employment of a tactic which was inappropriate at that time. The record will note that I did so in order to ease the tension in the Operations Room, which in my judgment was unacceptably high. Only one officer, a squadron leader serving as temporary advisor, understood my intention and replied in the same vein. I regret to say that the other officers in attendance did not have the presence of mind to understand the humor of the situation. And yet they offered no objection to what would certainly have been a tactical error. I will not state they were nearing panic; that is not my area of expertise. But I do state that their reaction was shocking, and would have offended any reasonable and competent officer.

" 'Further: At that critical moment I suffered the recurrence of an injury which had come about from severe strain and overwork. Three physicians have testified to the following, and their reports are included with this text: that this injury and its recurrence resulted from my staff's failure to provide the assistance and support necessary to carry out the duties I have assumed on behalf of the council. Further: Following my incapacitation and in my absence, my senior staff allowed an inferior force of Enemy ships to inflict heavy casualties upon five of our companies, and then to escape. Further: One or more of my senior staff has caused the monitor tapes of the entire incident to be purged from the memory of this flagship.' " Smothe looked up at Shimas. Seeing no reaction, he continued. " 'Therefore, for causes enumerated and pending investigations into charges of incompetence, conspiracy, and treason, all of my former senior staff are incarcerated under guard.

" 'I regret to report to you, Generals and fellow council members, that First Adjutant Brotman Nandes is gravely ill and is not expected to regain his former capacities. I therefore appoint to assume his duties and authority an officer whom I personally elevated from the lower ranks and trained to be my advisor. Former Squadron Leader Buto Shimas, service number as provided following text, has agreed to assume the permanent rank of major general and to fulfill the duties of first adjutant, effective with the transmission of this message. Company Leader Jenny Marsham, service number as provided after text, has accepted equal rank, with time of elevation one minute prior to that of her husband.' End of text."

Smothe set the message down. "I am to ask you, First Adjutant, if you have questions at this time. Or would you prefer to wait until the Fleet Leader is able to answer you without further injury to herself?"

"No questions," Shimas said. "Thank you, Fleet Leader. I'll be in the Operations Room." More than at the dizzying elevation in rank and duties—with Jenny still senior, as they both wanted—he was gratified that Mestoeffer had come to realize what he'd been pondering for the past five hours: that using the Sphere at that time would have been ridiculous, but was not itself the issue. What mattered was that not one of her senior staff had offered her a word of counsel about it. He was not comfortable with his complicity in her lie, but the message had been sent already; his only alternative to accepting the new position was to join those officers under incarceration. In his mind, their fate was well deserved. Their behavior had been inexcusable. No matter how intimidated they might have been by Mestoeffer, they'd owed her the benefit of their collective and individual experience. That was their job; they'd accepted the privileges, but not the responsibilities. They had done nothing for her. Nor had they once risked a word of support for Brotman Nandes. For them, he had neither respect nor pity.

After he'd gone, Arlana Mestoeffer removed the towels from her eyes and throat. She gestured for Smothe to come closer and took his hand. "You were right," she said in a bare whisper. "Shimas and Marsham are the only ones I can trust now. Those others would have been only too happy to see me make a mistake, and laugh about it later. Traitors!"

"Traitors indeed, dear one."

"But as you said, Marsham is terrified for her son. And Shimas will do nothing to jeopardize either of them. And he did save me from an embarrassing error. Terago, you are more valuable to me than I ever realized."

"Thank you, Arlana," he said, delighting at the sound of his real name, used for the first time in seven years. Bending down to kiss her forehead, he yelped as she squeezed his hand powerfully.

"But tell me again, dear one, why you left my side for twenty minutes to speak with that young female attendant. Was it really about my birthday? Or, as you grow older, do you miss the companionship of Grounders?"

For his own life as well as Dane's, he put on his best hurt-and-shocked expression. "Arlana, really!"

# ⇥29⇤

## DAY FOUR—Confrontation

Dane Steppart returned from checking on Brotman Nandes and was cleaning the stateroom of Jenny Marsham and Buto Shimas when she stumbled suddenly in the center of the compartment. She crossed the room unsteadily and sat at Marsham's desk.

Aware of the monitors watching and recording her every move, she closed her eyes and imagined a pleasurable warmth filling her as she created a mental image of her mother. She concentrated, calling forth emotion as if she were in an actual dream. For success, her plan required that she deceive the monitors—and to some extent herself, as well. There was a good chance that she would later be interrogated about this incident. If so, she needed part of her mind to believe that the experience had been genuine. It was not difficult. After a few moments the thoughts and emotions seemed very real.

In Dane's "dream" Linda looked good, despite circles under her eyes that told of fatigue, and new wrinkles around them that told of too much worry. Dane imagined her mother as appearing thinner than she'd been in years. But as she would in reality, Linda smiled when confronted with concern about her health; she said there was nothing like a War every few centuries to test a person's stamina. That familiar laughter, clear and hearty, assured Dane that as much as could be hoped for, her mother was doing well. The deception was working. Dane found herself believing in part that she was somehow linked to her mother. But she needed to make it more real, with more depth. She concentrated even harder. Now she imagined them speaking of her older brother Alfred; of hearing that he was safely home again and working too hard, and once again thinking of politics as a career; of old friends and the Hardaway farm; of a beautiful, warm smile and her mother saying that very soon they would be sharing a special dinner to celebrate Dane's last birthday; of Linda saying at last that she had to return to work.

The "dream" was working. The tears streaming down her cheeks came naturally as she watched her mother go. It was time for Dane to move on, as well.

Now she imagined herself sitting in the middle of *Dalkag*'s War Table. Jenny Marsham and Buto Shimas were standing together next to it, holding hands. Believing the dream more and more, she saw that they were deeply worried; their concern was visible in the way they looked at one another, and then looked above her where a hemisphere of blackness should be. There was nothing there at all. Even the normal Operations Room lighting was gone. In its place was a grayness that stretched beyond *Dalkag* and so far into the distance that she knew there was no end to it. Dane looked through her imagination down at her attendant's uniform of the same grayness, and saw it begin to collapse inward. With an eerie sense of calm she understood that the uniform was empty; she was no longer in it. She raised her hands to her face and couldn't see them. Shimas and Marsham were staring at something in their hands, mouths agape. Both said *"How?"* without making a sound.

Losing herself in the performance, Dane "watched" as the pervasive grayness lowered to cover the two officers, and they were gone. *No!* she thought with a start—the grayness had not come down; she was rising into it. So empty was the color that engulfed her, she could not know if her vision was measured in inches or light-years. Everything there was, was nothing.

And then it began.

In Dane's mind the nothing slowly became everything again, and everything was blackness. Soon, there was depth. Infinite depth with stars as she had never seen them, surrounding her, blinding her, all rushing toward her so fast that she knew she must move out of the way or be killed. But she had no self to move. When it seemed that she must be consumed in their fire, the stars veered away. Half went to her left and half went to her right. They came to a stop to form starscapes that glittered with color. To her left, gold. To her right, silver.

She had a body again. And weight. She plunged, spinning end over end, into the cluster of silver stars. Toward one in particular. She braced for an impact that never came.

Dane snapped her eyes open. She clung to the desk as the stateroom walls tumbled together and fit themselves into position around her. She was shaking, perspiring heavily, pale, dizzy, and only dimly aware for the time being that everything she had just experienced had come directly from her imagination. Perfect.

One of Marsham's folders dropped from her lap as she stood slowly, letting the dizziness pass. When it was gone she bent and lifted the folder from the floor. And stared, mouth agape, at a drawing she'd made on it. There was another one, quite different, on the other side. Without making a sound she raised her face to the ceiling above one of the monitors and said, *"How?"*

With the report folder in hand she left the stateroom, satisfied that under interrogation, a part of her mind would believe that what the monitors had just recorded had been spontaneous, and not the first step in the greatest deception she had ever attempted.

Lieutenant General Harriet Hopkis sipped tea and watched the thousand gold motes above her War Table. Their formation was the same as before, a forward-pointing pyramid. As she opened the comm link to deliver an hourly status report to the new first adjutant, four of the Gold Fleet ships broke formation and streaked directly toward her companies.

"Yes, General Hopkis," came the voice of Buto Shimas. "I see them. What are your thoughts on those four?"

"I assume they're the new type, with the long-range capability. I'll dispatch . . . *Whoa!* Did you see that?"

"Hyperspace," Shimas replied.

"Agreed. I've been expecting them to do this. But why did they wait until we could see them?"

"A challenge, I suppose. Are you ready to respond?"

"Yes, sir. I have seven volunteers. Officers and crews were unanimous in every case."

"Use only the first two, General. And send me the personnel files of everyone aboard."

"I'm giving the order now. Dispatching ships *Wendal* and *Venor.*"

"Understood."

Both officers watched on their respective War Tables as two ships of Sovereign Command came to full speed and, minutes later, disappeared. In a short time the two would leave hyperspace and do their best to survive for a few minutes. With luck, that would be long enough to send back a full picture of the Gold Fleet's main formations.

Buto Shimas called down this new information to Mestoeffer. "She heard you, sir," Fotey Smothe said when the brief report was complete. "And she agrees with your recommendation. Have the flanks begin closing in on us now at standard maneuvering speed."

"Understood." Shimas turned to Jenny Marsham, who was already issuing the order.

Around them were seven officers. With the exception of Jarred Marsham, all were newly appointed to their personal staff. One of these, Giel Hormat, wore a new insignia of rank that still felt strange to her; the jump from lieutenant to colonel had come as a shock. It gave her an understanding of how Shimas must have felt, rising from squadron leader to major general in the space of a heartbeat. Wasn't war wonderful?

Hormat was standing at the controls of the War Table. She was anxious to change the display to depict the entire Fleet, so that she could see the four Gold Fleet ships appear from hyperspace. Would they be caught in time? Probably not; not all four. Even with every ship in the Fleet alerted and waiting, it was likely that at least one would come out at the proper distance and survive for the few minutes needed to gather the intelligence it was after and broadcast it back to the Gold Fleet.

Within hours, she thought excitedly, the real killing would begin.

Minutes later, Hormat was the first to see the attendant enter the Operations Room. Aware of the special status and privilege of immediate access the young woman had with Shimas and Marsham, she asked politely, "Is something wrong, CJ? You don't look well." The attendant nodded toward her but said nothing, to Hormat's displeasure. Was she expected to accept insolence from a Grounder?

Dane offered the report folder she was carrying to Shimas. "Sir, would you look at this?"

"CJ," he said brusquely, "this is not a good time. Is it important?"

"I believe it is, sir."

"Very well." He accepted the folder and looked at it. "Dots and squares," he said irritably. "Here, take this with you and report to a doctor. That concussion . . ." He stopped suddenly and looked more closely at what she'd given him. "How . . .? It's been hours since . . . Where did this come from?"

"From me, sir. I drew it ten minutes ago. I saw this in a dream. Is it accurate?"

Marsham took the folder from her husband's hand and studied it, raising her eyebrows. "Colonel Hormat," she said, "change the display. Full presentation."

Instantly the entire Silver Fleet seemed to be hovering over the War Table, in miniature.

"Back it up ten minutes," Shimas said.

The companies of silver motes that had been moving relative to the rest reversed themselves and came to a stop. Marsham looked at the display, and down to the folder, then back again as Shimas did the same.

"She's even got the flanks in the right position," Marsham said, passing the report cover back to Shimas. "They'd just started to move ten minutes ago!"

"CJ," Shimas said, "you couldn't possibly have seen this from our stateroom, even if you switched on the screen. The display here has been centered on our advance ships for hours. Wait! Did you open up a link to another ship's War Table?"

"No, sir," she said truthfully. She hoped fervently that no one would think to check the monitors in Brotman Nandes's stateroom; she'd been able to use his own small War Table successfully, but was not certain that she'd shut down all the monitors first; the former first adjutant had rewired the room not long ago. Pressing ahead before they could think of all the possibilities, she asked Shimas, "Would you look there," she said, pointing, "on the other side?"

Turning the folder over, Shimas gaped. "Are you trying to tell me that this . . . this is the Gold Fleet?"

"Yes," Dane said emphatically. "I don't understand it, sir." And she didn't; *how* had Momed done it? "But that *is* the Gold Fleet formation."

"If that's true . . ." Marsham began, and stopped. What they were both looking at was so clear that no words to Shimas were necessary. The formation was nothing like they'd anticipated. "Jarred," she said, "take over the display controls. Colonel Hormat, go to our stateroom and check. I want to know if a link has been opened up recently. Go, hurry!"

"We can't wait," Shimas said. He remembered very clearly the last dream CJ had told him about. It had called her to *Pacal*'s Control Compartment, and prevented his assassination. And then there was the "feeling" she'd had about his dinner knife. That too had saved him. Both incidents were impossible to explain, but neither could be doubted; they had happened. And now, this. He could see no alternative; he had to trust her again. "Nandes and I were both wrong," he said. "We've got to start moving our ships immediately. If this is accurate and they're . . . CJ, did you get an impression of Enemy speed?"

She'd forgotten about that. But then, she wasn't sure what a satisfactory answer to that question would be. "No, sir."

"Then we must assume the worst. If we're lucky we'll have barely enough time to redeploy—"

"Before we have to go to speed to meet them." Marsham finished the thought. "I'll inform the Fleet Leader—"

"No," Shimas said, deciding instantly. "I'll do that. As soon as I have a moment. But for now . . ." He opened up a Fleetwide comm link and began issuing orders for a radical change in ship deployment. His first instruction was to General Hopkis, calling her companies back immediately. He regretted that he could not now call back the two ships they'd sent into hyperspace. He was equally concerned about the forty-one surviving ships of Buto's Bandits. Moments before he'd first spoken to Hopkis, he'd received a position report from them: still hours away from reentering hyperspace, due to severe damage on nine of the ships. He'd ordered them to remain together and to return to normal space far away from the Fleet; they were too few to approach the battle safely.

"We're going to use Nandes's original formation," Shimas announced. "But with the bulk of us right, not center." From the corner of his eye he saw Dane slump. "CJ?"

"Nothing, sir." She had breathed a sigh of genuine relief, her knees nearly buckling; this was a slight variation of the Fleet disposition she'd explained to Momed Pwanda after Jarred Marsham had revealed it to her, the same one she'd seen again aboard Tam Sepal's flagship. This formation was the one that Momed would be expecting, in setting the Gold Fleet's final posture. Each formation neutralized the other, almost perfectly. "It's just that in the dream, I heard you say those words. I remember that it felt . . . right. Oh, and there was something else too, about the worlds. A new—"

"That doesn't concern us for now, CJ. Tell me about it when this is over."

"Yes, sir."

Marsham eased her son aside and took the War Table's

controls. She divided the presentation into halves: a real-time display, and another that she programmed as Shimas spoke, projecting the formations as they would appear when each change he ordered was complete. "This will take approximately four and a half hours," she called out.

Shimas acknowledged her with a wave, and ordered that all evolutions be carried out at the maximum safe speed. It helped that the overall formation he was working toward was nearly identical to one that he and Marsham were familiar with, as would be all senior officers in the Fleet. From the beginning, he thought, Brotman Nandes had been right—almost. But that "almost" would have cost Sovereign Command everything.

Giel Hormat ran into the Operations Room to report that none of the screens in the stateroom had been activated during the past seven hours. Additionally, she'd fast-played the monitor record; CJ had gone into some sort of a sleeping state and made the two drawings, just as she'd told Shimas. Dane nodded to Hormat and the officer nodded back, with none of the irritation she'd felt before.

"Good," Shimas said, relieved that his decision to move the Fleet had been correct. He was not a believer, as his own mother and brothers had been, in dreams predicting reality. But then, he reminded himself again, he was alive this day because Dane Steppart could dream in a way he didn't understand—but had to accept, because the proof was undeniable. Dane . . . ? He was startled to realize that he'd thought of her by name, and not identifier.

"There's one!" Jarred Marsham shouted. Above the portion of the War Table giving a real-time display, a flickering gold speck appeared deep within a transiting company. Everyone watching understood that the ship had come in too close to gain the overall perspective it needed. "Another one!" This speck, highlighted as the other was, was farther out, but still too close. Both ships disappeared almost immediately.

Severing the comm link, Shimas turned toward the display. He hoped to hear from *Wendal* or *Venor* soon. But he was certain that if one or both were successful, what they sent back would exactly match the drawing he held. Another Gold Fleet ship came into view. Like the others, it arrived at a point not offering an adequate perspective. And like the others, it was gone within moments. He found himself hoping that the last of them would succeed. He would not order his own ships to hold fire against a target that would certainly be shooting at them. But if it was successful, the Enemy vessel would transmit to the Gold Fleet a picture not only useless, but misleading.

*Dalkag* accelerated and turned as each of those in the Operations Room compensated automatically. Even Dane barely noticed the strong pull toward the rear of the compartment, or the abrupt change in angle.

"There's the last one!" Jarred called out.

Shimas watched the flickering mote and was disappointed to see that like the others, it had come in too close. For the first time in his life he was sorry to see a Gold Fleet ship die. Its death meant that the Enemy would come in blind, until the last moments and, knowing that it was blind, would not make the mistakes he was hoping for. Still, he had the Enemy formations; that would be enough.

Realizing that he could wait no longer to report to the Fleet Leader without her bringing charges against him, he went to the comm console and called Mestoeffer's stateroom. She could easily watch the shifting formations on her own display, but he'd learned long ago that Arlana Mestoeffer required formality. And unending explanations.

Fotey Smothe's voice answered. "She is sleeping, First Adjutant. A doctor is here with her. She left orders that she is not to be disturbed, under any circumstances."

"Is that order recorded, Smothe?"

"The doctor can verify it, sir."

Shimas smiled at the indignation in Smothe's voice. Another voice, which he recognized as belonging to Chief Physician Bretta Bator, could be heard in the background. "The order was given, First Adjutant. I've administered a sedative to ease the Fleet Leader's pain and allow her to sleep."

"Understood, Doctor." Shimas broke the connection. He

was grateful for the luck; there was too much for the Fleet to do, in too little time. Any interference now could be fatal.

"Incoming data to the War Table," Jarred announced.

"Let's see it, Lieutenant."

All eyes watched as the Gold Fleet began to take shape in the blackness. The display was still building when it stopped abruptly. "Which ship was that?" Shimas asked.

"*Wendal*, sir. With a good position report."

*Good*, Shimas thought. Now they knew the Enemy's distance and speed. It came as no surprise to him that what little they saw could have been taken directly from the drawing he still held in his hand.

"Buto," Jenny Marsham said, "we have at least five hours before commencing hostilities. Why don't you go and rest? I'll monitor the change in our formations and call you if you're needed."

"No," he said. "But you go ahead."

"We'll compromise. I'll have a cot brought in here. We can alternate."

"Jenny, I really don't need to—"

"Don't argue with me, First Adjutant."

"Understood."

Dane turned for the doorway, and was stopped by Marsham's voice. "Where are you going?"

"To bring a cot, General."

Marsham shook her head. "You're needed here. In fact, we'll have one brought for you also."

Shimas nodded. "You do look tired, Dane."

"Sir?"

"That is your name, isn't it?"

"It was, sir."

"It *is*," he said. Looking around the room, he waited for an objection. None came, and he nodded. "Good."

"That's a good name," Marsham said, never having heard it spoken before. Like her husband, she no longer found it possible to think of the young woman as a Grounder. Or an attendant.

•　　•　　•

As *Wendal*'s final moments of life had confirmed it would, the first wave of the attack appeared above the War Table five hours eleven minutes later. Three Gold Fleet formations, numbering fifteen thousand ships each, came in like widely separated points of an isosceles triangle. The "top" of the triangle Shimas designated Enemy One, the "left" Enemy Two, and the "right" Enemy Three. With only *Wendal*'s limited report to go by, the Gold Fleet's ruse would have been successful, with deadly effect: Shimas would have assumed the strongest possible use of the triangle, which would have placed another one hundred fifty thousand in its center, to emerge as the three points drew off and engaged ships from the core of the Silver Fleet. His response would have been to all but dismiss the three points as diversions and marshal his forces to meet the hundred fifty thousand as they arrived. In fact, only thirty thousand Gold Fleet ships would emerge from that center. But because of Dane's drawing, that fatal mistake was not made.

The Silver Fleet was drawn up into four segments, all but the one containing *Dalkag* traveling at half engagement speed. Enemy One and Enemy Two, at the top and left of the triangle, would be met in equal numbers by the first two segments.

Corresponding to the center of the Gold Fleet triangle were two Silver Fleet echelons of seventy-five hundred each. These, the third segment, were intended to give the false impression of leading the bulk of the Silver Fleet. They would initially engage twice their number of Gold Fleet ships. Half were expected to survive, and then to turn on signal to enter the real fight. Behind them was nothing but empty space.

Enemy Three was the vanguard of the real Gold Fleet attack. As Shimas had constructed the diagram above the War Table, he'd judged that Enemy Three would aim directly for the empty space beyond his own third segment. Well behind Enemy Three were one hundred twenty thousand Gold Fleet ships, stretched out in an elongated column to hide their numbers for as long as possible. Obviously their intent was to wait for Shimas to commit his forces to a fatal error, and then to emerge from behind Enemy Three to deliver a devastating blow to the Silver Fleet's core—which, thanks to Dane, was not where it was expected to be.

In fact that core, one hundred forty-five thousand strong, was the fourth segment. Led by *Dalkag*, these ships were moving at maximum engagement speed to run far outside Enemy Three and to surprise the main attacking force at its most vulnerable time. Driving like twin wedges into the sides of the Enemy's advancing column, this fourth segment would immediately split its target into three weakened and outnumbered fragments. Forty minutes after this penetration, thousands more Silver Fleet ships—the ones called in from the false fight at the triangle's center—would arrive. These were to divide into company strength and take out targets of opportunity at the rear of the embattled Enemy fragments.

In this way Shimas planned to divert more than forty thousand of the Enemy into empty space, while providing all of his own ships with real targets—most of them caught off guard and badly outnumbered.

From her position at the War Table between Marsham and Shimas, Dane watched the display as it ran through repeated fast-time scenarios of the strategy. She could find no flaw in it, nor, she knew, would the thousands of other eyes watching from the far-flung ships of Sovereign Command. They believed that victory was imminent; she believed that an easy Gold Fleet triumph had been averted—nothing more. For unlike Dane, the officers of Sovereign Command were reckoning without two vital factors.

One of them entered the equation immediately. Trailing Fotey Smothe by the hand, Arlana Mestoeffer strode into the Operations Room. Pointing at the mote-filled blackness above the War Table, she demanded, "What is all of this? Explain, Shimas."

Dane moved away and looked up at a chronometer. Seconds passed, ending one day and beginning the next. At that moment the second factor was looking down at a very different display.

# ⇒30⇐

## DAY FIVE—Destruction

"This is wrong, No'ln Beviney," Pwanda said. "Look at the way we're spread out along our main attacking force."

"So? That's by design, Momed. Your design. We don't want the Enemy to see all of us at once, do we? That would give them too much time to react."

"With respect, now that we see how many of the Enemy are coming to meet us here, here, and here," he said, indicating the three points of the triangle, "I think the opposite is true. We expected virtually no resistance, remember?" *Unless*, he thought, *Dane was successful.* And quite obviously, she was. Now it was time to adjust. "They're supposed to believe we're trying to draw them away so that we can come at them en masse from here." He put a finger over the center of the triangle. "But if they really *do* split their forces . . ." He adjusted the display to reflect his idea. "You see? There will be no Enemy center to attack. By the time we arrive in full force, we'll be a staggered column, under simultaneous and concentrated attack on either three or four different fronts. As you can see, those Enemy formations will consist of up to fifty thousand ships each, against our total of one hundred twenty thousand. Which will be too spread out to fight effectively. Everything else we have will be scattered into four small groups, and another larger one that won't be able to reach us in time to do any good."

Beviney examined the table. "It all depends," she said,

"on how much resistance we meet at the points. Which right now is—"

"Better than twelve, ten, and nine thousand Enemy, respectively," Pwanda said. "With more appearing as we watch. No'ln Beviney," he said, lying carefully, "we were both wrong. The Enemy is doing exactly the opposite of what we expected. For that reason we've got to close up our main force right now. When we hit them, we'd better all be there at once." Or, he thought, this battle will have a clear winner; that wasn't the idea at all.

"I agree," Beviney said after a moment's thought. Taking the table controls, she issued the signals that would unite the Gold Fleet column into a more compact and deadly force. When she was finished she put her hand on his. "Momed, I'm beginning to think that the Nomarch was correct. You were born to the Gold Fleet, and stolen as a child by Dirts."

"Please, No'ln Beviney," Pwanda said dryly. "You do me too much honor."

Laughing, she squeezed his hand. "Now I'm sure you're one of us."

The forty-one surviving ships of Buto's Bandits were billions of miles away, having just returned to normal space at the safe distance ordered by Shimas. What they saw on their visual screens was already hours old. And fascinating to watch. Looking into the emptiness between galaxies, the ships' personnel were witness to the instantaneous birth of three new stars. More astounding, the three growing lights, seen from their angle, exactly described the points of an isosceles triangle. Not long afterward they could see a fourth star burst into being from the precise center of the triangle. Each of those lights represented hundreds, perhaps thousands, of ships meeting their deaths. Moving at the maximum speed allowed by their nine damaged comrades, they hoped they would not be too late to share in the glory.

•　　•　　•

"Fleet Leader, we must not break off now," Buto Shimas insisted. "Not for a day, not for a minute." He was supported by Jenny Marsham and all of the new senior staff, none of whom regarded their own careers as more important than the winning of this lethal encounter. Six hours into the battle, casualties were mounting with every passing second. At last report Sovereign Command had lost more than twenty-two thousand ships at the four points of ongoing Enemy engagement. Gold Fleet casualties were slightly higher; clearly they had not been expecting such heavy resistance to their advance so soon.

Shimas was trying to explain to Mestoeffer that given the disposition of Enemy ships, this was an advantage that could make all the difference. Thirty-nine thousand Gold Fleet ships had been successfully diverted into rushing past their lines, and were attacking emptiness. Unless those ships entered hyperspace and emerged close enough to disrupt their own forces, it would be hours before they could rejoin the battle. All that remained now was to throw the main force of Sovereign Command, one hundred forty-five thousand strong, against one hundred twenty thousand Gold Fleet ships.

"But look at them," Mestoeffer argued, dismayed by the solidarity of the officers opposing her point of view; it was unheard of to challenge a council member in this way. She was pointing to the War Table's display of the principal Gold Fleet formation. Unlike the weak column Shimas had prepared her to expect, this was a tight, well-organized unit that showed no hesitation to meet a numerically superior force. "They can see us as clearly as we see them. And don't forget their long-range weapons capability. We have no more surprises to hit them with."

Marsham said, "From what we're seeing, they have that capability on only a few ships. Enhanced range won't do them any good once we close in. Also, we don't need surprise now. All we need is a direct attack." And courage, she added mentally.

"You!" Mestoeffer whirled in her chair and glared at

Dane. "You're the one who sees everything, knows everything. What do *you* say?"

To Mestoeffer's astonishment, the young woman did not flinch. "Fleet Leader," Dane answered evenly, "I'm not a strategist. But it's clear, even to me, that we have to go ahead. If we hesitate, the Enemy will have all the time it needs to regroup and—"

"That's enough!" Mestoeffer looked away in disgust. How was it possible that she could no longer frighten even a worthless attendant?

"*I* believe you're right," Fotey Smothe said, rubbing her shoulders gently.

Mestoeffer slapped his hands away. "Your opinion is as worthless as theirs is insubordinate," she said angrily, frustrated as she had never been before. "Get away from me, *Grounder*."

Smothe turned pale and backed away, as if recoiling from a striking cobra. "What are you *saying?*" He tried to smile as if she'd been joking, but his lips were trembling. "I'm not . . . No, I was never . . ." He lapsed into silence and looked at those around him, feeling more naked and defenseless than he had in years. Near panic, he realized that none of the officers met his eyes; what did *those* butchers care that he'd just been condemned to death? They would enjoy watching him die! Turning to Dane, he mistook her look of encouragement for pity. It was enough to transform his terror into rage.

Shimas saw it coming. Before Smothe had taken a full step toward Mestoeffer, he was between them. The back of his right hand struck Smothe just below the temple. "There now," Shimas said softly, catching Smothe as a startled Mestoeffer turned around. "The poor man has fainted. Lieutenant Marsham, would you please take him to a doctor?"

"Fotey!"

For the first time in her life, Arlana Mestoeffer was appalled by something she'd done. Here was the only human being ever to offer her true loyalty and love, whose advice was given for her benefit, and no other's. In a careless moment she had destroyed him. And probably herself, as well. But also for the first time, Arlana Mestoeffer was not thinking of her own future. "Leave him alone, Lieutenant," she said quietly, standing. "I'll take him." Draping the barely conscious man's arm over her shoulder, she helped him toward the door. "It's all right, Terago," she whispered. "It's all right, I'll take care of you."

Mestoeffer was shocked to realize how much she cared for this man; more than anything else at that moment, she wanted him to live. That extraordinary revelation transformed itself into a rare and brutally honest appraisal of her own mind, and she realized something else: High rank and a lifelong hunger for glory were not enough to prevail over the Enemy. Her lover would certainly die—along with herself and those she was pledged to lead—unless the battle was led by someone more competent than she was. Framed in the doorway, Arlana Mestoeffer turned to face the officers watching her go. "Shimas. Marsham. Get this foolishness over with. Win!"

"He's a Grounder?" Jarred asked, grinning. "'Terago'? What have we got now, Grounders wearing uniforms? Grounders with *names?*" Blushing when no one laughed, he said, "I'm sorry, Dane. I meant no offense."

"Sir," Giel Hormat reported, "our forward ships are beginning to take fire from forty of their long-range shooters. Still too distant to have any effect."

"It appears they're becoming nervous," Shimas said, smiling. He was still thinking about Mestoeffer. She had just performed one of the most impressive acts of true leadership he had ever witnessed. "Very well. All formations but the leading squadron slow to forty percent speed. The rest as planned."

"Good," Marsham said, and issued the orders.

On the display, it appeared as though the leading one hundred ships were accelerating ahead of the Fleet. In fact they were slowing to seventy percent engagement speed. *Dalkag* slowed only to eighty percent, moving the flagship quickly up into the second echelon. The three-tiered maneuver was complete within fifty seconds. "All ships, re-sume previous speed," Shimas said.

"Here they come," Marsham announced. As anticipated, the leading Gold Fleet motes were opening a gap between themselves. Pouring through the gap came two hundred of the Enemy, accelerating to a speed that the Silver Fleet could not match—but was prepared to deal with.

The distances closed rapidly, with the Gold Fleet's long-range shooters effectively blocked by their own ships, now racing toward Sovereign Command's leading squadron. Having learned from analyses of recent experience that the increased speed and maneuverability of these ships came at the expense of shield and weapons power, Marsham and Shimas had worked out a way to neutralize the capability.

On command, the squadron formed a sphere that was opposite in intent from Nandes's and Shimas's original tactic. Above the War Table these one hundred ships seemed to close together into a tight ball. Firing as a single unit, they began taking a toll on the approaching craft, who realized quickly that the Silver Fleet squadron had left no maneuvering room between its ships. To approach that solid concentration of power with reduced weapons and shields was suicide. The officers in *Dalkag*'s Operations Room jeered as the specialized Enemy ships, so deadly when last engaged, turned and raced back toward their own lines. Of the original two hundred, forty-two had been the price paid by the Enemy to learn that the speed-enhanced ships were no longer an advantage: Only by penetrating the Fleet itself, where their vulnerability would be at its highest, could they hope to benefit from their new capability.

"That's all we'll see," Shimas remarked, "for a short while. Dane, may we borrow your cot?"

"Of course, sir." She was comfortably strapped into her chair, along with the officers present, and had no wish to move.

"Thank you," he said, standing. "I'm going to lie down, Jenny. You should do the same."

"I'm not tired, Buto."

Shrugging, he said to Hormat, "Please wake me in half an hour." Within a minute he was snoring softly and deep into a dreamless, renewing sleep.

Forty-three minutes later the moment arrived.

No human eye had ever witnessed the simultaneous clash of two hundred sixty thousand ships of war, each the final result of spacegoing technology developed over millennia. No human mind could comprehend the complexity of strike, counterstrike, maneuver, feint, thrust, formation, dissolution, attack, defend, on so great a scale. Nor could the War Tables. Within minutes of the Fleets coming together, all displays were overwhelmed with data and of necessity were lowered in scale to reflect only the nearest ten thousand ships.

The exceptions were aboard *Dalkag* and, Shimas assumed, aboard the Gold Fleet's own flagship. It was his responsibility, along with Marsham, to monitor the battle as a whole. This was an impossible task to accomplish in any detail. As the bodies of the Fleets pressed ever closer together, the fighting filled every inch of the display with silver and gold motes mingling in chaotic patterns that formed and dissolved too fast for the human senses to follow. Shimas had brought Sovereign Command into the fray with a strong numerical advantage. Now all a Fleet Leader or first adjutant could do was to issue very general orders and watch as the massive sweeps of glittering motes swirled within the display, with every fraction of a second marking the deaths of ships and those who rode in them.

At a nod from Marsham, Shimas turned to see Brotman Nandes standing there in the Operations Room, holding on with both hands to the sides of the doorway. The officer was not looking at the display, but at the people gathered there. He stared at Dane for a long moment, a look of total confusion in his eyes. This was the first time Shimas had ever thought of him as a very old man.

"Jarred," Shimas ordered, "Help the first adjutant to a

chair and strap him in securely." Nandes allowed himself to be led, making no comment. Almost immediately two more people entered. Arlana Mestoeffer walked alongside Fotey Smothe, the two taking seats at the side of the table next to Dane. Smothe strapped himself in and said, "My name is Terago Ninool." Neither of them spoke after that.

"Shimas!" Marsham called out. "*Dalkag*!"

He turned his attention to the silver mote representing the flagship of Sovereign Command and immediately saw the situation developing around it. Three Gold Fleet ships had penetrated *Dalkag*'s defensive outriders and were bearing in at accelerating speed. As he opened his mouth to give the warning Marsham shouted, "Brace! Brace for evasion and roll!"

*Dalkag* shifted in a violent swing that brought the floor vertical in a single second, as, two levels below in the Control Compartment, the ship's captain maneuvered to escape the oncoming Enemy. One of the three disappeared as *Dalkag* went into a roll and fired.

Dane felt the blood rush into her head and out again, leaving her disoriented. From next to her she heard quiet laughter. "Nothing to worry about, dear one," Smothe— Terago Ninool—said. "I've been in ocean storms much worse than this."

"Tell me about them later," Mestoeffer replied. "Much later."

*Dalkag* reversed its roll and pitched downward. A second Enemy ship disappeared from the display. At that moment, exactly as Dane remembered from aboard *Pacal*, they seemed to slam against a massive celestial barrier that would not give an inch. *Dalkag* rolled again, this time forward. For a brief instant Dane felt as if she were a young child again, practicing tumbling exercises. The ship leveled out and decelerated. The display above the War Table flickered for a second, and then disappeared entirely.

"Damage, Captain Zelas?" Shimas said calmly into the comm console.

"This is Executive Officer Vonya Myter," a voice replied. "We had an overload. Captain Zelas is dead."

"Condition of the ship, Captain Myter," Shimas said. The War Table display came on again. The third Enemy ship was not to be seen.

"Structural damage, twenty-six compartments breached and sealed," Myter reported, and named the compartments involved. "Loss of all but emergency capability from the power plant. Weapons are down by eighty percent, shield off-line, hyperspace not possible at this time. Casualty reports still coming in, sir. Confirmed are three hundred two dead, five hundred nineteen injured and unable to perform duties. All ship's systems are being repaired at maximum possible speed, sir."

"Understood, Captain. Well done."

"Thank you, sir."

"First Adjutant," Jarred said, "I can be of help with the weapons systems."

"Yes," Jenny Marsham answered. "Go ahead." As her son stood to leave, the War Table display flickered off again. It was restored within a second. "Colonel Hormat," she asked, "is the data we see real-time?"

"Yes, General."

"Six more, then," Marsham said, pointing.

Advancing from the rear of the Gold Fleet, the flagship *Noldron* had defeated two Sovereign Command ships that had come against it, and was chasing a third. Momed Pwanda was directing a skirmish hundreds of miles away while No'ln Beviney took personal command of *Noldron*.

"This is fun!" she cried out, exhilarated by the fight. It had been years since she'd trusted anyone enough to delegate her usual responsibilities and savor the pleasure of individual combat. "Ooh, you're turning away much too slowly," she said. "No no, that just won't do." Cutting her helm hard to the right, she shot *Noldron* across the arc described by the Enemy's retreat. Twelve seconds later it was over. "Ha!"

With no other Enemy vessels close, Beviney turned control back over to the next senior supervisor and walked to Pwanda's station. "Good, Momed," she said after a few seconds. "Very good." Something at the outer edge of the display caught her attention. "Look at that," she said thoughtfully, while Pwanda ignored her and concentrated. "Look at that ship. It's barely moving, but it's surrounded by ten Enemy protectors. See? Six of ours are trying to get past them. Momed, that's got to be their flagship. And it's hurt! That's my next target."

The word "flagship" caught Pwanda's instant attention. *Dane*. There was no way to know for sure, but recent evidence of her influence on the Silver Fleet left him confident that she would be aboard it. He relinquished the skirmish he was working on by signaling the ships to take local control. Looking to see what Beviney was referring to, he thought furiously. "That's a ruse," he said finally. "A wounded beowolf."

"What are you talking about?"

"A forest animal," he explained, making it up as he went. "It fakes injury to draw a predator into a trap. When it gets there, the whole colony drops out of the trees and eats the predator alive."

"That's awful!"

"Just look," he said, indicating the display. He took it back ten minutes in time and brought it up to the present at twenty times the normal speed. Releasing a breath, he saw that he'd guessed correctly; those ships guarding the flagship were the best in the Silver Fleet. "See? In the last ten minutes eight of our ships have tried to get inside those 'protectors.' Three made it. But all eight are dead now, with only one 'protector' killed. And we're about to lose six more in the same way. That's a beowolf, No'In Beviney, and it's chewing into your flesh. It's eating you alive."

Beviney was pale. As he'd known it would, the thought of animals with minds revolted her. The image of being consumed alive by them was more than she could take. "Call them off," she said in a quavering voice. "Order all ships to leave that 'beowolf' alone." As he signaled the orders, she turned and ran from the Battle Control Center, on her way to being sick.

*You're welcome, Dane,* Pwanda thought, and turned his attention back to the display.

To everyone's surprise, *Dalkag*'s newest attackers broke away and fled. All but one. This ship had already penetrated the outriders and seemed determined to finish the fight.

The correct decision, Shimas thought dispassionately. No matter what course of action it took, the Enemy vessel could not escape now. The Gold Fleet ship came out of one last turn and bore directly down on *Dalkag*. "Stand by," he said. "It's going to ram us." He reached beside him to take Jenny's hand as the badly damaged *Dalkag* maneuvered futilely to move out of the way.

She bent her face to his and kissed him on the cheek. "I'm pregnant," she whispered into his ear. "A son. I hoped he'd have your eyes, Buto. I love the way they arch up at the sides when you smile. And I love the way they look at me."

"I'd agree to that," he answered, sliding a thick arm around her waist. "But only if he has your—"

"Look!" Hormat called out. From below *Dalkag* an outrider streaked ahead of them. Too late to deflect the ship with weapons fire, it threw itself directly into the Enemy's path. The resulting explosion registered on the display for a fraction of a second before *Dalkag* was rocked by speeding chunks of debris from both ships.

The Operations Room went to total blackness as *Dalkag* spun side over side. Losing all sense of position, Dane heard sharp snapping sounds—dry logs cracking open in a fire. The tumbling seemed to go on forever while she found herself struggling for each breath. Her mind replayed the death of Tam Sepal as she felt her eyes beginning to swell. Distantly, with consciousness easing away, she heard airtight doors slamming shut.

She awoke and tried unsuccessfully to open her eyes. It was several moments of staring into the darkness before she realized that they *were* open. The spinning had nearly stopped; *Dalkag* continued to roll, but very slowly now. Breathing was easier; each lungful of air was more satisfying than the last. Her chest and thighs ached fiercely where the straps held her against the chair. Suddenly her eyes were stung by pinpoints of intense light that came from everywhere at once. Concussion, she thought, until she adapted to the intensity and saw that the emergency lighting had come on.

Everything around her had changed. The walls and ceiling of the mammoth Operations Room had closed in on her. The War Table, to which her hands had clung while *Dalkag* spun endlessly, was gone. After a few seconds she realized where she was. This was a near-perfect duplication of *Pacal*'s Control Compartment, but larger in scale.

Turning her head slowly to one side and then to the other, she was relieved to discover that her neck was apparently undamaged. It was then she saw Buto Shimas and Jenny Marsham, strapped into identical chairs to her right. Each of them was manipulating switches and levers on twin consoles. Shimas was using only one arm.

"Are you two all right?" Dane asked.

Shimas turned. "General Marsham has a broken leg and cracked ribs," he said. "Not bad, considering. How are you, Dane?"

"If you knew what a carnival was, I could explain it better. But all right, I think. How long have I been unconscious? Where are the others?"

"Just under seven hours," he answered. "Three of our staff are dead, along with Captain Myter and the officers who were down here with her. The Fleet Leader and Smothe are in her stateroom. Brotman Nandes died of a broken neck. The rest are scattered throughout the ship, doing what they can." As he spoke, the rolling came to a gentle, final stop. "Nicely done, Jenny," he said, turning toward her. "Now let's get a doctor down here. The baby—"

"Our son is *our* son," Marsham said. "A little unpleasantness isn't going to upset him." To Dane she said, "In case you're curious, Dane, my husband carried both of us down here. Or I should say, 'hopped' us down here, one at a time, in the dark. His left leg is rebroken, along with his left arm."

"Thank you, sir," Dane said. "Is there any way I can find out—"

"The food-production compartments are in the center of the ship," Shimas said. "There were no fatalities there. Your friends are probably sore and disoriented, but they're all right. In total there are three hundred fifty-two officers and crew left, and one hundred eleven Grounders. All of the children are safe. But everyone else is dead."

"I hope you don't mind answering all these questions, sir, but—"

"I don't have much else to do for the moment. You're going to ask what's happening outside?"

"Yes, sir."

"We won't know until communications are restored. It defies belief, though, that we haven't been torn apart yet. For some reason the Gold Fleet is leaving us untouched. In the meantime, we're hoping that you can give us the answers."

"The drawings I made?"

"You're sitting on the folder," Marsham said. "Perhaps you can bring it up to date."

"It wasn't something I tried to do," Dane said, alarmed. "I was dizzy and sat down. I had a dream. When I woke up, the drawings were complete."

"We know," Shimas said. "We've replayed the monitor record several times now. Remarkable."

"Try to do it again, Dane," Marsham urged her. "It could help. And as Buto said, we don't have much else to do right now."

She was trapped. "All right," she said, retrieving the folder and marker from beneath her. She closed her eyes and found that the dizziness was real this time. Concentrating, she tried to imagine the results of a battle that itself could not be imagined. She made her best guess and began to draw. Minutes later she was finished.

"I hope you're wrong," she heard Shimas saying.

Dane opened her eyes to see the first adjutant's face near her own, looking down over her shoulder. "I hope you're very wrong," he said, lifting the folder from her hands. He crossed the floor, dragging his left leg. Passing the new drawing to Marsham, he said, "Look at this. If . . . Wait a minute." Turning back to Dane, he asked, "Is this our ships, or theirs? You only made the one drawing this time."

"I don't know, sir," she said, hoping she had not made a foolish error they would see immediately. "I wasn't even aware that I . . . I don't know. Could it be both?"

"That would explain the disarray," Marsham said. "But compare this with the first two she made, Buto. The dots were individual squadrons, the boxes were complete companies. There can't be more than forty thousand ships here."

"That's why she's got to be wrong," Shimas said. "Unless this is the Gold Fleet. Dane, think hard. Whose ships are these?"

"I'm trying to remember, sir."

Marsham said firmly, "If it's us, this is only a small part of the Fleet. And look, they're all distinct. No two dots close together, no two boxes."

"That means no fighting," Shimas said, "Whomever those ships belong to, they're separated. It's as if they've broken off from battle and are moving apart in scattered formations. Which means . . ." He put his right arm around her shoulders and laughed. "Jenny, I understand now. The battle is over. And think of this: Our ships would never have let it end unless . . . unless we'd won. Do you understand? It's over, Jenny. And we won. I only wish we could see the rest of our ships."

"Yes!" Marsham said triumphantly. "It has to mean that. Buto, you did it!"

"*We* did it," he said, grinning until his wide face seemed in danger of splitting in two. "And think about what this means. Now our son will be born to see the Gold Fleet exterminated forever! He and his generation will go on and finish—"

"No!" Dane could bear to hear no more of this. She willed her drawing to be at least partially correct: that the battle was over. Why else would *Dalkag* be both defenseless and untouched? She spoke with an anger she did not care to disguise. "You're wrong. You're both wrong!" Hearing Shimas plan for still more destruction, eagerly dedicating their unborn son to the carnage, had shocked her into recalling a warning she'd given herself many times before. *How can I forget even for a second who these people are?* Why was it that sometimes she actually *liked* them? They were monsters . . . but they were human. Over the centuries they'd killed millions of innocent people. But they laughed, and loved, and had their hearts broken, just as anyone would . . . How could that be? *How?* Making no attempt to soften her words, for them or for herself, she said what had to be true. "That drawing represents both sides. You're looking at all that's left of your great Fleets. Everyone else is dead."

Shimas went pale. "Then . . . are you telling us—"

"That's right. It's over. They lost. And so did you."

Dane Steppart was correct.

Although replacement personnel were soon transferred aboard, the damage to *Dalkag* required seventeen days to repair, using spare parts from its own supplies and from other surviving ships of Sovereign Command. While the repairs were going on, Dane learned how to access the ship's memory and exit undetected. She spent time each day reading and memorizing. And she told Marsham and Shimas the rest of her "dream"—the part dreamt up by herself and Momed Pwanda, and made believable by those agents of The Stem who had willingly sacrificed their lives above targeted worlds.

The dead were consigned with appropriate honors to the deep grave of space. Jarred Marsham spoke for all of them. He bid them good-bye and assured a ceremonial audience that as long as there was war, there would be a place for the bodies. "Space," he'd said, "awaits each of us as it always has, with infinite capacity and patience."

# EPILOGUE

"First I want to thank you," Linda Steppart said to Buto Shimas as they all took seats, "for bringing my daughter home again."

When Shimas gave a perfunctory nod, Jenny Marsham said, "We've returned all citizens of Walden who were still—"

"Yes, I know. Dane told me you'd gathered them from all surviving ships."

Shimas glanced sharply at the woman who'd dared to interrupt his wife. He was still indignant over their reception here. He and Marsham had been kept waiting for three hours before this president and her chief of staff arrived to meet with them. "And she told us," he said abruptly, "about a new weapon you have. That's nonsense, of course." At a warning glance from Jenny, he took a slow breath and modified his tone. "That is to say, it is difficult to believe. But," he continued, using the precise words Mestoeffer had ordered him to use, "we have reports of our ships detonating for no discoverable reason while conducting supply runs. Madam President, can you verify the existence of this capability?"

"Gladly," Johann Berger said. "Please designate any number of targets, and we will provide a demonstration you won't soon forget. But first, take the civilians off. You've murdered enough of them already."

Shimas glared at the man. He'd argued to Mestoeffer that the worlds must learn immediately that despite recent losses, most of Sovereign Command remained—and would accept no nonsense from Grounders. He wanted to provoke a showdown: here, now, while he had ships under his command. But with her career and life at stake, the Fleet Leader was eager to return to the council and formally present her report of the battle. And now that the worlds could defend themselves, she was unwilling to risk further losses. In answer to Berger's implied threat he said tightly, "We have not asked for a demonstration. Sir."

"Cowards, eh?" Berger laughed. "I'm not surprised. The Gold Fleet ship declined to test us as well, although we would certainly have obliged it."

Shimas leapt to his feet. "An Enemy ship, here? When? What did it want?"

"That is government business," Steppart said, politely but firmly. "I'm sure you understand."

"The Enemy is *our* business. If you're dealing with them, I promise you that we—"

"Of course we understand, Madam President," Marsham interrupted. She glanced meaningfully at Shimas, who sat down again. He took in a long breath and looked away from all of them. Marsham continued, "We asked for this meeting because we have thanks to offer, as well. Dane twice saved the life of my husband. And if not for her, none of us would have survived the battle."

"She didn't tell me about that," Steppart said truthfully. Dane had spent what little time they had together assuring her mother that she was well, and advising her how to deal with these people: Take a position of strength. Force them to wait for the meeting they would ask for. When it began, Johann Berger was to take a belligerent role, while she was to be forceful, but diplomatic. Above all they were to show no fear, no weakness. Then she'd told Linda about the "weapon," and gone off into isolation for nearly three hours. What Dane had said fit perfectly with the strange behavior of the Gold Fleet ship ten days before. The man who'd called her from the vessel had given assurances of peaceful intentions, and requested—requested—permission to send down a shuttle.

Shimas interrupted her thoughts. "We owed Dane a debt of honor," he said in a clipped, level tone. "She asked that your citizens be returned. On the recommendation of Major General Marsham and myself, the Fleet Leader agreed. We were instructed to accompany them here and to present a formal acknowledgment of Dane's service to Sovereign Command." He pulled a document from the folder in front of him and slid it to the center of the table. "We have now fulfilled the debt."

Berger stood to reach for the document. Steppart shook her head, and he sat down again, understanding the message she wanted to convey: No longer would the worlds jump when a Fleet officer spoke.

Steppart accepted this presentation as part of the reason they had requested this meeting. The rest, of course, was to confirm what Dane and others had convinced them was true: that the worlds could now defend themselves. Evidently, the Gold Fleet had the same fear. The shuttle it sent down had circled the Capitol Building once, dropped a small package onto the roof, and left immediately. The packet was wrapped in a printed request that it be held unopened for Dane, should she ever return to Walden. Linda had opened it immediately, thinking that it might contain news of her daughter. And it was an undeniable pleasure to defy one of the Fleets.

It was only a matter of time, she reflected as she studied the faces of Shimas and Marsham, before this new—and fictitious—balance of power was tested, somewhere. But before that occurred, she hoped, the fiction would become reality. For at least a short time, the worlds would be left alone to communicate and travel without interference. For the first time in centuries, the finest minds in existence would be free to collaborate. Surely they could build and then improve upon the armament diagrams and specifications that Dane had drawn out from memory. If they were successful—Was it too much to hope for?—new planetary associations could be formed for trade and mutual defense. So much could happen . . . Hope, she had read somewhere, was a thing always in shadow. But it was hope, nonetheless. They just needed enough time . . .

Time. Thinking again about what she'd found in the Gold Fleet packet, Linda felt the need to prolong the meeting. She began asking polite questions about Fleet life.

After a minute First Adjutant Shimas looked up impatiently at a wall-mounted chronometer.

"Your pardon, Madam President," Marsham said. "But our orders were to return to *Dalkag* by the end of this watch. That time has nearly expired. May we conclude our business here?"

Johann Berger stood and left the room in response to a nod from Steppart, who could not trust her voice.

"There it is!"

Dane Steppart raised her arm and pointed excitedly at the first sunrise she'd seen in nearly a year. Her small face, framed by black hair that once again nearly reached her neck, was bright with excitement. Standing next to her, Paul Hardaway grinned. Children no more, they watched as, far to the east, a thin crack of luminous yellow edged upward from behind the skyline of Vermilion City.

"Sorry," Paul said. "No Rainbow Ghosts this time."

"That's all right," Dane said. "I can see them any time I want. And when I do, you'll always be there with me. All of you."

Alfred Steppart was the image of his late father. Tall and slender, he bore a wide face and dark brown eyes. Turning to Dane, he asked, "Your decision is final, then?"

"Yes."

Carnie Niles drew in a sharp breath and turned away. She saw Johann Berger appear at the roof door. "Oh, no," she said. "Not already."

"Dane," Berger called. "They want to talk with you now."

Pulling Paul's face down to her own, Dane kissed his cheek. "Thank you, Paul. For everything."

The young man smiled. "When my father was a boy he used to raise chickens. He told me once that they were the dumbest animals anywhere, because they'd let the fox right in with them before they raised a squawk. I guess those Fleet people aren't much smarter." He lifted her, and they embraced warmly.

When he set her down she hugged Alfred and Carnie,

then followed Johann Berger without another word. What could be said had already passed among the four. Except for one thing.

Alfred opened the Gold Fleet packet that Dane had left with them. He extracted a note and read aloud,

*"Go up to your roof when it's dark and look around you, Dane. Look at your family, and your friends. Look down at the world that gave you life and taught you how to be human. What is all of that worth? What will you do, how far will you go, to keep all of that alive?*

*"Now look up, at the night sky. There is your answer. Come join me, Dane. The fun is just beginning.*

"It's signed, *'Momed.'*"

Paul shook his head. "I used to like him. Not anymore."

"This didn't influence her," Alfred said, refolding the note.

"Then why leave it with us?"

"Because it explains what she's always felt but would never say. My sister decided the course of her life many years ago, Paul. Now she's getting on with it."

Linda Steppart stood at the main entrance to the Capitol Building and watched as the three of them walked down the steps to a waiting shuttle. Her heart filled with pride, and then broke when the two officers extended an arm to Dane, and she accepted them. The last sound of Dane's voice she heard was her daughter saying to the man and the woman, "You're my family, now."